Charles Dickens

The Personal History and Experience of David Copperfield the Younger

COMPACT EDITIONS

PHOENIX

A PHOENIX PAPERBACK
COMPACT EDITIONS

This paperback edition first published in
Great Britain in 2007
by Phoenix,
an imprint of Orion Books Ltd,
Orion House, 5 Upper St Martin's Lane,
London WC2H 9EA

1 3 5 7 9 10 8 6 4 2

A CIP catalogue record for this book
is available from the British Library.

ISBN 978-0-7538-2268-5

Printed and bound in Great Britain by
Clays Ltd, St Ives plc

The Orion Publishing Group's policy is to use papers
that are natural, renewable and recyclable products and
made from wood grown in sustainable forests. The logging
and manufacturing processes are expected to conform to
the environmental regulations of the country of origin.

www.orionbooks.co.uk

Contents

About the Author

Charles Dickens was born in Portsmouth on 7 February 1812 but the family later settled in Chatham. These years were the happiest of Dickens' early life, for in 1824 his father, John Dickens, was imprisoned for debt in the Marshalsea and the twelve-year-old Charles was sent to work in a warehouse off the Strand. His sense of humiliation was acute. However, when his father was released from prison Charles was sent back to school. In 1827 he was articled as a solicitor's clerk in Gray's Inn. After a short time he became a journalist, first working in Doctors' Commons and then travelling the country in a stagecoach to cover elections. In his twenties he made a name for himself with his first novel *The Pickwick Papers* which was published in monthly instalments. It was followed by *Oliver Twist* in 1838 and *Nicholas Nickleby* in 1839. In 1836 he had married Catherine Hogarth and set up home with her in Bloomsbury. They went on to have ten children together.

Dickens' writing was immensely popular during his life and this enabled him to buy Gad's Hill Place in Kent. In 1850 he founded his own weekly magazine, *Household Words*, which carried the serialised *Hard Times* in 1854. Dickens separated from his wife in 1858 since he was having a clandestine relationship with the actress Ellen Ternan. In 1870 he began *The Mystery of Edwin Drood*, but had completed only half of it when he died of a stroke at Gad's Hill Place on 9 June.

Charles Dickens will always be remembered for *David Copperfield* (1850), *Bleak House* (1853), *Little Dorrit* (1857), *A Tale of Two Cities* (1859) and *Great Expectations* (1861) in addition to the works mentioned above.

Chronology of Dickens' Life

Year	Age	Life
1812		Dickens born in Portsea, Portsmouth, 7 February
1815	3	Dickens family move to London
1817	5	Dickens family move to Chatham
1822	10	Dickens family (now 6 children) moves to London
1824	12	Dickens works at Warren's Blacking John Dickens (father) in Marshalsea Debtors Prison
1825	13	Dickens starts school at Wellington House Academy
1827	15	Dickens becomes junior clerk in solicitor's office
1829	17	Dickens becomes a freelance reporter at Doctors' Commons
1831	19	Dickens falls in love with Maria Beadnell Appointed Parliamentary reporter
1833	21	Dickens' first story 'A Dinner at Poplar Walk'
1835	23	Dickens engaged to Catherine Hogarth
1836	24	Dickens marries Catherine
1837	25	*Pickwick Papers* completed Dickens becomes editor of *Bentley's Miscellany*
1838	26	*Oliver Twist*
1839	27	*Nicholas Nickleby*
1840	28	Dickens begins *Master Humphrey's Clock*
1841	29	*The Old Curiosity Shop*
1842	30	Dickens visits America (Jan–Jun) *American Notes*

Chronology of his Times

Year	Literary Context	Historical Events
1812	Byron, *Childe Harold I & II*	1811–20 Regency of George, Prince of Wales
1815		Battle of Waterloo
1817	Keats, *Poems* Jane Austen d.	
1818	Mary Shelley, *Frankenstein*	
1822	Byron, *Vision of Judgement* Shelley d.	Suicide of Prime Minister Castlereagh
1824	Byron d.	
1825	Hazlitt, *Spirit of the Age*	Stockton–Darlington railway opened
1827	Blake d.	University of London founded
1829	Jerrold, *Black-ey'd Susan*	
1831		First Cholera epidemic
1833		Abolition of slavery throughout Empire State funding of schools started
1834		Tolpuddle Martyrs New Poor Law
1837	Lockhart, *Life of Scott*	Accession of Victoria
1838		Anti-Corn Law League Chartist petitions published
1839	Carlyle, *Chartism*	First Factory Inspector's report
1840	Hardy b.	Penny postage introduced
1841		Peel becomes Prime Minister
1842	Tennyson, *Poems* Browning, *Dramatic Lyrics*	Chartist riots Report on Sanitary Conditions of Labouring Population

Year	Age	Life
1843	31	*A Christmas Carol*
1844	32	Dickens and family stay in Genoa *Martin Chuzzlewit* *The Chimes*
1845	33	*The Cricket on the Hearth*
1848	36	*Dombey and Son* *The Haunted Man*
1850	38	Dickens begins weekly miscellany, *Household Words* *David Copperfield*
1851	39	John Dickens d.
1853	41	*Bleak House* Dickens tours Italy and Switzerland with Wilkie Collins
1855	43	Dickens meets Maria Beadnell again Spends some months in Paris
1856	44	Buys Gad's Hill Place
1857	45	*Little Dorrit* Meets Ellen Ternan during performances of *The Frozen Deep*
1858	46	Dickens separates from his wife Begins public readings
1859	47	*A Tale of Two Cities* *Household Words* incorporated into new weekly magazine, *All the Year Round*
1861	49	*Great Expectations*
1865	53	*Our Mutual Friend* Staplehurst railway accident
1868	56	Dickens begins Farewell Reading Tour
1870	58	Begins *The Mystery of Edwin Drood* Dies 9 June

Year	Literary Context	Historical Events
1843	Wordsworth made Poet Laureate	
1844	Disraeli, *Coningsby* Elizabeth Barrett, *Poems*	Rochdale Pioneers founded Co-operative Store
1845	Disraeli, *Sybil*	Railway speculation
1848	Emily Brontë d. Thackeray, *Vanity Fair*	Cholera epidemic Pre-Raphaelite Brotherhood founded
1850	Tennyson, *In Memoriam* Wordsworth d.	Pope appoints Catholic Bishops to England
1851	Melville, *Moby-Dick*	Great Exhibition Gold discovered in New South Wales
1853	Charlotte Brontë, *Villette*	
1855	Gaskell, *North and South* Kingsley, *Westward Ho!*	
1856	Elizabeth Barrett Browning, *Aurora Leigh*	End of Crimean War
1857	Trollope, *Barchester Towers* Flaubert, *Madame Bovary*	Indian Mutiny
1858	George Eliot, *Scenes of a Clerical Life*	Indian Viceroyality established
1859	Tennyson, *Idylls of the King* Darwin, *Origin of the Species*	Rise of Fenianism in Ireland
1861	Reade, *The Cloister and the Hearth*	Death of the Prince Consort American Civil War
1865	Carroll, *Alice's Adventures in Wonderland*	President Lincoln assassinated Palmerston d.
1868	Collins, *The Moonstone*	Gladstone becomes PM
1870	D. G. Rossetti, *Poems*	Education Act Franco–Prussian War Fall of Napoleon III

CHAPTER 1

I am Born

Whether I shall turn out to be the hero of my own life, or whether that station will be held by anybody else, these pages must show. To begin my life with the beginning of my life, I record that I was born on a Friday, at twelve o'clock at night. It was remarked that the clock began to strike, and I began to cry, simultaneously.

In consideration of the day and hour of my birth, it was declared first, that I was destined to be unlucky in life; and secondly, that I was privileged to see ghosts and spirits.

I need say nothing here on the first head, because nothing can show better than my history whether that prediction was verified or falsified by the result. On the second branch of the question, I will only remark, that unless I ran through that part of my inheritance while I was still a baby, I have not come into it yet.

I was born at Blunderstone, in Suffolk. I was a posthumous child. My father's eyes had closed upon the light of this world six months, when mine opened on it. There is something strange to me, even now, in the reflection that he never saw me.

An aunt of my father's of whom I shall have more to relate by-and-by, was the principal magnate of our family. Miss Trotwood, or Miss Betsey, as my poor mother always called her, had been married to a husband younger than herself, who was very handsome, except in the sense of the homely adage, 'handsome is, that handsome does' – for he was strongly suspected of having beaten Miss Betsey, and even of having once made some hasty but determined arrangements to throw her out of a window. These evidences of an incompatibility of temper induced Miss Betsey to pay him off and effect a separation by mutual consent. He went to India with his capital and tidings of his death reached home within ten years. How they affected my aunt, nobody knew; for immediately upon the separation she took her maiden name again, bought a cottage a long way off, and was understood to live secluded, ever afterwards, in an inflexible retirement.

My father had once been a favourite of hers, I believe; but she was

1

mortally affronted by his marriage, on the ground that my mother was 'a wax doll'. She had never seen my mother, but she knew her to be not yet twenty. My father was double my mother's age when he married, and of but a delicate constitution. He died a year afterwards, as I have said, six months before I came into the world.

This was the state of matters on the afternoon of, what *I* may be excused for calling, that eventful and important Friday.

My mother was sitting by the fire, that bright, windy March afternoon, very timid and sad, and very doubtful of ever coming alive out of the trial that was before her, when she saw a strange lady coming up the garden.

My mother had a sure foreboding that it was Miss Betsey. The lady came walking up to the door with a fell rigidity of figure and composure of countenance that could have belonged to nobody else. When she reached the house, she looked in at the window, pressing the end of her nose against the glass to that extent that it became perfectly flat and white in a moment.

She gave my mother such a turn, that I have always been convinced I am indebted to Miss Betsey for having been born on a Friday.

My mother had left her chair in her agitation. Miss Betsey, looking round the room, made a frown and a gesture to my mother to come and open the door. My mother went.

'Mrs David Copperfield, I *think*,' said Miss Betsey; the emphasis referring, perhaps, to my mother's mourning weeds, and her condition.

'Yes,' said my mother, faintly.

'Miss Trotwood,' said the visitor. 'You have heard of her, I dare say?'

My mother answered she had had that pleasure.

'Now you see her,' said Miss Betsey. My mother bent her head, and begged her to walk in.

They went into the parlour and when they were both seated, my mother, after vainly trying to restrain herself, began to cry.

'Oh, tut, tut, tut!' said Miss Betsey, in a hurry. 'Don't do that! Take off your cap, child, and let me see you.'

My mother was too much afraid of her to refuse. Therefore she did as she was told, and did it with such nervous hands that her hair (which was luxuriant and beautiful) fell all about her face.

'Why, bless my heart!' exclaimed Miss Betsey. 'You are a very Baby!'

My mother was, no doubt, unusually youthful in appearance even for her years; she hung her head, as if it were her fault, poor thing, and said, sobbing, that indeed she was afraid she was but a childish widow, and would be but a childish mother if she lived. In a short pause which ensued, she had a fancy that she felt Miss Betsey touch her hair with no ungentle hand; but, looking at her, she found that lady sitting with the skirt of her dress tucked up and her feet upon the fender, frowning at the fire.

'In the name of Heaven,' said Miss Betsey, suddenly, 'why Rookery?'

'Do you mean the house, ma'am?' asked my mother. 'The name was Mr Copperfield's choice. When he bought the house, he liked to think that there were rooks about it.'

The evening wind made such disturbance just now, among some tall elm-trees at the bottom of the garden, that neither my mother nor Miss Betsey could forbear glancing that way. As the elms fell into a violent flurry, tossing their wild arms about, some ragged old rooks'-nest burdening their higher branches swung like wrecks upon a stormy sea.

'Where are the birds?' asked Miss Betsey.

'There have not been any since we have lived here,' said my mother. 'The nests were very old ones, and the birds have deserted them a long while.'

'David Copperfield all over!' cried Miss Betsey. 'Calls a house a rookery when there's not a rook near it, and takes the birds on trust, because he sees the nests!'

'Mr Copperfield,' returned my mother, 'is dead, and if you dare to speak unkindly of him to me –'

My poor dear mother, I suppose, had some momentary intention of committing an assault and battery upon my aunt, who could easily have settled her with one hand. But it passed with the action of rising from her chair, and she sat down again very meekly, and fainted.

When she came to herself, or when Miss Betsey had restored her, whichever it was, she found the latter standing at the window.

'Well?' said Miss Betsey, coming back to her chair, as if she had only been taking a casual look at the prospect; 'and when do you expect –'

'I am all in a tremble,' faltered my mother. 'I don't know what's the matter. I shall die, I am sure!'

'No, no, no,' said Miss Betsey. 'What do you call your girl?'

'I don't know that it will be a girl, yet, ma'am,' said my mother innocently.

'Bless the Baby!' exclaimed Miss Betsey, 'I don't mean that. I mean your servant.'

'Peggotty,' said my mother.

'Peggotty!' repeated Miss Betsey, with some indignation. 'Do you mean to say, child, that any human being has gone into a Christian church, and got herself named Peggotty?'

'It's her surname,' said my mother, faintly. 'Mr Copperfield called her by it, because her Christian name was the same as mine.'

'Here Peggotty!' cried Miss Betsey, opening the parlour-door. 'Tea. Your mistress is a little unwell. Don't dawdle.'

Having issued this mandate with as much potentiality as if she had been a recognised authority in the house, Miss Betsey shut the door again, and sat down as before; with her feet on the fender.

'You were speaking about its being a girl,' said Miss Betsey. 'I have a presentiment that it must be a girl. Now, child, from the moment of this girl's birth, I intend to be her friend. I intend to be her godmother, and I beg you'll call her Betsey Trotwood Copperfield. There must be no mistakes in life with *this* Betsey Trotwood. There must be no trifling with *her* affections, poor dear.'

There was a twitch of Miss Betsey's head, as if her own old wrongs were working within her, and she repressed any plainer reference to them by strong constraint. So my mother suspected as she observed her by the low glimmer of the fire.

'And was David good to you, child?' asked Miss Betsey.

'We were very happy,' said my mother. 'Mr Copperfield was only too good to me.'

'What, he spoilt you, I suppose?' returned Miss Betsey.

'I fear he did indeed,' sobbed my mother.

'Well! Don't cry!' said Miss Betsey. 'You were not equally matched, child, and so I asked the question. You were an orphan, weren't you? And a governess?'

'I was nursery-governess in a family where Mr Copperfield came to visit,' said my mother simply.

'Ha! Poor Baby!' mused Miss Betsey, with her frown still bent upon the fire. 'Do you know anything about keeping house?'

'Not so much as I could wish. But Mr Copperfield was teaching me and I hope I should have improved, if the great misfortune of his death' – my mother could get no farther.

'Well, well!' said Miss Betsey. 'Don't cry any more. You'll make yourself ill and you know that will not be good either for you or for my god-daughter.'

This argument had some share in quieting my mother. There was an interval of silence, only broken by Miss Betsey's occasionally ejaculating 'Ha!' as she sat with her feet upon the fender.

'David had bought an annuity for himself,' said she, by-and-by. 'What did he do for you?'

'Mr Copperfield was so considerate as to secure the reversion of a part of it to me.'

'How much?' asked Miss Betsey.

'A hundred and five pounds a year.'

'He might have done worse,' said my aunt.

The word was appropriate to the moment. My mother was so much worse that Peggotty, coming in with the tea-board and candles, and seeing at a glance how ill she was, conveyed her up-stairs to her own room with all speed; and immediately despatched Ham Peggotty, her nephew, to fetch the nurse and doctor.

Those allied powers were considerably astonished to find an unknown lady of portentous appearance sitting before the fire, with her bonnet tied over her left arm, stopping her ears with jewellers' cotton. Peggotty knowing nothing about her, and my mother saying nothing, she was quite a mystery in the parlour.

The doctor, having been up-stairs and come down again, laid himself out to be polite and social. He was the mildest of little men.

Mr Chillip, looking at my aunt with his head on one side, and making her a little bow, said, in allusion to the jewellers' cotton, as he softly touched his left ear:

'Some local irritation, ma'am?'

'What?' replied my aunt, pulling the cotton out of one ear like a cork.

Mr Chillip was so alarmed by her abruptness that it was a mercy he didn't lose his presence of mind. But he repeated sweetly: 'Some local irritation, ma'am?'

'Nonsense!' replied my aunt, and corked herself again, at one blow.

Mr Chillip could do nothing after this, but sit and look at her feebly until he was called up-stairs again. After some quarter of an hour's absence, he returned.

'Well?' said my aunt, taking the cotton out of the ear nearest to him.

'Well, ma'am,' returned Mr Chillip, 'we are progressing slowly, ma'am.'

'Ba – a – ah!' said my aunt. And corked herself as before.

Mr Chillip was almost shocked but he sat and looked at her, notwithstanding, for nearly two hours, until he was again called out. After another absence, he again returned.

'Well?' said my aunt.

'Well, ma'am,' returned Mr Chillip, 'we are progressing slowly.'

'Ya – a – ah!' said my aunt. With such a snarl at him, that Mr Chillip absolutely could not bear it. He preferred to go and sit upon the stairs, in the dark and a strong draught, until he was again sent for.

The mild Mr Chillip could not possibly bear malice at such a time. He sidled into the parlour as soon as he was at liberty:

'Well, ma'am, I am happy to congratulate you. All is now over, ma'am, and well over.'

'How is she?' said my aunt.

'Quite as comfortable as we can expect a young mother to be,' returned Mr Chillip.

'And *she*. How is *she*?' said my aunt, sharply.

Mr Chillip laid his head a little more on one side, and looked at my aunt like an amiable bird.

'The baby,' said my aunt. 'How is she?'

'Ma'am,' returned Mr Chillip, 'I apprehended you had known. It's a boy.'

My aunt said never a word, but took her bonnet by the strings, in the manner of a sling, aimed a blow at Mr Chillip's head with it, walked out, and never came back.

CHAPTER 2

I observe

The first objects that assume a distinct presence before me, as I look far back into the blank of my infancy, are my mother with her pretty hair and youthful shape, and Peggotty, with no shape at all, and cheeks and arms so hard and red that I wondered the birds didn't peck her in preference to apples.

I believe I can remember these two kneeling on the floor and I going unsteadily from the one to the other. I have an impression of the touch of Peggotty's forefinger and of its being roughened by needlework, like a pocket nutmeg-grater.

What else do I remember? Let me see.

Our house – on the ground-floor is Peggotty's kitchen, opening into a back yard; with a pigeon-house on a pole without any pigeons in it; a great dog-kennel without any dog; and a quantity of fowls walking about in a ferocious manner. Of the geese outside the side-gate who come waddling after me with their long necks stretched out, I dream at night; as a man environed by wild beasts might dream of lions.

Here is a long passage leading from Peggotty's kitchen to the front door. A dark store-room opens out of it, and that is a place to be run past at night; for I don't know what may be among those tubs and jars and old tea-chests, letting a mouldy air come out at the door, in which there is the smell of soap, pickles, pepper, candles, and coffee, all at one whiff. Then there are the two parlours: the parlour in which we sit of an evening and the best parlour where we sit on a Sunday; grandly, but not so comfortably. There is something of a doleful air about that room to me. One Sunday night my mother reads to Peggotty and me in there, how Lazarus was raised up from the dead. And I am so frightened that they are afterwards obliged to show me the quiet churchyard out of the bedroom window, with the dead all lying in their graves at rest, below the solemn moon.

There is nothing half so green that I know anywhere, as the grass of that churchyard; nothing half so shady as its trees; nothing half so quiet as its tombstones.

Here is our pew in the church. What a high-backed pew! With a window near it, out of which our house can be seen, and *is* seen many times during the morning's service, by Peggotty, who likes to make herself as sure as she can that it's not being robbed, or is not in flames. But though Peggotty's eye wanders, she is much offended if mine does. I look at my mother, but *she* pretends not to see me. I look at a boy in the aisle, and *he* makes faces at me. I look up at the monumental tablets on the wall, and try to think of Mr Bodgers late of this parish, and what the feelings of Mrs Bodgers must have been, when affliction sore, long time Mr Bodgers bore, and physicians were in vain. In time my eyes gradually shut up; and I fall off the seat with a crash, and am taken out by Peggotty.

And now I see the outside of our house, with the latticed bedroom windows standing open to let in the sweet-smelling air. I am in the garden at the back – a very preserve of butterflies, as I remember it, where the fruit clusters on the trees, riper and richer than fruit has ever been since, and where my mother gathers some in a basket, while I stand by, bolting furtive gooseberries. A great wind rises, and the summer is gone in a moment.

Peggotty and I were sitting one night by the parlour fire, alone. I had been reading to Peggotty about crocodiles. I was tired of reading, and dead sleepy; but having leave, as a high treat, to sit up until Mother came home from spending the evening at a neighbour's, would rather have died upon my own post than have gone to bed.

'Peggotty,' says I, suddenly, 'were you ever married?'

'Lord, Master Davy,' replied Peggotty. 'What's put marriage in your head?'

She answered with such a start, that it quite awoke me.

'But *were* you ever married, Peggotty?' says I. 'You are a very handsome woman, an't you?'

I thought her in a different style from my mother, certainly; but of another school of beauty, I considered her a perfect example.

'Me handsome, Davy?' said Peggotty. 'Lawk, no, my dear! What put marriage in your head?'

'I don't know! – You mustn't marry more than one person at a time, may you, Peggotty?'

'Certainly not,' says Peggotty, with the promptest decision.

'But if you marry a person, and the person dies, why then you may marry another person, mayn't you, Peggotty?'

'You MAY,' says Peggotty, 'if you choose, my dear. That's a matter of opinion.'

'But what is your opinion, Peggotty?' said I.

I asked her, and looked curiously at her, because she looked so curiously at me.

'My opinion is,' said Peggotty, 'that I never was married myself, Master Davy, and that I don't expect to be.'

'You an't cross, Peggotty, are you?' said I.

I really thought she was, but I was quite mistaken: for she laid aside her work and opening her arms wide, took my curly head within them, and gave it a good squeeze. I know it was a good squeeze, because, being very plump, whenever she made any little exertion, some of the buttons on the back of her gown flew off. And I recollect two bursting to the opposite side of the parlour.

'Now let me hear some more about the Crorkindills,' said Peggotty, 'for I an't heard half enough.'

We had exhausted the crocodiles, and begun with the alligators, when the garden-bell rang. There was my mother, looking unusually pretty, I thought, and with her a gentleman with beautiful black hair and whiskers.

He patted me on the head; but somehow, I didn't like him or his deep voice, and I was jealous that his hand should touch my mother's in touching me – which it did. I put it away as well as I could.

'Oh, Davy!' remonstrated my mother.

'Dear boy!' said the gentleman. 'I cannot wonder at his devotion!'

I never saw such a beautiful colour on my mother's face before. She gently chid me for being rude.

'Come! Let us be the best friends in the world!' said the gentleman, laughing. 'Shake hands!'

My right hand was in my mother's left, so I gave him the other.

'Why, that's the wrong hand, Davy!' laughed the gentleman.

My mother drew my right hand forward, but I gave him the other, and he shook it heartily, and said I was a brave fellow, and went away.

At this minute I see him turn round in the garden, and give us a last look with his ill-omened black eyes, before the door was shut.

Peggotty, who had not said a word, secured the fastenings instantly, and we all went into the parlour. My mother sat singing to herself.

'– Hope you have had a pleasant evening, ma'am,' said Peggotty, standing as stiff as a barrel in the centre of the room, with a candlestick in her hand. 'A stranger or so makes an agreeable change.'

'A very agreeable change, indeed,' returned my mother.

I fell asleep, though I was not so sound asleep but that I could hear voices. When I half awoke from this uncomfortable doze, I found Peggotty and my mother both in tears.

'Not such a one as this, Mr Copperfield wouldn't have liked,' said Peggotty. 'That I swear!'

'Good Heavens!' cried my mother, 'you'll drive me mad! How can you have the heart to say such bitter things to me, when you are well aware that I haven't, out of this place, a single friend to turn to?'

'The more's the reason,' returned Peggotty, 'for saying that it won't do. No! No price could make it do. No !' – I thought Peggotty would have thrown the candlestick away, she was so emphatic with it.

'How can you go on as if it was all settled and arranged, Peggotty, when I tell you over and over again, you cruel thing, that nothing has passed! You talk of admiration. What am I to do, I ask you? Would you wish me to shave my head and black my face? I dare say you would, Peggotty. I dare say you'd quite enjoy it.'

Peggotty seemed to take this aspersion very much to heart, I thought.

'And my dear boy,' cried my mother, caressing me, 'my own little Davy! Is it to be hinted to me that I am wanting in affection for my precious treasure!'

'Nobody never hinted no such a thing,' said Peggotty.

'You did, Peggotty!' returned my mother. 'What else was it possible to infer from what you said, when you know that on his account I wouldn't buy myself a new parasol, though that old green one is frayed the whole way up, and the fringe is perfectly mangy?' Then, turning to me, with her cheek against mine, 'Am I a nasty, cruel, selfish mama? Say "yes," dear boy, and Peggotty will love you; and Peggotty's love is a great deal better than mine, Davy. *I* don't love you at all, do I?'

At this, we all fell a-crying together. I think I was the loudest of the party. I am afraid that I called Peggotty a 'Beast.' That honest creature was in deep affliction, I remember, and must have become quite buttonless for a little volley of those explosives went off, when, after having made it up with my mother, she kneeled down and made it up with me.

Whether it was the following Sunday when I saw the gentleman I cannot recall. But there he was, in church, and he walked home with us afterwards. Peggotty began to be less with us of an evening, than she had always been. My mother deferred to her very much and we were all three excellent friends; still we were different from what we used to be. Sometimes I fancied that Peggotty objected to my mother's wearing all the pretty dresses she had in her drawers, or to her going so often to visit at that neighbour's; but I couldn't, to my satisfaction, make out how it was.

Gradually, I became used to seeing the gentleman with the black whiskers. I liked him no better than at first, but if I had any reason for it beyond a child's instinctive dislike, it certainly was not *the* reason that I might have found if I had been older. I could observe, in little pieces, as it were; but as to making a net of a number of these pieces, and catching anybody in it, that was beyond me.

One autumn morning I was with my mother in the front garden, when Mr Murdstone – I knew him by that name now – came by, on horseback. He said he was going to Lowestoft to see some friends who were there with a yacht, and merrily proposed to take me on the saddle before him if I would like the ride.

The horse seemed to like the idea of the ride so much himself, as he stood snorting at the garden-gate, that I had a great desire to go. So I was sent up-stairs to Peggotty to be made spruce; while my mother kept Mr Murdstone company. I recollect Peggotty and I peeping out at them from my little window; and how, from being in a perfectly angelic temper, Peggotty turned cross in a moment, and brushed my hair excessively hard.

Mr Murdstone and I were soon off. He held me quite easily with one arm, and I could not make up my mind to sit in front of him without turning my head sometimes, and looking up in his face. He had that kind of shallow black eye which seems, from some peculiarity of light, to be disfigured, for a moment at a time, by a cast. I wondered what he was thinking about so closely. His hair and whiskers were blacker and thicker, looked at so near. His regular eyebrows, and the rich white, and black, and brown, of his complexion – confound his complexion, and his memory! – made me think him, in spite of my misgivings, a very handsome man. I have no doubt that my poor dear mother thought him so too.

We went to an hotel by the sea, where two gentlemen were smoking cigars in a room by themselves. They both rolled on to their feet, in an untidy sort of manner, when we came in, and said, 'Halloa, Murdstone! We thought you were dead!'

'Not yet,' said Mr Murdstone.

'And who's this shaver?' said one of the gentlemen.

'That's Davy,' returned Mr Murdstone.

'Davy who?' said the gentleman. 'Jones?'

'Copperfield,' said Mr Murdstone.

'What! Bewitching Mrs Copperfield's incumbrance?' cried the gentleman. 'The pretty little widow?'

'Quinion,' said Mr Murdstone, 'take care, if you please. Somebody's sharp.'

'Who is?' asked the gentleman, laughing.

I looked up, quickly; being curious to know.

'Only Brooks of Sheffield,' said Mr Murdstone.

I was quite relieved to find that it was only Brooks of Sheffield; for, at first, I really thought it was I.

There seemed to be something very comical in the reputation of Mr Brooks of Sheffield, for both the gentlemen laughed heartily when he was mentioned. The gentleman called Quinion said: 'And what is the opinion of Brooks of Sheffield, in reference to the projected business?'

'Why, I don't know that Brooks understands much about it at present,' replied Mr Murdstone; 'but he is not generally favourable, I believe.'

There was more laughter at this, and Mr Quinion said he would ring the bell for some sherry in which to drink to Brooks. When the wine came, he made me have a little and say, 'Confusion to Brooks of Sheffield!' The toast was received with great applause, and such hearty laughter that it made me laugh too. In short, we quite enjoyed ourselves.

We walked about on the cliff after that, and sat on the grass, and looked at things through a telescope. I must not forget that we went on board the yacht, where they all three descended into the cabin, and were busy with some papers.

I observed all day that Mr Murdstone was graver and steadier than the two gentlemen. They were very gay and careless. It appeared to me that he was more clever and cold than they were, and that they regarded him with something of my own feeling. Nor do I recollect that Mr Murdstone laughed at all that day, except at the Sheffield joke – and that, by the by, was his own.

We went home early in the evening. When he was gone, my mother asked me all about the day I had had. I mentioned what they had said about her, and she laughed, and told me they were impudent fellows who talked nonsense – but I knew it pleased her.

I write of her just as she was when I had gone to bed after this talk, and she came to bid me good-night. She kneeled down playfully and laying her chin upon her hands said:

'What was it they said, Davy? Tell me again. I can't believe it.'

'"Bewitching—"' I began.

My mother put her hands upon my lips to stop me.

'It was never bewitching,' she said, laughing.

'Yes, it was. "Bewitching Mrs Copperfield,"' I repeated stoutly. 'And "Pretty little widow."'

'What foolish, impudent creatures!' cried my mother, covering her face. 'Don't tell Peggotty; she might be angry with them.'

I promised, of course; and we kissed one another over and over again, and I soon fell fast asleep.

It seems to me, at this distance of time, as if it were the next day when Peggotty broached the striking and adventurous proposition I am about to mention; but it was probably about two months afterwards.

We were sitting one evening when my mother was out as before.

'Master Davy, how should you like to go along with me and spend a fortnight at my brother's at Yarmouth? Wouldn't *that* be a treat?'

'Is your brother an agreeable man, Peggotty?' I inquired, provisionally.

'Oh, what an agreeable man he is!' cried Peggotty, holding up her hands. 'Then there's the sea; and the boats and ships; and the fishermen; and the beach; and Am to play with –'

Peggotty meant her nephew Ham, she spoke of him as a morsel of English Grammar.

I was flushed by her summary of delights, and replied that it would indeed be a treat, but what would my mother say?

'Why, I'll as good as bet a guinea,' said Peggotty, 'that she'll let us go.'

'But what's she to do while we are away?' said I, putting my small elbows on the table. 'She can't live by herself.'

If Peggotty were looking for a hole, all of a sudden, in the heel of that stocking, it must have been not worth darning. 'Oh don't you know? She's going to stay for a fortnight with Mrs Grayper.'

If that was it, I was quite ready to go. I waited until my mother came home to ascertain if we could get leave to carry out this great idea. Without being nearly so much surprised as I expected, my mother entered into it readily; it was all arranged that night.

The day soon came for our going, even to me, who was in a fever of expectation, and half afraid that an earthquake, or some other great convulsion of nature, might interpose to stop the expedition. It touches me nearly now, to recollect how eager I was to leave my happy home; to think how little I suspected what I did leave for ever.

I am glad to recollect that when the carrier's cart was at the gate, and my mother stood there kissing me, a grateful fondness for her and for the old place I had never turned my back upon before, made me cry. I am glad to know that my mother cried too, and that I felt her heart beat against mine.

I am glad to recollect that when the carrier began to move, my mother called to him to stop, that she might kiss me once more. I am glad to dwell upon the earnestness and love with which she lifted up her face to mine.

As we left her standing in the road, Mr Murdstone seemed to expostulate with her for being so moved. I was looking back round the awning of the cart, and wondered what business it was of his. Peggotty, who was also looking back, seemed anything but satisfied.

I sat looking at Peggotty for some time, in a reverie on this supposititious case: whether, if she were employed to lose me like the boy in the fairy tale, I should be able to track my way home again by the buttons she would shed.

CHAPTER 3

I have a Change

The carrier's horse was the laziest horse in the world, I should hope, and we made so many deviations up and down lanes, that I was very glad when we saw Yarmouth. It looked rather spongy and soppy, I thought, as I carried my eye over the great dull waste that lay across the river; as we drew a little nearer, and saw the whole adjacent prospect lying a straight low line under the sky, I hinted to Peggotty that a mound or so might have improved it. But Peggotty said, with greater emphasis than usual, that we must take things as we found them, and that, for her part, she was proud to call herself a Yarmouth Bloater.

When we got into the street and smelt the fish, and pitch, and oakum, and tar, and saw the sailors walking about, and the carts jingling up and down over the stones, I felt that I had done so busy a place an injustice; and said as much to Peggotty, who heard my expressions of delight with great complacency, and told me it was well known that Yarmouth was, upon the whole, the finest place in the universe.

Ham was waiting for us at the public-house. Our intimacy was much advanced by his taking me on his back to carry me home. He was a huge, strong fellow of six feet high, dressed in a canvas jacket, and a pair of such very stiff trousers that they would have stood quite as well, alone, without any legs in them.

We turned down lanes past boat-builders' yards, shipwrights' yards, caulkers' yards, and a great litter of such places, until we came out upon the dull waste I had already seen at a distance; when Ham said, 'Yon's our house, Mas'r Davy!'

I looked in all directions, but no house could *I* make out. There was a black barge, not far off, high and dry on the ground, with an iron funnel sticking out of it for a chimney and smoking very cosily; but nothing else in the way of habitation that was visible to *me*.

'That's it, Mas'r Davy,' returned Ham.

If it had been Aladdin's palace, I could not have been more charmed. There was a delightful door cut in the side, and it was roofed in, but the wonderful charm of it was that it was a real boat which had no doubt been upon the water hundreds of times.

It was beautifully clean inside, and as tidy as possible. There was a table, and a chest of drawers, and over the little mantel-shelf, was a picture of the Sarah Jane lugger, with a real little wooden stern stuck on to it; a work of art, combining composition with carpentry, which I considered to be one of the most enviable possessions that the world could afford. There were some lockers and boxes which served for seats and eked out the chairs.

Then Peggotty showed me my bedroom in the stern of the vessel; with a little window, where the rudder used to go through; a little bed, which there was just room enough to get into; and a nosegay of seaweed in a blue mug on the table. The walls were whitewashed as white as milk, and the patchwork counterpane made my eyes quite ache with its brightness.

One thing I particularly noticed in this delightful house, was the smell of fish. On my imparting the discovery to Peggotty, she informed me that her brother dealt in lobsters, crabs, and crawfish; and I afterwards found that a heap of these creatures, in a state of wonderful conglomeration with one another, were usually to be found in a little wooden outhouse where the pots and kettles were kept.

We were welcomed by a very civil woman in a white apron. Likewise by a most beautiful little girl with a necklace of blue beads on, who wouldn't let me kiss her when I offered to, but ran away. By-and-by, a hairy man with a good-natured face came home. As he called Peggotty 'Lass,' and gave her a hearty smack on the cheek, I had no doubt that he was her brother, and so he turned out – being introduced to me as Mr Peggotty, the master of his house.

'Glad to see you, sir,' said Mr Peggotty. 'You'll find us rough, sir, but you'll find us ready.'

I thanked him, and replied that I was sure I should be happy in such a delightful place.

'Well, sir, if you can make out here, for a fortnut, 'long wi' her,' nodding at his sister, 'and Ham, and little Em'ly, we shall be proud of your company.'

After tea, when the door was shut and all was made snug it seemed to me the most delicious retreat that the imagination of man could conceive. To hear the wind getting up out at sea, to know that the fog was creeping over the desolate flat outside, and to look at the fire and think that there was no house near but this one, and this one a boat, was like enchantment. Little Em'ly had overcome her shyness, and was sitting by my side. Mr Peggotty was smoking his pipe. I felt it was a time for conversation.

'Mr Peggotty!' says I. 'Did you give your son the name of Ham, because you lived in a sort of ark?'

Mr Peggotty seemed to think it a deep idea, but answered: 'No, sir. I never give him no name. His father giv it him.'

'I thought you were his father!'

'My brother Joe was *his* father,' said Mr Peggotty.

'Dead, Mr Peggotty?' I hinted, after a respectful pause.

'Drowndead,' said Mr Peggotty.

I was very much surprised that Mr Peggotty was not Ham's father, and began to wonder whether I was mistaken about his relationship to anybody else.

'Little Em'ly,' I said, glancing at her. 'She is your daughter, isn't she, Mr Peggotty?'

'No, sir. My brother-in-law, Tom, was *her* father.'

I couldn't help it. 'Dead, Mr Peggotty?' I hinted, after another respectful silence.

'Drowndead,' said Mr Peggotty.

I felt the difficulty of resuming the subject, but had not got to the bottom of it yet. So I said: 'Haven't you *any* children, Mr Peggotty?'

'No, master,' he answered, with a short laugh. 'I'm a bacheldore.'

'A bachelor!' I said, astonished. 'Why, who's that, Mr Peggotty?' Pointing to the person in the apron who was knitting.

'That's Missis Gummidge,' said Mr Peggotty.

At this point Peggotty made motions to me not to ask any more questions. In the privacy of my own little cabin, she informed me that Ham and Em'ly were an orphan nephew and niece, whom my host had at different times adopted in their childhood, when they were left destitute; and that Mrs Gummidge was the widow of his partner in a boat, who had died very poor. He was but a poor man himself, said Peggotty, but as good as gold and as true as steel – those were her similes. The only subject on which he ever showed a violent temper was this generosity of his; and if it were ever referred to, he struck the table a heavy blow with his right hand and swore a dreadful oath that he would be 'Gormed' if he didn't cut and run for good, if it was ever mentioned again. It appeared that nobody had the least idea of this terrible verb to be gormed; but that they all regarded it as constituting a most solemn imprecation.

As slumber gradually stole upon me, I heard the wind howling across the flat so fiercely that I had a lazy apprehension of the great deep rising in the night. But I bethought myself that I was in a boat, after all; and that a man like Mr Peggotty was not a bad person to have on board if anything did happen.

Nothing happened, however, worse than morning. Almost as soon as it shone I was out with little Em'ly, picking up stones upon the beach.

'You're quite a sailor, I suppose?' I said to Em'ly.

'No,' replied Em'ly, shaking her head, 'I'm afraid of the sea.'

'Afraid!' I said, with a becoming air of boldness, and looking very big at the mighty ocean. '*I* an't!'

'Ah! but it's cruel,' said Em'ly. 'I have seen it tear a boat as big as our house all to pieces.'

'I hope it wasn't the boat that –'

'That father was drownded in?' said Em'ly. 'No. Not that one, I never see that boat.'

'Nor him?' I asked her.

Little Em'ly shook her head. 'Not to remember!'

Here was a coincidence! I immediately went into an explanation how I had never seen my own father. But there were some differences between Em'ly's orphanhood and mine, it appeared. She had lost her mother before her father.

'Besides,' said Em'ly, 'your father was a gentleman and your mother is a lady; and my father was a fisherman and my mother was a fisherman's daughter.'

'You would like to be a lady?' I said.

Em'ly looked at me, and laughed and nodded 'yes.'

'I should like it very much. We would all be gentlefolks together, then. Me, and uncle, and Ham, and Mrs Gummidge. We wouldn't mind then, when there come stormy weather. – Not for our own sakes, I mean. We would for the poor fishermen's, to be sure, and we'd help 'em with money when they come to any hurt.'

This seemed to me to be a very satisfactory, and therefore not at all improbable, picture. I expressed my pleasure in the contemplation of it, and little Em'ly was emboldened to say, shyly,

'Don't you think you are afraid of the sea, now?'

I said 'No,' and added, 'You don't seem to be, either, though you say you are,' – for she was walking much too near the brink of a sort of old jetty we had strolled upon, and I was afraid of her falling over.

'I'm not afraid in this way,' said little Em'ly. 'Not a bit. Look here!'

She started from my side, and ran along a jagged timber which overhung the deep water at some height, without the least defence. The incident is impressed on my remembrance, little Em'ly springing forward to her destruction with a look that I have never forgotten, directed far out to sea.

The light, bold, fluttering little figure turned and came back safe to me. There have been times since, in my manhood, when I have thought, Is it possible that her life might have a chance of ending that day? There has been a time since when I have asked myself the question, would it have been better for little Em'ly to have had the waters close above her head that morning; and when I have answered Yes, it would have been.

This may be premature. I have set it down too soon, perhaps. But let it stand.

We strolled a long way, and loaded ourselves with things that we thought curious, and then made our way home to Mr Peggotty's dwelling. We stopped under the lee of the lobster-house to exchange an innocent kiss, and went in to breakfast glowing with health and pleasure.

Of course I was in love with little Em'ly. I am sure my fancy raised up something round that blue-eyed mite of a child, which made a very angel of her. We used to walk about that dim old flat at Yarmouth in a loving manner, hours and hours. As to any sense of inequality, or youthfulness, or other difficulty in our way, little Em'ly and I had no such trouble, because we had no future. We made no more provision for growing older, than we did for growing younger. We were the admiration of Mrs Gummidge and Peggotty, who used to whisper of an evening when we sat lovingly, on our little locker side by side.

I soon found out that Mrs Gummidge did not always make herself so agreeable. Mrs Gummidge's was rather a fretful disposition. I was very sorry for her; but there were moments when it would have been more agreeable if Mrs Gummidge had had a convenient apartment of her own to retire to.

Mr Peggotty went occasionally to a public-house called The Willing Mind. I discovered this on the second or third evening of our visit.

Mrs Gummidge had been in a low state all day, and had burst into tears in the forenoon, when the fire smoked. 'I am a lone lorn creetur',' were Mrs Gummidge's words, when that unpleasant occurrence took place, 'and everythink goes contrairy with me.'

Accordingly, when Mr Peggotty came home about nine o'clock, this unfortunate Mrs Gummidge was knitting in her corner, in a very wretched and miserable condition.

'Well, mates,' said Mr Peggotty, taking his seat, 'and how are you?'

We all said something to welcome him, except Mrs Gummidge, who only shook her head over her knitting.

'What's amiss?' said Mr Peggotty, with a clap of his hands. 'Cheer up, old mawther!'

Mrs Gummidge did not appear to be able to cheer up. She took out an old black silk handkerchief and wiped her eyes. 'You've come from The Willing Mind, Dan'l? I'm sorry I should drive you there,' said Mrs Gummidge.

'I don't want no driving,' returned Mr Peggotty with an honest laugh. 'I only go too ready.'

'Very ready,' said Mrs Gummidge, shaking her head, and wiping her eyes. 'I am sorry it should be along of me that you're so ready.'

'It an't along o'you!'

'Yes, it is,' cried Mrs Gummidge. 'I know what I am. I know that I am a lone lorn creetur', and not only that everythink goes contrairy with me, but that I go contrairy with everybody. I make the house uncomfortable. I've made your sister so all day, and Master Davy.'

Here I was suddenly melted, and roared out, 'No, you haven't, Mrs Gummidge,' in great mental distress.

'It's far from right that I should do it,' said Mrs Gummidge. 'I'd better go into the house, and die and be a riddance!'

Mrs Gummidge retired with these words, and betook herself to bed. When she was gone, Mr Peggotty, who had not exhibited a trace of any feeling but the profoundest sympathy, looked round upon us, and said in a whisper: 'She's been thinking of the old 'un!'

I did not quite understand what old one Mrs Gummidge was supposed to have fixed her mind upon, until Peggotty, on seeing me to bed, explained that it was the late Mr Gummidge; and that her brother always took that for a received truth on such occasions. And whenever Mrs Gummidge was overcome during the remainder of our stay he always said the same thing in extenuation of the circumstance, and always with the tenderest commiseration.

So the fortnight slipped away, varied by nothing but the variation of the tide, which altered Mr Peggotty's times of going out and coming in, and altered Ham's engagements also. When the latter was unemployed, he sometimes walked with us to show us the boats and ships, and once or twice he took us for a row. I never hear the name of Yarmouth, but I am reminded of a certain Sunday morning on the beach, the bells ringing for church, little Em'ly leaning on my shoulder, Ham lazily dropping stones into the water, and the sun, away at sea, just breaking through the heavy mist.

At last the day came for going home. I bore up against the separation from Mr Peggotty and Mrs Gummidge, but my agony of mind at leaving little Em'ly was piercing. We were greatly overcome at parting; and if ever in my life I have had a void made in my heart, I had one made that day.

Now, all the time I had been on my visit, I had been ungrateful to my home and had thought little about it. But I was no sooner turned towards it, than I felt, all the more for the sinking of my spirits, that it was my nest, and that my mother was my comforter and friend.

This gained upon me as we went along; so that the nearer we drew, the more excited I was to get there, and to run into her arms. But Peggotty, instead of sharing in these transports, looked confused and out of sorts.

Blunderstone Rookery would come, however, in spite of her. How well I recollect it, on a cold grey afternoon, and with a dull sky, threatening rain!

The door opened, and I looked for my mother. It was not she, but a strange servant.

'Why, Peggotty!' I said, ruefully, 'isn't she come home?'

She took me by the hand; led me into the kitchen; and shut the door.

'Peggotty!' said I, quite frightened. 'What's the matter?'

'Nothing's the matter, bless you, Master Davy dear!' she answered, assuming an air of sprightliness.

'Something's the matter, I'm sure. Where's mama? Oh, she's not dead, Peggotty?'

Peggotty cried out No! with an astonishing volume of voice and then sat down, and said I had given her a turn. 'You see, dear, I should have told you before now but I couldn't azackly bring my mind to it.'

'Go on, Peggotty,' said I, more frightened than before.

'Master Davy,' said Peggotty, speaking in a breathless sort of way. 'What do you think? You have got a Pa! A new one.'

'A new one?' I repeated.

Peggotty gave a gasp, as if she were swallowing something that was very hard, and, putting out her hand, said: 'Come and see him.'

'I don't want to see him.'

'And your mama,' said Peggotty.

I ceased to draw back, and we went straight to the best parlour, where she left me. On one side of the fire, sat my mother; on the other, Mr Murdstone. My mother dropped her work, and arose hurriedly, but timidly I thought.

'Now, Clara my dear,' said Mr Murdstone. 'Recollect! Control yourself. Davy boy, how do you do?'

I gave him my hand. After a moment of suspense, I went and kissed my mother: she kissed me, patted me gently on the shoulder, and sat down again to her work. I could not look at her, I could not look at him, I knew quite well that he was looking at us both; and I turned to the window and looked out there at some shrubs that were drooping their heads in the cold.

As soon as I could, I crept up-stairs. My old dear bedroom was changed, and I was to lie a long way off. I rambled downstairs to find anything that was like itself, so altered it all seemed; and roamed into the yard. I very soon started back from there, for the empty dog-kennel was filled up with a great dog – deep-mouthed and black-haired like Him – and he was very angry at the sight of me, and sprang out to get at me.

CHAPTER 4

I fall into Disgrace

If the room to which my bed was removed were a sentient thing, I might appeal to it to bear witness for what a heavy heart I carried to it. I rolled myself up in a corner of the counterpane, and cried myself to sleep.

I was awakened by somebody saying 'Here he is!' and uncovering my head. My mother and Peggotty had come to look for me.

'Davy,' said my mother. 'Davy, my child!'

I dare say no words she could have uttered would have affected me so much, then, as her calling me her child. I hid my tears in the bedclothes, and pressed her from me with my hand.

'This is your doing, Peggotty!' said my mother. 'How can you reconcile it to your conscience, to prejudice my own boy against me? What do you mean by it, Peggotty?'

Poor Peggotty only answered, in a sort of paraphrase of the grace I usually repeated after dinner, 'Lord forgive you, Mrs Copperfield, and for what you have said this minute, may you never be truly sorry!'

'Davy, you naughty boy! Peggotty, you savage creature! Oh, dear me!' cried my mother, turning from one of us to the other, in her pettish, wilful manner. 'What a troublesome world this is, when one has the most right to expect it to be as agreeable as possible!'

I felt the touch of a hand that I knew was neither hers nor Peggotty's. It was Mr Murdstone's hand, and he kept it on my arm as he said:

'What's this? Clara, my love, have you forgotten? – Firmness, my dear!'

'I am very sorry, Edward,' said my mother. 'I meant to be very good, but I am so uncomfortable.'

'Indeed!' he answered. 'That's a bad hearing, so soon, Clara.'

He drew her to him, whispered in her ear. I knew, when I saw my mother's head lean down upon his shoulder, he could mould her pliant nature into any form he chose.

'Go you below, my love,' said Mr Murdstone. 'My friend,' turning a darkening face on Peggotty, 'do you know your mistress's name?'

'She has been my mistress a long time, sir,' answered Peggotty. 'I ought to.'

'That's true,' he answered. 'But I thought I heard you address her by a name that is not hers. She has taken mine, you know. Will you remember that?'

Peggotty curtseyed herself out of the room without replying. When we two were left alone, he looked steadily into my eyes.

'David,' he said, 'if I have an obstinate horse or dog to deal with, what do you think I do?'

'I don't know.'

'I beat him. I say to myself, "I'll conquer that fellow;" and if it were to cost him all the blood he had, I should do it. You understood me very well, I see. Come down with me.'

'Clara, my dear,' he said, when he walked me into the parlour, with his hand still on my arm; 'you will not be made uncomfortable any more, I hope. We shall soon improve our youthful humours.'

God help me, I might have been improved for my whole life, by a kind word at that season. A word of encouragement and explanation, of welcome home, of reassurance to me that it *was* home, might have made me respect instead of hate him. But the word was not spoken, and the time for it was gone.

We dined alone, we three together. I gathered that an elder sister of his was coming to stay and that she was expected that evening. After dinner, a coach drove up and Mr Murdstone went out to receive the visitor. My mother followed and I was timidly following her, when she turned round and, taking me in her embrace as she had been used to do, whispered me to love my new father and be obedient to him. She did this hurriedly and secretly, as if it were wrong.

Miss Murdstone was a gloomy-looking lady; dark, like her brother, with very heavy eyebrows. She brought with her two hard black boxes, with her initials on the lids in hard brass nails. When she paid the coachman she took a hard steel purse out of a very jail of a bag which hung upon her arm by a heavy chain. I had never seen such a metallic lady altogether as Miss Murdstone was.

She was brought into the parlour and there formally recognised my mother as a new and near relation. Then she looked at me, and said: 'Is that your boy, sister-in-law?'

My mother acknowledged me.

'Generally speaking,' said Miss Murdstone, 'I don't like boys. How d'ye do, boy?'

Under these encouraging circumstances, I replied that I was very well, and that I hoped she was the same; with such an indifferent grace, that Miss Murdstone disposed of me in two words:

'Wants manner!'

As well as I could make out, she had come for good, and had no intention of ever going again. On the very first morning after her arrival she was up and ringing her bell at cock-crow. When my mother came down to breakfast and was going to make the tea, Miss Murdstone said: 'Now, Clara, I am come here to relieve you of all the trouble I can. If you'll be so good as give me your keys, my dear, I'll attend to all this sort of thing in future.'

My mother did not suffer her authority to pass from her without a shadow of protest. One night when Miss Murdstone had been developing certain household plans to her brother, my mother said she thought she might have been consulted.

'Clara!' said Mr Murdstone sternly. 'I wonder at you.'

'Oh, it's very well to say you wonder, Edward!' cried my mother, 'and it's very well for you to talk about firmness, but you wouldn't like it yourself.'

Firmness, I may observe, was the grand quality on which both Mr and Miss Murdstone took their stand. However I might have expressed my comprehension of it at that time, I nevertheless did clearly comprehend that it was another name for tyranny.

'It's very hard,' said my mother, 'that in my own house –'

'*My* own house?' repeated Mr Murdstone. 'Clara!'

'*Our* own house, I mean,' faltered my mother, evidently frightened – 'it's very hard that I may not have a word to say about domestic matters. I am sure I managed very well before we were married. There's evidence,' said my mother sobbing; 'ask Peggotty if I didn't do very well when I wasn't interfered with!'

'Edward,' said Miss Murdstone, 'let there be an end of this. I go tomorrow.'

'Jane Murdstone,' said her brother, 'be silent!'

'I am sure,' my poor mother went on with many tears, 'I don't want anybody to go. I only want to be consulted sometimes. I thought you were pleased, once, with my being a little inexperienced but you seem to hate me for it now, you are so severe.'

'Edward,' said Miss Murdstone again, 'let there be an end of this. I go to-morrow.'

'Jane Murdstone,' thundered Mr Murdstone. 'Will you be silent? Clara,' he continued, looking at my mother, 'you astound me! Yes, I had a satisfaction in the thought of marrying an artless person, and forming her character. But when Jane Murdstone is kind enough to come to my assistance in this endeavour, and when she meets with a base return –'

'Oh, pray, Edward,' cried my mother, 'don't accuse me of being ungrateful. I have many faults, but not that.'

'When Jane Murdstone meets, I say,' he went on, 'with a base return, that feeling of mine is chilled and altered.'

'Don't, my love, say that!' implored my mother very piteously. 'Pray let us be friends.'

'Jane Murdstone,' said Mr Murdstone to his sister, 'any harsh words between us are, I hope, uncommon. It is not my fault that so unusual an occurrence has taken place to-night. I was betrayed into it by another. Let us both try to forget it. And as this,' he added, after these magnanimous words, 'is not a fit scene for the boy – David, go to bed!'

Going down next morning I paused outside the parlour-door on hearing my mother's voice. She was humbly entreating Miss Murdstone's pardon, which that lady granted, and a perfect reconciliation took place. I never knew my mother afterwards to give an opinion on any matter, without first appealing to Miss Murdstone.

There had been some talk on occasions of my going to boarding-school. Mr and Miss Murdstone had originated it, and my mother had of course agreed with them. Nothing, however, was concluded on the subject yet. In the meantime I learnt lessons at home.

Shall I ever forget those lessons! They were presided over nominally by my mother, but really by Mr Murdstone and his sister, who were always present, and found them a favourable occasion for giving my mother lessons in that miscalled firmness, which was the bane of both our lives. I had been apt enough to learn, when my mother and I had lived alone together. But these solemn lessons, I remember as a grievous daily drudgery and misery. They were very long, very numerous, very hard and I was generally as much bewildered by them as I believe my poor mother was herself.

Let me remember how it used to be. I come into the parlour after breakfast, with my books, and an exercise-book, and a slate. My mother is ready for me at her writing-desk, but not half so ready as Mr Murdstone in his easy-chair by the window, or as Miss Murdstone, sitting near my mother stringing steel beads. The very sight of these two has such an influence over me, that I begin to feel the words I have been at infinite pains to get into my head, all sliding away.

I hand the first book to my mother. I take a last drowning look at the page as I give it into her hand, and start off aloud at a racing pace while I have got it fresh. I trip over a word. Mr Murdstone looks up. I trip over another word. Miss Murdstone looks up. I redden, tumble over half-a-dozen words, and stop. I think my mother would show me the book if she dared.

'Now, Clara,' says Mr Murdstone, 'be firm with the boy. He knows his lesson, or he does not know it.'

'He does *not* know it,' Miss Murdstone interposes awfully.

'Now, Davy,' says my mother. 'Try once more, and don't be stupid.'

I obey the first clause of the injunction but am not so successful with the second, for I am very stupid. The despairing way in which my mother and I look at each other, as I blunder on, is truly melancholy. But the greatest effect in these miserable lessons is when my mother tries to give me the cue by the motion of her lips. At that instant Miss Murdstone, who has been lying in wait for nothing else all along, says in a deep warning voice: 'Clara!'

Mr Murdstone comes out of his chair, takes the book, throws it at me or boxes my ears with it, and turns me out of the room by the shoulders.

It seems to me, at this distance of time, as if my unfortunate studies generally took this course. I could have done very well if I had been without the Murdstones; but the influence of the Murdstones upon me was like the fascination of two snakes on a wretched young bird.

The natural result of this treatment, continued, I suppose, for some six months or more, was to make me sullen, dull and dogged. I was not made the less so by my sense of being daily more and more shut out and alienated from my mother. I believe I should have been almost stupefied but for one circumstance.

It was this. My father had left a small collection of books in a little room up-stairs, to which I had access. From that blessed little room, Roderick Random, Peregrine Pickle, Tom Jones, and Robinson Crusoe, came out to keep me company. They kept alive my hope of something beyond that place and time. When I think of it, the picture always rises in my mind of a summer evening, the boys at play in the churchyard, and I sitting on my bed, reading as if for life.

One morning when I went into the parlour with my books, I found my mother looking anxious, Miss Murdstone looking firm, and Mr Murdstone binding a lithe and limber cane, which he left off binding when I came in, and switched in the air.

'Now, David,' he said 'you must be far more careful to-day than usual.' He gave the cane another switch; and laid it down beside him.

This was a good freshener to my presence of mind, as a beginning. I felt the words of my lesson slipping off, not one by one, or line by line, but by the entire page; I tried to lay hold of them; but they seemed to have put skates on, and to skim way from me with a smoothness there was no checking. We began badly, and went on worse. My mother burst out crying.

'Clara!' said Miss Murdstone, in her warning voice.

'I am not quite well, my dear Jane, I think,' said my mother.

I saw Mr Murdstone wink, solemnly, at his sister, as he rose and said, taking up the cane: 'David, you and I will go up-stairs, boy.'

As he took me out at the door, my mother ran towards us. Miss Murdstone said, 'Clara! are you a perfect fool?' I saw my mother stop her ears then, and I heard her crying.

He walked me up to my room slowly and gravely – I am certain he had a delight in that formal parade of executing justice – and when we got there, suddenly twisted my head under his arm.

'Mr Murdstone! Sir!' I cried to him. 'Pray don't beat me! I have tried to learn, sir, but I can't while you and Miss Murdstone are by.'

'Can't you, indeed, David?' he said.

He had my head as in a vice, but I twined round him somehow, and stopped him for a moment. It was only for a moment for he cut me heavily an instant afterwards, and in the same instant I caught the hand with which he held me in my mouth, between my teeth, and bit it through. It sets my teeth on edge to think of it.

He beat me then, as if he would have beaten me to death. Above all the noise we made, I heard them running up the stairs – I heard my mother crying out – and Peggotty. Then he was gone; and the door was locked outside; and I was lying, fevered and hot, and torn, and sore, and raging in my puny way, upon the floor.

How well I recollect, when I became quiet, what an unnatural stillness seemed to reign through the whole house! How well I remember, when my smart and passion began to cool, how wicked I began to feel! My stripes were sore and stiff, and made me cry afresh, when I moved; but they were nothing to the guilt I felt. It lay heavier on my breast than if I had been a most atrocious criminal, I dare say.

It had begun to grow dark, when the key was turned and Miss Murdstone came in with some bread and meat, and milk. These she put down upon the table without a word, glaring at me with exemplary firmness, and then retired, locking the door after her.

Long after it was dark I sat there, wondering fearfully what would be done to me. Whether it was a criminal act that I had committed? Whether I should be taken into custody, and sent to prison? Whether I was at all in danger of being hanged?

I never shall forget the waking next morning; the being cheerful for the first moment, and then the being weighed down by the dismal oppression of remembrance. Miss Murdstone reappeared before I was out of bed; told me, in so many words, that I was free to walk in the garden for half an hour and no longer.

My imprisonment lasted five days. The length of those five days I can convey no idea of to any one. They occupy the place of years in my remembrance. On the last night of my restraint, I was awakened by hearing my name spoken in a whisper. It must have come through the keyhole.

I groped my way to the door, and putting my own lips to the keyhole, whispered:

'Is that you, Peggotty dear?'

'Yes, my own precious Davy,' she replied. 'Be as soft as a mouse, or the Cat'll hear us.'

I understood this to mean Miss Murdstone, her room being close by.

'How's mama, dear Peggotty? Is she very angry with me?'

'No. Not very.'

'What is going to be done with me?'

'School. Near London.'

'When, Peggotty?'

'To-morrow.'

'Shan't I see mama?'

'Yes,' said Peggotty. 'Morning.'

Then Peggotty fitted her mouth close to the keyhole, and delivered these words through it with as much feeling and earnestness as a keyhole has ever been the medium of communicating.

'Davy, dear. If I ain't been azackly as intimate with you. Lately, as I used to be. It ain't because I don't love you. It's because I thought it better for you. And for some one else besides. Davy, my darling, are you listening?'

'Ye – ye – ye – yes, Peggotty!' I sobbed.

'What I want to say, is. That you must never forget me. For I'll never forget you. And I'll take as much care of your mama, Davy. As ever I took of you. And I won't leave her. The day may come when she'll be glad to lay her poor head. On her stupid, old Peggotty's arm again. And I'll write to you, my dear.'

'Thank you, dear Peggotty!' said I. 'Oh, thank you! Will you write and tell Mr Peggotty and little Em'ly, and Mrs Gummidge and Ham, that I am not so bad as they might suppose, and that I sent 'em all my love – especially to little Em'ly?'

The kind soul promised, and we both of us kissed the keyhole with the greatest affection. From that night there grew up in my breast a feeling for Peggotty which I cannot very well define. She did not replace my mother; but she came into a vacancy in my heart, and I felt towards her something I have never felt for any other human being.

In the morning Miss Murdstone appeared as usual, and told me I was going to school; which was not altogether such news to me as she supposed. I was to come down-stairs into the parlour. There I found my mother, very pale and with red eyes: into whose arms I ran, and begged her pardon from my suffering soul.

'Oh, Davy!' she said. 'That you could hurt any one I love! Try to be better! I forgive you; but I am so grieved that you should have such bad passions in your heart.'

They had persuaded her that I was a wicked fellow, and she was more sorry for that, than for my going away. I felt it sorely. I tried to eat my parting breakfast, but my tears dropped upon my bread-and-butter.

'Master Copperfield's box there!' said Miss Murdstone, when wheels were heard at the gate.

My former acquaintaince, the carrier, was at the door; the box was taken out to his cart, and lifted in.

'Clara!' said Miss Murdstone, in her warning note.

'Ready, my dear Jane,' returned my mother. 'Good-bye, Davy, you are going for your own good. Good-bye, my child. You will come home in the holidays, and be a better boy.'

Miss Murdstone was good enough to take me out to the cart, and to say on the way that she hoped I would repent, before I came to a bad end; and then I got into the cart, and the lazy horse walked off with it.

CHAPTER 5

I am sent away from Home

We might have gone about half a mile, and my pocket-handkerchief was quite wet through, when I saw, to my amazement, Peggotty burst from a hedge and climb into the cart. She took me in her arms, and squeezed me to her stays. She brought out some paper bags of cake which she crammed into my pockets, and a purse which she put into my hand, but not one word did she say. After a final squeeze, she got down from the cart and ran away; and my belief is without a solitary button on her gown. I picked up one and treasured it as a keepsake for a long time.

The carrier looked at me, as if to inquire if she were coming back. I shook my head, and said I thought not. 'Then, come up,' said the carrier to the lazy horse; who came up accordingly.

Having by this time cried as much as I possibly could, I began to think it was of no use crying any more, especially as Roderick Random never cried in trying situations. The carrier proposed that my pocket-handkerchief should be spread upon the horse's back to dry; and particularly small it looked, under those circumstances.

I had now leisure to examine the purse. It had three bright shillings in it, but its most precious contents were two half-crowns folded together in a bit of paper, on which was written, in my mother's hand, 'For Davy. With my love.' I was so overcome by this, that I asked the carrier to reach me my handkerchief again; but he said he thought I had better do without, so I wiped my eyes on my sleeve.

After we had jogged on for some little time, I asked the carrier if he was going all the way?

'All the way where?' inquired the carrier (whose name was Mr Barkis).

'Near London,' I said.

'Why that horse,' said the carrier, 'would be deader than pork afore he got over half the ground.'

'Are you only going to Yarmouth, then?' I asked.

'That's about it,' said the carrier. 'And there I shall take you to the stage-cutch.'

I offered him a cake which he ate at one gulp, exactly like an elephant.

'Did *she* make 'em, now?' said Mr Barkis.

'Peggotty, do you mean, sir? She makes all our pastry and does all our cooking.'

'Do she though?' said Mr Barkis.

He made up his mouth as if to whistle. By-and-by, he said: 'No sweethearts, I b'lieve?'

'Oh, no. She never had a sweetheart.'

'Didn't she, though?' said Mr Barkis. Again he made up his mouth to whistle. 'So she makes, all the apple parsties, and does all the cooking, do she?'

I replied that such was the fact.

'Well, I'll tell you what,' said Mr Barkis. 'If you was writin' to her, p'raps you'd recollect to say that Barkis was willin'; would you?'

'That Barkis was willing,' I repeated, innocently. 'Is that all the message?'

'Ye – es,' he said, considering. 'Ye – es, Barkis is willin'.'

'But you will be at Blunderstone again to-morrow, Mr Barkis,' I said, 'and could give your own message so much better.'

As he repudiated this suggestion, however, I readily undertook its transmission. While waiting for the coach at the hotel at Yarmouth that very afternoon, I wrote a note to Peggotty, which ran thus: 'My dear Peggotty. I have come here safe. Barkis is willing. My love to mama. Yours affectionately. P.S. He particularly wants you to know – *Barkis is willing.*'

I slept soundly until we got to Yarmouth. The coach was in the yard, but without any horses to it as yet; and it looked as if nothing was more unlikely than its ever going to London. I was wondering what would become of me, when a lady looked out of a bow-window and said: 'Is that the little gentleman from Blunderstone?'

'Yes, ma'am,' I said.

The lady rang a bell, and called out 'William! show the coffee-room!' upon which a waiter came running to show it, and seemed a good deal surprised when he was only to show it to me.

It was a large long room with some large maps in it. I doubt if I could have felt much stranger if the maps had been real foreign countries, and I cast away in the middle of them. The waiter brought me some chops and vegetables, putting a chair for me at the table, and saying very affably, 'Now, six-foot! come on!'

I took my seat at the board; but found it extremely difficult to handle my knife and fork with anything like dexterity while he was staring so hard. After watching me into the second chop, he said: 'There's half a pint of ale for you. Will you have it now?'

I thanked him and said, 'Yes.' Upon which he poured it into a large tumbler and held it up against the light.

'My eye!' he said. 'It seems a good deal, don't it?'

'It does seem a good deal,' I answered with a smile. For it was quite delightful to me to find him so pleasant.

'There was a gentleman here yesterday,' he said – 'a stout gentleman, by the name of Topsawyer – perhaps you know him?'

'No,' I said bashfully, 'I haven't the pleasure –'

'He came in here,' said the waiter, looking at the light through the tumbler, 'ordered a glass of this ale – drank it, and fell dead. It was too old for him.'

I was very much shocked to hear of this melancholy accident, and said I had better have some water.

'I'll drink it, if you like,' said the waiter. 'I'm used to it. I don't think it'll hurt me, if I throw my head back, and take it off quick. Shall I?'

I replied that if he thought he could do it safely, but by no means otherwise. When he did take it off quick, I had a horrible fear of seeing him fall lifeless on the carpet. But it didn't hurt him. On the contrary, I thought he seemed the fresher for it.

'What have we got here?' he said, putting a fork into my dish. 'Not chops? Why a chop's the very thing to take off the bad effects of that beer! Ain't it lucky?'

So he took a chop by the bone in one hand, and a potato in the other, and ate away with a very good appetite, to my extreme satisfaction. He afterwards took another chop, and another potato; and after that another. When he had done, he brought me a pudding.

'Why, a batter-pudding,' he said, taking up a table-spoon, 'is my favourite pudding! Ain't that lucky? Come on, little 'un, and let's see who'll get most.'

The waiter certainly got most, what with his tablespoon to my tea-spoon, and his appetite to my appetite, I was left far behind at the first mouthful. I never saw any one enjoy a pudding so much, I think.

It was then I asked for the pen and paper to write to Peggotty. When I had finished, he asked me where I was going to school.

I said, 'Near London,' which was all I knew.

'Oh! my eye!' he said, shaking his head, 'that's the school where they broke the boy's ribs – a little boy he was. How old are you, about?'

I told him between eight and nine.

'That's just his age,' he said. 'He was eight years and six months old when they broke his first rib; eight years and eight months when they broke his second, and did for him.'

I could not disguise that this was an uncomfortable coincidence, and inquired how it was done. His answer was not cheering to my spirits, for it consisted of two dismal words, 'With whopping.'

The blowing of the coach-horn in the yard was a seasonable diversion, which made me get up and hesitatingly inquire if there were anything to pay.

'There's a sheet of letter-paper,' he returned. 'It's dear,' he said, 'on account of the duty. Threepence. That's the way we're taxed in this country. Never mind the ink. *I* lose by that.'

'How much ought I to – what would it be right to pay the waiter, if you please?' I stammered.

'If I hadn't a family, and that family hadn't the cowpock,' said the waiter, 'I wouldn't take a sixpence. If I didn't support an aged pairint' – here the waiter was greatly agitated – 'I wouldn't take a farthing. If I was treated well here, I should beg acceptance of a trifle. But I live on broken wittles – and I sleep on the coals' – here the waiter burst into tears.

I was very much concerned for his misfortunes, therefore I gave him one of my three bright shillings, which he spun up with his thumb, directly afterwards, to try the goodness of.

It was a little disconcerting to me, to find, when I was being helped up behind the coach, that I was supposed to have eaten all the dinner without any assistance. I discovered this, from overhearing the lady in the bow-window say to the guard, 'Take care of that child, or he'll burst!' and from observing that the women-servants who were about the place came out to look at me as a young phenomenon. I felt it rather hard, to be made the subject of jokes between the coachman and guard as to the coach drawing heavy behind, on account of my sitting there. The story of my supposed appetite getting wind among the passengers, they were merry upon it likewise; and asked me whether I was going to be paid for, at school, as two brothers or three. But the worst of it was, that I knew I should be ashamed to eat anything, when an opportunity offered, and that, after a rather light dinner, I should remain hungry all night – for I had left my cakes behind, at the hotel. When we stopped for supper I couldn't muster courage to take any, though this did not save me from more jokes; for a husky-voiced gentleman said I was like a boa-constrictor, who took enough at one meal to last him a long time.

We had started from Yarmouth at three o'clock in the afternoon, and we were due in London about eight next morning. It was Midsummer weather, and the evening was very pleasant. When we passed through a village and boys came running after us, I wondered whether their fathers were alive, and whether they were happy at home. I had plenty to think of, besides my mind running continually on the kind of place I was going to – which was an awful speculation. Sometimes, I resigned myself to thoughts of home and Peggotty; and to endeavouring to recall what sort of boy I used to be before I bit Mr Murdstone.

The night was not so pleasant as the evening, for it got chilly; and being put between two gentlemen I was nearly smothered by their falling asleep. At last the sun rose. What an amazing place London was to me when I saw it in the distance. We approached it by degrees, and got, in due time, to the inn in the Whitechapel district, for which we were bound.

The guard's eye lighted on me as he was getting down, and he said at the booking-office door:

'Is there anybody here for a yoongster from Bloonderstone, Sooffolk, to be left till called for?'

No. There was nobody. I went into the booking-office, and, by invitation of the clerk on duty, sat down on the scale at which they weighed the luggage. Here, as I sat looking at the parcels, inhaling the smell of stables (ever since associated with that morning), a procession of considerations began to march through my mind. Supposing nobody should ever fetch me, how long would they consent to keep me there? Supposing there was no mistake in the case, and Mr Murdstone had devised this plan to get rid of me, what should I do? If I tried to walk back home, how could I ever find my way? These thoughts made me giddy with apprehension and dismay. I was in the height of my fever when a man entered and whispered to the clerk, who presently slanted me off the scale, as if I were weighed, bought and paid for.

This new acquaintance was a gaunt young man, with hollow cheeks, dressed in a suit of black clothes which were rather rusty and short in the sleeves and legs.

'You're the new boy?' he said.

I supposed I was. I didn't know.

'I'm one of the masters at Salem House,' *he* said.

I made him a bow and felt very much overawed. I was so faint and tired, that I took heart to tell him that if he would allow me to buy something to eat, I should be very much obliged to him. After considering for a few moments, he said he wanted to call on an old person who lived not far off, and that the best way would be for me to make my breakfast at her house, where we could get some milk.

Accordingly we looked in at a baker's window, and decided in favour of a nice little loaf of brown bread, which cost me threepence. Then, at a grocer's shop, we bought an egg and a slice of streaky bacon. These provisions laid in, we went on through a great noise and uproar and over a bridge which, no doubt, was London Bridge, until we came to the poor person's house, which was a part of some alms-houses, as I knew by an inscription over the gate, which said they were established for twenty-five poor women.

The Master went into the little house of one of these poor old women, who was blowing a fire to make a little saucepan boil. The old woman stopped and said something that sounded like 'My Charley!' but on seeing me she got up and made a confused sort of half curtsey.

'Can you cook this young gentleman's breakfast for him, if you please?' said the Master at Salem House.

'Can I?' said the old woman. 'Yes can I, sure!'

I sat down to my brown loaf, my egg, and my rasher of bacon, with a basin of milk besides, and made a most delicious meal. While I was yet in the full enjoyment of it, the old woman said to the Master:

'Have you got your flute with you?'

The Master, upon this, put his hand underneath the skirts of his coat, and brought out his flute in three pieces, which he screwed together, and began immediately to play. My impression is, after many years of consideration, that there never can have been anybody in the world who played worse. The influence upon me was, first, to make me think of all my sorrows until I could hardly keep my tears back; then to take away my appetite; and lastly, to make me so sleepy that I couldn't keep my eyes open.

I dreamed that once while he was blowing the old woman leaned over the back of his chair and gave him an affectionate squeeze round the neck. When I seemed to have been dozing a long while, the Master took me away. We found the coach very near at hand, where I slept profoundly, until I found we were going at a footpace up a steep hill among green leaves. Presently, it stopped.

A short walk brought us to Salem House, which was enclosed with a high brick wall, and looked very dull. Through a grating in the door we were surveyed by a surly face, which belonged to a stout man with a bull-neck, a wooden leg, and his hair cut close all round his head.

'The new boy,' said the Master.

The man with the wooden leg eyed me all over and locked the gate behind us, and took out the key. We were going up to the house when he called after my conductor.

We looked back, and he was standing with a pair of boots in his hand. 'The cobbler's been, Mr Mell, and he says he can't mend 'em any more. He says there ain't a bit of the original boot left.'

With these words he threw the boots towards Mr Mell. I observed then, for the first time, that the boots he had on were a good deal the worse for wear, and that his stocking was just breaking out in one place, like a bud.

Salem House was a square brick building of a bare and unfurnished appearance. All about it was so very quiet, that I said to Mr Mell I supposed the boys were out; but he seemed surprised at my not knowing that all the boys were at their several homes. That Mr Creakle, the proprietor, was down by the sea-side with Mrs and Miss Creakle. And that I was sent in holiday-time as a punishment for my misdoing. All of which he explained to me as we went along.

I gazed upon the schoolroom into which he took me, as the most forlorn and desolate place I had ever seen. I see it now. A long room, with three long rows of desks, and six of forms, and bristling all round with pegs for hats and slates. Scraps of old copy-books and exercises litter the dirty floor. There is a strange unwholesome smell, like mildewed corduroys, sweet apples wanting air, and rotten books.

I went softly to the upper end of the room, observing all this as I crept along. Suddenly I came upon a pasteboard placard, beautifully written, which was lying on the desk, and bore these words: '*Take care of him. He bites.*'

I got upon the desk immediately, apprehensive of at least a great dog underneath. But I could see nothing of him. Mr Mell asked me what I did up there?

'I beg your pardon, sir,' says I, 'if you please, I'm looking for the dog.'

'Dog?' says he. 'What dog?'

'Isn't it a dog, sir? That's to be taken care of, that bites?'

'No, Copperfield,' says he, gravely, 'that's not a dog. That's a boy. My instructions are to put this placard on your back. I am sorry to make such a beginning with you, but I must do it.'

With that he tied the placard on my shoulders like a knap-sack; and wherever I went I had the consolation of carrying it.

What I suffered from that placard nobody can imagine. Whether it was possible for people to see me or not, I always fancied that somebody was reading it. That cruel man with the wooden leg aggravated my sufferings. If he saw me leaning against a tree, or a wall, he roared out 'Hallo, you Copperfield! Show that badge conspicuous, or I'll report you!' I knew that everybody who came to the house read that I was to be taken care of, for I bit. I recollect that I positively began to have a dread of myself, as a kind of wild boy who did bite.

There was an old door on which the boys had a custom of carving their names. In my dread of their coming back, I could not read a boy's name, without inquiring with what emphasis *he* would read, 'Take care of him. He bites.' I have looked at that door until the owners of all the names – there were five-and-forty of them in the school then, Mr Mell said – seemed to send me to Coventry by general acclamation, and to cry out, each in his own way, 'Take care of him. He bites!'

In the monotony of my life, and in my constant apprehension of the re-opening of the school, it was such an insupportable affliction! I had long tasks every day to do with Mr Mell; but I got through them without disgrace. Before, and after them, I walked about – how vividly I call to mind the damp about the house and the green cracked flagstones in the court. All day long, Mr Mell worked hard, making out the bills (as I found) for last half-year. When he had put up his things for the night, he took out his flute, and blew at it, until I almost thought he would gradually blow his whole being into the large hole at the top.

Mr Mell never said much to me, but he was never harsh to me. I suppose we were company to each other, without talking. I forgot to mention that he would talk to himself sometimes, and pull his hair in an unaccountable manner. But he had these peculiarities. At first they frightened me, though I soon got used to them.

CHAPTER 6

I enlarge my Circle of Acquaintance

One day I was informed by Mr Mell, that Mr Creakle would be home that evening. Before bed-time, I was fetched by the man with the wooden leg to appear before him.

I went on my way, trembling, to Mr Creakle's presence: which so abashed me, when I was ushered into it, that I hardly saw Mrs Creakle or Miss Creakle (who were both there, in the parlour), or anything but Mr Creakle, a stout gentleman in an arm-chair.

'So!' said Mr Creakle. 'This is the young gentleman whose teeth are to be filed! Turn him round.'

The wooden-legged man turned me about so as to exhibit the placard; and turned me about again and posted himself at Mr Creakle's side. Mr Creakle's face was fiery, and his eyes were small; he had thick veins in his forehead, and was bald on the top of his head. But the circumstance which impressed me most, was that he had no voice, but spoke in a whisper. The exertion this cost him made his angry face much more angry, and his thick veins much thicker.

'Now,' said Mr Creakle. 'What's the report of this boy?'

'There's nothing against him yet,' returned the man with the wooden leg. 'There has been no opportunity.'

I thought Mr Creakle was disappointed. I thought Mrs and Miss Creakle (who were both thin and quiet) were not disappointed.

'Come here, sir!' said Mr Creakle, beckoning to me.

'Come here!' said the man with the wooden leg, repeating the gesture.

'I have the happiness of knowing your father-in-law,' whispered Mr Creakle, taking me by the ear; 'and a worthy man he is, a man of strong character. He knows me, and I know him. Do *you* know me? Hey?' said Mr Creakle, pinching my ear.

'Not yet, sir,' I said, flinching with the pain.

'I'll tell you what I am,' whispered Mr Creakle, letting go with a screw at parting that brought water into my eyes. 'I'm a Tartar.'

'A Tartar,' said the man with the wooden leg.

'I am a determined character,' said Mr Creakle. 'My flesh and blood,' he looked at Mrs Creakle as he said this, 'when it rises against me, is not my flesh and blood. I discard it. Now you have begun to know me too, my young friend, and you may go.'

I was very glad to be ordered away, but I had a petition on my mind which concerned me so nearly, that I couldn't help saying, 'If you please, sir, if I might be allowed to take this writing off, before the boys come back –'

Whether Mr Creakle was in earnest, or whether he only did it to frighten me, I don't know, but he made a burst out of his chair, before which I precipitately retreated, and never stopped until I reached my bedroom.

Next morning Mr Sharp, the first master, came back. He was a limp, delicate-looking gentleman, I thought, with a way of carrying his head on one side, as if it were a little too heavy for him. His hair was very wavy; but I was informed by the first boy who came back that it was a wig.

It was no other than Tommy Traddles who gave me this piece of intelligence. He enjoyed my placard so much, that he saved me from the embarrassment of disclosure by presenting me to every other boy on his arrival, in this form of introduction, 'Look here! Here's a game!' Happily, the greater part of the boys were not so boisterous at my expense as I had expected. Some of them certainly did dance about me like wild Indians, and the greater part could not resist the temptation of pretending that I was a dog, and calling me Towzer. On the whole it was much better than I had anticipated.

I was not considered as being formally received into the school, however, until J. Steerforth arrived. Before this boy, who was reputed to be a great scholar, and at least half-a-dozen years my senior, I was carried as before a magistrate. He inquired into the particulars of my punishment, and was pleased to express his opinion that it was 'a jolly shame;' for which I became bound to him ever afterwards.

'What money have you got, Copperfield?' he said, walking aside with me.

I told him seven shillings.

'You had better give it to me to take care of,' he said. 'At least, you can if you like.'

I hastened to comply with his friendly suggestion.

'Perhaps you'd like to spend a couple of shillings or so, in a bottle of currant wine up in the bedroom?' said Steerforth. 'You belong to my bedroom, I find?'

I said, Yes, I should like that.

'Very good,' said Steerforth. 'You'll be glad to spend another shilling or so, in almond cakes, I dare say?'

I said, Yes, I should like that, too.

'And another shilling or so in biscuits, and another in fruit, eh?' said Steerforth 'I say, young Copperfield, you're going it!'

He was as good as his word. When we went up-stairs to bed, he produced the whole seven shillings worth, and laid it out on my bed, saying:

'There you are, young Copperfield, and a royal spread you've got.'

I begged him to do me the favour of presiding; and my request being seconded by the other boys, he sat upon my pillow, handing round the viands and dispensing the wine.

How well I recollect our sitting there, talking in whispers: the moonlight painting a pale window on the floor. I heard all kinds of things about the school. I heard that Mr Creakle was the most severe of masters; that he knew nothing himself, but the art of slashing; that he had taken to the schooling business after being bankrupt in hops, and making away with Mrs Creakle's money. I heard that the man with the wooden leg, Tungay, was an obstinate barbarian who had formerly assisted in the hop business, but had come into the scholastic line with Mr Creakle, in consequence of having done a deal of dishonest work for him, and knowing his secrets. I heard that Mr Creakle had a son who, assisting in the school, had once held some remonstrance with his father on an occasion when its discipline was cruelly exercised, and was supposed, besides, to have protested against his father's usage of his mother. I heard that Mr Creakle had turned him out of doors, in consequence, and that Mrs and Miss Creakle had been in a sad way, ever since.

But the greatest wonder that I heard of Mr Creakle was there being one boy in the school on whom he never ventured to lay a land, and that boy being J. Steerforth. Steerforth himself confirmed this and said that he should like to begin to see him do it. On being asked how he would proceed if he did begin to see him do it, he said he would commence by knocking him down with a blow on the forehead from the seven-and-sixpenny ink-bottle that was always on the mantelpiece.

I heard that Mr Sharp and Mr Mell were both wretchedly paid; I heard that Miss Creakle was regarded by the school in general as being in love with Steerforth and, as I sat in the dark thinking of his fine face and easy manner, I thought it very likely. I heard that Mr Mell was not a bad sort of fellow, but hadn't a sixpence to bless himself with; and that there was no doubt that old Mrs Mell, his mother, was as poor as Job. I thought of my breakfast then, but was, I am glad to remember, as mute as a mouse about it.

The hearing of all this outlasted the banquet some time and we at last betook ourselves to bed.

'Good-night, young Copperfield,' said Steerforth. 'I'll take care of you.'

'You're very kind,' I gratefully returned.

'You haven't got a sister, have you?'

'No,' I answered.

'That's a pity,' said Steerforth. 'If you had, I should have liked to know her.'

I thought of him very much after I went to bed, and raised myself to look at him in the moonlight, with his handsome face turned up. He was a person of great power in my eyes; that was, of course, the reason of my mind running on him. No veiled future dimly glanced upon him in the moonbeams. There was no shadowy picture of his footsteps, in the garden that I dreamed of walking in all night.

CHAPTER 7

My 'First Half' at Salem House

School began in earnest next day. I remember the roar of voices in the schoolroom suddenly becoming hushed as death when Mr Creakle entered and stood in the doorway looking upon us like a giant in a story-book surveying his captives.

'Now, boys, this is a new half. Come fresh up to the lessons, I advise you, for I come fresh up to the punishment. I won't flinch. Now get to work, every boy!'

When this dreadful exordium was over Mr Creakle came to where I sat, and told me that if I were famous for biting, he was famous for biting, too. He then showed me the cane, and asked me what I thought of *that* for a tooth? Was it a sharp tooth, hey? Did it bite? At every question he gave me a fleshy cut that made me writhe.

Not that these were special marks of distinction. A large majority of the boys (especially the smaller ones) were visited with similar instances of notice, as Mr Creakle made the round of the schoolroom. Half the establishment was writhing and crying, before the day's work began.

I should think there never can have been a man who enjoyed his profession more than Mr Creakle. He had a delight in cutting at the boys, which was like the satisfaction of a craving appetite. When I think of the fellow now, my blood rises hotly, because I know him to have been an incapable brute, who had no more right to be possessed of the great trust he held, than to be Lord High Admiral, or Commander-in-chief – in either of which capacities, it is probable, that he would have done infinitely less mischief.

Here I sit at the desk again, watching his eye. I don't watch his eye in idleness, but because I am morbidly attracted to it, in a dread desire to know what he will do next, and whether it will be my turn to suffer, or somebody else's. A lane of small boys beyond me watch it too. Now he throws his eye sideways down our lane, and we all droop over our books and tremble. An unhappy culprit, found guilty of imperfect exercise, approaches at his command. The culprit professes a determination to do better to-morrow. Mr Creakle cuts a joke before he beats him, and we laugh at it, – miserable little dogs, we laugh, with our hearts sinking into our boots.

Poor Traddles! He was always being caned – I think he was caned every day that half-year. After laying his head on the desk for a little while, he would begin to laugh again, and draw skeletons all over his slate, before his eyes were dry. I used to wonder what comfort Traddles found in drawing skeletons; but I believe he only did it because they were easy, and didn't want any features.

He was very honourable, Traddles was, and held it as a solemn duty in the boys to stand by one another. He suffered for this when Steerforth laughed in church, and the Beadle thought it was Traddles, and took him out. He never said who was the real offender, though he smarted for it next day, and was imprisoned so many hours that he came forth with a whole churchyardful of skeletons swarming all over his Latin Dictionary. But he had his reward. Steerforth said there was nothing of the sneak in Traddles, and we all felt that to be the highest praise.

To see Steerforth walk to church arm-in-arm with Miss Creakle was one of the great sights of my life. I didn't think Miss Creakle equal to little Em'ly in point of beauty, but I thought her a young lady of extraordinary attractions, and in point of gentility not to be surpassed. When Steerforth, in white trousers, carried her parasol for her, I felt proud to know him; and believed that she could not choose but adore him with all her heart.

Steerforth couldn't – or at all events he didn't – defend me from Mr Creakle, who was very severe with me; but whenever I had been treated worse than usual, he always told me that I wanted a little of his pluck, and that he wouldn't have stood it himself; which I felt he intended for encouragement. There was one advantage in Mr Creakle's severity. He found my placard in his way when he wanted to make a cut at me in passing; for this reason it was soon taken off.

An accidental circumstance cemented the intimacy between Steerforth and me. On one occasion, when he was talking to me in the playground, I hazarded the observation that something or somebody – I forget what now – was like something or somebody in Peregrine Pickle. When I was going to bed at night, he asked me if I had got that book?

I explained how it was that I had read it, and all those other books of which I have made mention.

'And do you recollect them?' Steerforth said.

Oh, yes, I replied; I believed I recollected them very well.

'Then you shall tell 'em to me, young Copperfield,' said Steerforth. 'I can't get to sleep at night, and I wake rather early in the morning. We'll go over 'em one after another.'

I felt extremely flattered by this arrangement, and we commenced it that very evening. The drawback was that I was often sleepy and then it was rather hard work, but Steerforth was resolute; and as he explained to me, in return, my sums and exercises, I was no loser by the transaction. Let me do myself justice, however. I was moved by no selfish motive. I admired and loved him, and his approval was return enough.

We seem to have been months over Peregrine, and months more over the other stories. Whatever I had within me that was romantic and dreamy was encouraged by so much story-telling in the dark. This accomplishment of mine was bruited about among the boys, and attracted a good deal of notice to me though I was the youngest there. In a school carried on by sheer cruelty, there is not likely to be much learnt. But my little vanity, and Steerforth's help, urged me on somehow; and made me an exception to the general body, insomuch that I did steadily pick up some crumbs of knowledge.

In this I was much assisted by Mr Mell, who had a liking for me that I am grateful to remember. It always gave me pain to observe that Steerforth treated him with systematic disparagement, and seldom lost an occasion of wounding his feelings. This troubled me the more because I had told Steerforth, from whom I could no more keep such a secret than I could keep a cake, about the two old women Mr Mell had taken me to see; and I was always afraid that Steerforth would twit him with it.

One day when Mr Creakle kept the house from indisposition, which naturally diffused a lively joy through the school, there was a good deal of noise in the course of the morning's work. It was, properly, a half-holiday, being Saturday. But as the weather was not favourable for going out walking, we were ordered into school in the afternoon, and Mr Mell, who always did the drudgery, kept school by himself.

If I could associate the idea of a bear with any one so mild as Mr Mell, I should think of him, in connexion with that afternoon when the uproar was at its height, as of one of those animals, baited by a thousand dogs. There were laughing boys, singing boys, howling boys; boys whirled about him, making faces, mimicking his poverty, his boots, everything belonging to him that they should have had consideration for.

'Silence!' cried Mr Mell, suddenly rising up, and striking his desk.

As I stood beside him, I saw the boys all stop. Steerforth was lounging with his back against the wall, and his hands in his pockets, and looked at Mr Mell with his mouth shut up as if he were whistling.

'Silence, Mr Steerforth!' said Mr Mell.

'Silence yourself,' said Steerforth.

'Sit down,' said Mr Mell.

'Sit down yourself,' said Steerforth, 'and mind your business.'

There was a titter, and some applause; but Mr Mell was so white that silence immediately succeeded.

'If you think, Steerforth,' said Mr Mell, 'that I have not observed you urging your juniors on to every sort of outrage against me, you are mistaken.'

'I don't give myself the trouble of thinking at all about you,' said Steerforth, coolly; 'so I'm not mistaken, as it happens.'

'And when you make use of your position of favouritism here, sir,' pursued Mr Mell, with his lip trembling very much, 'to insult a gentleman –'

'A what? – where is he?' said Steerforth.

– 'To insult one who is not fortunate in life, sir, and who never gave you the least offence,' said Mr Mell, with his lips trembling, 'you commit a mean and base action.'

'I tell you what, Mr Mell,' said Steerforth, coming forward up the room. 'When you take the liberty of calling me mean or base, you are an impudent beggar. You are always a beggar, you know; but when you do that, you are an impudent beggar.'

I saw a rigidity come upon the whole school as if they had been turned into stone, and found Mr Creakle in the midst of us, with Tungay at his side, and Mrs and Miss Creakle looking in at the door as if they were frightened.

'Mr Mell,' said Mr Creakle, shaking him by the arm; 'you have not forgotten yourself, I hope?'

'No, sir, no,' returned the Master, shaking his head, in great agitation. 'I have remembered myself, I – I – could wish – you had remembered me a little sooner, Mr Creakle. It – it – would have been more kind, sir.'

Mr Creakle turned to Steerforth, and said: 'Now, sir, as he don't condescend to tell me, what *is* this?'

'What did he mean by talking about favourites?' said Steerforth, at length.

'And pray, what did you mean by that, sir?' demanded Mr Creakle, turning angrily on his assistant.

'I meant, Mr Creakle,' Mr Mell returned in a low voice, 'as I said; that no pupil had a right to avail himself of his position of favouritism to degrade me.'

'To degrade *you*?' said Mr Creakle. 'But give me leave to ask whether, when you talk about favourites, you showed proper respect to me? To me, sir,' said Mr Creakle, darting his head at him suddenly, 'the principal of this establishment, and your employer?'

'It was not judicious, sir, I am willing to admit,' said Mr Mell.

Here Steerforth struck in. 'He said I was mean, and then he said I was base, and then I called him a beggar. If I had been cool, perhaps I shouldn't have called him a beggar. But I did, and I am ready to take the consequences of it.'

Without considering, perhaps, whether there were any consequences to be taken, I felt quite in a glow at this gallant speech.

'I am surprised, Steerforth – although your candour does you honour,' said Mr Creakle, 'that you should attach such an epithet to any person employed in Salem House, sir.'

'Let him deny it,' said Steerforth. 'If he's not a beggar himself, his near relation's one. His mother lives on charity in an alms-house.'

Mr Creakle turned to his assistant: 'Now you hear what this gentleman says, Mr Mell. Have the goodness, if you please, to set him right.'

'He is right, sir, without correction,' returned Mr Mell, 'what he has said is true.'

'Be so good then as to declare publicly, will you,' said Mr Creakle, putting his head on one side, and rolling his eyes round the school, 'whether it ever came to my knowledge until this moment?'

'I apprehend you never supposed my worldly circumstances to be very good,' replied the assistant. 'You know what my position is, and always has been here.'

'I apprehend, if you come to that,' said Mr Creakle, with his veins swelling bigger than ever, 'that you've been in a wrong position altogether, and mistook this for a charity school. Mr Mell, we'll part, if you please.'

'There is no time like the present,' answered Mr Mell. 'James Steerforth, the best wish I can leave you is that you may come to be ashamed of what you have done to-day. At present I would prefer to see you anything rather than a friend, to me, or to any one in whom I feel an interest.'

He laid his hand upon my shoulder; and then taking his flute and a few books from his desk, he went out of the school, with his property under his arm. Mr Creakle then made a speech, through Tungay, in which he thanked Steerforth for asserting the respectability of Salem House, which he wound up by shaking hands with Steerforth, while we gave three cheers – I did not quite know what for, but I supposed for

Steerforth, and so joined in them ardently, though I felt miserable. Mr Creakle then caned Tommy Traddles for being discovered in tears on account of Mr Mell's departure.

For myself, I felt so much self-reproach for my part in what had happened, that nothing would have enabled me to keep back my tears but the fear that Steerforth, who often looked at me, I saw, might think it unfriendly – or, I should rather say, undutiful – if I showed the emotion which distressed me. He was very angry with Traddles, and said he was glad he had caught it.

Poor Traddles, who was relieving himself as usual with a burst of skeletons, said he didn't care. Mr Mell was ill-used.

'Who has ill-used him, you girl?' said Steerforth.

'Why, you have,' returned Traddles. 'You have lost him his situation.'

'Do you suppose I am not going to write home, and take care that he gets some money?'

We thought this intention very noble in Steerforth, whose mother was a widow, and rich, and would do almost anything, it was said, that he asked her. We were all extremely glad to see Traddles so put down, and exalted Steerforth to the skies; but I must say that when I was going on with a story in the dark that night, Mr Mell's old flute seemed more than once to sound mournfully in my ears.

I soon forgot him in the contemplation of Steerforth, who, in an easy amateur way, took some of his classes until a new master was found. The new master came from a grammar-school, and Steerforth approved of him highly, and told us he was a Brick. Without exactly understanding what distinction was meant by this, I respected him greatly for it; though he never took the pains with me that Mr Mell had taken.

There was only one other event in this half-year that made an impression upon me which still survives.

One afternoon, Tungay came in, and called out in his usual strong way: 'Visitors for Copperfield!' Then I was told to get a clean frill on, before I repaired to the dining-room. These orders I obeyed, in such a flutter and hurry of my young spirits as I had never known before; and when I got to the parlour-door and the thought came into my head that it might be my mother I stopped to have a sob before I went in.

There, to my amazement, were Mr Peggotty and Ham, ducking at me with their hats. I could not help laughing; but it was more in the pleasure of seeing them, than at the appearance they made. We shook hands in a very cordial way; and I laughed and laughed, until I pulled out my pocket-handkerchief and wiped my eyes.

'Cheer up, Mas'r Davy bor'!' said Ham. 'Why, how you have growed!'

'Am I grown?' I said. I was not crying at anything particular but somehow it made me cry, to see old friends.

'Do you know how mama is, Mr Peggotty?' I said. 'And how my dear, dear, old Peggotty is?'

'Oncommon,' said Mr Peggotty.

'And little Em'ly, and Mrs Gummidge?'

'On – common,' said Mr Peggotty.

There was a silence. Mr Peggotty, to relieve it, took two prodigious lobsters, and an enormous crab, and a large canvas bag of shrimps, out of his pockets.

'You see,' said Mr Peggotty, 'knowing as you was partial to a little relish with your wittles when you was along with us, we took the liberty. Mrs Gummidge biled 'em.'

I expressed my thanks.

Mr Peggotty said: 'We come in one of our Yarmouth lugs to Gravesen'. My sister wrote to me as if ever I chanced to come to Gravesen', I was to come over and inquire for Mas'r Davy, and give her dooty, and reporting of the fam'ly as they was oncommon toe-be-sure. Little Em'ly, you see, she'll write to my sister when I go back as you was similarly oncommon, and so we make it quite a merry-go-rounder.'

I thanked him heartily; and said that I supposed little Em'ly was altered too, since we used to pick up shells and pebbles on the beach.

'She's getting to be a woman, that's wot she's getting to be. Her pretty face!' said Mr Peggotty, with his own shining like a light.

It was perfectly delightful to behold with what enthusiasm Mr Peggotty became inspired when he thought of his little favourite. Ham was quite as earnest as he. I dare say they would have said much more about her, if they had not been abashed by the unexpected coming in of Steerforth.

I said, 'Don't go, Steerforth, if you please. These are two Yarmouth boatmen – very kind, good people – who are relations of my nurse, and have come from Gravesend to see me.'

'Aye, aye?' said Steerforth. 'I am glad to see them. How are you both?'

There was an ease in his manner – a gay and light manner it was, but not swaggering – which I still believe to have borne a kind of enchantment with it. I could not but see how pleased they were with him, and how they seemed to open their hearts to him in a moment.

'You must let them know at home, if you please, Mr Peggotty,' I said, 'that Mr Steerforth is very kind to me, and that I don't know what I should ever do here without him.'

'Nonsense!' said Steerforth, laughing.

'And if Mr Steerforth ever comes into Norfolk or Suffolk,' I said, 'you may depend upon it I shall bring him to Yarmouth to see your house. You never saw such a good house, Steerforth. It's made out of a boat!'

'Made out of a boat, is it?' said Steerforth. 'It's the right sort of house for such a thorough-built boatman.'

'Well, sir,' said Mr Peggotty, bowing and chuckling, 'I thankee, sir! I do my endeavours in my line of life, sir.'

'The best of men can do no more, Mr Peggotty,' said Steerforth. He had got his name already.

'I'll pound it, it's wot you do yourself, sir,' said Mr Peggotty, shaking his head, 'I'm obleeged to you, sir, for your welcoming manner of me. I'm rough, sir, but I'm ready. I wish you both well, and I wish you happy!'

Ham echoed this sentiment, and we parted with them in the heartiest manner. I was almost tempted that evening to tell Steerforth about pretty little Em'ly, but I was too timid of mentioning her name. I remember that I thought a good deal about Mr Peggotty having said that she was getting on to be a woman; but I decided that was nonsense.

We transported the shell-fish up into our room unobserved, and made a great supper that evening. But Traddles was too unfortunate even to come through a supper like anybody else. He was taken ill in the night in consequence of Crab; and after being drugged with black draughts and blue pills, received a caning and six chapters of Greek Testament for refusing to confess.

The rest of the half-year is a jumble in my recollection of the daily strife and struggle of our lives; of the waning summer and the changing season; of the frosty mornings when we were rung out of bed, and the cold, cold smell of the dark nights when we were rung into bed; of the evening schoolroom dimly lighted and indifferently warmed, and the morning schoolroom which was nothing but a great shivering-machine; of dog's-eared lesson-books, tear-blotted copybooks, canings, hair-cuttings, rainy Sundays, suet-puddings, and a dirty atmosphere of ink surrounding all.

I well remember though, how the distant idea of the holidays, after seeming for an immense time to be a stationary speck, began to come towards us, and to grow and grow. How from counting months, we came to weeks, and then to days; how the breaking-up day changed its place fast, from the week after next to next week, this week, the day after to-morrow, to-morrow, to-day, to-night – when I was inside the Yarmouth mail, and going home.

CHAPTER 8

My Holidays.
Especially one Happy Afternoon

When we arrived before day at the inn where the mail stopped, I was shown up to a nice little bedroom; and very glad I was to pull the blankets round my head, and go to sleep.

Mr Barkis the carrier was to call for me in the morning at nine o'clock.

'I gave your message, Mr Barkis,' I said: 'I wrote to Peggotty.'

'Ah!' said Mr Barkis drily.

'Wasn't it right, Mr Barkis?' I asked, after a little hesitation.

'Why, no,' said Mr Barkis. 'No answer.'

'There was an answer expected, was there, Mr Barkis?' said I. For this was a new light to me.

'When a man says he's willin',' said Mr Barkis, turning his glance slowly on me, 'it's as much as to say, that man's a waitin' for a answer.'

'Have you told her so, Mr Barkis?'

'N – no,' growled Mr Barkis, reflecting about it. 'I ain't got no call to go and tell her so. I never said six words to her myself.'

'Would you like me to do it, Mr Barkis?' said I, doubtfully.

'You might tell her, if you would, that Barkis was a waitin' for a answer. Says you – what name is it?'

'Peggotty.'

'Chrisen name? Or nat'ral name?' said Mr Barkis.

'Oh, it's not her Christian name. Her Christian name is Clara.'

'Is it though?' said Mr Barkis.

He seemed to find an immense fund of reflection in this circumstance, and sat pondering and inwardly whistling for some time.

'Well!' he resumed at length. 'Says you, "Peggotty! Barkis is a waitin' for a answer." Says she, perhaps, "Answer to what?" Says you, "To what I told you." "What is that?" says she. "Barkis is willin'," says you.'

This extremely artful suggestion, Mr Barkis accompanied with a nudge of his elbow that gave me quite a stitch in my side. After that, he made no other reference to the subject except, taking a piece of chalk and writing up, inside the tilt of the cart, 'Clara Peggotty' – apparently as a private memorandum.

Ah, what a strange feeling it was to be going home when it was not home, and to find that every object I looked at reminded me of the happy old home, which was like a dream I could never dream again! The days when my mother and I and Peggotty were all in all to one another, and there was no one to come between us, rose up before me so sorrowfully on the road, that I am not sure but that I would rather have remained away. But soon I was at our house.

The carrier put my box down at the garden-gate, and left me. I walked along the path towards the house, and went in with a quiet, timid step.

God knows how infantine the memory may have been, that was awakened within me by the sound of my mother's voice in the old parlour. She was singing in a low tone. I think I must have heard her singing so to me when I was but a baby. The strain was new and yet so old that it filled my heart brimful; like a friend come back from a long absence.

I went softly into the room. She was sitting by the fire, suckling an infant, whose tiny hand she held against her neck. Her eyes were looking down upon its face, and she sat singing to it.

She started and cried out; and coming half across the room to meet me, kneeled down upon the ground and kissed me, and laid my head down on her bosom near the little creature that was nestling there, and put its hand up to my lips.

I wish I had died. I wish I had died then, with that feeling in my heart! I should have been more fit for Heaven than I ever have been since.

'He is your brother,' said my mother, fondling me. 'Davy, my pretty boy! My poor child!' Then she kissed me more and more, and clasped me round the neck. This she was doing when Peggotty came running in, and bounced down on the ground beside us, and went mad about us both for a quarter of an hour.

It seemed that I had not been expected so soon, the carrier being much before his usual time. It seemed, too, that Mr and Miss Murdstone had gone out upon a visit, and would not return before night. I had never hoped for this. I had never thought it possible that we three could be together undisturbed once more; and I felt, for the time, as if the old days were come back.

We dined together by the fireside. Peggotty was in attendance to wait upon us, but my mother wouldn't let her do it, and made her dine with us. While we were at table, I thought it a favourable occasion to tell

Peggotty about Mr Barkis, who, before I had finished what I had to tell her, began to laugh, and throw her apron over her face.

'What are you doing, you stupid creature?' said my mother, laughing.

'Oh, drat the man!' cried Peggotty. 'He wants to marry me.'

'It would be a very good match for you; wouldn't it?' said my mother.

'Oh! I don't know,' said Peggotty. 'Don't ask me. I wouldn't have him if he was made of gold. Nor I wouldn't have anybody.'

'Then, why don't you tell him so, you ridiculous thing?' said my mother.

'Tell him so,' retorted Peggotty. 'He has never said a word to me about it.'

I remarked that my mother became more serious and thoughtful. I had seen at first that she was changed. Her face looked careworn, and her hand was so thin and white that it seemed to me to be almost transparent. At last she said, putting out her hand, and laying it affectionately on her old servant:

'Don't leave me, Peggotty. Stay with me. It will not be for long, perhaps.'

'Me leave you, my precious!' cried Peggotty. 'Not for all the world and his wife. Peggotty go away from you? No, no, no. It isn't that there ain't some Cats that would be well enough pleased if she did, but they shan't be pleased. I'll stay with you till I am a cross cranky old woman. And when I'm too deaf, and too lame to be of any use at all, then I shall go to my Davy, and ask him to take me in.'

'And Peggotty,' says I, 'I shall be glad to see you, and I'll make you as welcome as a queen.'

'Bless your dear heart!' cried Peggotty. 'I know you will!'

We sat round the fire, and talked delightfully. I told them what a hard master Mr Creakle was and what a fine fellow Steerforth was, and I took the little baby in my arms and nursed it lovingly. When it was asleep, I crept close to my mother's side, according to my old custom, and sat with my arms embracing her waist, and my cheek on her shoulder, and once more felt her beautiful hair drooping over me – like an angel's wing as I used to think – and was very happy indeed.

'I wonder,' said Peggotty, 'what's become of Davy's great-aunt?'

'Lor, Peggotty!' observed my mother, 'Miss Betsey is not likely ever to trouble us again.'

'I wonder,' mused Peggotty, 'if she was to die, whether she'd leave Davy anything?'

'Good gracious me, Peggotty,' returned my mother, 'what a nonsensical woman you are! when you know that she took offence at the poor dear boy's ever being born at all.'

'I suppose she wouldn't be inclined to forgive him now that he's got a brother,' said Peggotty.

My mother immediately began to cry, and wondered how Peggotty dared to say such a thing.

'As if this poor little innocent in its cradle had ever done any harm to you or anybody else, you jealous thing!' said she. 'You had better go and marry Mr Barkis. Why don't you?'

'I should make Miss Murdstone happy, if I was to,' said Peggotty.

'What a bad disposition you have, Peggotty!' returned my mother. 'You are as jealous of Miss Murdstone as it is possible to be. You want to keep the keys yourself, I suppose? When you know that she only does it out of kindness and the best intentions!'

Peggotty muttered something to the effect that there was a little too much of the best intentions going on.

'Haven't you heard her say, over and over again,' returned my mother, 'that she wishes to spare me a great deal of trouble which she thinks I am not suited for. And isn't she up early and late, and going to and fro continually – and do you mean to insinuate that there is not a sort of devotion in that?'

'I don't insinuate at all,' said Peggotty.

'You do, Peggotty,' returned my mother. 'You are always insinuating. And when you talk of Mr Murdstone's good intentions –'

'I never talked of 'em,' said Peggotty.

'No, Peggotty,' returned my mother, 'but you insinuated. When you talk of Mr Murdstone's intentions and pretend to slight them, you must be as well convinced as I am how good they are. If he seems to have been at all stern with a certain person, it is solely because he is satisfied that it is for a certain person's benefit. He is better able to judge of it than I am; for I very well know that I am a weak, girlish creature, and that he is a firm, serious man.'

Peggotty sat looking silently at the fire.

'There, Peggotty,' said my mother, changing her tone, 'don't let us fall out with one another, for I couldn't bear it. You are my true friend and always have been, ever since the night when Mr Copperfield first brought me home here, and you came out to the gate to meet me.'

Peggotty was not slow to respond, and ratify the treaty of friendship by giving me one of her best hugs. When we had had our tea, I read Peggotty a chapter out of the Crocodile Book, in remembrance of old times – and then we talked about Salem House, which brought me round again to Steerforth, who was my great subject. We were very happy; and that evening, as the last of its race, and destined evermore to close that volume of my life, will never pass out of my memory.

It was almost ten o'clock before we heard the sound of wheels. We all got up then; and my mother said hurriedly that, as it was so late, perhaps I had better go to bed. I kissed her, and went up-stairs directly, before they came in. It appeared to my childish fancy as I ascended that they brought a cold blast of air into the house which blew away the old familiar feeling like a feather.

I felt uncomfortable about going down to breakfast in the morning, as I had never set eyes on Mr Murdstone since the day when I committed my memorable offence.

He was standing before the fire with his back to it, while Miss Murdstone made the tea. He looked at me steadily as I entered, but made no sign of recognition whatever.

I went up to him, after a moment of confusion, and said: 'I beg your pardon, sir. I am very sorry for what I did, and I hope you will forgive me.'

'I am glad to hear you are sorry, David,' he replied.

The hand he gave me was the hand I had bitten. I could not restrain my eye from resting for an instant on a red spot upon it; but it was not so red as I turned, when I met that sinister expression in his face.

'How do you do, ma'am?' I said to Miss Murdstone.

'Ah, dear me!' sighed Miss Murdstone. 'How long are the holidays?'

'A month, ma'am.'

'Oh!' said Miss Murdstone. 'Then here's *one* day off.'

It was on this very first day that I had the misfortune to throw her into a state of violent consternation. I came into the room where she and my mother were sitting; and the baby being on my mother's lap, I took it very carefully in my arms. Suddenly Miss Murdstone gave such a scream that I all but dropped it.

'Good heavens, Clara, he's got it!' cried Miss Murdstone. 'The boy has got the baby!'

She was limp with horror; but stiffened herself to make a dart at me, and take it out of my arms. I was solemnly interdicted by her from touching my brother any more on any pretence whatever.

On another occasion, when we three were together, this same dear baby was the innocent occasion of Miss Murdstone's going into a passion. My mother, who had been looking at its eyes as it lay upon her lap, said:

'Davy! come here!' and looked at mine.

I saw Miss Murdstone lay her beads down.

'I declare,' said my mother, gently, 'they are wonderfully alike.'

'What are you talking about, Clara?' said Miss Murdstone.

'My dear Jane,' faltered my mother, 'I find that the baby's eyes and Davy's are exactly alike.'

'Clara!' said Miss Murdstone, rising angrily, 'you are a positive fool sometimes. Who else could compare my brother's baby with your boy? They are utterly dissimilar in all respects. I will not sit here, and hear such comparisons made.' With that she stalked out.

I was not a favourite with Miss Murdstone. In short, I was not a favourite with anybody, not even with myself; for those who did like me could not show it, and those who did not showed it so plainly that I had a consciousness of always appearing boorish, and dull.

I felt that I made them as uncomfortable as they made me. If I came into the room where they were, and they were talking together and my mother seemed cheerful, an anxious cloud would steal over her face. If Mr Murdstone were in his best humour, I checked him. If Miss Murdstone were in her worst, I intensified it. I had perception enough to know that my mother was the victim always; that she was afraid to speak to me, or be kind to me, lest she should give them some offence. Therefore I resolved to keep myself as much out of their way as I could; and many a wintry hour did I hear the church clock strike, when I was sitting in my cheerless bedroom.

In the evening, sometimes, I sat with Peggotty in the kitchen. There I was comfortable, and not afraid of being myself. But neither of these resources was approved of in the parlour. I was still held to be necessary to my poor mother's training, and, as one of her trials, could not be suffered to absent myself.

'David,' said Mr Murdstone one day, 'I am sorry to observe that you are of a sullen disposition.'

'As sulky as a bear!' said Miss Murdstone.

I stood still, and hung my head.

'This is not a character that I can suffer to develop beneath my eyes without an effort at improvement,' said Mr Murdstone. 'You must endeavour, sir, to change it. We must endeavour to change it for you.'

'I beg your pardon, sir,' I faltered. 'I have never meant to be sullen.'

'Don't take refuge in a lie, sir!' he returned fiercely. 'You have withdrawn yourself in your sullenness to your own room. You know now that I require you to be here, and not there. Further, that I require you to bring obedience here. You know me, David. I will have it done.'

Miss Murdstone gave a hoarse chuckle.

'I will have a respectful, prompt, and ready bearing towards myself,' he continued, 'and towards Jane Murdstone, and towards your mother. I will not have this room shunned as if it were infected. Sit down.'

He ordered me like a dog, and I obeyed like a dog.

'One thing more,' he said. 'I observe that you have an attachment to low and common company. You are not to associate with servants. The kitchen will not improve you, in the many respects in which you need improvement. Of the woman who abets you, I say nothing – since you, Clara,' addressing my mother in a lower voice, 'from old associations have a weakness respecting her which is not yet overcome.'

'A most unaccountable delusion it is!' cried Miss Murdstone.

'I only say,' he resumed, addressing me, 'that I disapprove of your preferring such company as Mistress Peggotty, and that it is to be abandoned. Now, David, you know what will be the consequence if you fail to obey me to the letter.'

I knew well – better perhaps than he thought, as far as my poor mother was concerned – and I obeyed him to the letter. I retreated to my own room no more; I took refuge with Peggotty no more; but sat wearily in the parlour day after day looking forward to bedtime.

What irksome constraint I underwent, sitting in the same attitude hours upon hours, listening to the ticking of the clock and watching Miss Murdstone's shiny steel beads as she strung them.

What walks I took alone, down muddy lanes, in the bad winter weather, carrying that parlour, and Mr and Miss Murdstone in it, everywhere. What meals I had in silence and embarrassment, always feeling that there were a knife and fork too many, and those mine. What a blank space I seemed, which everybody overlooked, and yet was in everybody's way. What a heavy relief it was to hear Miss Murdstone hail the first stroke of nine at night, and order me to bed!

Thus the holidays lagged away, until the morning came when Miss Murdstone said: 'Here's the last day off!'

Again Mr Barkis appeared at the gate, and again Miss Murdstone in her warning voice, said: 'Clara!' when my mother bent over me, to bid me farewell.

I kissed her, and my baby brother, and was very sorry then; but not sorry to go away, for the gulf between us was there, and the parting was there, every day. And it is not so much the embrace she gave me, that lives in my mind, though it was as fervent as could be, as what followed.

I was in the cart when I heard her calling to me. I looked out, and she stood at the garden-gate alone, holding her baby up in her arms for me to see. It was cold still weather; and not a hair on her head, nor a fold of her dress, was stirred, as she looked intently at me, holding up her child.

So I saw her afterwards, in my sleep at school – a silent presence near my bed – looking at me with the same intent face – holding up her baby in her arms.

CHAPTER 9

I have a Memorable Birthday

I pass over all that happened at school until the anniversary of my birthday came round in March.

How well I recollect the kind of day it was! I look along the dim perspective of the schoolroom, with a sputtering candle here and there to light up the foggy morning, and the breath of the boys smoking in the raw cold as they blow upon their fingers.

It was after breakfast, when Mr Sharp entered and said: 'David Copperfield is to go into the parlour.' I expected a hamper from Peggotty, and brightened at the order. Some of the boys about me put in their claim not to be forgotten in the distribution of the good things, as I hurried away to the parlour; and there I found Mr Creakle, sitting at his breakfast, and Mrs Creakle with an opened letter in her hand. But no hamper.

'David Copperfield,' said Mrs Creakle, leading me to a sofa, and sitting down beside me. 'I have something to tell you, my child.'

Mr Creakle, at whom of course I looked, stopped up a sigh with a large piece of buttered toast.

'You are too young to know how the world changes,' said Mrs Creakle, 'and how the people in it pass away. But we all have to learn it, David.'

I looked at her earnestly.

'I grieve to tell you,' said she, 'that I hear this morning your mama is very ill.'

A mist rose between Mrs Creakle and me. Then I felt the burning tears run down my face.

'She is dead.'

There was no need to tell me so. I had already broken out into a desolate cry, and felt an orphan in the wide world.

She was very kind to me. She kept me there all day; and I cried, and wore myself to sleep, and awoke and cried again. When I could cry no more, I began to think; and then the oppression on my breast was heaviest, and my grief a dull pain that there was no ease for.

I thought of our house shut up and hushed. I thought of the little baby, who, Mrs Creakle said, they believed would die too. I thought of my father's grave in the churchyard, by our house, and of my mother lying there beneath the tree I knew so well.

I left Salem House upon the morrow afternoon. I little thought then that I left it, never to return. We travelled very slowly all night, and did not get into Yarmouth before nine or ten o'clock in the morning. I looked out for Mr Barkis, but instead of him a fat, short-winded, merry-looking man in black came puffing up.

'Master Copperfield? Come with me, young sir, if you please.'

I put my hand in his and we walked away to a shop in a narrow street, on which was written OMER, DRAPER, HABERDASHER, FUNERAL FURNISHER, &C. We went into a little back-parlour behind the shop, where we found three young women at work on a quantity of black materials, which were heaped upon the table.

The three, who appeared to be very industrious and comfortable, raised their heads to look at me, and then went on with their work. Stitch, stitch, stitch. At the same time there came from a workshop across a little yard outside the window, a regular sound of hammering that kept a kind of tune: RAT – tat-tat, RAT – tat-tat, RAT – tat-tat, without any variation.

'Well,' said my conductor to one of the three young women. 'How do you get on, Minnie?'

'We shall be ready by the trying-on time,' she replied gaily, without looking up. 'Don't you be afraid, father.'

Mr Omer took off his broad-brimmed hat. 'I think I'll measure this young scholar. Would you walk into the shop, Master Copperfield?'

I preceded Mr Omer, in compliance with his request; and after showing me a roll of cloth which he said was extra super, and too good mourning for anything short of parents, he took my various dimensions, and put them down in a book.

He took me back into the parlour and called down a little break-neck range of steps behind a door: 'Bring up that tea and bread-and-butter!' which, after some time, during which I sat listening to the stitching in the room and the tune that was being hammered across the yard, appeared on a tray, and turned out to be for me.

'I have been acquainted with you a long time, my young friend,' said Mr Omer.

'Have you, sir?'

'All your life,' said Mr Omer. 'I knew your father before you. He was five foot nine and a half, and he lays in five-and-twenty foot of ground.'

'RAT – tat-tat, RAT – tat-tat, RAT – tat-tat,' across the yard.

'Do you know how my little brother is, sir?' I inquired.

'He is in his mother's arms,' said he. 'The baby's dead.'

My wounds broke out afresh at this intelligence. I left the scarcely tasted breakfast and rested my head on another table in a corner which Minnie hastily cleared, lest I should spot the mourning that was lying there with my tears.

Presently a good-looking young fellow came across the yard into the room. He had a hammer in his hand.

'Well, Joram!' said Mr Omer. 'How do *you* get on?'

'All right,' said Joram. 'Will you give me your opinion of it?'

'I will,' said Mr Omer, rising and he turned to me; 'would you like to see your –'

'No, father,' Minnie interposed.

I can't say how I knew it was my dear, dear mother's coffin that they went to look at but it came into my mind what the noise was; and when the young man entered, I am sure I knew what he had been doing.

The work being now finished, the two girls went into the shop to put that to rights. Minnie stayed behind to fold up what they had made, humming a lively little tune the while. Joram came in and stole a kiss from her while she was busy (he didn't appear to mind me, at all), and said her father was gone for the chaise.

All this I observed, sitting at the table in the corner with my head leaning on my hand, and my thoughts running on very different things. The chaise soon came round to the front of the shop, and the baskets being put in first, I was put in next, and those three followed.

I do not think I have ever experienced so strange a feeling in my life as that of being with them, remembering how they had been employed, and seeing them enjoy the ride. I was not angry with them; I was more afraid of them, as if I were cast away among creatures with whom I had no community of nature. They were very cheerful. So, when we reached home, I dropped out of the chaise as quickly as possible, that I might not be in their company before those solemn windows, looking blindly on me like closed eyes once bright.

I was in Peggotty's arms before I got to the door, and she took me into the house. Her grief burst out when she first saw me; but she controlled it soon, and spoke in whispers, and walked softly, as if the dead could be disturbed.

Mr Murdstone took no heed of me when I went into the parlour, but sat by the fireside, weeping silently. Miss Murdstone, who was busy at her writing-desk, asked me, in an iron whisper, if I had been measured for my mourning.

I said: 'Yes.'

'And your shirts,' said Miss Murdstone; 'have you brought 'em home?'

'Yes, ma'am. I have brought home all my clothes.'

This was all the consolation that her firmness administered to me.

In these days before the funeral, I saw but little of Peggotty, except that, in passing up or down stairs, I always found her close to the room where my mother and her baby lay. A day or two before the burial she took me into the room. I only recollect that underneath some white covering on the bed, there seemed to me to lie embodied the solemn stillness that was in the house; and that when she would have turned the cover back, I cried: 'Oh no!' and held her hand.

If the funeral had been yesterday, I could not recollect it better. The very air of the best parlour, when I went in at the door, the bright condition of the fire, the patterns of the glasses and plates, the odour of Miss Murdstone's dress, and our black clothes.

And now the bell begins to sound, and Mr Omer and another come to make us ready. As Peggotty was wont to tell me, long ago, the followers of my father to the same grave were made ready in the same room.

There are Mr Murdstone, our neighbour Mr Grayper, Mr Chillip, and I. The Bearers and their load are in the garden; and they move before us past the elms, and through the gate, and into the churchyard, where I have so often heard the birds sing on a summer morning.

We stand around the grave. The day seems different to me from every other day, and the light not of the same colour. While we stand bare-headed, I hear the voice of the clergyman, saying: 'I am the Resurrection and the Life, saith the Lord!' Then I hear sobs; and I see that good and faithful servant, whom of all the people upon earth I love the best.

It is over, and the earth is filled in, and we turn to come away. Before us stands our house, so pretty and unchanged, so linked in my mind with the young idea of what is gone, that all my sorrow has been nothing to the sorrow it calls forth.

All this, I say, is yesterday's event. Events of later date have floated from me to the shore where all forgotten things will reappear, but this stands like a high rock in the ocean.

I knew that Peggotty would come to me in my room. She sat down upon my little bed; and holding my hand, told me all that had happened.

'She was never well. She was uncertain in her mind, and not happy. When her baby was born, she was more delicate, and sunk a little every day. I think she got to be more timid, and more frightened-like, of late;

and that a hard word was like a blow to her. But she was always the same to me.

'The last time that I saw her like her own old self, was the night when you came home, my dear. The day you went away, she said to me, "I shall never see my pretty darling again."

'She never told her husband what she had told me till one night, a little more than a week before it happened, when she said to him: "My dear, I think I am dying."

'"It's off my mind now, Peggotty," she told me that night. "I am very tired. God bless both my children! God protect and keep my fatherless boy!"

'On the last night, in the evening, she said: "If my baby should die too, Peggotty, please let them lay him in my arms, and bury us together. Let my dearest boy go with us to our resting-place and tell him that his mother blessed him not once, but a thousand times."

'Daybreak had come, when she said to me, how kind and considerate Mr Copperfield had always been to her, and how he had told her, when she doubted herself, that a loving heart was stronger than wisdom. "Peggotty, my dear," she said then, "lay your good arm underneath my neck for your face is going far off, and I want it to be near." I put it as she asked; and oh Davy! she died, like a child that had gone to sleep!'

Thus ended Peggotty's narration. From the moment of my knowing of the death of my mother, I remembered her only as the young mother of my earliest impressions, who had been used to dance with me at twilight in the parlour. In her death she winged her way back to her calm untroubled youth, and cancelled all the rest.

The mother who lay in the grave was the mother of my infancy; the little creature in her arms, was myself, as I had once been, hushed for ever on her bosom.

CHAPTER 10

I become Neglected,
and am Provided for

The first act of business Miss Murdstone performed when the day of the solemnity was over was to give Peggotty a month's warning. As to me, not a word was said. Happy they would have been, I dare say, if they could have dismissed me at a month's warning too. I mustered courage to ask Miss Murdstone when I was going back to school; and she answered drily, she believed I was not going back at all.

There was one change in my condition: the constraint that had been put upon me was quite abandoned. I was so far from being warned off from Peggotty's society, that, provided I was not in Mr Murdstone's, I was never sought out or inquired for. At first I was in daily dread of his taking my education in hand again, but I soon began to think that all I had to anticipate was neglect.

'Peggotty,' I said in a thoughtful whisper, one evening, when I was warming my hands at the kitchen fire, 'what do you mean to do?'

'I expect I shall be forced to go to Yarmouth,' replied Peggotty, 'and live there.'

'You might have gone farther off,' I said, brightening a little. 'I shall see you sometimes, my dear old Peggotty.'

'As long as you are here, my pet, I shall come over every week of my life to see you,' cried Peggotty, with great animation.

I felt a great weight taken off my mind by this promise; but this was not all, for Peggotty went on to say: 'I'm a going to my brother's, first, for another visit. I have been thinking that perhaps you might be let go along with me.'

If anything could have given me a sense of pleasure at that time, it would have been this. It was ruffled by a doubt of Miss Murdstone giving her consent; but even that was set at rest for she came out to the store-closet while we were yet in conversation, and Peggotty, with a boldness that amazed me, broached the topic on the spot.

'The boy will be idle there,' said Miss Murdstone, looking into a

65

pickle-jar, 'but it is of paramount importance that my brother should not be disturbed. I suppose I had better say yes.'

I thanked her, without making any demonstration of joy, lest it should induce her to withdraw her assent. Nor could I help thinking this a prudent course, when she looked at me out of the pickle-jar, with as great an access of sourness as if her black eyes had absorbed its contents.

When the month was out, Peggotty and I were ready to depart. Mr Barkis came into the house for Peggotty's boxes and he gave me a look as he shouldered the largest box which I thought had meaning in it, if meaning could ever be said to find its way into Mr Barkis's visage.

Peggotty was naturally in low spirits at leaving what had been her home so many years and she got into the cart with her handkerchief at her eyes.

So long as she remained in this condition, Mr Barkis gave no signs of life but when she began to look about her, he nodded his head and grinned. I have not the least notion at whom, or what he meant by it.

'Peggotty is quite comfortable now, Mr Barkis,' I remarked, for his satisfaction.

After reflecting about it, Mr Barkis eyed her and said: '*Are* you pretty comfortable?'

Peggotty laughed, and answered in the affirmative.

'But really and truly, are you?' growled Mr Barkis, sliding nearer to her on the seat. 'Are you? Really and truly? Eh?' At each of these inquiries Mr Barkis shuffled nearer to her, so that we were all crowded together in the corner of the cart. I could not help observing that he seemed to think he had hit upon a wonderful expedient for expressing himself without the inconvenience of inventing conversation.

Mr Peggotty and Ham waited for us at the old place. They received me and Peggotty in an affectionate manner. They each took one of Peggotty's trunks, and we were going away when Mr Barkis made a sign to me to come under an archway.

'I say,' growled Mr Barkis, 'it was all right.'

I looked up into his face, and answered, with an attempt to be very profound: 'Oh!'

'It didn't come to a end there,' said Mr Barkis, nodding confidentially. 'It was all right. I'm a friend of your'n. You made it all right, first.'

In his attempts to be lucid, Mr Barkis was extremely mysterious. As we were going along, Peggotty asked me what he had said; and I told her he had said it was all right.

'Like his impudence,' said Peggotty, 'but I don't mind that! Davy dear, what should you think if I was to think of being married?'

'If you were thinking of being married – to Mr Barkis?'

'Yes,' said Peggotty.

'I should think it would be a very good thing. For then you would always have the horse and cart to bring you over to see me.'

'Yes, my precious,' cried Peggotty, 'and I should be more independent altogether, you see; let alone my working with a better heart in my own house, than I could in anybody else's now. And I shall be always near my pretty's resting-place and when *I* lie down to rest, I may be laid not far off from my darling girl! But I wouldn't so much as give it another thought,' said Peggotty, cheerily, 'if my Davy was anyways against it.'

'Look at me, Peggotty,' I replied; 'and see if I don't truly wish it!' As indeed I did, with all my heart.

'Well, I'll speak to my brother and in the meantime we'll keep it to ourselves, you and me. Barkis is a good plain creatur',' said Peggotty, 'and if I tried to do my duty by him, I think it would be my fault if I wasn't – if I wasn't pretty comfortable,' said Peggotty, laughing heartily.

This quotation from Mr Barkis tickled us both so much, that we were quite in a pleasant humour when we came within view of Mr Peggotty's cottage.

It looked just the same, except that it may, perhaps, have shrunk a little in my eyes; and Mrs Gummidge was waiting at the door as if she had stood there ever since. But there was no little Em'ly to be seen.

'She's at school, sir,' said Mr Peggotty, 'she'll be home, from twenty minutes to half-an-hour's time. We all on us feel the loss of her, bless ye!'

I knew the way by which little Em'ly would come, and presently found myself strolling along the path to meet her. A figure appeared in the distance before long, and I soon knew it to be Em'ly. But when she drew nearer, and I saw her blue eyes looking bluer, and her dimpled face looking brighter, and her whole self prettier and gayer, a curious feeling came over me that made me pretend not to know her, and pass by as if I were looking at something a long way off.

Little Em'ly didn't care a bit. She saw me well enough; but instead of calling after me, ran away laughing. This obliged me to run after her, and she ran so fast that we were very near the cottage before I caught her.

'Oh, it's you, is it?' said little Em'ly.

'Why, you knew who it was, Em'ly,' said I.

'And didn't *you* know who it was?' said Em'ly. I was going to kiss her, but she covered her cherry lips with her hands, and ran away into the house. She seemed to delight in teasing me, which was a change in her I wondered at very much.

Little Em'ly was spoiled by them all, but she was so affectionate and sweet-natured, and had such a pleasant manner of being both sly and shy at once, that she captivated me more than ever. She was tender-hearted, too; for when, as we sat round the fire after tea, an allusion was made by Mr Peggotty to the loss I had sustained, the tears stood in her eyes, and she looked at me so kindly across the table, that I felt quite thankful to her.

'Ah!' said Mr Peggotty, taking up her curls, and running them over his hand like water, 'here's another orphan, you see, sir. And here,' said Mr Peggotty, giving Ham a back-handed knock in the chest, 'is another of 'm, though he don't look much like it.'

'If I had you for my guardian, Mr Peggotty,' said I, shaking my head, 'I don't think I should *feel* much like it.'

'Well said, Mas'r Davy, bor!' cried Ham in an ecstasy. 'Horrah! well said!'

'And how's your friend, sir?' said Mr Peggotty to me.

'Steerforth?' said I. 'He was very well indeed when I came away.'

'There's a friend!' said Mr Peggotty, stretching out his pipe. 'Why, Lord love my heart alive, if it ain't a treat to look at him!'

'He's such a generous, fine, noble fellow,' said I, quite carried away by my favourite theme, 'that it's hardly possible to give him as much praise as he deserves. I can never feel thankful enough for the generosity with which he has protected me, so much younger and lower in the school than himself.'

I was running on, very fast indeed, when my eyes rested on little Em'ly's face, listening with the deepest attention, her breath held, her blue eyes sparkling like jewels.

'Em'ly is like me,' said Peggotty, 'and would like to see him.'

I lay down in the old little bed in the stem of the boat, and the wind came moaning on across the flat as it had done before. But I could not help fancying, now, that it moaned of those who were gone; and I thought of the sea that had risen since I last heard those sounds and drowned my happy home. I recollect petitioning that I might grow up to marry little Em'ly, and so dropping lovingly asleep.

The days passed pretty much as they had passed before, except that little Em'ly and I seldom wandered on the beach now. She had tasks to learn, and needlework to do; and was absent during a great part of each day. Em'ly was more of a little woman than I had supposed. She seemed to have got a great distance away from me, in little more than a year. She liked me, but she laughed at me, and tormented me. The best times were when she sat quietly at work in the doorway, and I sat on the wooden steps at her feet, reading to her. It seems to me that I have never seen such a sunny little figure sitting in the doorway of the old boat; that I have never beheld such sky, such water, such glorified ships sailing away into golden air.

On the very first evening after our arrival, Mr Barkis appeared with a bundle of oranges tied up in a handkerchief for Peggotty. After that occasion he appeared every evening with a little bundle, which he regularly put behind the door, and left there. Among them I remember a pair of jet earrings, some Spanish onions, a canary bird and cage, and a leg of pickled pork.

At length, when the term of my visit was nearly expired, it was given out that Peggotty and Mr Barkis were going to make a day's holiday together, and that little Em'ly and I were to accompany them. While we were yet at breakfast, Mr Barkis appeared in the distance, driving a chaise-cart towards the object of his affections.

Peggotty was dressed as usual, in her neat and quiet mourning; but Mr Barkis bloomed in a new blue coat, of which the tailor had given him such good measure, that the cuffs would have rendered gloves unnecessary in the coldest weather, while the collar was so high that it pushed his hair up on end on the top of his head. I thought Mr Barkis a phenomenon of respectability.

When we were all in a bustle outside the door, I found that Mr Peggotty was prepared with an old shoe, which was to be thrown after us for luck, and which he offered to Mrs Gummidge.

'No. It had better be done by somebody else, Dan'l,' said Mrs Gummidge. 'I'm a lone lorn creetur' myself, and everythink that reminds me of creeturs that ain't lone and lorn, goes contrairy with me.'

'Come, old gal!' cried Mr Peggotty. 'Take and heave it.'

But here Peggotty called out from the cart, in which we all were by this time, that Mrs Gummidge must do it. So Mrs Gummidge did it; and immediately burst into tears, sinking into the arms of Ham, with the declaration that she knowed she was a burden, and had better be carried to the house at once. Which I really thought was a sensible idea.

Away we went, however, on our holiday excursion; and the first thing we did was to stop at a church, where Mr Barkis tied the horse to some rails, and went in with Peggotty, leaving little Em'ly and me alone in the chaise. I took that occasion to put my arm round Em'ly's waist, and propose that as I was going away soon, we should determine to be very affectionate to one another. Little Em'ly allowing me to kiss her, I informed her that I never could love another, and that I was prepared to shed the blood of anybody who should aspire to her affections.

How merry little Em'ly made herself about it! The fairy woman said I was 'a silly boy;' and then laughed so charmingly that I forgot the pain of being called by that disparaging name, in the pleasure of looking at her.

Mr Barkis and Peggotty were a good while in the church, but came out at last. As we were going along, Mr Barkis turned to me, and said, with a wink, 'What name was it as I wrote up in the cart?'

'Clara Peggotty,' I answered.

'What name would it be as I should write up now?'

'Clara Peggotty, again?' I suggested.

'Clara Peggotty BARKIS!' He turned, and burst into a roar of laughter that shook the chaise.

In a word, they were married, and had gone into the church for no other purpose. We drove to a little inn in a by-road, where we had a very comfortable dinner, and passed the day with great satisfaction.

I have often thought, since, what an odd, innocent, out-of-the-way kind of wedding it must have been! We got into the chaise again soon after dark, and drove cosily back.

Little Em'ly and I made a cloak of an old wrapper, and sat under it for the rest of the journey. Ah, how I loved her!! What happiness (I thought) if we were going away to live among the trees and in the fields, never growing older, never growing wiser, children ever, rambling hand in hand among flowery meadows, laying down our heads on moss at night in a sweet sleep of purity and peace and buried by the birds when we were dead! Some such picture, with no real world in it, was in my mind all the way. I am glad to think there were two such guileless hearts at Peggotty's marriage as little Em'ly's and mine.

Well, we came to the old boat again in good time at night; and there Mr and Mrs Barkis bade us good-bye, and drove away snugly to their own home. I felt then, for the first time, that I had lost Peggotty. I should have gone to bed with a sore heart indeed under any other roof but that which sheltered little Em'ly's head.

Mr Peggotty and Ham knew what was in my thoughts and were ready with some supper and their hospitable faces to drive it away. Little Em'ly sat beside me on the locker and it was altogether a wonderful close to a wonderful day.

With morning came Peggotty; who took me to her own home, and a beautiful little home it was. I took leave of Mr Peggotty, and Ham, and Mrs Gummidge, and little Em'ly, that day; and passed the night at Peggotty's in a little room in the roof which was to be always mine, Peggotty said.

'Young or old, Davy dear, as long as I am alive and have this house over my head,' said Peggotty, 'you shall find it as if I expected you here directly.'

I felt the truth and constancy of my dear old nurse, with all my heart. I went home in the morning, with herself and Mr Barkis in the cart. They left me at the gate, and it was a strange sight to me to see the cart go on, taking Peggotty away, and leaving me looking at the house in which there was no face to look on mine with love or liking any more.

And now I fell into a solitary condition which seems to cast its gloom upon this paper as I write. What would I have given, to have been sent to the hardest school that ever was kept! I think Mr Murdstone's means were straitened at about this time; but it is little to the purpose. He could not bear me; and in putting me from him, he tried, as I believe, to put away the notion that I had any claim upon him – and succeeded.

I approach a period of my life, which I can never lose the remembrance of, while I remember anything; and the recollection of which has often come before me like a ghost, and haunted happier times.

I had been out, one day, loitering somewhere, when I came upon Mr Murdstone walking with a gentleman. I was going by them, when the gentleman cried: 'You are Brooks of Sheffield.'

At these words, I observed the gentleman more attentively. I knew him to be Mr Quinion, whom I had gone over to Lowestoft with Mr Murdstone to see.

'And how do you get on, and where are you being educated, Brooks?' said Mr Quinion.

I did not know what to reply, and glanced dubiously at Mr Murdstone.

'He is at home at present,' said the latter. 'I don't know what to do with him.'

'Humph!' said Mr Quinion. 'I suppose you are a pretty sharp fellow still?'

'Ay! He is sharp enough,' said Mr Murdstone, impatiently.

I made my way home. Looking back, I saw Mr Murdstone leaning against the wicket of the churchyard, and Mr Quinion talking to him. They were both looking after me.

Mr Quinion lay at our house that night. After breakfast, the next morning, I was going out of the room, when Mr Murdstone called me back. He then repaired to another table, where his sister sat herself at her desk. Mr Quinion, with his hands in his pockets, stood looking out of window; and I stood looking at them all.

'David,' said Mr Murdstone, 'to the young this is a world for action; not for moping and droning in. It is especially so for a boy of your disposition, which requires a great deal of correcting. I suppose you know that I am not rich. You have received some considerable education already. Education is costly; and I am of opinion that it would not be at all advantageous to you to be kept at a school. What is before you, is a fight with the world; and the sooner you begin it, the better.'

I think it occurred to me that I had already begun it, in my poor way.

'You have heard the "counting-house" mentioned sometimes,' said Mr Murdstone.

'The counting-house, sir?' I repeated.

'Of Murdstone and Grinby, in the wine trade,' he replied. 'Mr Quinion suggests that it gives employment to some other boys, and that he sees no reason why it shouldn't give employment to you.'

'He having,' Mr Quinion observed in a low voice, 'no other prospect, Murdstone.'

Though I quite understood that the purpose of this announcement was to get rid of me, I have no distinct remembrance whether it pleased or frightened me. Nor had I much time for the clearing of my thoughts, as Mr Quinion was to go upon the morrow.

Behold me, on the morrow, in a much-worn little white hat, with a black crape round it for my mother, a black jacket, and a pair of stiff corduroy trousers and with my little worldly all before me in a small trunk, in the post-chaise that was carrying Mr Quinion to the London coach at Yarmouth! See, how our house and church are lessening in the distance; how the grave beneath the tree is blotted out by intervening objects; how the spire points upwards from my old playground no more, and the sky is empty!

CHAPTER 11

I begin Life on my own Account, and don't like it

I know enough of the world now, to have almost lost the capacity of being much surprised by anything; but it is matter of some surprise to me, even now, that I can have been so easily thrown away at such an age. It seems wonderful to me that nobody should have made any sign in my behalf. But none was made; and I became, at ten years old, a little labouring hind in the service of Murdstone and Grinby.

Murdstone and Grinby's warehouse was in Blackfriars, the last house at the bottom of a narrow street, curving down hill to the river. It was a crazy old house with a wharf of its own, abutting on the water when the tide was in, and on the mud when the tide was out, and literally overrun with rats. Its panelled rooms, discoloured with the dirt of a hundred years; its decaying floors; the rottenness of the place; are all before me, just as they were in the evil hour when I went among them for the first time, with my trembling hand in Mr Quinion's.

An important branch of Murdstone and Grinby's trade was the supply of wines and spirits to certain packet ships. A great many empty bottles were one of the consequences of this traffic, and certain boys were employed to wash them. There were three or four of us, counting me.

My working place was established in a corner of the warehouse, where Mr Quinion could see me. Hither, on the first morning of my so auspiciously beginning life on my own account, the oldest of the regular boys was summoned to show me my business. Mick Walker wore a ragged apron and a paper cap. He informed me that his father was a bargeman, and that our principal associate would be another boy whom he introduced by the extraordinary name of Mealy Potatoes, on account of his complexion, which was pale or mealy.

No words can express the secret agony of my soul as I sunk into this companionship compared with Steerforth, Traddles, and the rest of those boys; and felt my hopes of growing up to be a learned and distinguished man crushed in my bosom. The deep remembrance of the sense I had, of being utterly without hope; of the shame I felt in my position; of the misery it was to believe that day by day what I had learned, and thought, and delighted in, would pass away from me, little by little, never to be brought back, cannot be written. I mingled my tears with the water in which I was washing the bottles; and sobbed as if there were a flaw in my own breast, and it were in danger of bursting.

The clock was at half-past twelve when Mr Quinion tapped at the counting-house window, and beckoned to me to go in. I found there a stoutish, middle-aged person, in black tights and shoes, with no more hair upon his head than there is upon an egg, and with a very extensive face, which he turned full upon me.

'This,' said the stranger, with a certain indescribable air of doing something genteel, which impressed me very much, 'is Master Copperfield. I hope I see you well, sir?'

I said I was very well, and hoped he was.

'This is Mr Micawber,' said Mr Quinion to me. 'He has been written to by Mr Murdstone, on the subject of your lodgings, and he will receive you as a lodger.'

'My address,' said Mr Micawber, 'is Windsor Terrace, City Road. I – in short,' said Mr Micawber, in a burst of confidence – 'I live there.'

I made him a bow.

'Under the impression,' said Mr Micawber, 'that your peregrinations in this metropolis have not as yet been extensive, and that you might have some difficulty in penetrating the arcana of the Modern Babylon in the direction of the City Road – in short,' said Mr Micawber, 'that you might lose yourself – I shall be happy to call this evening, and install you in the knowledge of the nearest way.'

I thanked him with all my heart, for it was friendly in him to offer to take that trouble.

Mr Quinion then formally engaged me in the warehouse of Murdstone and Grinby, at a salary, I think, of six shillings a week. At the appointed time in the evening, Mr Micawber reappeared and we walked to our house together; Mr Micawber impressing the names of streets, and the shapes of houses upon me, as we went, that I might find my way back in the morning.

At his house in Windsor Terrace he presented me to Mrs Micawber, a thin and faded lady with a baby at her breast. This baby was one of twins; and I may remark here that I hardly ever saw both the twins detached from Mrs Micawber at the same time. One of them was always taking refreshment.

There were two other children; Master Micawber, aged about four, and Miss Micawber, aged about three. These, and a dark-complexioned young woman, who was servant to the family, and informed me that she was 'a Orfling,' and came from St Luke's workhouse, completed the establishment. My room was at the top of the house, at the back and very scantily furnished.

'I never thought,' said Mrs Micawber, when she came up to show me the apartment, 'before I was married, when I lived with papa and mama, that I should ever find it necessary to take a lodger. But Mr Micawber being in difficulties, all considerations of private feeling must give way.'

I said: 'Yes, ma'am.'

'If Mr Micawber's creditors *will not* give him time,' said Mrs Micawber, 'they must take the consequences. Blood cannot be obtained from a stone, neither can anything be obtained at present from Mr Micawber.'

Poor Mrs Micawber! The only visitors I ever saw, or heard of, were creditors and some of them were quite ferocious. One dirty-faced man, a boot-maker, would roar up at the windows of the second floor, where he knew Mr Micawber was. At these times, Mr Micawber would be transported with grief and mortification but within half-an-hour he would go out, humming a tune with a greater air of gentility than ever. Mrs Micawber was quite as elastic. I have known her to be thrown into fainting fits by the king's taxes at three o'clock, and to eat lamb-chops breaded, and drink warm ale at four.

In this house, and with this family, I passed my leisure time. I was out at the warehouse all day, and had to support myself all the week. I was such a child that frequently when I went into a strange public-house for a glass of ale to moisten what I had had for dinner, they were afraid to give it me. I remember one hot evening I went into the bar and said to the landlord:

'What is your best – your *very best* – ale a glass?' For it was a special occasion. It may have been my birthday.

'Twopence-halfpenny,' says the landlord, 'is the price of the Genuine Stunning ale.'

'Then,' says I, producing the money, 'just draw me a glass of the Genuine Stunning, if you please, with a good head to it.'

The landlord looked at me from head to foot and said something to his wife. She joined him in surveying me. They asked me a good many questions; as, what my name was, how old I was, where I lived, how I was employed, and how I came there. To all of which, I invented appropriate answers. They served me with the ale, though I suspect it was not the Genuine Stunning; and the landlord's wife gave me my money back and gave me a kiss.

I know I do not exaggerate the scantiness of my resources or the difficulties of my life. I worked from morning until night, with common men and boys, a shabby child. I lounged about the streets, insufficiently and unsatisfactorily fed. I know that, but for the mercy of God, I might easily have been, for any care that was taken of me, a little robber or a little vagabond.

Yet I held some station at Murdstone and Grinby's too. I never said, to man or boy, how it was that I came to be there, or gave the least indication of being sorry that I was there. That I suffered in secret, no one ever knew. I kept my own counsel, and I did my work. I soon became at least as expeditious and skilful as the other boys. Though perfectly familiar with them, my conduct and manner were different enough from theirs to place a space between us.

My rescue from this kind of existence I considered quite hopeless. I am solemnly convinced that I never for one hour was reconciled to it, or was otherwise than miserably unhappy; but I bore it; and even to Peggotty never in any letter revealed the truth.

Mr Micawber's difficulties were an addition to the distressed state of my mind. In my forlorn state I became quite attached to the family. On a Saturday night, which was my grand treat – because it was a great thing to walk home with six shillings in my pocket, thinking what such a sum would buy – Mrs Micawber would make the most heart-rending confidences to me. It was nothing at all unusual for Mr Micawber to sob violently at the beginning of one of these Saturday night conversations, and sing about Jack's delight being his lovely Nan, towards the end of it. I have known him come home to supper with a declaration that nothing was now left but a jail; and go to bed making a calculation of the expense of putting bow-windows to the house, 'in case anything turned up,' which was his favourite expression. And Mrs Micawber was just the same.

A curious equality of friendship, originating, I suppose, in our respective circumstances, sprung up between me and these people. But I never allowed myself to be prevailed upon to accept any invitation to eat and drink with them out of their stock until Mrs Micawber took me into her entire confidence.

'Master Copperfield,' said Mrs Micawber, 'I make no stranger of you, and therefore do not hesitate to say that Mr Micawber's difficulties are coming to a crisis. With the exception of the heel of Dutch cheese – which is not adapted to the wants of a young family – there is nothing to eat in the house.'

'Dear me!' I said, in great concern.

I had two or three shillings of my week's money in my pocket and with heartfelt emotion begged Mrs Micawber to accept of them as a loan. But that lady replied that she couldn't think of it.

'No, my dear Master Copperfield,' said she, 'but you can render me another kind of service, if you will. There are still a few trifles that we could part with. Mr Micawber's feelings would never allow *him* to dispose of them; and Clicket' – this was the girl from the workhouse – 'would take painful liberties if so much confidence was reposed in her. Master Copperfield, if I might ask you – '

I understood Mrs Micawber now, and began to dispose of the more portable articles of property that very evening. Mr Micawber had a few books and those went first. I carried them to a bookstall in the City Road and sold them for whatever they would bring. At the pawnbroker's shop, too, I began to be very well known. After these occasions Mrs Micawber made a little treat, generally a supper; and there was a peculiar relish in these meals which I well remember.

At last Mr Micawber's difficulties came to a crisis, and he was arrested early one morning, and carried over to the King's Bench Prison in the Borough. He told me, as he went out of the house, that the God of day had now gone down upon him – and I really thought his heart was broken. But I heard, afterwards, that he was seen to play a lively game at skittles before noon.

On the first Sunday after he was taken there, I was to have dinner with him. We went up to his room and cried very much. He solemnly conjured me to take warning by his fate; after which he borrowed a shilling of me for porter, and put away his handkerchief and cheered up.

We sat before a little fire until another debtor, who shared the room with Mr Micawber, came in from the bakehouse with the loin of mutton which was our joint-stock repast. Then I was sent up to Captain Hopkins in the room overhead, with Mr Micawber's compliments, and would Captain Hopkins lend me a knife and fork. There was something gipsy-like and agreeable in the dinner, and early in the afternoon I went home to comfort Mrs Micawber with an account of my visit.

I don't know how the household furniture came to be sold for the family benefit. Sold it was, however, and carried away in a van; except the bed, a few chairs, and the kitchen-table. With these possessions we encamped in the two parlours of the emptied house in Windsor Terrace; Mrs Micawber, the children, the Orfling, and myself; and lived in those rooms night and day. At last Mrs Micawber resolved to move into the prison, where Mr Micawber had now secured a room to himself. I was accommodated with an inexpensive lodging in the same neighbourhood, a quiet back-garret with a sloping roof, commanding a pleasant prospect of a timber-yard. I thought it quite a paradise.

All this time I was working at Murdstone and Grinby's in the same common way, and with the same sense of unmerited degradation as at first. The only changes I am conscious of are, firstly, that I had grown more shabby, and secondly, that I was now relieved of much of the weight of Mr and Mrs Micawber's cares; for some relatives or friends had engaged to help them and they lived more comfortably in the prison than they had lived out of it. I used to breakfast with them now, and in the evening I used to go back to the prison, and walk up and down the parade with Mr Micawber; or play casino with Mrs Micawber, and hear reminiscences of her papa and mama. Whether Mr Murdstone knew where I was, I am unable to say. I never told them at Murdstone and Grinby's.

Mr Micawber's affairs, although past their crisis, were very much involved by reason of a certain 'Deed,' of which I used to hear a great deal. At last this document ceased to be the rock ahead it had been; and Mrs Micawber informed me that 'her family' had decided that Mr Micawber should apply for his release under the Insolvent Debtors' Act, which would set him free, she expected, in about six weeks.

'And then,' said Mr Micawber, who was present, 'I have no doubt I shall, please Heaven, begin to live in a perfectly new manner, if – in short, if anything turns up.'

Mr Micawber, about this time, composed a petition to the House of Commons, praying for an alteration in the law of imprisonment for debt. There was a club in the prison, in which Mr Micawber was a great authority, and the club had strongly approved of this petition. Wherefore Mr Micawber set to work, engrossed it on an immense sheet of paper, and appointed a time for all within the walls if they chose, to come up to his room and sign it.

When I heard of this approaching ceremony, I was so anxious to see them all come in, that I established myself in a corner for that purpose. As many of the principal members of the club as could be got into the small room without filling it, supported Mr Micawber in front of the petition, while my old friend Captain Hopkins stationed himself close to it, to read it to all who were unacquainted with its contents. I remember a certain luscious roll he gave to such phrases as 'The people's representatives in Parliament assembled,' and 'His gracious Majesty's unfortunate subjects,' as if the words were delicious to taste.

As I walked to and fro daily between Southwark and Blackfriars,

I wonder how many of these people were wanting in the crowd that used to come filing before me in review again, to the echo of Captain Hopkins's voice! When I tread the old ground, I do not wonder that I seem to see and pity, going on before me, an innocent romantic boy, making his imaginative world out of such strange experiences and sordid things.

CHAPTER 12

Liking Life on my own Account no better, I form a great Resolution

In due time, Mr Micawber's petition was ripe for hearing; and that gentleman was ordered to be discharged, to my great joy.

Mr Micawber returned to the King's Bench when his case was over and the club held an harmonic meeting that evening in his honour; while Mrs Micawber and I had a lamb's fry in private, surrounded by the sleeping family.

As I could hardly hope for a more favourable opportunity of putting a question in which I had a near interest, I said to Mrs Micawber:

'May I ask, ma'am, what you and Mr Micawber intend to do, now that Mr Micawber at liberty?'

'My family,' said Mrs Micawber, 'are of opinion that Mr Micawber should quit London, and exert his talents in the country. Mr Micawber is a man of great talent, Master Copperfield.'

I said I was sure of that.

'My family are of opinion that something might be done for a man of his ability in the Custom House. It is their wish that Mr Micawber should go down to Plymouth. They think it indispensable that he should be upon the spot.'

'That he may be ready?' I suggested.

'Exactly,' returned Mrs Micawber. 'That he may be ready, in case of anything turning up.'

'And do you go too, ma'am?'

The events of the day had made Mrs Micawber hysterical, and she shed tears as she replied:

'I never will desert Mr Micawber. The pearl necklace and bracelets, which I inherited from mama, have been disposed of for less than half their value; and the set of coral, which was the wedding gift of my papa, has been actually thrown away for nothing. But I never will desert Mr Micawber. No!' cried Mrs Micawber, more affected than before, 'I never will do it! It's of no use asking me!'

Mrs Micawber having now raised her voice into a perfect scream, I was so frightened that I ran off to the club-room, and disturbed Mr Micawber in the act of leading the chorus of Gee up, Dobbin – with the tidings that Mrs Micawber was in an alarming state, upon which he immediately burst into tears, and came away with me.

'Emma, my angel!' cried Mr Micawber, running into the room; 'what is the matter?'

'I never will desert you, Micawber!' she exclaimed.

'My life!' said Mr Micawber, taking her in his arms.

'He is the parent of my children! He is the husband of my affections,' cried Mrs Micawber, struggling; 'and I ne – ver – will – desert Mr Micawber!'

Mr Micawber was so deeply affected by this proof of her devotion that he implored her to look up, and to be calm. But the more he asked Mrs Micawber to compose herself, the more she wouldn't. Consequently Mr Micawber was soon so overcome, that he mingled his tears with hers and mine; until he begged me to do him the favour of taking a chair on the staircase, while he got her into bed. So I sat at the staircase window, until he came out and joined me.

'How is Mrs Micawber now, sir?' I said.

'Very low,' said Mr Micawber, shaking his head. 'Ah, this has been a dreadful day!'

I was greatly touched, and disappointed too, for I had expected that we should be quite gay on this happy and long-looked-for occasion. But through all the confusion and lowness of spirits, I plainly discerned that Mr and Mrs Micawber were going away from London, and that a parting between us was near at hand. It was in my walk home that night, and in the sleepless hours which followed, that the thought first occurred to me which afterwards shaped itself into a settled resolution.

I had grown so accustomed to the Micawbers, and had been so intimate with them, that the prospect of being thrown upon some new shift for a lodging, and going once more among unknown people, was like being that moment turned adrift into my present life. That there was no hope of escape from it, unless the escape was my own act, I knew quite well. I rarely heard from Miss Murdstone, and never from Mr Murdstone; but two or three parcels of mended clothes had come up for me, and in each there was a scrap of paper to the effect that J. M. trusted D. C. was devoting himself wholly to his duties – not the least hint of my ever being anything else than the common drudge into which I was fast settling down.

The very next day showed me that Mrs Micawber had not spoken of their going away without warrant. They took a lodging in the house where I lived, for a week; at the expiration of which time they were to start for Plymouth.

I passed my evenings with Mr and Mrs Micawber, during the remaining term of our residence under the same roof; and I think we became fonder of one another as the time went on. On the last Sunday, they invited me to dinner; and we had a loin of pork and apple sauce, and a pudding.

'I shall never, Master Copperfield,' said Mrs Micawber, 'revert to the period when Mr Micawber was in difficulties, without thinking of you. Your conduct has always been of the most delicate and obliging description. You have never been a lodger. You have been a friend.'

I said I was very sorry we were going to lose one another.

'My dear young friend,' said Mr Micawber, 'I am a man of some experience in life. At present, and until something turns up (which I am, I may say, hourly expecting), I have nothing to bestow but advice. Still my advice is so far worth taking that – in short, that I have never taken it myself, and am the' – here Mr Micawber, who had been beaming up to the present moment, checked himself and frowned – 'the miserable wretch you behold.'

'My dear Micawber!' urged his wife.

'My advice is,' said Mr Micawber, smiling again, 'never do to-morrow what you can do to-day. Procrastination is the thief of time. Collar him!'

'My poor papa's maxim,' Mrs Micawber observed.

'My other piece of advice, Copperfield,' said Mr Micawber, 'annual income twenty pounds, annual expenditure nineteen nineteen and six, result happiness. Annual income twenty pounds, annual expenditure twenty pounds ought and six, result misery. The blossom is blighted, the leaf is withered, the God of day goes down upon the dreary scene, and – and in short you are for ever floored. As I am!'

To make his example the more impressive, Mr Micawber drank a glass of punch with an air of great satisfaction, and whistled the College Hornpipe.

Next morning I met the whole family at the coach-office, and saw them, with a desolate heart, take their places.

'Copperfield,' said Mr Micawber, 'farewell! If, in the progress of revolving years, I could persuade myself that my blighted destiny had been a warning to you, I should feel that I had not occupied another man's place in existence altogether in vain. In case of anything turning up (of which I am rather confident), I shall be extremely happy if it should be in my power to improve your prospects.'

I think, as I stood in the road looking wistfully at them, Mrs Micawber saw what a little creature I really was because she beckoned to me to climb up with quite a new and motherly expression in her face, and gave me just such a kiss as she might have given to her own boy. I had barely time to get down again before the coach started. It was gone in a minute. The Orfling and I stood looking vacantly at each other, and then said good-bye; she going back, I suppose, to St Luke's workhouse, as I went to begin my weary day at Murdstone and Grinby's.

But with no intention of passing many more weary days there. No. I had resolved to run away. – To go, by some means or other, down into the country, to the only relation I had in the world, my aunt, Miss Betsey.

Again and again, I had gone over that old story of my poor mother's about my birth. My aunt walked into that story, and walked out of it, a dread and awful personage; but there was one little trait in her behaviour which gave me some faint shadow of encouragement. I could not forget how my mother had thought that she felt her touch her hair with no ungentle hand; and though it might have been altogether my mother's fancy, I made a little picture out of it which softened the whole narrative.

As I did not even know where Miss Betsey lived, I wrote a long letter to Peggotty, and asked her, incidentally, if she remembered. I told Peggotty that I had a particular occasion for half a guinea; and that if she could lend me that sum until I could repay it, I should be very much obliged to her.

Peggotty's answer soon arrived, and was, as usual, full of affectionate devotion. She enclosed the half-guinea and told me that Miss Betsey lived near Dover, but whether at Dover itself, at Hythe, Sandgate, or Folkestone, she could not say. One of our men informing me that they were all close together, I resolved to set out at the end of that week.

Being unwilling to disgrace the memory I was going to leave behind me at Murdstone and Grinby's, I considered myself bound to remain until Saturday night; and, as I had been paid a week's wages in advance when I first came there, not to present myself in the counting-house at the usual hour, to receive my stipend. For this reason, I had borrowed the half-guinea, that I might not be without a fund for my travelling expenses. Accordingly, when the Saturday night came, I shook Mick Walker by the hand and, bidding a last good-night to Mealy Potatoes, ran away.

My box was at my old lodging over the water, and I looked about me for some one who would help me to carry it to the booking-office. There was a long-legged young man, with a little empty donkey-cart, standing in the Blackfriars Road, whose eye I caught. I stopped to assure him that I had not done so in bad manners, but uncertain whether he might or might not like a job.

'Wot job?' said the long-legged young man.

'To move a box,' I answered, which I wanted him to take to the Dover coach-office for sixpence.

'Done with you for a tanner!' said the young man, and directly got upon his cart, and rattled away at such a rate, that it was as much as I could do to keep pace with the donkey.

There was a defiant manner about this young man that I did not much like; as the bargain was made, however, I took him up-stairs to the room I was leaving, and we brought the box down, and put it on his cart. I was unwilling to put the direction-card on there, lest any of my landlord's family should fathom what I was doing, and detain me; so I said to the young man that I would be glad if he would stop when he came to the dead-wall of the King's Bench prison. The words were no sooner out of my mouth, than he rattled away and I was quite out of breath when I caught him at the place appointed.

Being much flushed and excited, I tumbled my half-guinea out of my pocket in pulling the card out. I put it in my mouth for safety, and had just tied the card on to my satisfaction, when I felt myself violently chucked under the chin by the young man, and saw my half-guinea fly into his hand.

'Wot!' said the young man, seizing me with a frightful grin. 'This is a pollis case, is it? You're going to bolt, are you?'

'You give me my money back, if you please,' said I, very much frightened.

The young man jumped into the cart, sat upon my box, and, exclaiming that he would drive to the pollis straight, rattled away harder than ever.

I ran after him as fast as I could. Now I lost him, now I saw him, now I lost him. At length, confused by fright and heat, I left the young man to go where he would with my box and money; and, panting and crying, but never stopping, faced about for Greenwich, which I had understood was on the Dover Road: taking very little more out of the world, towards the retreat of my aunt, than I had brought into it, on the night when my arrival gave her so much umbrage.

CHAPTER 13

The Sequel of my Resolution

For anything I know, I may have had some wild idea of running all the way to Dover, when I gave up the pursuit of the young man with the donkey-cart, and started for Greenwich. I came to a stop in the Kent Road. Here I sat down on a doorstep, with hardly breath enough to cry for the loss of my box and half-guinea.

It was by this time dark; I heard the clocks strike ten. But it was a summer night, fortunately, and fine weather. When I had recovered my breath, I rose up and went on. In the midst of my distress, I had no notion of going back.

But my standing possessed of only three-halfpence in the world troubled me. I trudged on miserably until I happened to pass a little shop, where it was written up that the best price was given for rags, bones, and kitchen-stuff. The master of this shop was sitting at the door in his shirt-sleeves, smoking.

My late experiences with Mr and Mrs Micawber suggested to me that here might be a means of keeping off the wolf for a little while.

I went up the next by-street, took off my waistcoat, and came back to the shop. 'If you please, sir,' I said. 'I am to sell this for a fair price.'

Mr Dolloby – the name over the shop-door, at least – went into the shop, followed by me, spread the waistcoat on the counter, looked at it and said:

'What do you call a price, now, for this here little weskit?'

'Would eighteenpence be?' – I hinted, after some hesitation.

Mr Dolloby gave it me back. 'I should rob my family,' he said, 'if I was to offer ninepence for it.'

This was a disagreeable way of putting the business; because it imposed upon me, a perfect stranger, the unpleasantness of asking Mr Dolloby to rob his family on my account. However, I walked out of the shop, the richer by that sum, and the poorer by a waistcoat. But when I buttoned my jacket, that was not much.

A plan had occurred to me for passing the night. This was, to lie behind the wall at the back of my old school. I imagined it would be a kind of company to have the boys so near me, although they would know nothing of my being there.

It cost me some trouble to find Salem House; but I found it, and lay down by it. Never shall I forget the lonely sensation of first lying down, without a roof above my head!

Sleep came upon me as it came on many other outcasts, against whom house-doors were locked, and I dreamed of lying on my old school-bed. I slept until the warm beams of the sun, and the ringing of the getting-up bell at Salem House, awoke me. If I could have hoped that Steerforth was there, I would have lurked about until he came out alone; but I knew he must have left long since. So I crept away and struck into the long dusty Dover Road.

I heard the church-bells ringing as I plodded on; and I met people who were going to church. The peace and rest of the old Sunday morning were on everything, except me. I felt quite wicked in my dirt and dust, with my tangled hair. But for the picture I had conjured up, of my mother in her youth and beauty, weeping by the fire, and my aunt relenting to her, I hardly think I should have had the courage to go on. But it always went before me, and I followed.

I got, that Sunday, through three-and-twenty miles on the straight road, though not very easily, for I was new to that kind of toil. I see my-self, as evening closes in, coming over the bridge at Rochester footsore and tired, and eating bread that I had bought for supper. I sought no shelter but the sky; and toiling into Chatham, crept, at last, upon a sort of grass-grown battery overhanging a lane. Here I lay down and slept soundly.

Very stiff and sore of foot I was in the morning. Feeling that I could go but a very little way that day, if I were to reserve any strength for getting to my journey's end, I resolved to make the sale of my jacket its principal business. Accordingly, I took the jacket off, and carrying it under my arm, began a tour of inspection of the various slop-shops.

It was a likely place to sell a jacket in; for the dealers in secondhand clothes were numerous, and were, generally speaking, on the look-out for customers at their shop-doors. But I was rendered timid by the costly nature of their merchandise.

This modesty of mine directed my attention to such shops as Mr Dolloby's, in preference to the regular dealers. At last I found one that I thought looked promising, at the corner of a dirty lane. Into this shop, which was low and small, I went with a palpitating heart; which was not relieved when an ugly old man with a stubbly grey beard, rushed out of a dirty den and seized me by the hair of my head.

'What do you want?' grinned this old man, in a fierce, monotonous whine. 'Oh, my eyes and limbs, what do you want?'

'I wanted to know,' I said, trembling, 'if you would buy a jacket.'

'Oh, let's see the jacket!' cried the old man. With that he took his trembling hands, which were like the claws of a great bird, out of my hair; and put on a pair of spectacles. 'How much?' he cried after examining it.

'Half-a-crown,' I answered, recovering myself.

'Oh, my lungs and liver,' cried the old man, 'no! Eighteenpence!'

'Well,' said I, glad to have closed the bargain, 'I'll take eighteenpence.'

'Oh, my liver!' cried the old man, throwing the jacket on a shelf. 'Don't ask for money; make it an exchange.'

I told him humbly that I wanted money, nothing else was of any use to me. So I went outside, and sat down in the shade in a corner. And I sat there so many hours, that the shade became sunlight, and the sunlight became shade again, and still I sat there waiting for the money.

There never was such another drunken madman in that line of business, I hope. That he was well known in the neighbourhood, I soon understood from the visits he received from the boys, who continually came skirmishing about the shop, calling to him to bring out his gold. As if this were not bad enough, the boys, connecting me with the establishment, pelted me, and used me very ill all day.

He made many attempts to induce me to consent to an exchange; at one time coming out with a fishing-rod, at another with a fiddle, but I resisted all these overtures. At last he began to pay me in halfpence at a time; and was full two hours getting by easy stages to a shilling.

'Oh, my eyes and limbs!' he cried, peeping hideously out of the shop, 'will you go for twopence more?'

'I would go for nothing, if I could,' I said, 'but I want the money badly.'

'Oh, will you go for fourpence?'

I was so faint and weary that I closed with this offer; and taking the money out of his claw, went away more hungry and thirsty than I had ever been. But at an expense of threepence I soon refreshed myself completely; and, being in better spirits then, limped seven miles upon my road.

My bed at night was under another haystack, where I rested comfortably, having washed my blistered feet in a stream. When I took the road again next morning, I found that it lay through a succession of hop-grounds and orchards.

The trampers inspired me with dread. Some of them were most ferocious-looking ruffians, who stared at me as I went by. I recollect one fellow who had a woman with him, and who roared to me in such a tremendous voice that I halted.

'Where are you going?' said the tinker, gripping the bosom of my shirt with his blackened hand.

'I am going to Dover,' I said.

'Have you got the price of a pint of beer about you?' said the tinker. 'Out with it, afore I take it away!'

I should certainly have produced it, but that I met the woman's look, and saw her form 'No!' with her lips.

'I am very poor,' I said, attempting to smile, 'and have got no money.'

'What do you mean,' said the tinker, 'by wearing my brother's silk handkercher? Give it over here!' And he had mine off my neck in a moment, and tossed it to the woman.

The woman tossed it back to me, and made the word 'Go!' with her lips. Before I could obey, however, the tinker seized the handkerchief out of my hand with a roughness that threw me away like a feather, and turned upon the woman with an oath, and knocked her down. I never shall forget seeing her fall backward on the hard road; nor, when I looked back from a distance, seeing her wiping blood from her face with a corner of her shawl, while he went on ahead.

This adventure frightened me so that, when I saw any of these people coming, I turned back until I could find a hiding-place, which happened so often that I was very seriously delayed. But under this difficulty, as under all the other difficulties of my journey, I seemed to be sustained by my fanciful picture of my mother. When I came, at last, upon the downs near Dover, it relieved the solitary aspect of the scene with hope; and not until I actually set foot in the town itself, on the sixth day of my flight, did it desert me.

I inquired about my aunt among the boatmen first, and received various answers, all equally jocose and disrespectful. The shopkeepers, not liking my appearance, replied without hearing what I had to say, that they had got nothing for me. I felt more miserable and destitute than I had done at any period of my running away. My money was all gone, I was hungry, thirsty, and worn out; and seemed as distant from my end as if I had remained in London.

I was sitting on the step of an empty shop when a fly-driver, coming by with his carriage, dropped a horsecloth. Something good-natured in the man's face, as I handed it up, encouraged me to ask him if he could tell me where Miss Trotwood lived.

'Trotwood,' said he. 'Old lady? Pretty stiff in the back? Is gruffish and comes down upon you, sharp?'

My heart sank within me as I acknowledged the undoubted accuracy of this description.

'Why then,' said he. 'If you go up there,' pointing with his whip towards the heights, 'and keep on till you come to some houses facing the sea I think you'll hear of her. My opinion is, she won't stand anything, so here's a penny for you.'

I accepted the gift thankfully, and bought a loaf with it. Despatching this refreshment by the way, I went in the direction my friend had indicated. At length I went into a little shop and inquired if they could have the goodness to tell me where Miss Trotwood lived. I addressed myself to a man behind the counter, who was weighing some rice for a young woman; but the latter turned round quickly.

'My mistress?' she said. 'What do you want with her, boy?'

'I want,' I replied, 'to speak to her, if you please.'

'To beg of her, you mean,' retorted the damsel.

'No,' I said, 'indeed.' But suddenly remembering that in truth I came for no other purpose, I held my peace in confusion, and felt my face burn.

My aunt's handmaid, as I supposed she was from what she had said, walked out of the shop, telling me that I could follow her. We soon came to a very neat little cottage with cheerful bow-windows: in front of it, a small garden full of flowers, carefully tended, and smelling deliciously.

'This is Miss Trotwood's,' said the young woman. With which words she hurried into the house, as if to shake off the responsibility of my appearance.

My shoes were by this time in a woeful condition. My shirt and trousers, stained with heat, dew, grass, and the Kentish soil on which I had slept, might have frightened the birds from my aunt's garden. My hair had known no comb or brush since I left London. From head to foot I was powdered almost as white with chalk and dust, as if I had come out of a limekiln. In this plight, I waited to make my first impression on my formidable aunt.

The unbroken stillness of the parlour-window leading me to infer that she was not there, I lifted up my eyes to the window above it, where I saw a florid gentleman, with a grey head, who shut up one eye in a grotesque manner, laughed, and went away.

I was so much discomposed by this behaviour that I was on the point of slinking off, when there came out of the house a lady with gardening gloves on her hands and carrying a great knife.

I knew her immediately to be Miss Betsey, for she came stalking out of the house exactly as my poor mother had so often described her stalking up our garden at Blunderstone Rookery.

'Go away!' said Miss Betsey, making a chop in the air with her knife. 'Go along! No boys here!'

I watched her as she marched to a corner of her garden, and stooped to dig up some little root there. Then, without a scrap of courage, but with a great deal of desperation, I went in and stood beside her, touching her with my finger.

'If you please, ma'am,' I began.

She started and looked up.

'If you please, aunt.'

'Eh?' exclaimed Miss Betsey, in a tone of amazement.

'If you please, aunt, I am your nephew.'

'Oh, Lord!' said my aunt. And sat flat down in the garden-path.

'I am David Copperfield, of Blunderstone, in Suffolk – where you came, on the night when I was born, and saw my dear mama. I have been very unhappy since she died. I have been taught nothing, and thrown upon myself, and put to work not fit for me. It made me run away to you. I was robbed at first setting out, and have walked all the way, and have never slept in a bed since I began the journey.' Here I broke into a passion of crying, which I suppose had been pent up within me all the week.

My aunt, with every sort of expression but wonder discharged from her countenance, sat staring at me, until I began to cry; when she got up in a great hurry, collared me, and took me into the parlour. Her first proceeding was to bring out several bottles, and pour some of the contents of each into my mouth. I am sure I tasted aniseed water, anchovy sauce, and salad dressing. When she had administered these restoratives, as I was still unable to control my sobs, she put me on the sofa, with a shawl under my head, and the handkerchief from her own head under my feet, lest I should sully the cover; and ejaculated at intervals, 'Mercy on us!' letting those exclamations off like minute guns.

After a time she rang the bell. 'Janet,' said my aunt, when her servant came in. 'Give my compliments to Mr Dick, and say I wish to speak to him.'

Janet looked a little surprised to see me lying on the sofa but went on her errand. My aunt walked up and down the room, until the gentleman who had squinted at me from the upper window came in.

'Mr Dick,' said my aunt, 'you have heard me mention David Copperfield? Now don't pretend not to have a memory, because you and I know better.'

'David Copperfield?' said Mr Dick. 'Oh yes, to be sure. David, certainly.'

'Well,' said my aunt, 'this is his son. He would be as like his father as it's possible to be, if he was not so like his mother, too.'

'His son?' said Mr Dick. 'Indeed!'

'Yes,' pursued my aunt, 'and he has done a pretty piece of business. He has run away. Ah! His sister, Betsey Trotwood, never would have run away.' My aunt shook her head firmly, confident in the character and behaviour of the girl who never was born. 'Now, here you see young David Copperfield, and the question I put to you is, what shall I do with him?'

'What shall you do with him?' said Mr Dick, feebly, scratching his head.

'Yes,' said my aunt, with a grave look. 'Come! I want some very sound advice.'

'Why, if I was you,' said Mr Dick, looking vacantly at me, 'I should –' The contemplation of me seemed to inspire him with a sudden idea, and he added, briskly, 'I should wash him!'

'Janet,' said my aunt, turning round with a quiet triumph, which I did not then understand, 'Mr Dick sets us all right. Heat the bath.'

My aunt was a tall, hard-featured lady, but by no means ill-looking. Her features were handsome though unbending and austere. I particularly noticed that she had a quick, bright eye. Her hair, which was grey, was arranged in two plain divisions, under what I believe would be called a mob-cap; her dress was of a lavender colour, and perfectly neat; but scantily made, as if she desired to be as little encumbered as possible.

Mr Dick, as I have already said, was grey-headed and florid, his eyes prominent, with a strange kind of watery brightness in them that made me, in combination with his vacant manner, his submission to my aunt, and his childish delight when she praised him, suspect him of being a little mad; though, if he were mad, how he came to be there puzzled me extremely.

Janet was a pretty blooming girl, of about nineteen or twenty. I may mention here what I did not discover until afterwards, namely, that she was one of a series of protégées whom my aunt had taken into her service expressly to educate in a renouncement of mankind, and who had generally completed their abjuration by marrying the baker.

Janet had gone away to get the bath ready, when my aunt, to my great alarm, became in one moment rigid with indignation, and had hardly voice to cry out, 'Janet! Donkeys!'

Upon which, Janet came running up the stairs as if the house were in flames, darted out on a little piece of green in front, and warned off two saddle-donkeys, that had presumed to set hoof upon it. To this hour I don't know whether my aunt had any lawful right of way over that patch of green; but it was all the same to her. The one great outrage of her life was the passage of a donkey over that immaculate spot. In whatever occupation she was engaged, a donkey turned the current of her ideas in a moment and she was upon him straight.

The bath was a great comfort. For I began to be sensible of acute pains in my limbs and was now so tired and low that I could hardly keep myself awake for five minutes together. When I had bathed, they enrobed me in a shirt and a pair of trousers belonging to Mr Dick, and tied me up in two or three great shawls. Feeling very faint and drowsy, I lay down on the sofa again and fell asleep.

It might have been a dream, originating in the fancy which had occupied my mind so long, but I awoke with the impression that my aunt had bent over me, and had put my hair away from my face, and had then stood looking at me. The words, 'Pretty fellow,' seemed to be in my ears, too.

We dined soon after I awoke, off a roast fowl and a pudding; I sitting at table, not unlike a trussed bird myself, and moving my arms with considerable difficulty. All this time, I was deeply anxious to know what she was going to do with me; but she took her dinner in profound silence.

The cloth being drawn, my aunt sent up for Mr Dick again, who joined us, and looked as wise as he could when she requested him to attend to my story, which she elicited from me, gradually, by a course of questions. During my recital, she kept her eyes on Mr Dick who, whensoever he lapsed into a smile, was checked by a frown from my aunt.

'Whatever possessed that poor unfortunate Baby, that she must be married again,' said my aunt.

'Perhaps she fell in love with her second husband,' Mr Dick suggested.

'Fell in love!' repeated my aunt. 'What do you mean?'

'Perhaps,' Mr Dick simpered, after thinking a little, 'she did it for pleasure.'

'Pleasure, indeed!' replied my aunt. 'A mighty pleasure for the poor Baby to fix her simple faith upon any dog of a fellow, certain to ill-use her in some way or other. She couldn't even have a baby like anybody else. Where was this child's sister, Betsey Trotwood? Not forthcoming. Don't tell me!'

Mr Dick seemed quite frightened.

'And then, as if this was not enough, she goes and marries a Murderer – or a man with a name like it – and stands in *this* child's light! And the natural consequence is, as anybody but a baby might have foreseen, that he prowls and wanders. And then there's that woman with the Pagan name, that Peggotty, *she* goes and gets married next. I only hope,' said my aunt, shaking her head, 'that her husband is one of those Poker husbands and will beat her well with one.'

I could not bear to hear my old nurse so decried, and told my aunt that she was mistaken. That Peggotty was the best, the most faithful and most self-denying friend in the world; who had ever loved me dearly. I broke down as I was trying to say that her home was my home, and that I would have gone to her for shelter, but for her humble station, which made me fear that I might bring some trouble on her.

'Well, well!' said my aunt, 'the child is right to stand by those who have stood by him – Janet! Donkeys!'

I thoroughly believe that but for those unfortunate donkeys, we should have come to a good understanding; for my aunt had laid her hand on my shoulder, and the impulse was upon me, thus emboldened, to embrace her and beseech her protection. But the interruption put an end to all softer ideas for the present.

After tea, we sat at the window – on the look-out, as I imagined, from my aunt's sharp expression, for more invaders – until dusk, when Janet set candles and pulled down the blinds.

'Now, Mr Dick,' said my aunt, 'I am going to ask you another question. Look at this child. What would you do with him, now?'

'Do with David's son?' said Mr Dick.

'Ay,' replied my aunt, 'with David's son.'

'Oh!' said Mr Dick. 'I should put him to bed.'

'Janet!' cried my aunt, with the same complacent triumph that I had remarked before. 'Mr Dick sets us all right. If the bed is ready, we'll take him up to it.'

Janet reporting it to be quite ready, I was taken up kindly, but in some sort like a prisoner; my aunt going in front, and Janet bringing up the rear. The only circumstance which gave me any new hope, was my aunt's stopping on the stairs to inquire about a smell of fire and Janet's replying that she had been making tinder of my old shirt. I heard them lock my door on the outside. Turning these things over in my mind, I deemed it possible that my aunt might suspect I had a habit of running away and took precautions to have me in safe keeping.

The room was a pleasant one, at the top of the house, overlooking the sea, on which the moon was shining brilliantly. I remember how I sat looking at the moonlight on the water, as if I could hope to read my fortune in it. I remember the sensation of gratitude and rest which the sight of the white-curtained bed inspired. I remember how I thought of all the solitary places under the night sky where I had slept, and how I prayed that I never might be houseless any more. I remember how I seemed to float, then, down the melancholy glory of that track upon the sea, away into the world of dreams.

CHAPTER 14

My Aunt makes up her Mind about me

On going down in the morning, I found my aunt musing so profoundly over the breakfast-table that the contents of the urn had overflowed the teapot. I felt sure that I had been the subject of her reflections, and was more than ever anxious to know her intentions towards me. Yet I dared not express my anxiety, lest it should give her offence.

When she had finished her breakfast, my aunt very deliberately leaned back in her chair and contemplated me at her leisure. I attempted to hide my confusion but my knife tumbled over my fork, and I choked myself with my tea.

'I have written to your father-in-law,' said my aunt. 'I have sent him a letter that I'll trouble him to attend to, or he and I will fall out, I can tell him!'

'Does he know where I am, aunt?' I inquired, alarmed.

'I have told him,' said my aunt, with a nod.

'Shall I – be given up to him?' I faltered.

'I don't know,' said my aunt. 'We shall see.'

'I can't think what I shall do,' I exclaimed, 'if I have to go back to Mr Murdstone!'

'I can't say, I am sure,' said my aunt, shaking her head. 'We shall see.'

My spirits sank under these words, and I became very downcast and heavy of heart.

My aunt brought out her work-box. 'I wish you'd go up-stairs,' she said as she threaded her needle, 'and give my compliments to Mr Dick, and I'll be glad to know how he gets on with his Memorial.'

I rose with all alacrity, to acquit myself of this commission.

'I suppose,' said my aunt, 'you think Mr Dick a short name, eh? Mr Richard Babley – that's the gentleman's true name.'

I was going to suggest that I had better give him the full benefit of that name, when my aunt went on to say:

'But don't you call him by it, whatever you do. He can't bear his name.'

I promised to obey, and went up-stairs with my message.

'Ha! Phoebus!' said Mr Dick, laying down his pen. 'How does the world go? I'll tell you what,' he added, in a lower tone, 'I shouldn't wish it to be mentioned, but it's a' – here he put his lips close to my ear – 'it's a mad world. Mad as Bedlam, boy!'

Without presuming to give my opinion on this question, I delivered my message.

'I believe I have made a start. Do you recollect the date,' said Mr Dick, looking earnestly at me, 'when King Charles the First had his head cut off?'

I said I believed it happened in the year sixteen hundred and forty-nine.

'Well,' returned Mr Dick, looking dubiously at me. 'So the books say; but I don't see how that can be. Because, if it was so long ago, how could the people about him have made that mistake of putting some of the trouble out of *his* head, after it was taken off, into *mine*?'

I was very much surprised by the inquiry; but could give no information on this point.

'It's very strange,' said Mr Dick, with a despondent look upon his papers, 'but no matter.'

I was going away when he directed my attention to a large paper kite in the corner.

'I made it. We'll go and fly it, you and I,' said Mr Dick.

He showed me that it was covered with manuscript, laboriously written; but so plainly, that as I looked along the lines, I thought I saw some allusion to King Charles the First's head.

'There's plenty of string,' said Mr Dick, 'and when it flies high, it takes the facts a long way. That's my manner of diffusing 'em.'

His face was so pleasant, and had something so reverend in it, though it was hale and hearty, that I was not sure but that he was having a good-humoured jest with me. So I laughed, and he laughed, and we parted the best friends possible.

'Well, child,' said my aunt, when I went down-stairs. 'What do you think of Mr Dick?'

I had some idea of endeavouring to evade the question by replying that I thought him a very nice gentleman; but my aunt was not to be put off.

'Come! Your sister Betsey Trotwood would have told me what she thought directly.'

'Is he – is Mr Dick at all out of his mind?' I stammered.

'Not a morsel,' said my aunt. 'He has been *called* mad, or I should

not have had the benefit of his society and advice for these last ten years
and upwards. Mr Dick is a sort of distant connexion of mine. If it hadn't
been for me, his own brother would have shut him up for life.'

Seeing that my aunt felt strongly on the subject, I tried to look as if I
felt strongly too.

'So I stepped in,' said my aunt, 'I said, "Your brother's sane. Let him
have his little income, and come and live with me." After a good deal of
squabbling, I got him; and he has been here ever since. Nobody knows
what that man's mind is, except myself. Did he say anything to you
about King Charles the First, child?'

'Yes, aunt.'

'Ah!' said my aunt, rubbing her nose as if she were a little vexed.
'That's his allegorical way of expressing it. He connects his illness with
great disturbance and that's the figure which he chooses to use. And
why shouldn't he, if he thinks proper?'

I said: 'Certainly, aunt.'

I must say that the generosity of her championship of poor harmless
Mr Dick, not only inspired my young breast with some selfish hope for
myself, but warmed it unselfishly towards her. I began to know that there
was something about my aunt, notwithstanding her many eccentricities
and odd humours, to be honoured and trusted in. Though she was just
as sharp that day as on the day before, she seemed to me to command
more of my respect, if not less of my fear.

At length the reply from Mr Murdstone came, and my aunt informed
me, to my infinite terror, that he was coming to speak to her himself
on the next day. On the next day, I sat counting the time, flushed and
heated by the conflict of sinking hopes and rising fears within me.

My aunt sat at work in the window, and I sat by, with my thoughts
running astray on all possible and impossible results of Mr Murdstone's
visit, when she gave a sudden alarm of donkeys, and to my consternation and amazement, I beheld Miss Murdstone, on a side-saddle, ride
deliberately over the sacred piece of green.

My aunt was so exasperated by the coolness with which Miss
Murdstone looked about her, that she was unable for the moment to
dart out according to custom. I seized the opportunity to inform her
who it was; and that the gentleman now coming near the offender was
Mr Murdstone himself.

'I don't care who it is!' cried my aunt. 'Janet, turn him round. Lead
him off!' and I saw, from behind my aunt, a sort of hurried battle-piece,
in which the donkey stood resisting everybody, while Janet tried to pull
him round by the bridle. Miss Murdstone struck at Janet with a parasol,

but my aunt, descrying the young malefactor who was the donkey's guardian, rushed out, dragged him into the garden, and called upon Janet to fetch the constables. This part of the business, however, did not last long; for the young rascal, being expert at a variety of dodges, soon went whooping away, taking his donkey in triumph with him.

Miss Murdstone was now waiting with her brother at the bottom of the steps. My aunt, a little ruffled by the combat, marched past them with great dignity, and took no notice of their presence, until they were announced by Janet.

'Shall I go away, aunt?' I asked, trembling.

'No, sir,' said my aunt. 'Certainly not!' With which she pushed me into a corner near her, and fenced me in with a chair.

Mr Murdstone began: 'Miss Trotwood!'

'I beg your pardon,' observed my aunt. 'You are the Mr Murdstone who married the widow of my late nephew, David Copperfield, of Blunderstone Rookery?'

'I am,' said Mr Murdstone.

'You'll excuse my saying, sir,' returned my aunt, 'that I think it would have been a much happier thing if you had left that poor child alone.'

'I so far agree with what Miss Trotwood has remarked,' observed Miss Murdstone, bridling, 'that I consider our lamented Clara to have been, in all essential respects, a mere child.'

'It is a comfort to you and me, ma'am,' said my aunt, 'who are getting on in life, and are not likely to be made unhappy by our personal attractions, that nobody can say the same of us.'

'No doubt!' returned Miss Murdstone, though not with a very gracious assent.

'Janet,' said my aunt, 'my compliments to Mr Dick, and beg him to come down.'

When he came, my aunt performed the ceremony of introduction.

'Mr Dick. An old and intimate friend. On whose judgment,' said my aunt, with emphasis, as an admonition to Mr Dick, who was biting his forefinger and looking rather foolish, 'I rely.'

Mr Dick took his finger out of his mouth with a grave and attentive expression of face. My aunt inclined her head to Mr Murdstone, who went on:

'Miss Trotwood. On the receipt of your letter, I considered it an act of greater justice to answer it in person, however inconvenient the journey, rather than by letter. This unhappy boy has been the occasion of much domestic trouble and uneasiness; both during the lifetime of my late dear wife, and since. He has a sullen, rebellious spirit; a violent temper;

and an untoward, intractable disposition. Both my sister and myself have endeavoured to correct his vices, but ineffectually.'

'I beg to observe,' said Miss Murdstone, 'that of all the boys in the world, I believe this is the worst boy.'

'I have my own opinions,' resumed Mr Murdstone, 'as to the best mode of bringing him up. It is enough that I place this boy under the eye of a friend of my own, in a respectable business; that he runs away from it; makes himself a common vagabond about the country; and comes here, in rags, to appeal to you, Miss Trotwood.'

'About the respectable business,' said my aunt. 'If he had been your own boy, you would have put him to it, just the same?'

'If he had been my brother's own boy,' returned Miss Murdstone, striking in, 'his character, I trust, would have been altogether different.'

'Or if the poor child, his mother, had been alive, he would still have gone into the respectable business, would he?' said my aunt.

'I believe,' said Mr Murdstone, with an inclination of his head, 'that Clara would have disputed nothing, which myself and my sister Jane Murdstone were agreed was for the best.'

Miss Murdstone confirmed this with an audible murmur.

'Humph!' said my aunt. 'Unfortunate baby! The poor child's annuity died with her?'

'Died with her,' replied Mr Murdstone.

'And there was no settlement of the little property – what's-its-name Rookery – upon her boy?'

'It had been left to her, unconditionally, by her first husband,' Mr Murdstone began, when my aunt caught him up with the greatest irascibility.

'But when she married again – did no one put in a word for the boy at that time?'

'My late wife loved her second husband, ma'am,' said Mr Murdstone, 'and trusted implicitly in him.'

'Your late wife, sir, was a most unworldly baby,' returned my aunt, shaking her head at him. 'And now, what have you got to say next?'

'Merely this, Miss Trotwood,' he returned. 'I am here to take David back unconditionally, to dispose of him as I think proper, and to deal with him as I think right. You may possibly have some idea, Miss Trotwood, of abetting him in his running away, and in his complaints to you. Now I must caution you that if you step in between him and me, now, you must step in for ever. I am here, for the first and last time, to take him away. Is he ready to go? If he is not my doors are shut against him henceforth, and yours, I take it for granted, are open to him.'

To this address, my aunt had listened with the closest attention, sitting perfectly upright, with her hands folded on one knee, and looking grimly on the speaker.

'And what does the boy say?' said my aunt. 'Are you ready to go, David?'

I answered no, and entreated her not to let me. I said that neither Mr nor Miss Murdstone had ever liked me, or had ever been kind to me. And I begged and prayed my aunt to befriend and protect me, for my father's sake.

'Mr Dick,' said my aunt; 'what shall I do with this child?'

Mr Dick considered, hesitated, brightened, and rejoined, 'Have him measured for a suit of clothes directly.'

'Mr Dick,' said my aunt triumphantly, 'give me your hand, for your common sense is invaluable.' Having shaken it with great cordiality, she pulled me towards her and said to Mr Murdstone:

'You can go when you like; I'll take my chance with the boy. If he's all you say he is, at least I can do as much for him as you have done. But I don't believe a word of it.'

'Miss Trotwood,' rejoined Mr Murdstone, shrugging his shoulders, as he rose, 'if you were a gentleman –'

'Bah! Stuff and nonsense!' said my aunt. 'Don't talk to me!'

'How exquisitely polite!' exclaimed Miss Murdstone, rising. 'Overpowering, really!'

'Do you think I don't know,' said my aunt, turning a deaf ear to the sister, 'what kind of life you must have led that poor, unhappy, misdirected baby? Who so smooth and silky as Mr Murdstone at first! The poor, benighted innocent had never seen such a man. He worshipped her. He doted on her boy – he was to be another father to him, and they were all to live together in a garden of roses, weren't they? Ugh! Get along with you, do!' said my aunt.

'I never heard anything like this person in my life!' exclaimed Miss Murdstone.

'Mr Murdstone,' Miss Betsey said, shaking her finger at him, 'you were a tyrant to the simple baby, and you broke her heart. She was a loving baby – I know that – and through the best part of her weakness you gave her the wounds she died of.'

He had stood by the door, all this while, with a smile upon his face, though his black eyebrows were heavily contracted. I remarked now, that he seemed to breathe as if he had been running.

'Good day, sir,' said my aunt, 'and good-bye! Good day to you, too, ma'am,' said my aunt, turning suddenly upon his sister. 'Let me see you ride a donkey over *my* green again, and as sure as you have a head upon your shoulders, I'll knock your bonnet off, and tread upon it!'

It would require a painter, and no common painter too, to depict my aunt's face, as she delivered herself of this very unexpected sentiment, and Miss Murdstone's face as she heard it. But the manner of the speech, no less than the matter, was so fiery, that Miss Murdstone, without a word in answer, discreetly put her arm through her brother's, and walked haughtily out of the cottage.

My aunt remained in the window looking after them. Her face gradually relaxed, and became so pleasant, that I was emboldened to kiss and thank her; which I did with great heartiness, and with both my arms clasped round her neck. I then shook hands with Mr Dick, who shook hands with me a great many times, and hailed this happy close of the proceedings with repeated bursts of laughter.

'You'll consider yourself guardian, jointly with me, of this child, Mr Dick,' said my aunt.

'I shall be delighted,' said Mr Dick, 'to be the guardian of David's son.'

'Very good,' returned my aunt, '*that's* settled. I have been thinking, do you know, Mr Dick, that I might call him Trotwood. Trotwood Copperfield.'

'Yes, to be sure,' said Mr Dick, a little abashed.

My aunt took so kindly to the notion, that some ready-made clothes were purchased for me that afternoon marked Trotwood Copperfield, in her own handwriting.

Thus I began my new life, in a new name, and with everything new about me. Now that the state of doubt was over, I felt, for many days, like one in a dream. I never thought that I had a curious couple of guardians, in my aunt and Mr Dick. The two things clearest in my mind were that a remoteness had come upon the old Blunderstone life and that a curtain had for ever fallen on my life at Murdstone and Grinby's. No one has ever raised that curtain since. The remembrance of that life is fraught with so much pain to me, with so much mental suffering and want of hope, that I have never had the courage even to examine how long I was doomed to lead it. Whether it lasted for a year, or more, or less, I do not know. I only know that it was, and ceased to be; and that I have written, and there I leave it.

CHAPTER 15

I make another Beginning

Mr Dick and I soon became the best of friends, and very often went out together to fly the great kite. It was quite an affecting sight, I used to think, to see him with the kite when it was up a great height in the air. He never looked so serene as he did then. I used to fancy, as I saw him watch the kite high in the quiet air, that it lifted his mind out of its confusion. As he wound the string in until it fluttered to the ground, and lay there like a dead thing, he seemed to wake gradually out of a dream; and I have seen him take it up, and look about him in a lost way, as if they had both come down together, so that I pitied him with all my heart.

While I advanced in friendship and intimacy with Mr Dick, I did not go backward in the favour of his staunch friend, my aunt. She took so kindly to me, that, in the course of a few weeks, she shortened my adopted name of Trotwood into Trot; and even encouraged me to hope, that if I went on as I had begun, I might take equal rank in her affections with my sister Betsey Trotwood.

'Trot,' said my aunt one evening, when the backgammon-board was placed as usual for herself and Mr Dick, 'we must not forget your education.'

This was my only subject of anxiety, and I felt quite delighted by her referring to it.

'Should you like to go to school at Canterbury?' said my aunt.

I replied that I should like it very much, as it was so near her.

'Good,' said my aunt. 'Janet, hire the grey pony and chaise to-morrow morning at ten o'clock, and pack up Master Trotwood's clothes to-night.'

I was greatly elated by these orders; but my heart smote me for my selfishness, when I witnessed their effect on Mr Dick, who was low-spirited at the prospect of our separation. But, on hearing that I should sometimes come over on a Saturday, and that he could come and see me on a Wednesday, he revived. In the morning we parted in a most affectionate manner, and Mr Dick did not go into the house until my aunt had driven me out of sight of it.

My aunt drove the grey pony through Dover in a masterly manner; making a point of not letting him have his own way in any respect. When we came into the country road, she permitted him to relax a little, however; and looking at me by her side, asked whether I was happy?

'Very happy indeed, thank you, aunt,' I said.

She was much gratified. 'We are going to Mr Wickfield's.'

'Does *he* keep a school?' I asked.

'No, Trot,' said my aunt. 'He keeps an office.'

At length we stopped before a very old house bulging out over the road. It was quite spotless in its cleanliness. The old-fashioned brass knocker on the low arched door twinkled like a star; the two stone steps descending to the door were as white as if they had been covered with fair linen; and all the angles and corners, and quaint little panes of glass, were as pure as any snow that ever fell upon the hills.

When the pony-chaise stopped at the door, I saw a cadaverous face appear at a small window on the ground floor and quickly disappear. The low arched door then opened, and the face came out. It was quite as cadaverous as it had looked in the window. It belonged to a youth of fifteen, as I take it now, but looking much older. He was high-shouldered and bony; dressed in black; and had a long, lank, skeleton hand.

'Is Mr Wickfield at home, Uriah Heep?' said my aunt.

'Mr Wickfield's at home, ma'am,' said Uriah Heep, 'if you'll please to walk in.'

We went into a long low parlour. Opposite to the tall old chimney-piece were two portraits: one of a gentleman with grey hair and black eyebrows, the other of a lady with a very placid and sweet expression.

A gentleman entered, at sight of whom I turned to the first-mentioned portrait to make sure that it had not come out of its frame. But as the gentleman advanced into the light, I saw that he was some years older than when he had had his picture painted.

'Miss Betsey Trotwood,' said the gentleman, 'pray walk in.'

Miss Betsey thanked him, and we went into his room, which was furnished as an office. It looked into a garden, and had an iron safe let into the wall.

'Well, Miss Trotwood,' said Mr Wickfield, for I soon found that it was he, and that he was a lawyer, 'what wind blows you here? Not an ill wind, I hope?'

'No,' replied my aunt, 'I have not come for any law. This is my grand-nephew.'

'Wasn't aware you had one, Miss Trotwood,' said Mr Wickfield.

'I have adopted him,' said my aunt with a wave of her hand, importing that his knowledge and his ignorance were all one to her, 'and I have brought him here, to put him to a school where he may be well taught, and well treated.'

'Before I can advise you properly,' said Mr Wickfield, 'what's your motive in this?'

'Deuce take the man!' exclaimed my aunt. 'Always fishing for motives. Why, to make the child happy and useful.'

'It must be a mixed motive, I think,' said Mr Wickfield, shaking his head and smiling incredulously.

'A mixed fiddlestick!' returned my aunt. 'You don't suppose, I hope, that you are the only plain dealer in the world?'

'Ay, but I have only one motive in life, Miss Trotwood,' he rejoined, smiling. 'Other people have hundreds. I have only one. However, that's beside the question. Whatever the motive, you want the best school?'

My aunt nodded assent.

'At the best we have,' said Mr Wickfield, considering, 'your nephew couldn't board just now.'

'But he could board somewhere else, I suppose?' suggested my aunt.

Mr Wickfield thought I could. After a little discussion, he proposed to take my aunt to the school, that she might judge it for herself; also, to take her to two or three houses where he thought I could be boarded. We were all three going out together, when he stopped.

'Our little friend here might have some motive, perhaps, for objecting to the arrangements. I think we had better leave him behind?'

My aunt seemed disposed to contest the point; but to facilitate matters I said I would gladly remain behind, and returned into Mr Wickfield's office, where I sat down again.

It so happened that the chair was opposite a narrow passage, which ended in the little circular room where I had seen Uriah Heep's pale face looking out of window. Uriah was at work at a desk in this room, which had a brass frame on the top to hang paper upon. Though his face was towards me, I thought, for some time, the writing being between us, that he could not see me; but looking that way more attentively, I observed that, every now and then, his sleepless eyes would come below the writing, like two red suns, and stealthily stare at me for a whole minute at a time, during which his pen went, or pretended to go, as cleverly as ever. Whenever I looked towards those two red suns, I was sure to find them, either just rising or just setting.

At length, my aunt and Mr Wickfield came back. They were not so successful as I could have wished; for though the advantages of the school were undeniable, my aunt had not approved of any of the boarding-houses proposed for me.

'I'll tell you what you can do, Miss Trotwood,' said Mr Wickfield. 'Leave your nephew here, for the present. He's a quiet fellow. He won't disturb me at all. It's a capital house for study.'

My aunt evidently liked the offer. So did I.

'Then come and see my little housekeeper,' said Mr Wickfield.

We accordingly went up a wonderful old staircase, and into a shady old drawing-room, which had old oak seats and great beams in the ceiling. It was a prettily furnished room with a piano, all old nooks and corners.

Mr Wickfield tapped at a door and a girl of about my own age came out. On her face, I saw immediately the placid and sweet expression of the lady whose picture had looked at me downstairs. Although her face was quite bright and happy, there was a tranquillity about it, and about her, that I never have forgotten; that I never shall forget.

This was his little housekeeper, his daughter Agnes, Mr Wickfield said. When I heard how he said it, and saw how he held her hand, I guessed what the one motive of his life was.

She listened to her father as he told her about me, and proposed to my aunt that we should go up-stairs and see my room. A glorious old room it was, with more oak beams, and diamond panes.

My aunt was as happy as I was, in the arrangement made for me. So we were left to take leave of one another.

She told me that everything would be arranged for me by Mr Wickfield, and that I should want for nothing.

'Trot,' said my aunt in conclusion, 'never be mean in anything; never be false; never be cruel. Avoid those three vices, and I can always be hopeful of you.'

I promised, as well as I could, that I would not abuse her kindness or forget her admonition.

'The pony's at the door,' said my aunt, 'and I am off!'

With these words she embraced me hastily, and went out of the room. I was startled by so abrupt a departure, and feared I had displeased her; but when I looked into the street, and saw how dejectedly she got into the chaise, I understood her better.

By five o'clock, which was Mr Wickfield's dinner-hour, I had mustered up my spirits again. Agnes sat opposite to him at table. I doubted whether he could have dined without her. After dinner, we came upstairs into the drawing-room, in one snug corner of which, Agnes set glasses for her father, and a decanter of port wine.

There he sat, taking his wine, a good deal of it, while Agnes played on the piano, and talked to him and me. Sometimes his eyes rested on her, and he fell silent. She always roused him with a question or caress. Then he came out of his meditation, and drank more wine.

In the course of the evening I had rambled a little way along the street, that I might have another peep at the old houses, and the grey Cathedral. As I came back, I saw Uriah Heep shutting up the office; and, feeling friendly towards everybody, spoke to him, and at parting, gave him my hand. But oh, what a clammy hand his was! as ghostly to the touch as to the sight! I rubbed mine afterwards, to warm it, *and to rub his off*.

It was such an uncomfortable hand, that, when I went to my room, it was still cold and wet upon my memory. Leaning out of window, and seeing one of the faces on the beam-ends looking at me sideways, I fancied it was Uriah Heep got up there somehow, and shut him out in a hurry.

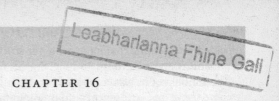

CHAPTER 16

I am a New Boy in more Senses than One

Next morning, after breakfast, I entered on school life again. I went, accompanied by Mr Wickfield, to the scene of my future studies and was introduced to my new master, Doctor Strong.

Doctor Strong looked almost as rusty, to my thinking, as the tall iron rails and gates outside the house. He was in his library with his clothes not particularly well brushed, and his shoes yawning like two caverns on the hearth-rug. Turning upon me a lustreless eye, that reminded me of a long-forgotten blind horse who used to crop the grass in Blunderstone churchyard, he said he was glad to see me.

But, sitting not far off was a very pretty young lady whom he called Annie, and who was his daughter, I supposed – who got down to put Doctor Strong's shoes on, which she did with great cheerfulness. When she had finished, I was much surprised to hear Mr Wickfield, address her as 'Mrs Strong;' and I was wondering could she be Doctor Strong's son's wife, when Doctor Strong himself unconsciously enlightened me.

'By-the-by, Wickfield,' he said, 'you have not found any suitable provision for my wife's cousin yet?'

'No,' said Mr Wickfield. 'Not yet.'

'I could wish it done as soon as it *can* be done, Wickfield,' said Doctor Strong, 'for Jack Maldon is needy, and idle; and of those two bad things, worse things sometimes come.'

'No,' said Mr Wickfield, 'I have not been able to dispose of Mr Jack Maldon yet. I believe, I penetrate your motive, and it makes the thing more difficult.'

'My motive,' returned Doctor Strong, 'is to make some suitable provision for a cousin, and an old playfellow, of Annie's.'

'Yes, I know,' said Mr Wickfield, 'at home or abroad.'

'Ay!' replied the Doctor.

'Your own expression, you know,' said Mr Wickfield. 'Or abroad.'

Doctor Strong regarded him with a puzzled look, which immediately subsided into a smile that gave me great encouragement; for it was full of amiability and sweetness.

The school-room was a pretty large hall, on the quietest side of the house. About five-and-twenty boys were studiously engaged at their books when we went in, but they rose to give the Doctor good morning, and remained standing when they saw Mr Wickfield and me.

'A new boy, young gentlemen,' said the Doctor; 'Trotwood Copperfield.'

One Adams, who was the head-boy, then welcomed me. He was very affable and good-humoured; and he showed me my place, and presented me to the masters, in a gentlemanly way that would have put me at my ease, if anything could.

It seemed to me so long, however, since I had been among such boys that I felt as strange as ever I have done in all my life. I was conscious of having acquired experiences foreign to my age, appearance, and condition as one of them, that I half believed it was an imposture to come there as an ordinary little schoolboy. I had become, in the Murdstone and Grinby time, so unused to games of boys, that I knew I was awkward and inexperienced in the commonest things belonging to them.

My mind ran upon what they would think, if they knew of my acquaintance with the King's Bench Prison? Was there anything about me which would reveal my proceedings in connexion with the Micawber family – all those pawnings, and sellings, and suppers – in spite of myself? Suppose some of the boys had seen me coming through Canterbury, wayworn and ragged, and should find me out? What would they say, who made so light of money, if they could know how I had scraped my halfpence together, for the purchase of my daily saveloy and beer, or my slices of pudding? All this ran in my head so much, on that first day at Doctor Strong's, that I shrunk within myself whensoever I was approached by one of my new schoolfellows; and hurried off, the minute school was over.

But there was such an influence in Mr Wickfield's old house, that when I knocked at it, with my new school-books under my arm, I began to feel my uneasiness softening away. I sat there, sturdily conning my books, until dinner-time and went down, hopeful of becoming a passable sort of boy yet.

Agnes was in the drawing-room. She asked me how I liked the school. I told her I should like it very much, I hoped; but I was a little strange to it at first.

'*You* have never been to school,' I said, 'have you?'

'Oh yes! Every day.'

'Ah, but you mean here, at your own home?'

'Papa couldn't spare me to go anywhere else,' she answered, smiling and shaking her head. 'His housekeeper must be in his house, you know.'

'He is very fond of you, I am sure,' I said.

'Mama has been dead ever since I was born,' she said, in her quiet way. 'I only know her picture, down-stairs. I saw you looking at it yesterday. Did you think whose it was?'

I told her yes, because it was so like herself.

'Papa says so, too,' said Agnes, pleased. 'Hark! That's papa now!'

He greeted me cordially; and told me I should certainly be happy under Doctor Strong, who was one of the gentlest of men.

'There may be some, perhaps, who abuse his kindness,' said Mr Wickfield. 'Never be one of those, Trotwood. He is the least suspicious of mankind and it deserves consideration in all dealings with the Doctor.'

He spoke, I thought, as if he were weary, or dissatisfied with something; but I did not pursue the question in my mind, for dinner was just then announced, and we went down and took the same seats as before.

We had scarcely done so, when Uriah Heep put in his red head and his lank hand at the door, and said:

'Here's Mr Maldon begs the favour of a word, sir.'

'I am but this moment quit of Mr Maldon,' said his master.

'I beg your pardon. It's only to say, on reflection,' observed a voice behind Uriah, 'that as it seems I have no choice in the matter, the sooner I go abroad the better. My cousin Annie did say that she liked to have her friends within reach rather than to have them banished, and Doctor Strong was of the same mind, I believed. But as it appears from the course you take with me that he has changed his mind, the sooner I am off, the better.'

'Have you dined?' asked Mr Wickfield, with a motion of his hand towards the table.

'Thank'ee. I am going to dine,' said Mr Maldon, 'with my cousin Annie. Good-bye!'

Mr Wickfield, without rising, looked after him thoughtfully as he went out. He was rather a shallow sort of young gentleman, I thought, with a handsome face and confident bold air.

When we had dined, we went up-stairs again, where everything went on exactly as on the previous day. Agnes set the glasses and decanters in the same corner, and Mr Wickfield sat down to drink, and Agnes played the piano and some games at dominoes with me.

The time having come for her withdrawal for the night, and she having left us, Mr Wickfield said: 'Should you like to stay with us, Trotwood, or to go elsewhere?'

'To stay,' I answered, quickly. 'If I may.'

'Why, it's but a dull life that we lead here, boy, I am afraid,' he said.

'Not more dull for me than Agnes, sir. Not dull at all!'

'Than Agnes,' he repeated, walking slowly to the great chimney-piece, and leaning against it. 'Than Agnes!'

He was musing, not speaking to me; so I remained quiet.

'A dull old house,' he said, 'and a monotonous life; but I must have her near me. If it is miserable to bear when she is here,' he said, 'what would it be, and she away? No, no, no. I cannot try that.'

At length he aroused himself, and looked about the room until his eyes encountered mine.

'Stay with us, Trotwood, eh?' he said in his usual manner. 'I am glad of it. You are company to us both. It is wholesome to have you here.'

'I am sure it is for me, sir,' I said. 'I am so glad to be here.'

'That's a fine fellow!' said Mr Wickfield. 'As long as you are glad to be here, you shall stay.' He clapped me on the back; and told me that when I wished to read for my own pleasure, I was free to come down to his room, and to sit with him. I thanked him for his consideration; and went down with a book in my hand to avail myself of his permission.

But seeing a light in the little round office, and immediately feeling myself attracted towards Uriah Heep, who had a sort of fascination for me, I went in there instead. I found Uriah reading a great fat book, with such demonstrative attention that his lank forefinger followed every line as he read, and made clammy tracks along the page (or so I fully believed) like a snail.

'You are working late,' says I.

'Yes, Master Copperfield,' says Uriah. 'I am improving my legal knowledge, going through Tidd's Practice. Oh, what a writer Mr Tidd is, Master Copperfield!'

'I suppose you are quite a great lawyer?' I said, after looking at him for some time.

'Me, Master Copperfield?' said Uriah. 'Oh, no! I'm a very umble person. My mother is likewise a very umble person. We live in a umble abode, Master Copperfield. My father's former calling was umble. He was a sexton.'

'What is he now?' I asked.

'He is a partaker of glory at present, Master Copperfield,' said Uriah

Heep. 'But we have much to be thankful for. How much have I to be thankful for in living with Mr Wickfield!'

I asked Uriah if he had been with Mr Wickfield long.

'Going on four year, Master Copperfield,' said Uriah; shutting up his book. 'Since a year after my father's death. How much have I to be thankful for, in Mr Wickfield's kind intention to give me my articles, which would otherwise not lay within the umble means of mother and self!'

'Perhaps you'll be a partner in Mr Wickfield's business, one of these days,' I said, to make myself agreeable; 'and it will be Wickfield and Heep.'

'Oh no, Master Copperfield,' returned Uriah, shaking his head, 'I am much too umble for that!'

He certainly did look uncommonly like the carved face on the beam outside my window, as he sat, in his humility, eyeing me sideways, with his mouth widened, and the creases in his cheeks.

'Mr Wickfield is a most excellent man, Master Copperfield,' said Uriah.

I replied that I was certain he was; but that I had not known him long myself, though he was a friend of my aunt's.

'Oh, indeed, Master Copperfield,' said Uriah. 'Your aunt is a sweet lady, Master Copperfield!'

He had a way of writhing when he wanted to express enthusiasm, which was very ugly; and which diverted my attention from the compliment he had paid my relation, to the snaky twistings of his throat and body.

'A sweet lady, Master Copperfield!' said Uriah Heep. 'She has a great admiration for Miss Agnes, I believe. I hope you have, too, Master Copperfield. But I am sure you must have.'

'Everybody must have,' I returned.

'Oh, thank you, Master Copperfield,' said Uriah Heep, 'for that remark! It is so true! Umble as I am, I know it is *so* true!'

He writhed himself quite off his stool in the excitement of his feelings, and, being off, began to make arrangements for going home.

'Mother will be expecting me,' he said, 'and getting uneasy; for though we are very umble, Master Copperfield, we are much attached to one another. If you would come and see us, any afternoon, and take a cup of tea at our lowly dwelling, mother would be as proud of your company as I should be.'

I said I should be glad to come.

'Thank you, Master Copperfield,' returned Uriah, putting his book away upon the shelf. – 'I suppose you stop here, some time, Master Copperfield?'

I said I was going to be brought up there, I believed, as long as I remained at school.

'Oh, indeed!' exclaimed Uriah. 'I should think *you* would come into the business at last, Master Copperfield!'

I protested that no such scheme was entertained in my behalf by anybody; but Uriah insisted on blandly replying to all my assurances, 'Oh, yes, Master Copperfield, I should think you would, indeed!' After shaking hands with me – his hand felt like a fish – he opened the door into the street and crept out.

I got a little the better of my uneasiness when I went to school next day, and so shook it off by degrees, that in less than a fortnight I was quite happy among my new companions. And, in a very little while, the Murdstone and Grinby life became so strange to me that I hardly believed in it, while my present life grew so familiar, that I seemed to have been leading it a long time.

Doctor Strong's was an excellent school; as different from Mr Creakle's as good is from evil. Some of the higher scholars boarded in the Doctor's house, and through them I learned some particulars of the Doctor's history. As, how he had not yet been married twelve months to the beautiful young lady I had seen in the study, whom he had married for love; for she had not a sixpence, and had a world of poor relations ready to swarm the Doctor out of house and home. Also, how the Doctor's cogitating manner was attributable to his being always engaged in looking out for Greek roots; which, in my ignorance, I supposed to be a botanical furor on the Doctor's part, especially as he always looked at the ground when he walked about, until I understood that they were roots of words, with a view to a new Dictionary which he had in contemplation. Adams, our head-boy, had made a calculation of the time this Dictionary would take in completing at the Doctor's rate of going. He considered that it might be done in one thousand six hundred and forty-nine years, counting from the Doctor's last birthday.

It was very pleasant to see the Doctor with his pretty young wife. He had a fatherly way of showing his fondness for her, which seemed in itself to express a good man. I often saw them walking in the garden. She appeared to take great care of the Doctor, and to like him very much.

I saw a good deal of Mrs Strong, both because she had taken a liking for me on the morning of my introduction to the Doctor; and because she was very fond of Agnes, and was often backwards and forwards at our house. There was a curious constraint between her and Mr Wickfield,

I thought. When she came there of an evening, she always shrunk from accepting his escort home, and ran away with me instead. And sometimes, as we were running gaily across the Cathedral yard together, we would meet Mr Jack Maldon, who was always surprised to see us.

Mrs Strong's mama was a lady I took great delight in. Her name was Mrs Markleham; but our boys used to call her the Old Soldier, on account of the skill with which she marshalled great forces of relations against the Doctor. She was a little, sharp-eyed woman, who used to wear one unchangeable cap, ornamented with two artificial butterflies.

I observed the Old Soldier to pretty good advantage, on a night which is made memorable to me by something else I shall relate. It was the night of a little party at the Doctor's, given on the occasion of Mr Jack Maldon's departure for India, whither he was going as a cadet: Mr Wickfield having at length arranged the business. It happened to be the Doctor's birthday, too. We had made presents to him in the morning and cheered him until we were hoarse. And now, in the evening, Mr Wickfield, Agnes, and I, went to have tea with him in his private capacity.

Mr Jack Maldon was there, before us. Mrs Strong, dressed in white, with cherry-coloured ribbons, was playing the piano, and he was leaning over her to turn the leaves. The clear red and white of her complexion was not so blooming as usual, I thought, but she looked wonderfully pretty.

'I have forgotten, Doctor,' said Mrs Strong's mama, when we were seated, 'to pay you the compliments of the day. Many, many happy returns. Not only for your own sake, but for Annie's and John Maldon's, and many other people's. You are a blessing to us. You really are a Boon, you know.'

'Nonsense, nonsense,' said the Doctor.

'No, no,' retorted the Old Soldier. 'I cannot consent to be put down. What I am saying, is what I said when you first overpowered me with surprise by proposing for Annie. Because, you having known her from a baby, I hadn't thought of you in such a light at all.'

'Aye, aye,' returned the Doctor, good-humouredly. 'Never mind.'

'But I *do* mind,' said the Old Soldier, laying her fan upon his lips. 'I recall these things that I may be contradicted if I am wrong. Well! Then I spoke to Annie, and said, "My dear, here's Doctor Strong has made you the subject of a handsome declaration and an offer." I said, "Now, Annie, tell me the truth this moment; is your heart free?" "Mama," she said crying, "I am extremely young" – which was perfectly true – "and I hardly know if I have a heart at all." "Then, my dear," I said, "you may rely upon it, it's free. At all events, my love," said I, "Doctor Strong is in an agitated state of mind, and must be answered." "Mama," said Annie, "would he be unhappy without me? If he would, I honour and respect him so much, that I think I will have him." So it was settled. And then, and not till then, I said to Annie, "Annie, Doctor Strong will not only be your husband, but he will represent your late father: he will represent the head of our family, he will represent the wisdom and station, and I may say the means, of our family; and will be, in short, a Boon to it.'"

The daughter had sat quite silent and still during this speech, with her eyes fixed on the ground; her cousin standing near her, and looking on the ground too. She now said very softly, in a trembling voice:

'Mama, I hope you have finished?'

Some more company coming in, the talk became general; and it naturally turned on Mr Jack Maldon, and his voyage, and the country he was going to, and his various plans and prospects. He was to leave that night, in a post-chaise, for Gravesend; where the ship, in which he was to make the voyage, lay; and was to be gone I don't know how many years. I recollect it was settled by general consent that India was quite a misrepresented country, and had nothing objectionable in it, but a tiger or two, and a little heat in the warm part of the day. For my own part, I looked on Mr Jack Maldon as a modern Sindbad.

Mrs Strong was a very pretty singer but she was out of voice that evening. She tried a duet, once, with her cousin Maldon, but could not so much as begin. The good Doctor said she was nervous, and, to relieve her, proposed a round game at cards. I remarked that the Old Soldier took him into custody directly, for her partner; and instructed him, as the first preliminary, to give her all the silver he had in his pocket. We had a merry game. Mrs Strong had declined to play, on the ground of not feeling very well; and her cousin Maldon had excused himself because he had some packing to do. When he had done it, however, he returned, and they sat together on the sofa.

At supper, we were hardly so gay. Every one appeared to feel that a parting of that sort was an awkward thing, and that the nearer it approached, the more awkward it was. Mr Jack Maldon tried to be very talkative, but was not at his ease, and made matters worse.

The Doctor, however, was well pleased, and had no suspicion but that we were all at the utmost height of enjoyment.

'Annie, my dear,' said he, looking at his watch, and filling his glass, 'it is past your cousin Jack's time, and we must not detain him, since time and tide – both concerned in this case – wait for no man. Mr Jack Maldon, you have a long voyage, and a strange country, before you. The winds you are going to tempt, have wafted thousands to fortune, and brought thousands happily back. Some of us can hardly expect to greet you on your return. The next best thing is to hope to do it, and that's my case. Farewell, Mr Jack,' said the Doctor, standing up; on which we all stood up. 'A prosperous voyage out, a thriving career abroad, and a happy return home!'

We all drank the toast, and all shook hands with Mr Jack Maldon; after which he hastily took leave. He got into the chaise with a tremendous broadside of cheers discharged by our boys, who had assembled on the lawn for the purpose. Running among them I was very near the chaise when it rolled away; and I had a lively impression made upon me of having seen Mr Jack Maldon rattle past with an agitated face, and something cherry-coloured in his hand.

I went back into the house, where I found the guests all standing in a group about the Doctor, discussing how Mr Jack Maldon had gone away, and how he had borne it, and all the rest of it. In the midst of these remarks, Mrs Markleham cried: 'Where's Annie?'

We found her lying on the hall floor in a swoon. When she opened her eyes and saw that we were all standing about her, she arose, turning her head to lay it on the Doctor's shoulder – or to hide it, I don't know which. We went into the drawing-room, and they brought her in, looking very white and weak, I thought, and sat her on a sofa.

'Annie, my dear,' said her mother. 'You have lost a bow. Will anybody be so good as find a cherry-coloured ribbon?'

It was the one she had worn at her bosom. We all looked for it but nobody could find it.

'Do you recollect where you had it last, Annie?' said her mother.

I wondered how I could have thought she looked white, or anything but burning red, when she answered that she had had it safe a little while ago, she thought, but it was not worth looking for.

We walked very slowly home, Mr Wickfield, Agnes, and I; Agnes and I admiring the moonlight, and Mr Wickfield scarcely raising his eyes from the ground. When we reached our own door, Agnes discovered that she had left her little reticule behind. Delighted to be of any service to her, I ran back to fetch it.

I went into the supper-room where it had been left, which was dark. But a door of communication between that and the Doctor's study being open, I passed on there to get a candle.

The Doctor was sitting in his easy-chair by the fireside, and his young wife was on a stool at his feet. The Doctor, with a complacent smile, was reading and she was looking up at him. But, with such a face as I never saw. It was so beautiful in its form, so ashy pale, so fixed in its abstraction, so full of a wild, sleep-walking, dreamy horror of I don't know what. Distinctly as I recollect her look, I cannot say of what it was expressive. I cannot even say of what it is expressive to me now, rising again before my older judgment. Penitence, humiliation, shame, pride, love, and trustfulness, I see them all; and in them all, I see that horror of I don't know what.

My entrance roused her. It disturbed the Doctor too, for when I went back to replace the candle he was patting her head in his fatherly way, saying he would have her go to bed.

But she asked him, in a rapid, urgent manner, to let her stay. To let her feel assured that she was in his confidence that night. And, as she turned again towards him, I saw her cross her hands upon his knee, and look up at him with the same face as he resumed his reading.

It made a great impression on me, and I remembered it a long time afterwards, as I shall have occasion to narrate when the time comes.

CHAPTER 17

Somebody turns up

It has not occurred to me to mention Peggotty since I ran away; but, of course, I wrote her a letter almost as soon as I was housed at Dover, and another when my aunt took me formally under her protection. On my being settled at Doctor Strong's I wrote to her again, detailing my happy condition and sending a gold half-guinea to discharge the sum I had borrowed of her.

To these communications Peggotty replied promptly. Her utmost powers of expression were exhausted in the attempt to write what she felt on the subject of my journey. Four sides of incoherent beginnings of sentences that had no end, except blots, were inadequate to afford her any relief. But the blots showed me that Peggotty had been crying all over the paper, and what could I have desired more?

She gave me one piece of intelligence which affected me very much, namely that Mr and Mrs Murdstone were gone away and the house was shut up, to be let or sold. It pained me to think of the dear old place as altogether abandoned. It seemed as if the house were dead too, now, and all connected with my father and mother were faded away.

Mr Barkis was an excellent husband, she said, and he sent his duty, and my little bedroom was always ready for me. Mr Peggotty was well, and Ham was well, and Mrs Gummidge was but poorly, and little Em'ly wouldn't send her love, but said that Peggotty might send it, if she liked.

All this intelligence I dutifully imparted to my aunt, only reserving to myself the mention of little Em'ly. I saw Miss Betsey on a Saturday, every third or fourth week, when I went over to Dover for a treat: and I saw Mr Dick every alternate Wednesday, when he arrived by stage-coach, to stay until next morning.

'Trotwood,' said Mr Dick, with an air of mystery one Wednesday; 'who's the man that hides near our house and frightens her?'

'Frightens my aunt, sir?'

Mr Dick nodded. 'The first time he came was very soon after the mistake was made of putting some of the trouble out of King Charles's head into my head. I was walking out with Miss Trotwood after tea, just at dark, and there he was, close to our house. He came up behind her, and whispered. Then she turned round and fainted, and he walked away; but that he should have been hiding ever since is the most extraordinary thing!'

'*Has* he been hiding ever since?' I asked.

'To be sure he has,' retorted Mr Dick, nodding his head gravely. 'Never came out, till last night! He came up behind her again, and I knew him again.'

'And did he frighten my aunt again?'

'All of a shiver,' said Mr Dick. 'Held by the palings. Cried. But, Trotwood,' getting me close to him that he might whisper very softly; 'why did she give him money, boy, in the moonlight?'

'He was a beggar, perhaps.'

Mr Dick shook his head. 'No beggar, sir!' He went on to say, that from his window he had afterwards seen my aunt give this person money outside the garden rails who then slunk away while my aunt came hurriedly back into the house, and had, even that morning, been quite different from her usual self.

I had not the least belief, in the outset of this story, that the unknown was anything but a delusion of Mr Dick's, but after some reflection I began to entertain the question whether an attempt might have been twice made to take poor Mr Dick himself from under my aunt's protection, and whether my aunt might have been induced to pay a price for his peace and quiet. As I was already much attached to Mr Dick, my fears favoured this supposition; and for a long time his Wednesday hardly ever came round, without my entertaining a misgiving that he would not be on the coach-box as usual. There he always appeared, however; and he never had anything more to tell of the man who could frighten my aunt.

These Wednesdays were the happiest days of Mr Dick's life. He was an universal favourite, and his ingenuity in little things was transcendent. He could turn crampbones into chessmen; fashion Roman chariots from old court cards; make spoked wheels out of cotton reels, and birdcages of old wire. But Mr Dick's renown was not long confined to us. Doctor Strong himself made some inquiries of me about him, and requested to be presented to him. This ceremony I performed; and it soon passed into a custom for Mr Dick to come into the school and wait. He would sit attentively listening, with a profound veneration for the learning he had never been able to acquire.

This veneration Mr Dick extended to the Doctor, whom he thought the most subtle and accomplished philosopher of any age. How it ever came about, that the Doctor began to read out scraps of the famous Dictionary in these walks, I never knew; perhaps he felt it all the same, at first, as reading to himself. However, it passed into a custom too; and Mr Dick, listening with a face shining with pride and pleasure, in his heart of hearts, believed the Dictionary to be the most delightful book in the world.

As I think of them going up and down before those school-room windows, I think of it as one of the pleasantest things, in a quiet way, that I have ever seen. I feel as if they might go walking to and fro for ever, and the world might somehow be the better for it.

Agnes was one of Mr Dick's friends, very soon; and in often coming to the house, he made acquaintance with Uriah. The friendship between himself and me was maintained on this odd footing: that, while Mr Dick came to look after me as my guardian, he always consulted me in any little matter of doubt; not only having a high respect for my native sagacity, but considering that I inherited a good deal from my aunt.

One Thursday morning, when I was about to walk with Mr Dick from the hotel to the coach-office, I met Uriah in the street, who reminded me of the promise I had made to take tea with himself and his mother: adding, with a writhe, 'But I didn't expect you to keep it, Master Copperfield, we're so very umble.'

I really had not yet been able to make up my mind whether I liked Uriah or detested him. But I felt it quite an affront to be supposed proud, and said I only wanted to be asked.

'Oh, if that's all, Master Copperfield,' said Uriah, 'will you come this evening?'

So, at six o'clock that evening, I announced myself as ready, to Uriah.

'Mother will be proud, indeed,' he said, as we walked away together. 'Or she would be proud, if it wasn't sinful.'

'Have you been studying much law lately?' I asked, to change the subject.

'Oh, Master Copperfield,' he said, with an air of self-denial, 'my reading is hardly to be called study. I have passed an hour or two in the evening, sometimes, with Mr Tidd.'

'Rather hard, I suppose?' said I.

'He is hard to *me*,' returned Uriah. 'There are expressions – Latin words and terms – that are trying to a reader of my umble attainments.'

'Would you like to be taught Latin?' I said, briskly. 'I will teach it you with pleasure, as I learn it.'

'Oh, thank you, Master Copperfield,' he answered, shaking his head, 'I am greatly obliged, but I am far too umble. There are people enough to tread upon me in my lowly state, without my doing outrage to their feelings by possessing learning. A person like myself had better not aspire. If he is to get on in life, he must get on umbly.'

I never saw his mouth so wide, or the creases in his cheeks so deep, as when he delivered himself of these sentiments: shaking his head all the time, and writhing modestly.

We entered a low, old-fashioned room from the street, and found there Mrs Heep, who was the dead image of Uriah, only short. She received me with the utmost humility. The tea-things were set upon the table, and the kettle was boiling on the hob. There was a chest of drawers with an escritoire top; there was a company of Uriah's books commanded by Mr Tidd; and there were the usual articles of furniture. I don't remember that any individual object had a bare, pinched, spare look; but I do remember that the whole place had.

It was perhaps a part of Mrs Heep's humility that, notwithstanding the lapse of time that had occurred since Mr Heep's decease, she still wore weeds. I think there was some compromise in the cap; but otherwise she was as weedy as in the early days of her mourning.

'This is a day to be remembered, my Uriah, I am sure,' said Mrs Heep, making the tea, 'when Master Copperfield pays us a visit. If I could have wished father to remain among us for any reason, it would have been that he might have known his company this afternoon.'

I felt embarrassed by these compliments; but I was sensible, too, of being entertained as an honoured guest, and I thought Mrs Heep an agreeable woman.

I found that Mrs Heep gradually got nearer to me, and that Uriah got opposite to me, and presently they began to talk about aunts, and then I told them about mine; and about fathers and mothers, and then I told them about mine; and then Mrs Heep began to talk about fathers-in-law, and then I began to tell her about mine; but stopped, because my aunt had advised me to observe a silence on that subject. A tender young cork, however, would have had no more chance against a pair of corkscrews, than I had against Uriah and Mrs Heep. They wormed things out of me that I had no desire to tell, with a certainty I blush to think of.

The skill with which the one followed up whatever the other said, was a touch of art which I was still less proof against. When there was nothing more to be got out of me about myself (for on the Murdstone and Grinby life, and on my journey, I was dumb), they began about Mr Wickfield and Agnes. Uriah threw the ball to Mrs Heep, Mrs Heep caught it and threw it back to Uriah. The ball itself was always changing too. Now it was Mr Wickfield, now Agnes, now the excellence of Mr Wickfield, now my admiration of Agnes; now the extent of Mr Wickfield's business and resources, now the wine that Mr Wickfield took, the reason why he took it, and the pity that it was he took so much. I found myself perpetually letting out something or other that I had no business to let out, and seeing the effect of it in the twinkling of Uriah's dinted nostrils.

I had begun to be a little uncomfortable, when a figure coming down the street passed the door – it stood open to air the room – came back and walked in, exclaiming loudly, 'Copperfield! Is it possible?'

It was Mr Micawber!

'My dear Copperfield,' said Mr Micawber, putting out his hand, 'this is indeed a meeting which is calculated to impress the mind with a sense of the instability and uncertainty of all human – in short, it is a most extraordinary meeting. Copperfield, dear fellow, how do you do?'

I was glad to see him too, and shook hands heartily, inquiring how Mrs Micawber was.

'She is tolerably convalescent. The twins no longer derive their sustenance from Nature's founts – in short,' said Mr Micawber, in one of his bursts of confidence 'they are weaned – and Mrs Micawber is, at present, my travelling companion. She will be rejoiced, Copperfield, to renew her acquaintance with one who has proved himself in all respects a worthy minister at the sacred altar of friendship.'

I said I should be delighted to see her.

Mr Micawber smiled and looked about him.

'I have discovered my friend Copperfield,' said Mr Micawber genteelly, 'partaking of a social meal in company with a widow lady, and one who is apparently her offspring – in short, her son. I shall esteem it an honour to be presented.'

I could do no less, under these circumstances, than make Mr Micawber known to Uriah Heep and his mother; which I accordingly did. As they abased themselves before him, Mr Micawber took a seat, and waved his hand in his most courtly manner.

'Any friend of my friend Copperfield's,' said Mr Micawber, 'has a personal claim upon myself.'

'We are too umble, sir,' said Mrs Heep, 'my son and me, to be the friends of Master Copperfield. We are thankful to him for his company; also to you, sir, for your notice.'

'Ma'am,' returned Mr Micawber, with a bow, 'you are very obliging: and what are you doing, Copperfield? Still in the wine trade?'

I replied that I was a pupil at Doctor Strong's.

'A pupil?' said Mr Micawber, raising his eyebrows. 'I am extremely happy to hear it. Although a mind like my friend Copperfield's' – to Uriah and Mrs Heep – 'does not require that cultivation which, without his knowledge of men and things, it would require, still it is a rich soil teeming with latent vegetation – in short, it is an intellect capable of getting up the classics to any extent.'

'Shall we go and see Mrs Micawber,' I said, to get Mr Micawber away.

It was a little inn where Mr Micawber put up, and he occupied a little room strongly flavoured with tobacco-smoke near the bar, on account of the smell of spirits and jingling of glasses. Here, recumbent on a small sofa, underneath a picture of a race-horse, with her head close to the fire, and her feet pushing the mustard off the dumb-waiter, was Mrs Micawber.

Mrs Micawber was amazed, but very glad to see me. I was very glad to see her too, and, after an affectionate greeting on both sides, sat down on the small sofa near her.

'I thought you were at Plymouth, ma'am,' I said to Mrs Micawber, as he went out to look at the paper.

'My dear Master Copperfield,' she replied, 'we went to Plymouth to be on the spot. But the local influence of my family was quite unavailing to obtain any employment in that department, for a man of Mr Micawber's abilities. They would rather *not* have a man of Mr Micawber's abilities. He would only show the deficiency of the others. Apart from which, when that branch of my family became aware that Mr Micawber was accompanied by myself, and by little Wilkins and his sister, and by the twins, they did not receive him with that ardour which he might have expected. In fact,' said Mrs Micawber, lowering her voice, – 'our reception was cool.'

'Dear me!' I said.

'Under such circumstances, what could a man of Mr Micawber's spirit do but borrow the money to return to London? Since then, I have consulted other branches of my family on the course which it is most expedient for Mr Micawber to take – for I maintain that he must take some course. It is clear that a family of six, not including a domestic, cannot live upon air.'

'Certainly, ma'am,' said I.

'The opinion of those other branches of my family,' pursued Mrs

Micawber, 'is, that Mr Micawber should immediately turn his attention to the Medway Coal Trade. We came and saw the Medway. My
opinion of the coal trade on that river is that it may require talent, but
that it certainly requires capital. Talent, Mr Micawber has; capital, Mr
Micawber has not. Being so near here, Mr Micawber was of opinion
that it would be rash not to come on, and see the Cathedral. Firstly, on
account of its being so well worth seeing, and secondly, on account of
the great probability of something turning up in a cathedral town. We
have been here three days. Nothing has, as yet, turned up; and it may
not surprise you to know that we are at present waiting for a remittance
from London to discharge our pecuniary obligations at this hotel. Until
the arrival of that remittance,' said Mrs Micawber with much feeling, 'I
am cut off from my home ((I allude to lodgings in Pentonville), from my
boy and girl, and from my twins.'

I felt the utmost sympathy for Mr and Mrs Micawber and said as
much to Mr Micawber, who now returned: adding that I only wished I
had money enough to lend them the amount they needed. When I took
my leave of them, they both pressed me to come and dine before they
went away. Accordingly I was called out of school next forenoon, and
found Mr Micawber in the parlour; who had called to say that the dinner would take place as proposed. When I asked him if the remittance
had come, he pressed my hand and departed.

As I was looking out of window that same evening, it surprised me,
and made me rather uneasy, to see Mr Micawber and Uriah Heep walk
past, arm in arm. But I was still more surprised, when I went to the little
hotel next day at the appointed dinner-hour, to find that he had gone
home with Uriah, and had drunk brandy-and-water at Mrs Heep's.

'And I'll tell you what, my dear Copperfield,' said Mr Micawber, 'your
friend Heep is a young fellow who might be attorney-general. If I had
known that young man, at the period when my difficulties came to a
crisis, all I can say is, that I believe my creditors would have been a great
deal better managed than they were.'

I hardly understood how this could have been, seeing that Mr
Micawber had paid them nothing at all as it was; but I did not like to
ask. Neither did I like to say, that I hoped he had not been too com-
municative.

We had a beautiful little dinner. Mr Micawber was uncommonly
convivial. I never saw him such good company. He made his face shine
with the punch, so that it looked as if it had been varnished all over.
He got cheerfully sentimental about the town, and proposed success to
it; observing that he never should forget the agreeable hours they had

passed in Canterbury. He proposed me afterwards. Then I proposed Mrs Micawber. On which Mr Micawber delivered an eulogium on Mrs Micawber's character, and said she had ever been his guide, philosopher, and friend, and that he would recommend me, when I came to a marrying-time of life, to marry such another woman, if such another woman could be found. We sang 'Auld Lang Syne', joining hands around the table, and were really affected.

In a word, I never saw anybody so thoroughly jovial as Mr Micawber, down to the very last moment of the evening, when I took a hearty farewell of himself and his amiable wife. Consequently, I was not prepared, at seven o'clock next morning, to receive the following communication, dated a quarter of an hour after I had left him: –

MY DEAR YOUNG FRIEND,

'The die is cast – all is over. Hiding the ravages of care with a sickly mask of mirth, I have not informed you, this evening, that there is no hope of the remittance! Under these circumstances, I have discharged the pecuniary liability at this establishment, by giving a note made payable fourteen days after date. When it becomes due, it will not be taken up. The result is destruction. The bolt is impending, and the tree must fall.

'Let the wretched man who now addresses you be a beacon to you through life. He writes with that intention, and in that hope. If he could think himself of so much use, one gleam of day might, by possibility, penetrate into the cheerless dungeon of his remaining existence – though his longevity is, at present (to say the least of it), extremely problematical.

'This is the last communication, my dear Copperfield, you will ever receive

From
The
Beggared Outcast,
WILKINS MICAWBER'

I was so shocked by the contents of this heartrending letter, that I ran off directly towards the little hotel with the intention of trying to soothe Mr Micawber with a word of comfort. But, half-way there, I met the London coach with Mr and Mrs Micawber up behind, Mr Micawber, the very picture of tranquil enjoyment, eating walnuts out of a paper bag, with a bottle sticking out of his breast pocket. As they did not see me, I thought it best, all things considered, not to see them. So, I turned into a by-street and felt, upon the whole, relieved that they were gone: though I still liked them very much, nevertheless.

CHAPTER 18

A Retrospect

My school-days! The silent gliding on of my existence from childhood up to youth! Let me think whether there are any marks along its course, by which I can remember how it ran.

A moment, and I occupy my place in the Cathedral, where we went every Sunday morning, assembling first at school for that purpose. I am not the last boy in the school. I have risen, in a few months, over several heads. But who is this that breaks upon me? This is Miss Shepherd, whom I love.

Miss Shepherd is a boarder at the Misses Nettingall's establishment. I adore Miss Shepherd. She is a little girl, with a round face and curly flaxen hair. The Misses Nettingall's young ladies come to the Cathedral too. I cannot look upon my book, for I must look upon Miss Shepherd.

At length, Fate being propitious, we meet at the dancing-school. I have Miss Shepherd for my partner. I touch Miss Shepherd's glove, and feel a thrill go up the right arm of my jacket, and come out at my hair. I say nothing tender to Miss Shepherd, but we understand each other. Once, I kiss Miss Shepherd in the cloak room. Ecstasy!

How do I ever come to break with her? I can't conceive. And yet a coolness grows. Whispers reach me of Miss Shepherd having avowed a preference for Jones – a boy of no merit whatever! One day, I meet the Misses Nettingall's establishment out walking. Miss Shepherd makes a face as she goes by, and laughs to her companion. All is over. The devotion of a life is at an end.

I am higher in the school, and I am not at all polite, now, to the Misses Nettingall's young ladies, and shouldn't dote on any of them, if they were twenty times as beautiful. I am growing great in Latin verses, and neglect the laces of my boots. Doctor Strong refers to me in public as a promising young scholar and my aunt remits me a guinea by the next post.

The shade of a young butcher rises, the terror of the youth of Canterbury. He is broad-faced, bull-necked, with rough red cheeks and an injurious tongue. His main use of this tongue is to disparage Doctor

Strong's young gentlemen. He waylays the smaller boys to punch their unprotected heads, and calls challenges after me in the open streets. For these sufficient reasons I resolve to fight the butcher.

It is a summer evening, down in a green hollow, at the corner of a wall and the butcher and myself stand face to face. In a moment the butcher lights ten thousand candles out of my left eyebrow. In another moment, I don't know where the wall is, or where I am, or where anybody is. I go in at the butcher madly, and cut my knuckles open against his face, without appearing to discompose him at all. At last I awake, very queer about the head, and see the butcher walking off, congratulated by two other butchers; from which I augur, justly, that the victory is his.

I am taken home in a sad plight, and I have beef-steaks put to my eyes, and am rubbed with vinegar and brandy. For three or four days I remain at home and I should be very dull, but that Agnes condoles with me, and makes the time light and happy. Agnes has my confidence completely; I tell her all about the butcher, and she thinks I couldn't have done otherwise than fight.

Time has stolen on unobserved – and what comes next! *I* am the head-boy, now! I look down on the line of boys below me, with a condescending interest in such of them as bring to my mind the boy I was myself, when I first came there. That little fellow seems to be no part of me; I remember him as something left behind upon the road of life and almost think of him as of some one else.

And the little girl I saw on that first day at Mr Wickfield's, where is she? Gone also. In her stead, Agnes, my sweet sister, my counsellor and friend, is quite a woman.

I wear a gold watch and chain, a ring upon my little finger, and a long-tailed coat; and I worship the eldest Miss Larkins.

The eldest Miss Larkins is a tall, black-eyed, fine figure of a woman. My passion for her takes away my appetite, and makes me wear my newest silk neck-kerchief continually. I have no relief but in putting on my best clothes, and having my boots cleaned over and over again. I seem, then, to be worthier of the eldest Miss Larkins.

I regularly take walks outside Mr Larkins's house in the evening, though it cuts me to the heart to see the officers go in, or to hear them up in the drawing-room, where the eldest Miss Larkins plays the harp. I even walk, in a sickly, spoony manner, round the house after the family are gone to bed, wishing that a fire would burst out; that the assembled crowd would stand appalled; that I, dashing through them with a ladder, might rear it against her window, save her in my arms, go back for something she had left behind, and perish in the flames.

Sometimes brighter visions rise before me. When I dress (the occupation of two hours), for a great ball given at the Larkins's (the anticipation of three weeks), I indulge my fancy with pleasing images. I picture myself taking courage to make a declaration to Miss Larkins. I picture Miss Larkins sinking her head upon my shoulder, and saying, 'Oh, Mr Copperfield, can I believe my ears!' I picture Mr Larkins waiting on me next morning, and saying, 'My dear Copperfield, my daughter has told me all. Youth is no objection. Here are twenty thousand pounds. Be happy!'

I repair to the enchanted house, where there are lights, chattering, music, and the eldest Miss Larkins, a blaze of beauty. She is dressed in blue, with blue flowers in her hair. It is the first really grown-up party that I have ever been invited to, and I am a little uncomfortable.

But after I have stood in the doorway for some time, and feasted my eyes upon the goddess of my heart, she approaches and asks pleasantly, if I dance?

I stammer, with a bow, 'With you, Miss Larkins.'

'With no one else?' inquires Miss Larkins.

'I should have no pleasure in dancing with any one else.'

Miss Larkins laughs and says, 'Do you waltz? If not, Captain Bailey –'

But I do waltz and I take Miss Larkins out. I swim about in space, with a blue angel, in a state of blissful delirium, until I find myself alone with her in a little room, resting on a sofa. She admires a flower in my buttonhole. I give it her, and say: 'I ask an inestimable price for it, Miss Larkins.'

'Indeed! What is that?'

'A flower of yours, that I may treasure it as a miser does gold.'

'You're a bold boy,' says Miss Larkins.

She gives it me, not displeased; and I put it to my lips. Miss Larkins, laughing, draws her hand through my arm, and says, 'Now take me back to Captain Bailey.'

I am lost in the recollection of this delicious interview when she comes to me again, with a plain elderly gentleman upon her arm, and says:

'Here is my bold friend! Mr Chestle wants to know you, Mr Copperfield.'

I feel at once that he is a friend of the family, and am much gratified.

'I admire your taste, sir,' says Mr Chestle. 'It does you credit. I suppose you don't take much interest in hops; but I am a pretty large grower myself; and if you ever like to come over to our neighbourhood we shall be glad for you to stop as long as you like.'

I thank Mr Chestle warmly, and shake hands. I go home in a state of unspeakable bliss, and waltz in imagination, all night long, with my arm round the blue waist of my dear divinity.

'Trotwood,' says Agnes, one day after dinner. 'Who do you think is going to be married to-morrow? The eldest Miss Larkins.'

'To – to Captain Bailey?' I have just enough power to ask.

'No. To Mr Chestle, a hop-grower.'

I am terribly dejected for about a week or two. I take off my ring, I wear my worst clothes, and I frequently lament over the late Miss Larkins's faded flower. Being, by that time, tired of this life, and having received new provocation from the butcher, I throw the flower away, go out with the butcher, and gloriously defeat him.

This, and the resumption of my ring, are the last marks I can discern, now, in my progress to seventeen.

CHAPTER 19

I look about me, and make a Discovery

I am doubtful whether I was at heart glad or sorry, when the time came for my leaving Doctor Strong's. I had been very happy there, I had a great attachment for the Doctor, and I was eminent in that little world. For these reasons I was sorry to go; but for other reasons, unsubstantial enough, I was glad. Misty ideas of being a young man at my own disposal, of the wonderful things to be seen and done by that magnificent animal, and the wonderful effects he could not fail to make upon society, lured me away.

My aunt and I had held many grave deliberations on the calling to which I should be devoted. But I had no particular liking, that I could discover, for anything.

'I tell you what, my dear,' said my aunt one morning. 'It has occurred to me that a little change may be useful, in helping you to know your own mind. Suppose you were to go down into the country and see that out-of-the-way woman with the savagest of names.' She could never thoroughly forgive Peggotty for being so called.

'Of all things in the world, aunt, I should like it best!'

'Well,' said my aunt, 'that's lucky, for I should like it too. But it's natural and rational that you should like it. And I am very well persuaded that whatever you do, Trot, will always be natural and rational.'

'I hope so, aunt.'

'Your sister, Betsey Trotwood,' said my aunt, 'would have been as natural and rational a girl as ever breathed. You'll be worthy of her, won't you?'

'I hope I shall be worthy of *you*, aunt. That will be enough for me.'

In pursuance of my aunt's kind scheme, I was shortly afterwards fitted out with a handsome purse of money, and a portmanteau, and tenderly dismissed upon my expedition. At parting, my aunt said that as her object was that I should look about me, she would recommend me to stay a few days in London either on my way down into Suffolk, or in coming back. In a word, I was at liberty to do what I would, for three weeks or a month; and no other conditions were imposed upon my freedom than a pledge to write three times a week and faithfully report myself.

I went to Canterbury first. Agnes was very glad to see me, and told me that the house had not been like itself since I had left it.

'I am sure I am not like myself when I am away,' said I. 'I seem to want my right hand, when I miss you, though that's not saying much. Every one who knows you, is guided by you, Agnes.'

'Every one who knows me, spoils me, I believe,' she answered, smiling.

'No. It's because you are so good, and so sweet-tempered. You have such a gentle nature, and you are always right.'

'You talk,' said Agnes, 'as if I were the late Miss Larkins.'

'Come! It's not fair to abuse my confidence,' I answered, reddening at the recollection of my blue enslaver. 'But I shall confide in you, just the same. I shall always tell you, if you'll let me – even when I come to fall in love in earnest.'

'Why, you have always been in earnest!' said Agnes, laughing.

'That was as a schoolboy,' said I, a little shamefaced. 'I suppose I shall be in a terrible state of earnestness one day or other. My wonder is, that you are not in earnest yourself, by this time, Agnes.'

Agnes shook her head.

'Oh, I know you are not!' said I, 'because if you had been, you would have told me. Or at least,' for I saw a faint blush in her face, 'you would have let me find it out for myself. But there is no one that I know of, who deserves to love *you*, Agnes. In the time to come, I shall have a wary eye on all admirers; and shall exact a great deal from the successful one, I assure you.'

Agnes, now suddenly lifting up her eyes to mine, said, 'Trotwood, there is something that I want to ask you. Have you observed any alteration in Papa?'

I had observed it, and must have shown as much in my face; for her eyes were in a moment cast down.

'Tell me what,' she said in a low voice.

'He is often very nervous. His hand trembles, his speech is not plain, and his eyes look wild. I have remarked that at those times he is most certain to be wanted on some business.'

'By Uriah,' said Agnes.

'Yes. Do not be alarmed by what I say, Agnes, but I saw him, the other evening, lay down his head upon his desk and shed tears like a child.'

Her hand passed softly before my lips while I was yet speaking, and in a moment she had met her father at the door. The expression of her face,

I felt to be very touching. There was such deep fondness for him, in her beautiful look; and a fervent appeal to me to deal tenderly by him.

We were to drink tea at the Doctor's, and round the study fireside found the Doctor, and his young wife, and her mother. The Doctor received me as an honoured guest.

'I shall not see many more new faces in Trotwood's stead, Wickfield,' said the Doctor, warming his hands; 'I shall relinquish all my young people in another six months, and lead a quieter life. I shall have nothing to think of, then, but my Dictionary and Annie.'

As Mr Wickfield glanced towards her, sitting at the tea-table by Agnes, she seemed to me to avoid his look.

'There is a post come in from India, I observe,' he said, after a short silence.

'By-the-by! and letters from Mr Jack Maldon!' said the Doctor.

'Poor dear Jack!' said Mrs Markleham, shaking her head. 'That trying climate! Like living, they tell me, on a sand-heap, underneath a burning-glass! He looked strong, but he wasn't.'

'Do I gather from what you say, ma'am, that Mr Maldon is ill?' asked Mr Wickfield.

'My dear sir, he's had dreadful strokes of the sun, no doubt, and jungle fevers and agues, and every kind of thing you can mention.'

'Does he say all this?' asked Mr Wickfield.

'Say? Not he. You might drag him at the heels of four wild horses rather than he say anything calculated to overturn the Doctor's plans.'

'Wickfield's plans,' said the Doctor, stroking his face, and looking penitently at his adviser. 'That is to say, our joint plans for him. I said myself, abroad or at home.'

'And I said,' added Mr Wickfield, gravely, 'abroad. I was the means of sending him abroad. It's my responsibility.'

'Oh! Responsibility!' said the Old Soldier. 'Everything was done for the best, my dear Mr Wickfield. But if the dear fellow can't live there, he'll die there and I know he'll die there, sooner than overturn the Doctor's plans.'

'Well, ma'am,' said the Doctor cheerfully, 'I am not bigoted to my plans. If Mr Jack Maldon comes home on account of ill health, we must endeavour to make some more suitable provision for him in this country.'

Mrs Markleham was so overcome by this generous speech (which, I need not say, she had not at all expected or led up to) that she could only tell the Doctor it was like himself, and gently chid her daughter for not being more demonstrative when such kindnesses were showered, for her sake, on her old playfellow: and entertained us with some particulars concerning other deserving members of her family, whom it was desirable to set on their deserving legs.

All this time, Annie never once spoke, or lifted up her eyes. Mr Wickfield had his glance upon her as she sat by his own daughter's side. Long after the subject was dismissed, he remained so; seldom raising his eyes, unless to rest them for a moment, with a thoughtful frown, upon the Doctor, or his wife, or both.

The Doctor was very fond of music. Agnes sang with great sweetness and expression, and so did Mrs Strong. They sang and played together and we had quite a little concert. But I remarked two things: first, that though Annie soon recovered her composure, there was a blank between her and Mr Wickfield; secondly, that Mr Wickfield seemed to dislike the intimacy between her and Agnes. And now, I must confess, the recollection of what I had seen on that night when Mr Maldon went away began to return upon me with a meaning it had never had. The innocent beauty of her face was not as innocent to me as it had been; I mistrusted the natural grace and charm of her manner; and when I looked at Agnes by her side, suspicions arose within me that it was an ill-assorted friendship.

The evening closed in an incident which I well remember. Agnes was going to embrace Annie and kiss her, when Mr Wickfield stepped between them, as if by accident, and drew Agnes away. Then I saw, as though I were still standing in the doorway on the night of the departure, the expression of that night in the face of Mrs Strong.

I cannot say how impossible I found it, when I thought of her afterwards, to remember her face in its innocent loveliness again. It haunted me when I got home. I seemed to have left the Doctor's roof with a dark cloud lowering on it.

But morning brought with it my parting from that old house, which Agnes had filled with her influence; and that occupied my mind sufficiently. I should be there again soon, no doubt; but the days of my inhabiting there were gone, and the old time was past. I was heavier at heart when I packed up than I cared to show to Uriah Heep: who was so officious to help me that I uncharitably thought him mighty glad that I was going.

I got away from Agnes and her father with an indifferent show of being very manly, and took my seat upon the box of the London coach. The main object on my mind, I remember, when we got fairly on the road, was to appear as old as possible to the coachman, and to speak extremely gruff. The latter point I achieved at great personal inconvenience: but I stuck to it, because I felt it was a grown-up sort of thing.

'You are going through, sir?' said the coachman.

'Yes, William,' I said, condescendingly (I knew him); 'I am going to London. I shall go down into Suffolk afterwards.'

'Is Suffolk your county, sir?' asked William.

'Yes,' I said, with some importance.

'I'm told the dumplings is uncommon fine down there,' said William. 'And the Punches. A Suffolk Punch is worth his weight in gold. Did you ever breed any Suffolk Punches yourself, sir?'

'N – no,' I said, 'not exactly.'

'Here's a gen'lm'n behind me,' said William, 'as has bred 'em by wholesale.'

The gentleman spoken of was a gentleman with a very unpromising squint, and a prominent chin, who had a tall white hat on and whose breath quite tickled the back of my head.

'Ain't you bred them Suffolk Punches by wholesale?' asked William.

'I should think so,' said the gentleman. 'There ain't no sort of orse that I ain't bred, and no sort of dorg. Orses and dorgs is wittles and drink to me – lodging, wife, and children – reading, writing, and 'rithmetic – snuff, tobacker, and sleep.'

'That ain't a sort of man to see sitting behind a coachbox, is it though?' said William in my ear, as he handled the reins.

I construed this remark into an indication of a wish that he should have my place, so I blushingly offered to resign it.

'Well, if you don't mind, sir,' said William, 'I think it *would* be more correct.'

I have always considered this as the first fall I had in life. When I booked my place at the coach-office I had had 'Box-Seat' written against the entry, and had given the book-keeper half-a-crown. I was got up in a special great-coat and shawl expressly and had felt that I was a credit to the coach. And here, in the very first stage, I was supplanted by a shabby man with a squint.

A distrust of myself, which has often beset me in life on small occasions, was assuredly not stopped in its growth by this little incident outside the Canterbury coach. It was in vain to take refuge in gruffness of speech. I spoke from the pit of my stomach for the rest of the journey, but I felt completely extinguished, and dreadfully young.

We went to the Golden Cross, at Charing Cross, then a mouldy sort of establishment in a close neighbourhood. A waiter showed me into the coffee-room; and a chambermaid introduced me to my small bedchamber, which smelt like a hackney-coach, and was shut up like a family vault. I was still painfully conscious of my youth, for nobody stood in any awe of me at all.

'Well now,' said the waiter, in a tone of confidence, 'what would you like for dinner? Have a fowl!'

I told him, as majestically as I could, that I wasn't in the humour for a fowl.

'Ain't you?' said the waiter. 'Have a weal cutlet!'

I assented to this proposal, in default of being able to suggest anything else.

He asked me what I would take with it; and on my replying 'Half a pint of sherry,' thought it a favourable opportunity, I am afraid, to extract that measure of wine from the stale leavings at the bottoms of several small decanters. When the wine came, I thought it flat; and it certainly had more English crumbs in it, than were to be expected in a foreign wine in anything like a pure state; but I was bashful enough to drink it.

Being then in a pleasant frame of mind (from which I infer that poisoning is not always disagreeable in some stages of the process), I resolved to go to Covent Garden Theatre and there I saw Julius Caesar. To have all those noble Romans alive before me was a most novel and delightful effect that when I came out into the rainy street, at twelve o'clock at night, I felt as if I had come from the clouds. But the unceremonious pushing and hustling that I received, soon recalled me to myself, and put me in the road back to the hotel; where, after some porter and oysters, I sat past one o'clock, with my eyes on the coffee-room fire.

I was so filled with the play that I didn't know when the figure of a handsome well-formed young man, became a real presence to me. But I recollect being conscious of his company without having noticed his coming in.

At last I rose to go to bed, much to the relief of the sleepy waiter. In going towards the door, I passed the person and saw him plainly. He did not know me, but I knew him in a moment.

At another time I might have wanted the confidence to speak to him, but, in the then condition of my mind, I went up to him at once with a fast-beating heart, and said:

'Steerforth! won't you speak to me?'

He looked at me but I saw no recognition in his face.

'You don't remember me, I am afraid,' said I.

'My God!' he suddenly exclaimed. 'It's little Copperfield!'

I grasped him by both hands. 'I never, never, never was so glad! My dear Steerforth, I am so overjoyed to see you!'

'And I am rejoiced to see you, too!' he said, shaking my hands heartily. 'Why, Copperfield, old boy, don't be overpowered!' And yet he was glad, too, I thought, to see how the delight I had in meeting him affected me.

I brushed away the tears that my utmost resolution had not been able to keep back, and I made a clumsy laugh of it, and we sat down together, side by side.

'Why, how do you come to be here?' said Steerforth, clapping me on the shoulder.

'I came here by the Canterbury coach to-day. I have been adopted by an aunt down in that part of the country, and have just finished my education there. How do *you* come to be here, Steerforth?'

'Well, I am what they call an Oxford man,' he returned; 'that is to say, I get bored to death down there, periodically – and I am on my way now to my mother's. You're a devilish amiable-looking fellow, Copperfield, now I look at you! Not altered in the least!'

'I knew *you* immediately,' I said; 'but you are more easily remembered.'

He laughed as he ran his hand through the clustering curls of his hair. 'I am on an expedition of duty. My mother lives a little way out of town; and the roads being in a beastly condition, I remained here to-night instead of going on. I have been dozing away at the play.'

'I have been at the play, too,' said I. 'At Covent Garden. What a delightful and magnificent entertainment!'

Steerforth laughed heartily. 'My dear young Davy, the daisy of the field, at sunrise, is not fresher than you are. I have been at Covent Garden, too, and there never was a more miserable business. Holloa, you sir!' This was addressed to the waiter. 'Where have you put my friend, Mr Copperfield?'

'Well, sir,' said the waiter, with an apologetic air. 'Mr Copperfield is at present in forty-four, sir.'

'And what the devil do you mean,' retorted Steerforth, 'by putting Mr Copperfield into a little loft over a stable?'

'Why, you see we wasn't aware, sir,' returned the waiter, 'as Mr Copperfield was anyways particular. We can give Mr Copperfield seventy-two, sir, if it would be preferred. Next you, sir.'

'Of course it would be preferred,' said Steerforth. 'And do it at once.'

The waiter immediately withdrew to make the exchange. Steerforth invited me to breakfast with him next morning at ten o'clock – an invitation I was only too happy to accept. It being now pretty late, we went up-stairs, where we parted with friendly heartiness and where I found my new room a great improvement on my old one, it having an immense four-post bedstead in it, which was quite a little landed estate. Here, among pillows enough for six, I soon fell asleep in a blissful condition.

CHAPTER 20

Steerforth's Home

It was not in the coffee-room that I found Steerforth but in a snug private apartment, where a fine hot breakfast was set forth on a table covered with a clean cloth. I was rather bashful at first, Steerforth being so superior to me in all respects, but his easy patronage soon made me quite at home.

'Now, Copperfield,' said Steerforth, 'I should like to hear all about you. I feel as if you were my property.'

Glowing with pleasure to find that he had still this interest in me, I told him how my aunt had proposed the little expedition that I had before me.

'As you are in no hurry, then,' said Steerforth, 'come home with me to Highgate, and stay a day or two. You will be pleased with my mother – every one who likes me, has a claim on her that is sure to be acknowledged.'

'Then I think I shall be a favourite,' said I.

After I had written to my aunt and told her of my fortunate meeting, we went out in a hackney-chariot, and took a walk through the Museum, where I could not help observing how much Steerforth knew on an infinite variety of subjects.

'You'll take a high degree at college, Steerforth,' said I.

'Not I!' cried Steerforth. 'My dear Daisy – will you mind my calling you Daisy?'

'Not at all.'

'I have not the least desire to distinguish myself in that way.'

I was abashed at having made so great a mistake, and was glad to change the subject. The short winter day wore away so fast, that it was dusk when the stage-coach stopped at an old brick house at Highgate on the summit of the hill. An elderly lady with a handsome face was in the doorway and folded Steerforth in her arms. To this lady he presented me as his mother, and she gave me a stately welcome.

It was a genteel old-fashioned house. From the windows of my room I saw all London lying in the distance like a great vapour, with here and there some lights twinkling through it. I had only time, in dressing, to glance at the solid furniture, and some pictures of ladies on the walls, when I was called to dinner.

There was a second lady in the dining-room, of a slight short figure, who attracted my attention. She had black hair and eager eyes, and was thin, and had a scar upon her lip which had once cut through her mouth. I concluded in my own mind that she was about thirty years of age.

She was introduced as Miss Dartle, and both Steerforth and his mother called her Rosa. I found that she had been for a long time Mrs Steerforth's companion. It appeared to me that she never said anything she wanted to say, outright; but hinted it, and made a great deal more of it by this practice. For example, before dinner was done, Mrs Steerforth speaking to me about my intention of going down into Suffolk, I said how glad I should be if Steerforth would only go there with me. I reminded him of the boatman whom he had seen at school.

'Oh! That bluff fellow!' said Steerforth. 'He had a son with him, hadn't he?'

'That was his nephew,' I replied. 'He has a pretty little niece too. In short, his house is full of people who are objects of his generosity and kindness. You would be delighted to see that household.'

'Should I?' said Steerforth. 'Well, I think I should. It would be worth a journey to see that sort of people together.'

Miss Dartle, whose sparkling eyes had been watchful of us, now broke in. 'Oh, but, really? Are they, though?' she said.

'Are who what?' said Steerforth.

'That sort of people. Are they really animals and clods, and beings of another order? I want to know so much.'

'Why, there's a pretty wide separation between them and us,' said Steerforth. 'They are not to be expected to be as sensitive as we are. Their delicacy is not to be shocked, or hurt very easily. They are wonderfully virtuous, I dare say. But they have not very fine natures, and they may be thankful that, like their coarse rough skins, they are not easily wounded.'

'Really!' said Miss Dartle. 'Well, I don't know, now, when I have been better pleased than to hear that. It's so consoling! It's such a delight to know that, when they suffer, they don't feel! Sometimes I have been quite uneasy for that sort of people; but now I shall just dismiss the idea of them altogether. I had my doubts, I confess, but now they're cleared up. I didn't know, and now I do know, and that shows the advantage of asking – don't it?'

I believed that Steerforth had said what he had, in jest, or to draw Miss Dartle out; and I expected him to say as much when she was gone. But he merely asked me what I thought of her.

'She is very clever, is she not?' I asked.

'Clever! She brings everything to a grindstone,' said Steerforth. 'She has worn herself away by constant sharpening. She is all edge.'

'What a remarkable scar that is upon her lip!' I said.

Steerforth's face fell. 'The fact is I did that.'

'By accident?'

'No. I was a young boy, and she exasperated me, and I threw a hammer at her. A promising young angel I must have been!'

I was deeply sorry to have touched on such a painful theme, but that was useless now.

'She has borne the mark ever since,' said Steerforth; 'and she'll bear it to her grave, if she ever rests in one; though I can hardly believe she will ever rest anywhere. She was the motherless child of a sort of cousin of my father's. He died one day. My mother, who was then a widow, brought her here to be company to her. She has a couple of thousand pounds of her own, and saves the interest of it. There's the history of Miss Rosa Dartle for you.'

'And I have no doubt she loves you like a brother?' said I.

'Humph!' retorted Steerforth. 'Some brothers are not loved over much – but help yourself, Copperfield! We'll drink the daisies of the field, in compliment to you; and the lilies of the valley that toil not, neither do they spin, in compliment to me – the more shame for me!' A moody smile that had overspread his features cleared off as he said this and he was his own winning self again.

I could not help glancing at the scar with a painful interest when we went in to tea. It was not long before I observed that it was the most susceptible part of her face, and when she turned pale, lengthened out to its full extent, like a mark in invisible ink brought to the fire. There was a little altercation between her and Steerforth about a cast of the dice at backgammon, when I thought her, for one moment, in a storm of rage; and then I saw it start forth like the old writing on the wall.

It was no matter of wonder to me to find Mrs Steerforth devoted to her son. She seemed to be able to speak or think about nothing else.

'It was at Mr Creakle's, my son tells me, that you first became acquainted,' said Mrs Steerforth. 'Indeed, I recollect his speaking, at that time, of a pupil younger than himself who had taken his fancy there.'

'He was very generous and noble to me in those days, I assure you, ma'am,' said I, 'I should have been quite crushed without him.'

'He is always generous and noble,' said Mrs Steerforth, proudly.

I subscribed to this with all my heart, God knows. She knew I did; for the stateliness of her manner already abated towards me.

'My son informs me, Mr Copperfield, that when you met yesterday you made yourself known to him with tears of joy. I cannot be indifferent to any one who is so sensible of his merit, and I am very glad to see you here, and can assure you that he feels an unusual friendship for you, and that you may rely on his protection.'

Miss Dartle played backgammon as eagerly as she did everything else. But I am very much mistaken if she missed a word of this, or lost a look of mine as I received it with the utmost pleasure, and, honoured by Mrs Steerforth's confidence, felt older than I had done since I left Canterbury.

When the evening was pretty far spent, Steerforth promised, over the fire, that he would seriously think of going down into the country with me. While we were talking, he more than once called me Daisy; which brought Miss Dartle out again.

'But really, Mr Copperfield,' she asked, 'is it a nick-name? And why does he give it you? Is it because he thinks you young and innocent?'

I coloured in replying that I believed it was.

'Oh!' said Miss Dartle. 'Now I am glad to know that! He thinks you young and innocent; and so you are his friend? Well, that's quite delightful!'

She went to bed soon after this, and Mrs Steerforth retired too. Steerforth and I, after lingering for half an hour, talking about Traddles and all the rest of them at old Salem House, went up-stairs together.

I found the fire burning in my room and the curtains drawn, giving it a very snug appearance. I sat down in a great chair upon the hearth to meditate on my happiness; when I found a likeness of Miss Dartle looking eagerly at me from above the chimney-piece.

It was a startling likeness. The painter hadn't made the scar, but *I* made it; and there it was, coming and going: now confined to the upper lip as I had seen it at dinner, and now showing the whole extent of the wound inflicted by the hammer, as I had seen it when she was passionate.

I wondered peevishly why they couldn't put her anywhere else instead of quartering her on me. To get rid of her, I went to bed. But, as I fell asleep, I could not forget that she was still there looking; and when I awoke in the night, I found that I was uneasily asking all sorts of people in my dreams whether it really was or not – without knowing what I meant.

CHAPTER 21

Little Em'ly

There was a servant in that house, a man who had come into Steerforth's service at the University. Littimer was soft-footed, deferential, observant, always at hand when wanted, and never near when not; but his great claim to consideration was his respectability. He surrounded himself with an atmosphere of respectability, and walked secure in it. I felt particularly young in this man's presence. How old he was himself, I could not guess. In the calmness of respectability he might have numbered fifty years as well as thirty.

Littimer got horses for us; and Steerforth, who knew everything, gave me lessons in riding. He provided foils and Steerforth gave me lessons in fencing – gloves, and I began, of the same master, to improve in boxing. I had no reason to believe that Littimer understood such arts himself; yet whenever he was by while we were practising, I felt myself the greenest of mortals.

I am particular about this man, because he made a particular effect on me at that time, and because of what took place thereafter.

The week passed away in a most delightful manner to one entranced as I was; and gave me so many occasions for knowing Steerforth better that at its close I seemed to have been with him for a much longer time. I believed that I was nearer to his heart than any other friend, and my own heart warmed with attachment to him.

He made up his mind to go with me into the country, and what I felt, in returning to the old familiar places, I shall not endeavour to describe. I was so concerned for the honour of Yarmouth, that when Steerforth said, as we drove through its dark streets to the inn, that it was a good, queer, out-of-the-way kind of hole, I was highly pleased. We went to bed on our arrival and breakfasted late in the morning. Steerforth, who was in great spirits, had been strolling about the beach before I was up. Moreover, he had seen, in the distance, what he was sure must be the house of Mr Peggotty.

'When do you propose to introduce me there, Daisy?' he said. 'I am at your disposal.'

'I was thinking that this evening would be a good time. I shall not give them any notice that we are here. We must take them by surprise.'

'Oh, of course!' said Steerforth. 'Let us see the natives in their aboriginal condition. Now, you are going to see your nurse, I suppose?'

'Why, yes,' I said, 'I must see Peggotty first.'

I gave him minute directions for finding the residence of Mr Barkis and went out alone. The streets looked small, of course. The streets that we have only seen as children always do, when we go back to them. But I had forgotten nothing in them, and found nothing changed, until I came to Mr Omer's shop. OMER AND JORAM was now written up, where OMER used to be.

I looked in. There was a pretty woman at the back of the shop, dancing a little child in her arms, while another little fellow clung to her apron. I had no difficulty in recognising Minnie. In the workshop across the yard I could faintly hear the old tune playing, as if it had never left off.

'Is Mr Omer at home?' said I, entering.

'Oh yes, sir,' said Minnie; 'Joe, call your grandfather!'

The little fellow who was holding her apron gave a lusty shout and soon Mr Omer, shorter-winded than of yore, but not much older-looking, stood before me.

'Servant, sir,' said Mr Omer. 'What can I do for you?'

'You can shake hands with me, if you please,' said I, putting out my own. 'You were very good-natured to me once.'

'I'm glad to hear it,' returned the old man, 'but I don't remember you.'

'Don't you remember your coming to the coach to meet me, and our riding out to Blunderstone together; you, and I, and Mrs Joram, and Mr Joram too – who wasn't her husband then?'

'Why, dear me, yes; the party was a lady, I think?'

'My mother,' I rejoined.

'To – be – sure,' said Mr Omer, 'and there was a little child too! Two parties! Why, in that very ride the day was named for my Minnie to marry Joram. And look here! The youngest!'

Minnie laughed as her father put one of his fat fingers into the hand of the child she was dancing on the counter.

'Let me see,' said Mr Omer. 'Peggotty, the boatman's sister – she had something to do with your family? She was in service there?'

My answering in the affirmative gave him great satisfaction.

'Well, sir, we've got a young relation of hers here, under articles to us, that has as elegant a taste in the dress-making business – I assure you I don't believe there's a Duchess in England can touch her.'

'Not little Em'ly?' said I.

'Em'ly's her name,' said Mr Omer, 'and she's little too. But if you'll believe me, she has such a face of her own that half the women in this town are mad against her.'

'Then she should have kept to her own station in life, father,' said Minnie, 'and not have given them any hold to talk about her, and then they couldn't have done it.'

'You see,' he said, 'an ill-natured story got about, that Em'ly wanted to be a lady. Then out of a very little, she could dress herself, you see, better than most others could out of a deal, and *that* made things unpleasant. Moreover, she was a little spoiled; and couldn't, at first, exactly bind herself down. So when she got a situation to keep a fractious old lady company, they didn't very well agree. At last she came here, and she has been as good a girl as ever was. Worth any six! Minnie, is she worth any six, now?'

'Yes, father,' replied Minnie. 'Never say *I* detracted from her!'

As they had spoken in a subdued tone, I had no doubt that she was near. On my asking, Mr Omer nodded towards the door of the parlour. Looking through the glass, I saw a most beautiful creature, with the cloudless blue eyes that had looked into my childish heart.

The tune across the yard was beating, softly, all the while.

'Wouldn't you like to speak to her?' said Mr Omer, but I was too bashful to do so and went away to my dear old Peggotty's.

The moment I knocked at the door she opened it. I had never ceased to write to her, but it must have been seven years since we had met.

'Is Mr Barkis at home, ma'am?' I said.

'He's at home, sir,' returned Peggotty, 'but he's bad abed with the rheumatics.'

'Don't he go over to Blunderstone now?' I asked. 'Because I want to ask a question about a house there – the Rookery.'

She took a step backward.

'Peggotty!' I cried to her.

She cried, 'My darling boy!' and we both burst into tears, and were locked in one another's arms.

What extravagances she committed; what laughing and crying over me I have not the heart to tell.

'Barkis will be so glad,' said Peggotty, wiping her eyes with her apron. 'Will you come up and see him, my dear?'

He received me with absolute enthusiasm. He was too rheumatic to be shaken hands with, but he begged me to shake the tassel on the top of his nightcap, which I did most cordially. When I sat down by the side of the bed, he said that it did him a world of good to feel as if he was driving me on the Blunderstone road again.

'What name was it as I wrote up in that cart, sir?' said Mr Barkis, with a slow rheumatic smile.

'Ah! Mr Barkis, we had some grave talks about that matter, hadn't we?'

'And I don't regret it,' said Mr Barkis. 'Do you remember what you told me once, about her making all the apple parsties?'

'Yes, very well,' I returned.

'It was as true,' said Mr Barkis, 'as taxes is. And nothing's truer than them. A man as poor as I am, finds that out in his mind when he's laid up.'

Here his right hand came slowly from under the bedclothes, and took hold of a stick. After some poking about with this instrument, Mr Barkis poked it against a box.

'Old clothes,' said Mr Barkis. 'I wish it was Money, sir, but it AIN'T.'

I expressed myself quite sure of that, and Mr Barkis, turning his eyes to his wife, said: 'She's the best of women, C. P. Barkis. My dear, you'll get a dinner to-day for company; something good to eat and drink, will you?'

I should have protested against this unnecessary demonstration in my honour, but that I saw Peggotty, on the opposite side of the bed, extremely anxious I should not. So I held my peace.

I prepared Peggotty for Steerforth's arrival, and it was not long before he came. His easy, spirited, good humour, and natural gift of adapting himself to whomsoever he pleased, bound her to him wholly in five minutes. We made merry in the little parlour, where the Book of Martyrs, unthumbed since my time, was laid out upon the desk as of old. When Peggotty spoke of what she called my room, and of her hoping I would occupy it, before I could so much as look at Steerforth, he was possessed of the whole case.

'Of course,' he said. 'You'll sleep here and I shall sleep at the hotel.'

'But to bring you so far,' I returned, 'and to separate, seems bad companionship, Steerforth.'

'Why, in the name of Heaven, where do you naturally belong?' he said. It was settled at once.

He maintained all his delightful qualities to the last, until we started forth, at eight o'clock, for Mr Peggotty's boat. If any one had told me, then, that all this was a brilliant game, played for the excitement of the moment, in a careless course of winning what was worthless to him, and next minute thrown away: if any one had told me such a lie that night,

I wonder in what manner of receiving it my indignation would have found a vent!

Probably only in an increase, had that been possible, of the romantic feelings of fidelity and friendship with which I walked beside him, over the dark wintry sands, towards the old boat.

'This is a wild kind of place, Steerforth, is it not?'

'Dismal enough in the dark,' he said, 'and the sea roars as if it were hungry for us.'

We said no more as we approached the light, but made softly for the door.

A murmur of voices had been audible on the outside, and, at the moment of our entrance, a clapping of hands. Mr Peggotty, laughing with all his might, held his rough arms wide open; Ham, with a mixed expression in his face of exultation and bashfulness, held little Em'ly by the hand; little Em'ly herself was stopped by our entrance (for she saw us first) in the very act of springing from Ham to nestle in Mr Peggotty's embrace. In the first glimpse we had of them all, this was the way in which they were all employed. Mrs Gummidge in the background, clapping her hands like a mad-woman.

The little picture was instantaneously dissolved by our going in. I was face to face with Mr Peggotty, holding out my hand to him, when Ham shouted: 'It's Mas'r Davy!'

In a moment we were all shaking hands with one another, and asking one another how we did, and all talking at once. Mr Peggotty was so proud and overjoyed to see us, that he kept ruffling his shaggy hair and laughing with such glee that it was a treat to see him.

'Why, that you two gent'lmen – gentl'men growed – should come to this here roof to-night, of all nights in my life,' said Mr Peggotty, 'is such a thing as never happened afore, I do rightly believe! Em'ly, my darling, come here! There's Mas'r Davy's friend, my dear! He comes to see you, along with Mas'r Davy, on the brightest night of your uncle's life as ever was or will be!'

After delivering this speech with extraordinary animation, Mr Peggotty put one of his large hands rapturously on each side of his niece's face and kissed it a dozen times. Then he let her go and she ran into the little chamber where I used to sleep.

'If you two gent'lmen growed,' said Mr Peggotty, 'don't excuse me for being in a state of mind, when you understand matters, I'll arks your pardon.

'There was a certain person as had know'd our Em'ly, from the time when her father was drownded. Not much of a person to look at, he warn't, but on the whole a honest sort of a chap, with his art in the right place.'

I thought I had never seen Ham grin to anything like the extent to which he sat grinning at us now.

'What does this here blessed tarpaulin go and do,' said Mr Peggotty, 'but he loses that there art of his to our little Em'ly. Well! I counsels him to speak. He's big enough, but he's bashfuller than a little un, so *I* speak. "What! *Him*!" says Em'ly. "*Him* that I've know'd so intimate so many years. Oh, Uncle! I never can have *him*." I says no more to her than "My dear, you're right to speak out." Then I aways to him, and says, "I wish it could have been so, but it can't. But wot I say to you is, Be as you was with her." And he was. For two year going on we was just the same at home here as afore.'

Mr Peggotty laid a hand upon my knee and a hand upon Steerforth's and divided the following speech between us.

'All of a sudden, one evening – as it might be to-night – comes little Em'ly from her work, and him with her! But this chap takes hold of her hand and cries out to me, joyful, "This is to be my little wife!" And she says, "Yes, Uncle! If you please, I have thought better of it, and I'll be as good a wife as I can to him, for he's a dear, good fellow!" Then Missis Gummidge, she claps her hands like a play, and you come in.'

Ham staggered under the blow Mr Peggotty dealt him in his un-bounded joy, but feeling called upon to say something, he said, with much faltering:

'I see her grow up – gent'lmen – like a flower. I'd lay down my life for her. There ain't a gent'lman in all the land that can love his lady more than I love her, though there's many a common man would say better what he meant.'

I thought it affecting to see such a sturdy fellow as Ham was now, trembling in the strength of what he felt for the pretty little creature who had won his heart. Whether I had come there with any lingering fancy that I was still to love little Em'ly, I don't know. I know that I was filled with pleasure by all this; but an indescribably sensitive pleasure that a very little would have changed to pain.

Therefore, if it had depended upon me to touch the prevailing chord among them with any skill, I should have made a poor hand of it. But Steerforth did it with such address, that in a few minutes we were all as easy and as happy as it was possible to be.

'Mr Peggotty,' he said, 'you are a thoroughly good fellow, and deserve to be as happy as you are to-night. My hand upon it! Ham, I give you joy, my boy. My hand upon that, too! Daisy, stir the fire, and make it a brisk one! and Mr Peggotty, unless you can induce your gentle niece to come back, I shall go.'

Presently they brought Little Em'ly to the fireside, very much confused, and very shy – but she soon became more assured when she found how gently Steerforth spoke to her; how easily he carried on, until he brought us, by degrees, into a charmed circle, and we were all talking away without any reserve.

As I remember, it was almost midnight when we took our leave. We parted merrily; and as they all stood crowded round the door to light us as far as they could upon our road, I saw the sweet blue eyes of little Em'ly peeping after us, from behind Ham, and heard her soft voice calling to us to be careful how we went.

'A most engaging little Beauty!' said Steerforth, taking my arm. 'Well! It's a quaint place, and they are quaint company; and it's quite a new sensation to mix with them.'

'How fortunate we are, too,' I returned, 'to have arrived to witness their happiness in that intended marriage! I never saw people so happy.'

'That's rather a chuckle-headed fellow for the girl; isn't he?' said Steerforth.

He had been so hearty with him, and with them all, that I felt a shock in this unexpected and cold reply. But seeing a laugh in his eyes, I answered, much relieved:

'Ah, Steerforth! It's well for you to joke about the poor! You may skirmish with Miss Dartle, or try to hide your sympathies in jest from me, but I know better. When I see how perfectly you understand them, how you can enter into happiness like this plain fisherman's, or humour a love like my old nurse's, I know that there is not a joy or sorrow of such people, that can be indifferent to you. And I admire and love you for it, Steerforth, twenty times the more!'

He stopped, and looking in my face, said: 'Daisy, I believe you are in earnest, and are good. I wish we all were!' Next moment he was gaily singing Mr Peggotty's song, as we walked at a round pace back to Yarmouth.

CHAPTER 22

Some old Scenes, and some new People

Steerforth and I stayed for more than a fortnight in that part of the country. We were very much together, but occasionally were asunder for some hours at a time. When he went out boating with Mr Peggotty, a favourite amusement of his, I generally remained ashore. My occupation of Peggotty's spare-room put a constraint upon me, from which he was free; for I did not like to remain out late whereas Steerforth had nothing to consult but his own humour. Thus I heard of his making little treats for the fishermen at The Willing Mind after I was in bed, and of his being afloat whole moonlight nights and coming back when the morning tide was at flood. By this time, however, I knew that his restless nature and bold spirits delighted in any means of excitement that presented itself freshly to him.

Another cause of our being sometimes apart was, that I had an interest in going over to Blunderstone, and revisiting the familiar scenes of my childhood. My occupation in my solitary pilgrimages was to haunt the old spots, of which I never tired. The grave where both my parents lay, I walked near, by the hour. My reflections at these times were always associated with the figure I was to make in life, and the distinguished things I was to do.

It was with a singular jumble of sadness and pleasure that I used to linger until the reddening winter sun admonished me that it was time to start on my return. My nearest way to Yarmouth was by a ferry. It landed me on the flat between the town and the sea. Mr Peggotty's house being not a hundred yards out of my tract, I always looked in as I went by. Steerforth was pretty sure to be there expecting me.

One dark evening when I was later than usual, I found him alone in Mr Peggotty's house, sitting thoughtfully before the fire, quite unconscious of my approach.

He gave such a start when I put my hand upon his shoulder, that he made me start too.

'You come upon me,' he said, almost angrily, 'like a reproachful ghost!'

'I was obliged to announce myself, somehow.'

'I detest this mongrel time,' he returned, 'neither day nor night. I have been sitting here, thinking that all the people we found so glad on the night of our coming down, might – to judge from the present wasted air of the place – be dead, or come to I don't know what harm. David, I wish to God I had had a judicious father these last twenty years!'

'My dear Steerforth, what is the matter?'

'I wish with all my soul I had been better guided!' he exclaimed. 'I wish with all my soul I could guide myself better!'

There was a passionate dejection in his manner that quite amazed me. He was more unlike himself than I could have supposed possible.

'It would be better to be this poor Peggotty, or his lout of a nephew,' he said, 'than to be myself, twenty times richer and twenty times wiser.'

I begged him, with all the earnestness I felt, to tell me what had occurred to cross him so unusually, and to let me sympathise with him, if I could not hope to advise him. Before I had well concluded, he began to laugh.

'Tut, it's nothing, Daisy!' he replied. 'I told you, I am heavy company for myself, sometimes. But I tell you, my good fellow, once more, that it would have been well for me (and for more than me) if I had had a steadfast father!'

His face was always full of expression, but I never saw it express such a dark kind of earnestness as when he said these words, with his glance bent on the fire.

'So much for that!' he said.

The advent of Mrs Gummidge with a basket, explained how the house had happened to be empty. She had hurried out to buy something that was needed, against Mr Peggotty's return with the tide. Steerforth, after very much improving Mrs Gummidge's spirits by a cheerful salutation, took my arm, and hurried me away.

He had improved his own spirits, no less than Mrs Gummidge's.

'And so,' he said, gaily, 'we abandon this buccaneer life to-morrow, do we?'

'So we agreed,' I returned. 'And our places by the coach are taken, you know.'

'Ay! there's no help for it, I suppose,' said Steerforth. 'I have almost forgotten that there is anything to do in the world but to go out tossing on the sea here. I wish there was not.'

'As long as the novelty should last,' said I, laughing.

'Like enough,' he returned; 'though there's a sarcastic meaning in that observation for an amiable piece of innocence like my young friend. You know I have bought a boat down here?'

'What an extraordinary fellow you are, Steerforth!' I exclaimed, for this was the first I had heard of it. 'When you may never care to come near the place again!'

'I don't know that,' he returned. 'I have taken a fancy to the place. At all events I have bought a boat – a clipper – and Mr Peggotty will be master of her in my absence.'

'Now I understand you, Steerforth!' said I, exultingly. 'You pretend to have bought it for yourself, but you have really done so to confer a benefit on him. My dear kind Steerforth, how can I tell you what I think of your generosity?'

'Tush!' he answered, turning red. 'The less said, the better.'

'Didn't I say that there was not a joy, or sorrow, or any emotion of such honest hearts that was indifferent to you?'

'Aye, aye,' he answered, 'you told me all that. There let it rest. We have said enough!'

Afraid of offending him by pursuing the subject when he made so light of it, I only pursued it in my thoughts as we went on.

'She must be newly rigged,' said Steerforth, 'and I shall leave Littimer behind to see it done. Did I tell you Littimer had come down this morning, with a letter from my mother?'

I observed that he was pale even to his lips, and feared that some difference between him and his mother might have led to his being in the frame of mind in which I found him. I hinted so.

'Oh no!' he said, shaking his head, and giving a slight laugh. 'Nothing of the sort! Yes. Littimer is come down. He shall see to the boat being fresh named. She's the Stormy Petrel now. I'll have her christened again.'

'By what name?' I asked.

'The Little Em'ly.'

I could not help showing in my face how much it pleased me, but I said little, and he resumed his usual smile, and seemed relieved.

'But see here,' he said, looking before us, 'where the original little Em'ly comes! And that fellow with her – he never leaves her!'

Ham was in his working-dress, and looked a very fit protector for the blooming little creature at his side. Indeed, there was an undisguised show of his pride in her, and his love for her, which were, to me, the best of good looks. I thought, as they came towards us, that they were well matched.

She withdrew her hand from his arm as we stopped to speak to them, and blushed as she gave it to Steerforth and to me. When they passed on, after we had exchanged a few words, she walked by herself. I thought all this very pretty and engaging, and Steerforth seemed to think so too, as we looked after them.

Suddenly there passed us – evidently following them – a young woman whose approach we had not observed.

'That is a black shadow to be following the girl,' said Steerforth. 'Where the Devil did it come from, I wonder!'

'From the shadow of this wall, I think,' said I, as we emerged upon a road on which a wall abutted.

'It's gone!' he returned, looking over his shoulder. 'And all ill go with it.'

But, he looked again over his shoulder towards the sea-line glimmering afar off; and yet again. And he only seemed to forget it when the light of fire and candle shone upon us, seated warm and merry at table.

Littimer was there. We had almost finished dinner, when taking a step towards the table from the corner where he kept watch upon us, he said to his master:

'I beg your pardon, sir. Miss Mowcher is here.'

'Why, what on earth does *she* do here?' said Steerforth.

'She informs me that she makes one of her professional visits here, every year, sir. I met her in the street this afternoon, and she wished to know if she might have the honour of waiting on you after dinner, sir.'

'Do you know the Giantess in question, Daisy?' inquired Steerforth.

I was obliged to confess that Miss Mowcher and I were wholly unacquainted.

'Then you shall know her,' said Steerforth, 'for she is one of the seven wonders of the world. When Miss Mowcher comes, show her in.'

I felt some curiosity and excitement about this lady, especially as Steerforth positively refused to answer any question of which I made her the subject. I remained, therefore, in a state of considerable expectation until Littimer announced: 'Miss Mowcher!'

I looked at the doorway and saw nothing. I was still looking at the doorway, thinking that Miss Mowcher was a long while making her appearance, when, to my infinite astonishment, there came waddling round a sofa a dwarf, of about forty or forty-five, with a very large head and face, a pair of roguish grey eyes, and such extremely little arms, that, to enable herself to lay a finger archly against her snub nose as she ogled Steerforth, she was obliged to meet the finger half-way, and lay her nose against it. Legs she had none worth mentioning; for she was so short that she stood at a common-sized chair as at a table, resting a bag she carried on the seat. After ogling Steerforth for a few moments, this lady broke into a torrent of words.

'Oh, you naughty boy, fie for shame, what do you do so far away from home? Up to mischief, I'll be bound. Oh, you're a downy fellow, Steerforth, so you are, and I'm another, ain't I? You'd have betted a hundred pound to five, that you wouldn't have seen me here, wouldn't you? Bless you, man alive, I'm everywhere. I'm here, and there, and where not, like the conjurer's half-crown in the lady's hankercher. Talking of hankerchers – *and* talking of ladies – what a comfort you are to your blessed mother, ain't you, my dear boy, over one of my shoulders, and I don't say which!'

Miss Mowcher untied her bonnet, at this passage of her discourse, and sat down on a footstool in front of the fire.

'Oh, my stars and what's-their-names!' she went on, glancing shrewdly at me. 'If you saw me looking out of an upper window, you'd think I was a fine woman, wouldn't you?'

'I should think that, wherever I saw you,' replied Steerforth.

'Go along, you dog, do!' cried the little creature, 'and don't be impudent!'

I never beheld anything approaching to Miss Mowcher's wink, except Miss Mowcher's self-possession. She had a wonderful way too of pausing with her head cunningly on one side, and one eye turned up like a magpie's. Altogether I was lost in amazement, and sat staring at her, quite oblivious, I am afraid, of the laws of politeness.

She had by this time drawn the chair to her side, and was busily engaged in producing from the bag (plunging in her short arm to the shoulder, at every dive) a number of small bottles, sponges, combs, brushes and other instruments, which she tumbled in a heap upon the chair. From this employment she suddenly desisted, and said to Steerforth, 'Who's your friend?'

'Mr Copperfield,' said Steerforth, 'he wants to know you.'

'Well, then, he shall! I thought he looked as if he did!' returned Miss Mowcher, waddling up to me. 'Face like a peach!' standing on tiptoe to pinch my cheek as I sat. 'Happy to make your acquaintance, Mr Copperfield, I'm sure.'

I said that I congratulated myself on having the honour to make hers, and that the happiness was mutual.

'Oh, my goodness, how polite we are!' exclaimed Miss Mowcher, making a preposterous attempt to cover her large face with her morsel of a hand. 'Come, Steerforth, let's explore the polar regions, and have it over.'

She then selected two or three of the little instruments, and a little bottle, and asked (to my surprise) if the table would bear. On Steerforth's replying in the affirmative, she pushed a chair against it, and begging the assistance of my hand, mounted up, pretty nimbly, to the top, as if it were a stage.

'If either of you saw my ankles,' she said, when she was safely elevated, 'say so, and I'll go home and destroy myself.'

'I did not,' said Steerforth.

'Well then,' cried Miss Mowcher, 'I'll consent to live. Now, ducky, come to Mrs Bond and be killed.'

This was an invocation to Steerforth to place himself under her hands; who, accordingly, sat himself down, with his back to the table, and his laughing face towards me, and submitted his head to her inspection. To see Miss Mowcher standing over him, looking at his rich profusion of brown hair through a large round magnifying glass, which she took out of her pocket, was a most amazing spectacle.

'*You're* a pretty fellow!' said Miss Mowcher, after a brief inspection. 'Just half-a-minute, my young friend, and we'll give you a polishing that shall keep your curls on for the next ten years!'

With this, she tilted some of the contents of the little bottle on to one of the little bits of flannel, and, again imparting some of the virtues of that preparation to one of the little brushes, began rubbing and scraping away with both on the crown of Steerforth's head in the busiest manner I ever witnessed.

'I haven't seen a pretty woman since I've been here, Jemmy.'

'No?' said Steerforth.

'Not the ghost of one,' replied Mowcher.

'We could show her the substance of one, I think?' said Steerforth, addressing his eyes to mine. 'Eh, Daisy?'

'Yes, indeed,' said I.

'Aha!' cried the little creature. 'A sister of yours, Mr Copperfield?'

'No,' said Steerforth, before I could reply. 'Nothing of that sort. On the contrary, Mr Copperfield used – or I am much mistaken – to have a great admiration for her.'

'Why, hasn't he now?' returned Miss Mowcher. 'Is he fickle? Oh, for shame! Did he sip every flower, and change every hour, until Polly his passion requited? – Is her name Polly?'

The Elfin suddenness with which she pounced upon me with this question, and a searching look, quite disconcerted me for a moment.

'No, Miss Mowcher,' I replied. 'Her name is Emily.'

'Aha?' she cried exactly as before. 'What a rattle I am! Mr Copperfield, ain't I volatile?'

Her tone and look implied something that was not agreeable to me in connexion with the subject. So I said, in a graver manner: 'She is engaged to be married to a most worthy and deserving man in her own station of life. I esteem her for her good sense, as much as I admire her for her good looks.'

'Well said!' cried Steerforth. 'Hear, hear! Now I'll quench the curiosity of this little Fatima, my dear Daisy, by leaving her nothing to guess at. She is at present apprenticed, or articled, or whatever it may be, to Omer and Joram, Haberdashers, Milliners, and so forth, in this town. Do you observe? Omer and Joram. The promise of which my friend has spoken, is entered into with her cousin; Christian name, Ham; surname, Peggotty; occupation, boat-builder. She lives with a relative; surname, Peggotty; occupation, seafaring. She is the prettiest and most engaging little fairy in the world. I admire her – as my friend does – exceedingly. If it were not that I might appear to disparage her intended, which I know my friend would not like, I would add, that to *me* she seems to be throwing herself away; that I am sure she might do better; and that I swear she was born to be a lady.'

Miss Mowcher listened to these words, which were very slowly and distinctly spoken, with her head on one side, and her eye in the air, as if she were still looking for that answer. When he ceased she became brisk again in an instant, and rattled away with surprising volubility.

'Oh! And that's all about it, is it?' she exclaimed, trimming his whiskers with a little restless pair of scissors. 'What's that game at forfeits? I love my love with an E, because she's enticing; I hate her with an E, because she's engaged. I took her to the sign of the exquisite, and treated her with an elopement; her name's Emily, and she lives in the east? Ha! ha! Mr Copperfield, ain't I volatile?'

Merely looking at me with extravagant slyness, she continued, without drawing breath: 'There! if ever any scapegrace was trimmed and touched up to perfection, you are, Steerforth. If I understand any noddle in the world, I understand yours. Do you hear me when I tell you that, my darling? Now if Mr Copperfield will take the chair I'll operate on him.'

'Thank you, Miss Mowcher, not this evening.'

'Don't say no,' returned the little woman, looking at me with the aspect of a connoisseur; 'a little bit more eyebrow?'

'Thank you,' I returned, 'some other time.'

Miss Mowcher, finding that I was not at present disposed for any decoration within the range of her art, requested the aid of my hand to descend from her elevated station.

'The fee,' said Steerforth, 'is –'

'Five bob,' replied Miss Mowcher, 'and dirt cheap, my chicken. Ain't I volatile, Mr Copperfield?'

I replied politely: 'Not at all.' But I thought she was rather so, when she tossed up his two half-crowns like a goblin pieman, caught them, dropped them in her pocket, and gave it a loud slap.

'That's the till!' observed Miss Mowcher, standing at the chair again, and replacing in the bag a miscellaneous collection of little objects she had emptied out of it. 'Now, I know I'm going to break your hearts, but I am forced to leave you. You must call up all your fortitude, and try to bear it. Good-bye, Mr Copperfield! How I *have* been rattling on!'

With the bag slung over her arm, and rattling as she waddled to the door, she departed.

Steerforth told me that Miss Mowcher had quite an extensive connexion, and made herself useful to a variety of people in a variety of ways. Some people trifled with her as a mere oddity, he said; but she was as shrewdly and sharply observant as any one he knew, and as long-headed as she was short-armed. He told me that what she had said of being here, and there, and everywhere, was true enough; for she made little darts into the provinces, and seemed to pick up customers everywhere, and to know everybody. She was the principal theme of our conversation until we parted for the night.

I was surprised, when I came to Mr Barkis's house, to find Ham in front of it, and still more surprised to learn from him that little Em'ly was inside.

'You see, Mas'r Davy,' he rejoined, in a hesitating manner, 'Em'ly, she's talking to some 'un in here. A young woman, that Em'ly knowed once, and doen't ought to know no more.'

When I heard these words, a light began to fall upon the figure I had seen following them, some hours ago.

'Did I see her to-night, Ham, on the sands, after we met you?'

'It's like you did, Mas'r Davy. She was theer, sir, creeping soon arterwards under Em'ly's winder and whisp'ring "Em'ly, Em'ly, for Christ's sake, have a woman's heart towards me. I was once like you!" Those was solemn words, Mas'r Davy, fur to hear.'

'They were indeed, Ham. What did Em'ly do?'

'Says Em'ly, "Martha, is it you?" For they had sat at work together, many a day, at Mr Omer's. She wanted to speak to Em'ly. Em'ly couldn't speak to her theer, for her uncle was come home, and he wouldn't – no, Mas'r Davy,' said Ham, with great earnestness, 'he couldn't see them two together, side by side, for all the treasures that's wrecked in the sea.'

I felt how true this was. I knew it, on the instant, quite as well as Ham.

'So Em'ly writes in pencil on a bit of paper,' he pursued, 'and gives it to her out o' window to bring here. "Show that," she says, "to my aunt, Mrs Barkis, and she'll set you down by her fire, till I can come." By-and-by she asks me to bring her. What can I do? I can't deny her, when the tears is on her face.'

The door opened then, and Peggotty appeared, beckoning to Ham to come in. I would have kept away, but she entreated me to come in too.

The girl – the same I had seen upon the sands – was near the kitchen fire. She was sitting on the ground, with her head and one arm lying on a chair. I fancied, from the disposition of her figure, that Em'ly had but newly risen from the chair, and that the forlorn head might perhaps have been lying on her lap. I saw but little of the girl's face, over which her hair fell loose and scattered, but I saw that she was young, and of a fair complexion. Peggotty had been crying. So had little Em'ly.

Em'ly spoke first.

'Martha wants to go to London.'

'Why London?' returned Ham.

'Better there than here,' said a third voice – Martha's, though she did not move. 'No one knows me there. Everybody knows me here.'

'What will she do there?' inquired Ham.

'She will try to do well,' said little Em'ly.

'I never can do worse than I have done here,' said Martha. 'Take me out of these streets, where the whole town knows me from a child!'

Em'ly went to Martha. What she gave her, I don't know. I saw her stooping over her, and putting money in her bosom. She asked was that enough? 'More than enough,' the other said, and took her hand and kissed it.

Then Martha arose, and gathering her shawl about her, covering her face with it, and weeping aloud, went slowly to the door. No word passed her lips.

As the door closed, little Em'ly hid her face in her hands, and fell to sobbing.

'Doen't, Em'ly!' said Ham, tapping her gently on the shoulder. 'You doen't ought to cry so, pretty!'

'Oh, Ham!' she exclaimed, still weeping pitifully. 'I am not as good a girl as I ought to be! I know I have not the thankful heart, sometimes, I ought to have!'

'Yes, yes, you have, I'm sure,' said Ham.

'No! no! no!' cried little Em'ly, 'I try your love too much. I'm often cross and changeable with you. Why am I ever so to you, when I should think of nothing but how to make you happy!'

'You always make me so,' said Ham. 'I am happy, all day long, in the thoughts of you.'

'That is because you are good; not because I am! Oh, my dear, it might have been a better fortune for you, if you had been fond of some one else – of some one steadier and much worthier than me, who was never vain and changeable!'

'Poor little tender-heart,' said Ham, in a low voice. 'Martha has overset her, altogether.'

Peggotty had hastened to the chair before the fire. Em'ly, with her arms around her neck, kneeled by her, looking up most earnestly into her face.

'Oh, pray, aunt, try to help me! Ham, dear, try to help me! Mr David, for the sake of old times, do, please, try to help me! I want to be a better girl than I am. I want to feel what a blessed thing it is to be the wife of a good man, and to lead a peaceful life. Oh my heart, my heart!'

She dropped her face on Peggotty's breast, and wept silently while my old nurse hushed her like an infant.

She got calmer by degrees, and then we soothed her; now talking encouragingly, and now jesting a little with her, until she began to raise her head and speak to us. So we got on, until she was able to smile, and then to laugh, and then to sit up, half ashamed.

I saw her do, that night, what I had never seen her do before. I saw her innocently kiss her chosen husband on the cheek, and creep close to his bluff form as if it were her best support. When they went away together, in the waning moonlight, I saw that she held his arm with both her hands, and kept close to him.

CHAPTER 23

I corroborate Mr Dick, and choose a Profession

When I awoke in the morning I thought of little Em'ly. I had no gentler feeling towards any one than the pretty creature who had been my play-mate. The repetition to any ears – even to Steerforth's – of what she had been unable to repress when her heart lay open to me by an accident, I felt would be unworthy of our pure childhood. I made a resolution, therefore, to keep it in my own breast.

While we were at breakfast, a letter was delivered to me from my aunt. As it contained matter on which I thought Steerforth could advise me as well as any one, I resolved to make it a subject of discussion on our journey home. For the present we had enough to do, in taking leave of all our friends, and we departed to the regret and admiration of all concerned.

For some time we held no conversation, I being sufficiently engaged in wondering when I should see the old places again. At length Steerforth pulled me by the arm: 'Find a voice, David. What about the letter you were speaking of at breakfast?'

'Oh!' said I, taking it out of my pocket. 'My aunt asks me if I should like to be a proctor. What *is* a proctor, Steerforth?'

'A sort of monkish attorney,' replied Steerforth. 'He is, to some faded courts held in Doctors' Commons – a lazy old nook near St Paul's Churchyard – what solicitors are to the courts of law and equity. It's a place that has an ancient monopoly in suits about people's wills and people's marriages, and disputes among ships and boats.'

I made allowance for Steerforth's light way of treating the subject and did not feel indisposed towards my aunt's suggestion; which she left to my free decision, making no scruple of telling me that it had occurred to her, on her lately visiting her own proctor in Doctors' Commons for the purpose of settling her will in my favour.

'That's a laudable proceeding on the part of our aunt, at all events,' said Steerforth, when I mentioned it; 'and one deserving of all encouragement. Daisy, my advice is that you take kindly to Doctors' Commons.'

My aunt was in town awaiting me at a kind of private hotel in Lincoln's Inn Fields, where there was a stone staircase, and a convenient door in the roof; my aunt being firmly persuaded that every house in London was going to be burnt down every night.

If I had been round the world since we parted, we could hardly have been better pleased to meet again. My aunt cried outright as she embraced me.

Supper was comfortably served and hot, though my aunt's rooms were very high up, and consisted of a roast fowl, a steak, and some vegetables, which were all excellent. But my aunt had her own ideas concerning London provision, and ate but little.

'I suppose this unfortunate fowl was born and brought up in a cellar,' said my aunt.

'Don't you think it may have come out of the country?' I hinted.

'Certainly not,' returned my aunt. 'It would be no pleasure to a London tradesman to sell anything which was what he pretended it was.'

I did not venture to controvert this opinion, but made her, according to certain established regulations from which no deviation could ever be permitted, a glass of hot white wine and water, and a slice of toast cut into long thin strips. With these accompaniments, my aunt looked benignantly on me, from among the borders of her nightcap.

'Well, Trot,' she began, 'what do you think of the proctor plan?'

'I like it very much indeed, aunt. I have only one difficulty.'

'Say what it is,' she returned.

'I want to ask, as this seems to be a limited profession, whether my entrance into it would not be very expensive?'

'It will cost, to article you, just a thousand pounds.'

'My dear aunt,' said I, drawing my chair nearer, 'I am uneasy about that. It's a large sum of money. You have expended a great deal on my education, and have always been as liberal to me in all things, as it was possible to be. Surely there are some ways in which I might begin life with hardly any outlay, yet with a good hope of getting on by resolution and exertion. Are you sure it would not be better to try that course?'

My aunt finished eating the piece of toast on which she was then engaged, and replied as follows:

'Trot, my child, if I have any object in life, it is to provide for your being a good, sensible and happy man. I am bent upon it – so is Dick. Perhaps I might have been better friends with your poor father. Perhaps I might have been better friends with that poor child your mother. When you came to me, a little runaway boy, all dusty and way-worn, perhaps I thought so. From that time until now, Trot, you have ever been a credit to me and a pride and a pleasure. I have no other claim upon my means; at least' – here to my surprise she hesitated, and was confused – 'no, I have *no* other claim upon my means – and you are my adopted child. Only be loving to me in my age, and bear with my whims and fancies; and you will do more for an old woman whose prime of life was not so happy as it might have been than ever that old woman did for you.'

It was the first time I had heard my aunt refer to her past history. There was a magnanimity in her quiet way of doing so, which would have exalted her in my respect and affection, if anything could.

'All is agreed and understood between us now, Trot,' said my aunt, 'and we need talk of this no more. We'll go to the Commons after breakfast to-morrow.'

At about mid-day, we set out for the office of Messrs Spenlow and Jorkins, in Doctors' Commons. My aunt, who had this other general opinion in reference to London, that every man she saw was a pickpocket, gave me her purse to carry, which had ten guineas in it and some silver.

We were crossing Ludgate Hill, when I found that my aunt greatly accelerated her speed, and looked frightened. I observed, at the same time, that a lowering ill-dressed man was coming so close after us, as to brush against her.

'Don't be alarmed,' said I. 'I'll soon get rid of this fellow.'

'No, no!' she returned. 'Don't speak to him for the world. I entreat, I order you!'

'Good Heaven, aunt! He is nothing but a sturdy beggar.'

'You don't know what he is!' replied my aunt. 'You don't know what you say!'

We had stopped in an empty doorway and he had stopped too.

'Don't look at him!' said my aunt, 'but get me a coach, and wait for me in St Paul's Churchyard. I must go with him.'

'With him, aunt? This man?'

'I am in my senses,' she replied, 'and I tell you I *must*. Get me a coach!'

However much astonished I might be, I was sensible that I had no right to refuse such a peremptory command. I called a hackney chariot which was passing. My aunt sprang in and the man followed. Confounded, I turned from them at once. In doing so, I heard her say to the coachman, 'Drive anywhere!' and presently the chariot passed me, going up the hill.

What Mr Dick had told me now came into my mind. I could not doubt that this person was the person of whom he had made such mysterious mention, though what the nature of his hold upon my aunt could possibly be, I was unable to imagine. After half an hour's cooling in the churchyard, I saw the chariot coming back.

My aunt had not yet sufficiently recovered from her agitation to be quite prepared for the visit we had to make. She desired me to tell the coachman to drive slowly up and down a little while. She said no more, except, 'My dear child, never ask me what it was, and don't refer to it,' until she had perfectly regained her composure. On her giving me her purse, to pay the driver, I found that all the guineas were gone, and only the loose silver remained.

Doctors' Commons was approached by a little low archway. A few dull courts and narrow ways brought us to the skylighted offices of Spenlow and Jorkins; in the vestibule three or four clerks were at work. One of these rose to receive my aunt and show us into Mr Spenlow's room.

We were left to look about us while Mr Spenlow was fetched. The furniture of the room was old-fashioned and dusty; and the green baize on the top of the writing-table was as pale as an old pauper. There were a great many bundles of papers on it, and sundry immense Books of Evidence tied together in massive sets. I was casting my eyes over these and similar objects, when hasty footsteps were heard in the room outside, and Mr Spenlow, in a black gown trimmed with white fur, came hurrying in.

He was a little light-haired gentleman, with the stiffest of white cravats. He was got up with such care, and was so stiff, that he could hardly bend himself; being obliged, when he glanced at some papers after sitting down, to move his whole body from the bottom of his spine, like Punch.

'And so, Mr Copperfield, you think of entering into our profession?'

I said that I was strongly inclined to like it. That I could not absolutely pledge myself until I knew something more about it. I presumed I should have an opportunity of trying how I liked it, before I bound myself to it irrevocably.

'We always, in this house, propose a month,' said Mr Spenlow. 'I should be happy, myself, to propose two months – three – an indefinite period, in fact – but I have a partner, Mr Jorkins.'

'And the premium, sir,' I returned, 'is a thousand pounds.'

'And the premium, Stamp included, is a thousand pounds,' said Mr Spenlow. 'As I have mentioned to Miss Trotwood, I am actuated by no mercenary considerations; few men are less so, I believe; but I am bound to respect Mr Jorkins's opinions.'

'I suppose, sir,' said I, still desiring to spare my aunt, 'that it is not the custom here, if an articled clerk were particularly – I suppose it is not the custom, in the later years of his time, to allow him any –'

Mr Spenlow lifted his head far enough out of his cravat to shake it, and answered, anticipating the word 'salary' – 'No. I will not say what consideration I might give to that point myself, Mr Copperfield, if I were unfettered. Mr Jorkins is immovable.'

I was quite dismayed by the idea of this terrible Jorkins. But I found out afterwards that he was a mild man whose place was to keep himself in the background, and be constantly exhibited by name as the most obdurate and ruthless of men. The heart and hand of the good angel Spenlow would have been always open, but for the restraining demon Jorkins.

It was settled that I should begin my month's probation as soon as I pleased. Mr Spenlow offered to take me into Court and conducted me through a paved courtyard into a large dull room. There, on two sides of a raised platform, were sundry gentlemen in red gowns and grey wigs, whom I found to be the Doctors aforesaid. Blinking over a little desk was an old gentleman, whom, if I had seen him in an aviary, I should certainly have taken for an owl, but who, I learned, was the presiding judge. On the level of the floor were sundry other gentlemen of Mr Spenlow's rank, in black gowns. The public, represented by a boy with a comforter, and a shabby-genteel man secretly eating crumbs out of his coat pockets, was warming itself at a stove in the centre. The languid stillness of the place was only broken by the voice of one of the Doctors, who was wandering slowly through a perfect library of evidence, and stopping to put up at little roadside inns of argument on the journey. Altogether, I have never, on any occasion, made one at such a cosey, dosey, old-fashioned, time-forgotten, sleepy-headed little family-party in all my life; and I felt it would be quite a soothing opiate to belong to it in any character – except perhaps as a suitor.

My aunt and I had another long talk about my plans, when we were safely housed; and as I knew she was anxious to get home, and, between fire, food, and pickpockets, could never be considered at her ease for half-an-hour in London, I urged her to leave me to take care of myself.

'I have been considering that too, my dear,' she returned. 'There is a furnished little set of chambers to be let in the Adelphi, Trot, which ought to suit you to a marvel.'

With this brief introduction, she produced from her pocket an advertisement cut out of a newspaper, setting forth that in Buckingham Street in the Adelphi there was to be let furnished a singularly desirable and compact set of chambers, forming a genteel residence for a young gentleman. Terms moderate, and could be taken for a month only, if required.

Away we went. The advertisement directed us to apply to Mrs Crupp, a stout lady with a flounce of flannel petticoat below a nankeen gown. We went up-stairs.

The chambers were on the top of the house and consisted of a little half-blind entry where you could see hardly anything, a little stone-blind pantry where you could see nothing at all, a sitting-room, and a bedroom. The furniture was faded, but quite good enough for me; and the river was outside the windows.

My aunt, seeing how enraptured I was with the place, took it for a month, with leave to remain for twelve months when that time was out. Mrs Crupp was to find linen, and to cook; and I was to take possession the day after to-morrow. Mrs Crupp said, thank Heaven she had now found summun she could care for!

On the way back, my aunt informed me how she confidently trusted that the life I was now to lead would make me self-reliant, which was all I wanted. She repeated this next day, in the intervals of our arranging for the transmission of my clothes and books from Mr Wickfield's; relative to which, I wrote a long letter to Agnes. I need only add that she made a handsome provison for all my possible wants during my month of trial; that I saw her safely seated in the Dover coach, and that when the coach was gone, I turned my face to the Adelphi, pondering on the old days when I used to roam about its subterranean arches, and on the happy changes which had brought me to the surface.

CHAPTER 24

My first Dissipation

It was a wonderfully fine thing to have that lofty castle to myself. It was a wonderfully fine thing to walk about town with the key of my house in my pocket. It was a wonderfully fine thing to come and go without a word to any one; but I must say, too, that there were times when it was very dreary.

It was fine in the morning, but as the day declined, the life seemed to go down too. I wanted somebody to talk to, then. I missed Agnes. After two days and nights, I felt as if I had lived there for a year.

Steerforth not yet appearing, I walked out to Highgate. Mrs Steerforth was very glad to see me, and said that he had gone away with one of his Oxford friends to see another who lived near St Albans, but that she expected him to return to-morrow. I was so fond of him, that I felt quite jealous of his Oxford friends.

As she pressed me to stay to dinner, I remained, and I believe we talked about nothing but him all day. I told her how much the people liked him at Yarmouth. Miss Dartle took a great interest in all our proceedings there, and got everything out of me she wanted to know. The society was so agreeable that I felt myself falling a little in love with her. I could not help thinking what delightful company she would be in Buckingham Street.

I was taking my coffee and roll in the morning, before going to the Commons, when Steerforth himself walked in. I showed him over the establishment with no little pride, and he commended it highly. 'I tell you what, old boy,' he added, 'I shall make quite a town-house of this place, unless you give me notice to quit.'

This was a delightful hearing.

'But you shall come to dinner,' said I.

'There's nothing I should like better, but I *must* remain with these two fellows.'

'Then bring them here to dinner,' I returned. It occurred to me that I really ought to have a little house-warming, and that there never could be a better opportunity. I had a new pride in my rooms after his approval of them, and therefore made him promise positively in the names of his two friends, and we appointed six o'clock as the dinner-hour.

One of Steerforth's friends was named Grainger, and the other Markham. They were both very gay and lively fellows; Grainger, something older than Steerforth; Markham, youthful-looking, and I should say not more than twenty. I observed that the latter always spoke of himself indefinitely, as 'a man,' and seldom or never in the first person singular.

'A man might get on very well here, Mr Copperfield,' said Markham – meaning himself.

'I hope you have both brought appetites with you?' said Steerforth.

'Upon my honour,' returned Markham, 'town seems to sharpen a man's appetite. A man is hungry all day along. A man is perpetually eating.'

I made Steerforth take the head of the table when dinner was announced, and seated myself opposite to him. Everything was very good; we did not spare the wine; and he exerted himself so brilliantly to make the thing pass off well, that there was no pause in our festivity.

When the cloth was cleared, and the dessert put on the table, I abandoned myself to enjoyment and held forth in a most unwonted manner, passing the wine faster and faster. I proposed Steerforth's health. I said he was my dearest friend, the protector of my boyhood, and the companion of my prime. I finished by saying, 'I'll give you Steerforth! God bless him! Hurrah!' We gave him three times three, and another, and a good one to finish with. I broke my glass in going round the table to shake hands with him, and I said (in two words) 'Steerforth, you'retheguidingstarofmyexistence.'

Somebody was smoking. We were all smoking. I was smoking, and trying to suppress a rising tendency to shudder. Somebody was leaning out of my bedroom window, refreshing his forehead against the cool stone of the parapet, and feeling the air upon his face. It was myself. Now, somebody was unsteadily contemplating his features in the looking-glass. That was I too. My eyes had a vacant appearance; and my hair – only my hair – looked drunk.

Somebody said to me, 'Let us go to the theatre, Copperfield!' The theatre? To be sure. The very thing. Come along!

A very foggy night, with great rings round the lamps in the streets! There was an indistinct talk of its being wet. I considered it frosty. Steerforth put my hat into shape, then said, 'You are all right, Copperfield, are you not?' and I told him, 'Neverberrer.'

Shortly afterwards, we were very high up in a very hot theatre. There was an abundance of bright lights and there was music, and there were ladies down in the boxes, and I don't know what more. The whole building looked to me as if it were learning to swim.

On somebody's motion, we resolved to go down-stairs to the dress-boxes, where the ladies were. Then I was being ushered into one of these boxes, and found myself saying something as I sat down, and people about me crying 'Silence!' to somebody, and ladies casting indignant glances at me, and – what! yes! – Agnes, sitting on the seat before me, in the same box, with a lady and gentleman beside her, whom I didn't know. I see her face now, better than I did then, I dare say, with its indelible look of regret and wonder turned upon me.

'Agnes!' I said, thickly, 'Lorblessmer! Agnes!'

'Hush!' she answered, I could not conceive why. 'You disturb the company.'

I looked at her again and saw her put her gloved hand to her forehead.

'Agnes!' I said. 'I'mafraidyou'renorwell.'

After she had looked at me attentively for a little while, she replied in a low tone:

'I know you will do as I ask you. For my sake, Trotwood, ask your friends to take you home.'

I felt ashamed, and got up and went away. I stepped at once out of the box-door into my bedroom, where only Steerforth was with me, helping me to undress, and where I was by turns telling him that Agnes was my sister, and adjuring him to bring the corkscrew, that I might open another bottle of wine.

How somebody, lying in my bed, lay saying and doing all this over again, at cross purposes, in a feverish dream all night – the bed a rocking sea that was never still! How, as that somebody slowly settled down into myself, did I begin to parch, and feel as if my outer covering of skin were a hard board; my tongue the bottom of an empty kettle, furred with long service; the palms of my hands, hot plates of metal which no ice could cool!

But the agony of mind, the remorse, and shame I felt, when I became conscious next day! My recollection of that indelible look which Agnes had given me – the torturing impossibility of communicating with her, not knowing, Beast that I was, how she came to be in London, or where she stayed – my disgust of the very sight of the room where the revel had been held – my racking head – the smell of smoke, the sight of glasses, the impossibility of going out, or even getting up! Oh, what a day it was!

CHAPTER 25

Good and bad Angels

I was going out at my door in the morning after that deplorable day of sickness and repentance, when I saw a ticket-porter coming up-stairs, with a letter in his hand.

'T. Copperfield, Esquire,' he said, touching his hat with his little cane, and gave me the letter, which he said required an answer.

All it said was, 'My dear Trotwood. I am staying at the house of papa's agent, Mr Waterbrook, in Ely-place, Holborn. Will you come and see me to-day, at any time you like to appoint? Ever yours affectionately, AGNES.'

It took me such a long time to write an answer at all to my satisfaction, that I don't know what the ticket-porter can have thought, unless he thought I was learning to write. After many attempts, I wrote, 'My dear Agnes. Your letter is like you, and what could I say of it that would be higher praise than that? I will come at four o'clock. Affectionately and sorrowfully, T. C.' With this missive the ticket-porter at last departed.

Although I left the office at half-past three, the appointed time was exceeded by a full quarter of an hour before I could muster up sufficient desperation to pull the bell-handle of Mr Waterbrook's house. I was shown into a pretty drawing-room, and there sat Agnes, netting a purse.

Nobody being by, I yielded to my self-reproach and shame, and – in short – made a fool of myself. I cannot deny that I shed tears.

'If it had been any one but you, Agnes,' said I, turning away my head, 'I should not have minded it half so much.'

She put her hand upon my arm for a moment; and I felt so befriended and comforted, that I could not help moving it to my lips, and gratefully kissing it.

'Don't be unhappy, Trotwood,' said Agnes, cheerfully. 'If you cannot trust me, whom will you trust?'

'Ah, Agnes!' I returned. 'You are my good Angel!'

She smiled rather sadly, I thought, and shook her head. 'If I were, indeed, there is one thing that I should set my heart on very much.'

I looked at her inquiringly; but already with a foreknowledge of her meaning.

'On warning you,' said Agnes, with a steady glance, 'against your bad Angel.'

'My dear Agnes,' I began, 'if you mean Steerforth –'

'I do, Trotwood,' she returned.

'Then, Agnes, you wrong him very much. Is it not unjust, and unlike you, to judge him from what you saw of me the other night?'

'I do not judge him from what I saw of you the other night,' she quietly replied. 'But from many things – trifles in themselves, but they do not seem to me to be so, when they are put together. I judge him, partly from your account of him, Trotwood, and your character, and the influence he has over you.'

There was always something in her modest voice that seemed to touch a chord within me, and Steerforth, in spite of all my attachment to him, darkened in that tone.

'It is very bold in me,' said Agnes, 'who can know so little of the world, to give you my advice so confidently. But I am certain that what I say is right. I feel as if it were some one else speaking to you, and not I, when I caution you that you have made a dangerous friend.'

Again his image, though it was still fixed in my heart, darkened.

'Do you forgive me?' said Agnes after a little while.

'I will forgive you,' I replied, 'when you come to do Steerforth justice, and to like him as well as I do.'

'Not until then?' said Agnes.

I saw a passing shadow on her face when I made this mention of him, but she returned my smile, and we were again as unreserved in our mutual confidence as of old.

'You must not forget,' said Agnes, calmly changing the conversation, 'that you are always to tell me, not only when you fall into trouble, but when you fall in love. Who has succeeded to Miss Larkins?'

'No one, Agnes.'

'Some one, Trotwood,' said Agnes, laughing, and holding up her finger.

'No, upon my word! There is a lady at Mrs Steerforth's house who is very clever and whom I like to talk to – Miss Dartle – but I don't adore her.'

Agnes told me she thought she should keep a little register of my violent attachments, with the date, duration, and termination of each, like the table of the reigns of the kings and queens, in the History of England. Then she asked me if I had seen Uriah.

'No. Is he in London?'

'He comes to the office downstairs, every day,' returned Agnes. 'I am afraid on disagreeable business. I believe he is going to enter into partnership with papa.'

'What? That mean, fawning fellow worm himself into such promotion!' I cried, indignantly. 'You must prevent it, Agnes.'

Agnes shook her head. 'Uriah has made himself indispensable to papa. He has mastered papa's weaknesses and taken advantage of them, until papa is afraid of him. He professes humility and gratitude but his position is really one of power, and I fear he makes a hard use of his power.'

I said he was a hound, which, at the moment, was a great satisfaction to me.

'Oh, Trotwood!' cried Agnes. 'I almost feel as if I had been papa's enemy, instead of his loving child. For I know how he has altered, in his devotion to me. I know what a multitude of things he has shut out for my sake, and how his anxious thoughts of me have weakened his strength. If I could ever work out his restoration, as I have so innocently been the cause of his decline!'

I had never seen Agnes grieve like this. It made me so sorry that I could only say, in a helpless manner, 'Pray, Agnes, don't! Don't, my dear sister!'

But Agnes was too superior to me in character and purpose to be long in need of my entreaties. The beautiful, calm manner, which makes her so different in my remembrance from everybody else, came back again, as if a cloud had passed from a serene sky.

'We are not likely to remain alone much longer,' said Agnes; 'and while I have an opportunity, let me earnestly entreat you, Trotwood, to be friendly to Uriah. Don't repel him. Don't resent what may be uncongenial to you in him. He may not deserve it, for we know no certain ill of him. In any case, think first of papa and me!'

Agnes had not time to say more, for Mrs Waterbrook came sailing in. I had a dim recollection of having seen her at the theatre; but she appeared to remember me perfectly, and still to suspect me of being in a state of intoxication.

Finding by degrees, however, that I was sober, and (I hope) that I was a modest young gentleman, Mrs Waterbrook softened towards me considerably, and invited me to dinner next day. I accepted the invitation, and took my leave, making a call on Uriah in the office as I went out, and leaving a card for him in his absence.

When I went to dinner next day, I found Mr Waterbrook to be a middle-aged gentleman, with a good deal of shirt-collar, who only wanted a black nose to be the portrait of a pug-dog. He told me he was happy to have the honour of making my acquaintance.

I found Uriah Heep among the company, in a suit of black. He told me, when I shook hands, that he felt obliged to me for my condescension. I could have wished he had been less obliged, for he hovered about me in his gratitude all the rest of the evening; and whenever I said a word to Agnes, was sure, with his shadowless eyes and cadaverous face, to be looking gauntly down upon us from behind.

There were other guests – all iced for the occasion, as it struck me, like the wine. But, there was one who attracted my attention before he came in, on account of my hearing him announced as Mr Traddles. He was a young man of retiring manners, with a comic head of hair, and he got into an obscure corner so soon, that I had some difficulty in making him out. At length I had a good view of him, and either my vision deceived me, or it was the old unfortunate Tommy.

I made my way to Mr Waterbrook, and said that I believed I had the pleasure of seeing an old schoolfellow there, the gentleman named Traddles.

'Indeed!' said my host, with much diminished interest. 'It is a coincidence that Traddles should be here at all: as he was only invited this morning, when a place became vacant.'

I inquired what Mr Traddles was by profession.

'Traddles,' returned Mr Waterbrook, 'is a young man reading for the bar. He is quite a good fellow – nobody's enemy but his own.'

'Is he his own enemy?' said I, sorry to hear this.

'Well,' returned Mr Waterbrook, 'I should say he would never be worth five hundred pound. He has a kind of talent, for drawing briefs, and stating a case in writing. Yes.'

When dinner was announced, Uriah, Traddles, and I, as the junior part of the company, went down last. It gave me an opportunity of making myself known to Traddles, who greeted me with great fervour: while Uriah writhed with such obtrusive self-abasement, that I could gladly have pitched him over the banisters.

Traddles and I were separated at table, being billeted in two remote corners. The dinner was very long, and the conversation was about the Aristocracy – and Blood. Mrs Waterbrook repeatedly told us, that if she had a weakness, it was Blood. We might have been a party of Ogres, the conversation assumed such a sanguine complexion.

I was very glad indeed to get up-stairs to talk to Agnes and to introduce Traddles, who was shy, but agreeable, and the same good-natured creature still. As he was going away next morning for a month, we exchanged addresses, and promised ourselves the pleasure of another meeting when he should come back to town. He was greatly interested to hear that I knew Steerforth, and spoke of him with warmth. But Agnes only looked at me the while, and very slightly shook her head.

As she was not among people with whom I believed she could be much at home, I was almost glad to hear that she was going away within a few days, though I was sorry at the prospect of parting from her again so soon. This caused me to remain until all the company were gone. Conversing with her and hearing her sing, I could have remained there half the night; but, having no excuse for staying any longer, I took my leave. I felt then, more than ever, that she was my better Angel.

I have said that the company were all gone; but I ought to have excepted Uriah, who had never ceased to hover near us. He was close beside me, when I walked away from the house, slowly fitting his long skeleton fingers into a great Guy Fawkes pair of gloves.

It was in remembrance of the entreaty Agnes had made to me, that I asked him if he would come home to my rooms, and have some coffee.

'Oh, really, Master Copperfield,' he rejoined, – 'I beg your pardon, Mister Copperfield, but the other comes so natural, – I don't like that you should put a constraint upon yourself to ask a numble person like me to your ouse.'

'There is no constraint in the case,' said I. 'Will you come?'

'I should like to, very much,' replied Uriah, with a writhe.

'Well, then, come along!' said I.

I could not help being rather short with him, but he appeared not to mind it. We went the nearest way, without conversing much upon the road, and I conducted him to my fireside. When I lighted my candles, he fell into meek transports with the room that was revealed to him; and when I heated the coffee he professed so much emotion, that I could joyfully have scalded him.

'Oh, really, Master Copperfield, – I mean Mister Copperfield,' said Uriah, 'to see you waiting upon me is what I never could have expected! But, so many things happen to me which I never could have expected, I am sure, in my umble station, that it seems to rain blessings on my ed.'

As he sat on my sofa, with his long knees drawn up under his coffee-cup, his spoon going softly round and round, his shadowless red eyes turned towards me and a snaky undulation pervading his frame from his chin to his boots, I decided that I disliked him intensely. It made me very uncomfortable to have him for a guest.

'You have heard something, I des-say, of a change in my expectations, Mister Copperfield?' observed Uriah.

'Yes,' said I, 'something.'

'What a prophet you have shown yourself, Mister Copperfield! Don't you remember saying to me once, that perhaps I should be a partner in Mr Wickfield's business, and perhaps it might be Wickfield and Heep? *You* may not recollect it; but when a person is umble, Master Copperfield, a person treasures such things up!'

'I recollect talking about it,' said I, 'though I certainly did not think it very likely then.'

'Oh! who *would* have thought it likely, Mister Copperfield!' returned Uriah, enthusiastically. 'I recollect saying with my own lips that I was much too umble. But the umblest persons may be the instruments of good. I am glad to think I have been the instrument of good to Mr Wickfield. Oh what a worthy man he is, Mister Copperfield, but how imprudent he has been!'

'I am sorry to hear it,' said I. I could not help adding, rather pointedly, 'on all accounts.'

'Decidedly so, Mister Copperfield,' replied Uriah. 'On all accounts. Miss Agnes's above all! You don't remember your own eloquent expressions, Master Copperfield; but *I* remember how you said one day that everybody must admire her, and how I thanked you for it! You have forgot that, I have no doubt, Master Copperfield?'

'No,' said I, drily.

'Oh how glad I am you have not!' exclaimed Uriah. 'To think that you should be the first to kindle the sparks of ambition in my umble breast, and that you've not forgot it!'

Something in the emphasis he laid upon the kindling of those sparks made me start with a sudden sense of being no match for him, and a suspicious anxiety as to what he might be going to say next. He said nothing at all but he left the renewal of the conversation to me.

'So, Mr Wickfield,' said I, at last, 'who is worth five hundred of you – or me; has been imprudent, has he, Mr Heep?'

'I wish you'd call me Uriah, if you please. It's like old times.'

'Well! Uriah,' said I, bolting it out with some difficulty. 'About Mr Wickfield.'

'Oh! Yes, truly. Great imprudence. If any one else had been in my place during the last few years, by this time he would have had Mr Wickfield under his thumb. Un – der – his thumb,' said Uriah, very slowly, as he stretched out his cruel-looking hand above my table, and pressed his own thumb down upon it, until it shook, and shook the room.

If I had been obliged to look at him with his splay foot on Mr Wickfield's head, I think I could scarcely have hated him more.

'Oh, dear, yes, Master Copperfield,' he proceeded, in a soft voice, 'there would have been loss, disgrace, I don't know what all. Mr Wickfield knows it. I am the umble instrument of umbly serving him, and he puts me on an eminence I hardly could have hoped to reach. How thankful should I be!'

I recollect well how indignantly my heart beat, as I saw his crafty face preparing for something else.

'Master Copperfield,' he began 'You will not think the worse of my umbleness, if I make a little confidence to you?'

'Oh no,' said I, with an effort.

'Thank you!' He took out his pocket-handkerchief, and began wiping the palms of his hands. 'Miss Agnes, Master Copperfield –'

'Well, Uriah?'

'Oh, how pleasant to be called Uriah, spontaneously!' he cried; and gave himself a jerk, like a convulsive fish. 'You thought her looking very beautiful to-night, Master Copperfield?'

'I thought her looking as she always does: superior, in all respects, to every one around her,' I returned.

'Oh, it's so true! Umble as I am,' he wiped his hands harder, 'the image of Miss Agnes has been in my breast for years. Oh, Master Copperfield, with what a pure affection do I love the ground my Agnes walks on!'

I believe I had a delirious idea of seizing the red-hot poker out of the fire, and running him through with it. He seemed to swell and grow before my eyes; the room seemed full of the echoes of his voice. I asked him, with a better appearance of composure than I could have thought possible, whether he had made his feelings known to Agnes.

'Oh no, Master Copperfield!' he returned. 'Not to any one but you. You see I am only just emerging from my lowly station. I rest a good deal of hope on her observing how useful I am to her father. She's so much attached to her father, that I think she may come, on his account, to be kind to me.'

I fathomed the depth of the rascal's whole scheme, and understood why he laid it bare.

'If you'll have the goodness to keep my secret, Master Copperfield,' he pursued, 'and not, in general, to go against me, I shall take it as a particular favour. You wouldn't wish to make unpleasantness. I know what a friendly heart you've got; but having only known me on my umble footing (on my umblest, I should say, for I am very umble still), you might, unbeknown, go against me rather, with my Agnes. I call her mine, you see, Master Copperfield. There's a song that says, "I'd crowns resign, to call her mine!" I hope to do it, one of these days.'

Dear Agnes! Too good for any one that I could think of, was it possible that she was reserved to be the wife of such a wretch as this!

'There's no hurry at present, you know, Master Copperfield,' Uriah proceeded, in his slimy way. 'My Agnes is very young still; and mother and me will have to make a good many new arrangements, before it would be quite convenient. So I shall have time gradually to make her familiar with my hopes, as opportunities offer. I'm so much obliged to you for this confidence! It's such a relief to know that you understand our situation, and are certain (as you wouldn't wish to make unpleasantness in the family) not to go against me!'

He took the hand which I dared not withhold, and having given it a damp squeeze, referred to his pale-faced watch.

'Dear me!' he said, 'it's past one. The ouse that I am stopping at will have gone to bed these two hours.'

'I am sorry,' I returned, 'that there is only one bed here, and that I–'

'Don't think of mentioning beds, Master Copperfield!' he rejoined ecstatically. 'But *would* you have any objections to my laying down before the fire?'

As no arguments I could urge, in my bewildered condition, had the least effect in inducing him to accept my bedroom, I was obliged to make the best arrangements I could, for his repose before the fire. The mattress of the sofa, the sofa pillows, a blanket and a great-coat made him a bed for which he was more than thankful.

I never shall forget that night, how I wearied myself with thinking about Agnes and this creature; how I considered what could I do, and could come to no other conclusion than that the best course was to keep to myself what I had heard. When I awoke, the recollection that Uriah was lying in the next room oppressed me as if I had had some meaner quality of devil for a lodger.

When I saw him going downstairs early in the morning (for, thank Heaven! he would not stay to breakfast), it appeared to me as if the night was going away in his person. When I went out to the Commons, I charged Mrs Crupp with particular directions to leave the windows open, that my sitting-room might be aired, and purged of his presence.

CHAPTER 26

I fall into Captivity

I saw no more of Uriah Heep until the day Agnes left town. I was at the coach-office to take leave of her and there was he, returning to Canterbury by the same conveyance. It was some small satisfaction to me to observe his high-shouldered, mulberry-coloured great-coat perched up on the roof, while Agnes was, of course, inside. At the coach-window he hovered about us like a great vulture; gorging himself on every syllable that I said to Agnes, or Agnes said to me.

I had thought very much of the words Agnes had used in reference to the partnership: 'Feeling sure it was necessary for papa's peace that the sacrifice should be made, I entreated him to make it.' A miserable foreboding that she would yield to the same feeling in reference to any sacrifice for his sake had oppressed me ever since. I had no consolation in seeing how different she was from this detestable Rufus with the mulberry-coloured coat, for I felt that in the self-denial of her pure soul and the sordid baseness of his, the greatest danger lay. All this, doubtless, he knew thoroughly, and had, in his cunning, considered well.

Yet, I was so certain that the prospect of such a sacrifice cast no shadow on her yet, that I could as soon have injured her, as given her any warning. Thus we parted without explanation; she smiling farewell from the coach-window; her evil genius writhing on the roof, as if he had her in his clutches.

I could not get over this farewell glimpse of them for a long time. I had ample leisure to refine upon my uneasiness: for Steerforth was at Oxford and, when I was not at the Commons, I was very much alone.

In the meantime, days and weeks slipped away. I was articled to Spenlow and Jorkins. On the day when I was articled, no festivity took place, beyond my having sandwiches and sherry into the office for the clerks, and going alone to the theatre at night. Mr Spenlow remarked, on this occasion, when we concluded our business, that he should have been happy to have seen me at his house at Norwood to celebrate our becoming connected, but for his domestic arrangements being in some disorder, on account of the expected return of his daughter from finishing her education at Paris. I knew that he was a widower with one daughter, and expressed my acknowledgments.

In a week or two, he said that if I would do him the favour to come down next Saturday, and stay till Monday, he would be extremely happy. Of course I said I *would* do him the favour; and he was to drive me down in his phaeton, and to bring me back.

The phaeton was a very handsome affair; the horses arched their necks and lifted up their legs as if they knew they belonged to Doctors' Commons. We were very pleasant, going down, and Mr Spenlow gave me some hints in reference to my profession. He said it was the genteelest profession in the world, and must on no account be confounded with the profession of a solicitor: being quite another sort of thing, infinitely more exclusive, less mechanical, and more profitable.

There was a lovely garden to Mr Spenlow's house, and I was quite enchanted. There was a charming lawn, there were clusters of trees, and there were perspective walks that I could just distinguish in the dark, arched over with trellis-work.

We went into the house and into a hall where there were all sorts of hats, caps, whips, and walking-sticks. 'Where is Miss Dora?' said Mr Spenlow to the servant. 'Dora!' I thought. 'What a beautiful name!'

We turned into a room near at hand and I heard a voice say, 'Mr Copperfield, my daughter Dora, and my daughter Dora's confidential friend!' It was, no doubt, Mr Spenlow's voice, but I didn't care whose it was. All was over in a moment. I was a captive and a slave. I loved Dora Spenlow to distraction!

I was swallowed up in an abyss of love in an instant. There was no pausing on the brink; no looking down, or looking back; I was gone, headlong, before I had sense to say a word to her.

'*I*,' observed a well-remembered voice, when I had bowed and murmured something, 'have seen Mr Copperfield before.'

The speaker was not Dora. No; the confidential friend, Miss Murdstone!

I don't think I was much astonished. There was nothing worth mentioning in the material world, but Dora Spenlow, to be astonished about. I said, 'How do you do, Miss Murdstone? I hope you are well.' She answered, 'Very well.' I said, 'How is Mr Murdstone?' She replied, 'My brother is robust, I am obliged to you.'

Mr Spenlow then put in his word.

'I am glad to find,' he said, 'Copperfield, that you and Miss Murdstone are already acquainted.'

'Mr Copperfield and myself,' said Miss Murdstone, with severe composure, 'were once slightly acquainted. It was in his childish days. I should not have known him.'

I replied that I should have known her anywhere.

'My daughter Dora having, unhappily, no mother,' said Mr Spenlow, 'Miss Murdstone is obliging enough to become her companion and protector.'

A passing thought occurred to me that Miss Murdstone was not so much designed for purposes of protection as of assault. But as I had none but passing thoughts for any subject save Dora, I glanced at her and saw, in her prettily pettish manner, that she was not much inclined to be confidential to her companion and protector, when the dinner-bell rang.

There was some company. I don't remember who was there, except Dora. I have not the least idea what we had for dinner, besides Dora. My impression is that I dined off Dora entirely, and sent away half-a-dozen plates untouched. I sat next to her. I talked to her. She had the most delightful little voice, the gayest little laugh, the pleasantest and most fascinating little ways that ever led a lost youth into hopeless slavery.

When she went out of the room with Miss Murdstone, I fell into a reverie, only disturbed by the cruel apprehension that Miss Murdstone would disparage me to her. My apprehensions of being disparaged were revived when we went into the drawing-room, but I was relieved of them in an unexpected manner.

'David Copperfield,' said Miss Murdstone, beckoning me aside. 'A word.'

I confronted Miss Murdstone alone.

'David Copperfield,' said Miss Murdstone, 'I do not wish to revive the memory of past differences, or of past outrages. I have received outrages from a person who is not to be mentioned without scorn and therefore I would rather not mention her.'

I felt very fiery on my aunt's account; but I said it would certainly be better, if Miss Murdstone pleased, *not* to mention her. I could not hear her disrespectfully mentioned, I added.

Miss Murdstone disdainfully inclined her head, then resumed: 'I shall not attempt to disguise the fact that I formed an unfavourable opinion of you in your childhood. It may have been a mistaken one, or you may have ceased to justify it. That is not in question between us now. I may have my opinion of you. You may have your opinion of me.'

I inclined my head, in my turn.

'But it is not necessary,' said Miss Murdstone, 'that these opinions should come into collision here. As the chances of life have brought us together again, I would say let us meet here as distant acquaintances. It is quite unnecessary that either of us should make the other the subject of remark. Do you approve of this?'

'Miss Murdstone,' I returned, 'I think you and Mr Murdstone used me very cruelly, and treated my mother with great unkindness. I shall always think so, as long as I live. But I quite agree in what you propose.'

Miss Murdstone bent her head. Then, just touching the back of my hand with the tips of her cold, stiff fingers, she walked away, arranging the little fetters on her wrists.

All I know of the rest of the evening is that I heard the empress of my heart sing enchanted ballads in the French language, generally to the effect that, whatever was the matter, we ought always to dance, Ta ra la, Ta ra la! That when Miss Murdstone took her into custody and led her away, she smiled and gave me her delicious hand. That I caught a view of myself in a mirror, looking perfectly idiotic. That I retired to bed in a most maudlin state of mind, and got up in a crisis of feeble infatuation.

It was a fine morning, and I thought I would take a stroll down one of those wire-arched walks. The garden was cool and solitary. I walked about, wondering what my feelings of happiness would be, if I could ever become engaged to this dear wonder. To be allowed to call her 'Dora,' to write to her, to dote upon and worship her, to have reason to think that when she was with other people she was yet mindful of me, seemed to me the summit of human ambition. There is no doubt that I was a lackadaisical young spooney but there was a purity of heart in all this, that prevents my having quite a contemptuous recollection of it, let me laugh as I may.

I had not been walking long, when I turned a corner, and met her.

'You – are – out early, Miss Spenlow,' said I.

'It's so stupid at home,' she replied, 'and Miss Murdstone talks such nonsense about its being necessary for the day to be aired, before I come out. Aired!' (She laughed, here, in the most melodious manner.) 'On a Sunday morning, I must do something. Besides, it's the brightest time of the whole day. Don't you think?'

I hazarded that it was very bright to me then, though it had been very dark to me a minute before.

'Do you mean a compliment?' said Dora, 'or that the weather has really changed?'

I stammered worse than before, in replying that I meant no compliment, but the plain truth; though I was not aware of any change having taken place in the weather. It was in the state of my own feelings, I added bashfully; to clench the explanation.

I never saw such curls as those she shook out to hide her blushes. As to the straw hat and blue ribbons which was on the top of the curls, if I could only have hung it up in my room in Buckingham Street, what a priceless possession it would have been!

She was shaking the curls again, when her little dog came running along the walk. He was mortally jealous of me, and persisted in barking. She took him up in her arms but he persisted upon barking still. At length he was quiet – well he might be with her dimpled chin upon his head! – and we walked away to look at a greenhouse.

'You are not very intimate with Miss Murdstone, are you?' said Dora.

'No,' I replied. 'Not at all so.'

'She is a tiresome creature,' said Dora, pouting. 'I can't think what papa can have been about, when he chose such a vexatious thing to be my companion. Papa calls her my confidential friend, but I am sure she is no such thing. We are not going to confide in any such cross people, Jip and I. We mean to find out our own friends, instead of having them found out for us – don't we, Jip?'

Jip made a comfortable noise, in answer, a little like a tea-kettle when it sings.

The greenhouse contained quite a show of beautiful geraniums. We loitered along and Dora stopped to admire this one or that one, and I stopped to admire the same one, and Dora, laughing, held the dog up childishly, to smell the flowers; and if we were not all three in Fairyland, certainly *I* was.

Miss Murdstone found us here and marched us into breakfast as if it were a soldier's funeral.

We had a quiet day. No company, a walk, a family dinner of four, and an evening of looking over books and pictures; Miss Murdstone with a homily before her, and her eye upon us, keeping guard. Ah! little did Mr Spenlow imagine, when he sat opposite to me after dinner that day, how fervently I was embracing him, in my fancy, as his son-in-law!

We departed early in the morning, for we had a Salvage case coming on at the Admiralty court. Dora was at the breakfast-table and I had the melancholy pleasure of taking off my hat to her in the phaeton, as she stood on the door-step with Jip in her arms.

What the Admiralty was to me that day; what nonsense I made of our case in my mind, as I listened to it; and how I felt when Mr Spenlow went home without me; I shall make no fruitless effort to describe. If that sleepy old court could rouse itself, and present in any visible form the daydreams I have had in it about Dora, it would reveal my truth.

I don't mean the dreams that I dreamed on that day alone, but day after day, from week to week, and term to term. I went there, not to attend to what was going on, but to think about Dora.

Within the first week of my passion, I bought four sumptuous waist-coats – not for myself; *I* had no pride in them; for Dora – and took to wearing straw-coloured kid gloves in the streets. I walked miles upon miles daily in the hope of seeing her. Not only was I soon as well known on the Norwood Road as the postmen, but I pervaded London likewise. I walked about the streets where the best shops for ladies were. I haunted the Bazaar like an unquiet spirit, I fagged through the Park again and again. Sometimes, on rare occasions, I saw her. Perhaps I met her and spoke to her. In the latter case I was always very miserable afterwards, to think she had no idea of the extent of my devotion. I was always looking out for another invitation to Mr Spenlow's house. I was always being disappointed, for I got none.

Mrs Crupp must have been a woman of penetration; for when this attachment was but a few weeks old she found it out.

'Cheer up, sir,' said Mrs Crupp. 'I can't abear to see you so, sir. I know what it is, sir.'

'Mrs Crupp?' I returned, reddening.

'Oh, bless you!' said Mrs Crupp, nodding encouragement. 'If she don't smile upon you, there's a many as will. You are a young gentleman to *be* smiled on, Mr Copperfull, and you must learn your walue, sir.'

Mrs Crupp always called me Mr Copperfull: firstly, no doubt, because it was not my name; and secondly, I am inclined to think, in some indistinct association with a washing-day.

'What makes you suppose there is any young lady in the case, Mrs Crupp?' said I.

'Sir,' said Mrs Crupp, in a tone approaching to severity, 'I've laundressed other young gentlemen besides yourself. A young gentleman may be over-careful of himself, or he may be under-careful of himself. He may brush his hair too regular, or too unregular. But let him go to which extreme he may, sir, there's a young lady in both of 'em.'

Mrs Crupp shook her head in such a determined manner, that I had not an inch of 'vantage-ground left.

'You are a young gentleman, Mr Copperfull, and my adwice to you is, to cheer up and to know your own walue,' said Mrs Crupp. 'If you was to take to skittles now, which is healthy, you might find it divert your mind, and do you good.'

With these words, Mrs Crupp retired. As her figure disappeared into the gloom of the entry, this counsel certainly presented itself to my mind in the light of a slight liberty on Mrs Crupp's part; but, at the same time, I was content to receive it, in another point of view, as a word to the wise, and a warning in future to keep my secret better.

CHAPTER 27

Tommy Traddles

It may have been for no better reason than because there was a certain similarity in the sound of the word skittles and Traddles, that it came into my head, next day, to go and look after my old schoolfellow. He lived near the Veterinary College at Camden Town, which was principally tenanted, as one of our clerks informed me, by gentlemen students, who bought live donkeys, and made experiments on those quadrupeds in their private apartments.

I found that the street was not as desirable as I could have wished it to be, for the sake of Traddles. The inhabitants appeared to have a propensity to throw any little trifles they were not in want of, into the road: which not only made it rank and sloppy, but untidy too, on account of the cabbage-leaves.

The general air of the place reminded me forcibly of the days when I lived with Mr and Mrs Micawber. An indescribable character of faded gentility attached to the house I sought. Happening to arrive at the door as it was opened to the afternoon milkman, I was reminded of Mr and Mrs Micawber more forcibly yet.

'Now,' said the milkman to a very youthful servant girl. 'Has that there little bill of mine been heerd on?'

'Oh, master says he'll attend to it immediate,' was the reply.

'Because,' said the milkman, speaking, as I judged from his tone for the edification of somebody within the house, 'because that there little bill has been running so long, that I begin to believe it's run away altogether, and never won't be heerd of.'

The voice of the youthful servant became faint, but she seemed to me again to murmur that it would be attended to immediate.

'I tell you what,' said the milkman, taking her by the chin, 'are you fond of milk?'

'Yes, I likes it,' she replied.

'Good,' said the milkman. 'Then you won't have none to-morrow. D'ye hear?'

I thought she seemed, upon the whole, relieved, by the prospect of having any to-day. The milkman released her chin and with anything rather than good-will opened his can, and deposited the usual quantity in the family jug. This done, he went away, muttering.

'Does Mr Traddles live here?' I then inquired.

Upon which the youthful servant replied 'Yes.'

I walked in, and in pursuance of the servant's directions walked up-stairs. Traddles was on the landing to meet me. He gave me welcome, with great heartiness, to his little room. It was extremely neat, though sparely furnished. His table was covered with papers, and he was hard at work in an old coat.

'Traddles,' said I, shaking hands with him again, after I had sat down, 'I am delighted to see you.'

'I am delighted to see *you*, Copperfield,' he returned. 'It was because I was thoroughly glad to see you when we met that I gave you this address instead of my chambers.'

'Oh! You have chambers?' said I.

'I have the fourth of a room and a passage, and the fourth of a clerk,' returned Traddles. 'Three others and myself unite to have a set of chambers – to look business-like – and we quarter the clerk too. Half-a-crown a week he costs me.'

'You are reading for the bar, Mr Waterbrook informed me?' I said.

'Why, yes,' said Traddles. 'The fact is, I have just begun to keep my terms, after rather a long delay. It's some time since I was articled, but the payment of that hundred pounds was a great pull. A great pull!' said Traddles, with a wince, as if he had had a tooth out.

'Do you know, Traddles, I can't help thinking of that sky-blue suit you used to wear.'

'Lord, to be sure!' cried Traddles, laughing. 'Those were happy times, weren't they?'

'I think our schoolmaster might have made them happier, without doing any harm to any of us,' I returned.

'But there was a good deal of fun going on. Do you remember the nights in the bedroom? When you used to tell the stories? Old Creakle! I should like to see him again, too!'

'He was a brute to you, Traddles,' said I, indignantly.

'Do you think so?' returned Traddles. 'Perhaps he was, rather. But it's all over, a long while.'

'You were brought up by an uncle, then?' said I.

'He died soon after I left school. I had never been brought up to any profession, and at first I was at a loss what to do for myself. However, I began, with the assistance of the son of a professional man, who had been to Salem House, to copy law writings. Then I began to state cases for them, and make abstracts, and do that sort of work. I got a good many jobs. I was fortunate enough to become acquainted with a person who was getting up an Encyclopaedia, and he set me to work; and, indeed' (glancing at his table), 'I am at work for him at this minute. I am not a bad compiler, Copperfield,' said Traddles, preserving the same air of cheerful confidence in all he said, 'but I have no invention at all; not a particle.'

As Traddles seemed to expect that I should assent to this as a matter of course, I nodded; and he went on, 'Now, Copperfield, it's so pleasant to see you, that I shan't conceal anything. Therefore you must know that I am engaged.

'She's a curate's daughter, one of ten, down in Devonshire. She is such a dear girl! A little older than me, but the dearest girl! I dare say ours is likely to be a rather long engagement, but our motto is "Wait and hope!" And she would wait, Copperfield, till she was sixty – any age you can mention – for me! In the meantime, and this is the end of my prosing about myself, I get on as well as I can. I don't make much, but I don't spend much. I board with the people down-stairs, who are very agreeable. Both Mr and Mrs Micawber have seen a good deal of life, and are excellent company.'

'Mr and Mrs Micawber!' I repeated. 'Why, I am intimately acquainted with them!'

An opportune double knock at the door, which I knew well, resolved any doubt in my mind as to their being my old friends. I begged Traddles to ask his landlord to walk up and Mr Micawber, not a bit changed, came into the room.

'I beg your pardon, Mr Traddles,' said Mr Micawber, with the old roll in his voice, 'I was not aware that there was any individual, alien to this tenement, in your sanctum.'

'How do you do, Mr Micawber?' said I.

He examined my features, fell back, cried, 'Is it possible! Have I the pleasure of again beholding Copperfield!' and shook me by both hands with the utmost fervour.

'Good Heaven, Mr Traddles!' said Mr Micawber, 'to think that I should find you acquainted with the friend of my youth, the companion of earlier days! My dear!' calling over the banisters to Mrs Micawber, while Traddles looked not a little amazed at this description of me, 'Here is a gentleman in Mr Traddles's apartment, whom he wishes to have the pleasure of presenting to you, my love!'

Mr Micawber immediately reappeared, and shook hands with me again.

'You find us, Copperfield,' said Mr Micawber, with one eye on Traddles, 'at present established, on what may be designated as a small and unassuming scale; but, you are aware that I have, in the course of my career, surmounted difficulties, and conquered obstacles. You are no stranger to the fact, that there have been periods of my life, when it has been requisite that I should pause, until certain expected events should turn up; when it has been necessary that I should fall back, before making what I trust I shall not be accused of presumption in terming – a spring. The present is one of those momentous stages in the life of man. You find me, fallen back, *for* a spring; and I have every reason to believe that a vigorous leap will shortly be the result.'

I was expressing my satisfaction, when Mrs Micawber came in.

'My dear,' said Mr Micawber, leading her towards me. 'Here is a gentleman of the name of Copperfield who wishes to renew his acquaintance with you.'

It would have been better, as it turned out, to have led gently up to this announcement, for Mrs Micawber was taken so unwell, that Mr Micawber was obliged to run down to the water-butt in the back yard and draw a basinful to lave her brow with. She presently revived, however, and was really pleased to see me. We had half-an-hour's talk, all together; and I asked her about the twins, who, she said, were 'grown great creatures,' and after Master and Miss Micawber, whom she described as 'absolute giants,' but they were not produced on that occasion.

Mr Micawber was very anxious that I should stay to dinner. I should not have been averse to do so, but that I imagined I detected calculation relative to the extent of the cold meat, in Mrs Micawber's eye. I therefore pleaded another engagement; but I told Traddles, and Mr and Mrs Micawber, that they must appoint a day when they would come and dine with me. An appointment was made for the purpose, that suited us all, and then I took my leave.

Mr Micawber, under pretence of showing me a nearer way than that by which I had come, accompanied me to the corner of the street.

'My dear Copperfield,' said Mr Micawber, 'I need hardly tell you that to have beneath our roof a mind like that which gleams in your friend Traddles, is an unspeakable comfort. You may imagine that his society is a source of consolation to myself and to Mrs Micawber. I am at present, my dear Copperfield, engaged in the sale of corn upon commission. It is not an avocation of a remunerative description – in other words, it does *not* pay – and some temporary embarrassments of a pecuniary nature have been the consequence. I am, however, delighted to add that I have now an immediate prospect of something turning up, which I trust will enable me to provide, permanently, both for myself and for your friend Traddles, in whom I have an unaffected interest. You may, perhaps, be prepared to hear that Mrs Micawber is in a state of health which renders it not wholly improbable that an addition may be ultimately made to those pledges of affection which – in short, to the infantine group. Mrs Micawber's family have been so good as to express their dissatisfaction at this state of things. I have merely to observe, that I am not aware it is any business of theirs, and that I repel that exhibition of feeling with scorn, and with defiance!'

Mr Micawber then shook hands with me again, and left.

CHAPTER 28

Mr Micawber's Gauntlet

Until the day arrived on which I was to entertain my newly-found old friends, I lived principally on Dora and coffee. In my love-lorn condition, my appetite languished; for I felt as though it would have been an act of perfidy towards Dora to have a natural relish for my dinner.

On the occasion of this domestic little party, I provided a pair of soles, a small leg of mutton, and a pigeon-pie. Mrs Crupp broke out into rebellion on my first hint in reference to the cooking of the fish and joint. But, in the end, a compromise was effected; and Mrs Crupp consented to achieve this feat, on condition that I dined from home for a fortnight afterwards.

Having laid in the materials for a bowl of punch; having provided a bottle of lavender-water, two wax candles and a pincushion, to assist Mrs Micawber in her toilette at my dressing-table; and having laid the cloth with my own hands, I awaited the result with composure.

At the appointed time, my three visitors arrived together. Mr Micawber with more shirt-collar than usual; Mrs Micawber with her cap in a paper parcel; Traddles supporting Mrs Micawber on his arm. They were all delighted with my residence.

'My dear Copperfield,' said Mr Micawber, 'this is luxurious. This is a way of life which reminds me of the period when I was myself in a state of celibacy, and Mrs Micawber had not yet been solicited to plight her faith at the Hymeneal altar.'

'He means, solicited by him, Mr Copperfield,' said Mrs Micawber, archly. 'He cannot answer for others.'

'My dear,' returned Mr Micawber with sudden seriousness, 'I have no desire to answer for others. I am too well aware that when you were reserved for me, it is possible you may have been reserved for one destined to fall a victim to pecuniary involvements of a complicated nature. I understand your allusion, my love. I regret it, but I can bear it.'

'Micawber!' exclaimed Mrs Micawber, in tears. 'Have I deserved this! I, who never have deserted you; who never *will* desert you, Micawber!'

'My love,' said Mr Micawber, much affected, then embraced Mrs Micawber, and pressed my hand.

To divert his thoughts from this melancholy subject, I informed Mr Micawber that I relied upon him for a bowl of punch, and led him to the lemons. His recent despondency was gone in a moment. I never saw a man so thoroughly enjoy himself amid the odour of burning rum as Mr Micawber did that afternoon. It was wonderful to see his face shining at us as he stirred, and mixed, and tasted. As to Mrs Micawber, I don't know whether it was the effect of the lavender-water or the wax candles, but she came out of my room, comparatively speaking, lovely. And the lark was never gayer than that excellent woman.

I suppose – I never ventured to inquire – that Mrs Crupp, after frying the soles, was taken ill. Because we broke down at that point. The leg of mutton came up very red within, and very pale without: besides having a foreign substance of a gritty nature sprinkled over it, as if it had had a fall into ashes. The pigeon-pie was not bad, but delusive: the crust being like a disappointing head, phrenologically speaking: full of lumps and bumps, with nothing particular underneath. In short, the banquet was such a failure that I should have been quite unhappy if I had not been relieved by a bright suggestion from Mr Micawber.

'My dear friend Copperfield,' said Mr Micawber, 'accidents will occur in the best-regulated families. If the young person in attendance could produce a gridiron, I would put it to you that this little misfortune may be easily repaired.'

There was a gridiron in the pantry, on which my morning rasher of bacon was cooked. We had it in, in a twinkling, and immediately applied ourselves to carrying Mr Micawber's idea into effect. Traddles cut the mutton into slices; Mr Micawber covered them with pepper, mustard, salt, and cayenne; I put them on the gridiron and took them off, under Mr Micawber's direction; and Mrs Micawber heated some mushroom ketchup in a little saucepan. When we had slices enough done to begin upon, we fell to.

What with the novelty of this cookery, the bustle of it, the being so flushed with the fire, so amused, and in the midst of such a tempting noise and savour, we reduced the leg of mutton to the bone. My own appetite came back miraculously. I am ashamed to record it, but I really believe I forgot Dora for a little while. Mr and Mrs Micawber could not have enjoyed the feast more, if they had sold a bed to provide it. Traddles laughed as heartily as he ate and worked. Indeed, we all did, and I dare say there never was a greater success.

We were at the height of our enjoyment, when I was aware of a strange presence in the room, and my eyes encountered those of the staid Littimer, standing hat in hand before me.

'I beg your pardon, sir, I was directed to come in. Is my master not here, sir?'

'No.'

'Have you not seen him, sir?'

'No; don't you come from him?'

'Not immediately so, sir. But I should think he might be here to-morrow, as he has not been here to-day.'

With which he took the fork from my unresisting hand, and bent over the gridiron.

We should not have been much discomposed, I dare say, by the appearance of Steerforth himself, but we became in a moment the meekest of the meek before his respectable serving-man. I was a mere infant at the head of my own table; and hardly ventured to glance at the respectable phenomenon, who had come from Heaven knows where, to put my establishment to rights.

Meanwhile he took the mutton off the gridiron, and gravely handed it round. We all took some, but our appreciation of it was gone. As we severally pushed away our plates, he removed them, and set on the cheese. He took that off, too, when it was done with; cleared the table; gave us our wine-glasses; and, of his own accord, wheeled the dumb-waiter into the pantry. All this was done in a perfect manner, yet, his very elbows, when he had his back towards me, seemed to teem with the expression of his fixed opinion that I was extremely young.

'Can I do anything more, sir?'

I thanked him and said, No; but would he take no dinner himself?

'None, I am obliged to you, sir. I wish you good-night, sir.'

He comprehended everybody present, in the respectful bow with which he followed these words, and disappeared. My visitors seemed to breathe more freely when he was gone.

'Punch, my dear Copperfield,' said Mr Micawber, tasting it, 'like time and tide, waits for no man. Ah! it is at the present moment in high flavour. My love, will you give me your opinion?'

Mrs Micawber pronounced it excellent.

'Then I will drink,' said Mr Micawber, 'to the days when my friend Copperfield and myself were younger, and fought our way in the world side by side.'

Mr Micawber took a pull at his punch. So we all did: Traddles evidently lost in wondering at what distant time Mr Micawber and I could have been comrades in the battle of the world.

'As we are quite confidential here, Mr Copperfield,' said Mrs Micawber, 'Mr Traddles being a part of our domesticity, I should much like to have your opinion on Mr Micawber's prospects. For corn,' said Mrs Micawber argumentatively, 'as I have repeatedly said to Mr Micawber, may be gentlemanly, but it is not remunerative. Commission to the extent of two and ninepence in a fortnight cannot, however limited our ideas, be considered remunerative.'

We were all agreed upon that.

'Then,' said Mrs Micawber, who prided herself on taking a clear view of things, 'I ask myself this question. If corn is not to be relied upon, what is? I naturally look round the world, and say, "What is there in which a person of Mr Micawber's talent is likely to succeed?" Now I am convinced, myself, that things cannot be expected to turn up of themselves. We must assist to turn them up. I may be wrong, but I have formed that opinion.'

Both Traddles and I applauded it highly.

'Very well,' said Mrs Micawber. 'Here is Mr Micawber, with great talent – *I* should say, with genius, but that may be the partiality of a wife -'

Traddles and I both murmured 'No.'

'And here is Mr Micawber without any suitable position or employment. Where does that responsibility rest? Clearly on society. Then I would boldly challenge society to set it right. It appears to me, my dear Mr Copperfield,' said Mrs Micawber, forcibly, 'that what Mr Micawber has to do, is to throw down the gauntlet to society, and say, in effect, "Show me who will take that up. Let the party immediately step forward."'

I ventured to ask Mrs Micawber how this was to be done.

'By advertising,' said Mrs Micawber. 'It appears to me, that what Mr Micawber has to do, is to advertise in all the papers; to describe himself plainly as so-and-so, with such and such qualifications, and to put it thus: "*Now* employ me, on remunerative terms, and address, post-paid, to W. M., Post Office, Camden Town."'

'This idea of Mrs Micawber's, my dear Copperfield,' said Mr Micawber, glancing at me sideways, 'is, in fact, the Leap to which I alluded, when I last had the pleasure of seeing you.'

'Advertising is rather expensive,' I remarked, dubiously.

'Exactly so!' said Mrs Micawber, preserving the same logical air. 'It is for that reason especially, that I think Mr Micawber ought to raise a certain sum of money – on a bill.'

Mr Micawber, leaning back in his chair, cast his eyes up at the ceiling;

but I thought him observant of Traddles, too, who was looking at the fire.

'If no member of my family,' said Mrs Micawber, 'is possessed of sufficient natural feeling to negotiate that bill then my opinion is that Mr Micawber should go into the City, and should dispose of it for what he can get. If the individuals in the Money Market oblige Mr Micawber to sustain a great sacrifice, that is between themselves and their consciences. I recommend Mr Micawber to do the same; to regard it as an investment which is sure of return, and to make up his mind to *any* sacrifice.'

I felt, I don't know why, that this was self-denying and devoted in Mrs Micawber, and I uttered a murmur to that effect. Traddles did likewise.

'I will not,' said Mrs Micawber, finishing her punch, 'protract these remarks on the subject of Mr Micawber's pecuniary affairs. I am aware that I am merely a female; still I must not forget that my papa was in the habit of saying, "Emma's form is fragile, but her grasp of a subject is inferior to none." That my papa was too partial, I well know; but that he was an observer of character in some degree, my duty and my reason forbid me to doubt.'

With these words, Mrs Micawber retired to my bedroom. And really I felt that she was a noble woman who might have been a Roman matron, and done all manner of heroic things, in times of public trouble.

In the fervour of this impression, I congratulated Mr Micawber on the treasure he possessed. So did Traddles. Mr Micawber extended his hand to each of us. He was full of eloquence. He gave us to understand that in our children we lived again, and that any accession to their number was doubly welcome. He said that Mrs Micawber had latterly had her doubts on this point, but he had dispelled them. As to her family, their sentiments were utterly indifferent to him, and they might – I quote his own expression – go to the Devil.

Mr Micawber then delivered a warm eulogy on Traddles. He feelingly alluded to the young lady, unknown, whom Traddles had honoured with his affection. Mr Micawber pledged her. So did I.

Mr Micawber took an early opportunity after that of hinting at the state of *my* affections. After a good deal of blushing, stammering, and denying, I said, having my glass in my hand, 'Well! I would give them D!' which so excited and gratified Mr Micawber, that he ran with a glass of punch into my bedroom, in order that Mrs Micawber might drink D, who drank it with enthusiasm, crying from within, 'My dear Mr Copperfield, I am delighted.'

Our conversation afterwards took a more worldly turn; Mr Micawber telling us that he found Camden Town inconvenient, and that the first thing he contemplated doing, when the advertisement should have been the cause of something satisfactory turning up, was to move. He mentioned a terrace at the western end of Oxford Street, fronting Hyde Park, but which he did not expect to attain immediately. There would probably be an interval, in which he should content himself – say in Piccadilly – which would be a cheerful situation where they might live comfortably for a few years. Wherever his abode might be, we might rely on this – there would always be a room for Traddles, and a knife and fork for me. We acknowledged his kindness.

It was between ten and eleven o'clock when Mrs Micawber put on her bonnet. Mr Micawber took the opportunity of Traddles putting on his great-coat, to slip a letter into my hand, with a whispered request that I would read it at my leisure. I also took the opportunity to detain Traddles for a moment on the top of the stairs.

'Traddles,' said I, 'Mr Micawber don't mean any harm, poor fellow: but, if I were you, I wouldn't lend him anything.'

'My dear Copperfield,' returned Traddles, smiling, 'I haven't got anything to lend.'

'You have got a name, you know,' said I.

'Oh!' said Traddles. 'I am afraid I have lent him that already.'

'To the bill that is to be a certain investment?'

'No,' said Traddles. 'Mine's another.'

'I hope there will be nothing wrong about it,' said I.

'I should think not, because he told me that it was provided for. That was Mr Micawber's expression, "Provided for."'

Mr Micawber looking up at this juncture to where we were standing, I had only time to repeat my caution. Traddles thanked me, and descended. But I was much afraid, when I observed the good-natured manner in which he gave Mrs Micawber his arm, that he would be carried into the Money Market neck and heels.

I returned to my fireside, and was musing on the character of Mr Micawber, when I heard a quick step ascending the stairs. At first, I thought it was Traddles coming back for something but as the step approached, I knew it, and felt my heart beat high, for it was Steerforth's.

I was never unmindful of Agnes, but when he stood before me with his hand out, I felt ashamed of having doubted one I loved so heartily.

'Why, Daisy, old boy!' laughed Steerforth, shaking my hand heartily, and throwing it away. 'Have I detected you in another feast? How are you, my Bacchanal?'

'I am very well,' said I; 'and not at all Bacchanalian to-night, though I confess to another party of three.'

'All of whom I met in the street, talking loud in your praise,' returned Steerforth. 'Who's our friend in the tights?'

I gave him the best idea I could, in a few words, of Mr Micawber. He laughed heartily at my feeble portrait of that gentleman, and said he was a man to know.

'But who do you suppose our other friend is?' said I.

'Not a bore, I hope? I thought he looked a little like one.'

'Traddles!' I replied, triumphantly.

'Who's he?' asked Steerforth, in his careless way.

'Don't you remember Traddles? Traddles in our room at Salem House?'

'Oh! That fellow!' said Steerforth. 'Where the deuce did you pick *him* up?'

I extolled Traddles in my reply, as highly as I could; for I felt that Steerforth rather slighted him. Steerforth, dismissing the subject with a smile, inquired if I could give him anything to eat? I got out the remains of the pigeon-pie, and so forth.

'Why, Daisy, here's a supper for a king!' he exclaimed, starting out of his silence, with a burst, and taking his seat at the table. 'I shall do it justice, for I have come from Yarmouth.'

'Littimer was here to-day, to inquire for you,' I remarked.

'Littimer is a greater fool than I thought him, to have been inquiring for me at all,' said Steerforth, jovially pouring out a glass of wine.

'So you have been at Yarmouth, Steerforth!'

'An *escapade* of a week or so.'

'And how are they all? Of course, little Emily is not married yet?'

'Not yet. Going to be, I believe – in so many weeks, or months, or something or other. I have not seen much of 'em. By-the-by;' he began feeling in his pockets; 'I have a letter for you from your old nurse. Old what's-his-name's in a bad way.'

'Barkis, do you mean?'

'Yes! It's all over with poor Barkis, I am afraid. Here it is.'

The letter was from Peggotty; something less legible than usual, and brief. It informed me of her husband's hopeless state. It said nothing of her weariness and watching, and praised him highly. It was written with a plain, unaffected, homely piety and ended with 'my duty to my ever darling' – meaning myself.

While I deciphered it, Steerforth continued to eat and drink. 'It's a bad job,' he said, when I had done; 'but the sun sets every day, and people die every minute, and we mustn't be scared by the common lot. No! Ride on! Rough-shod if need be, smooth-shod if that will do, but ride on! Ride on over all obstacles, and win the race!'

'And win what race?' said I.

'The race that one has started in,' said he. 'Ride on!'

'I tell you what, Steerforth,' said I, 'if your high spirits will listen to me –'

'They are potent spirits, and will do whatever you like,' he answered.

'I will go down and see my old nurse. She will take it so kindly, that it will be a comfort and support to her.'

'Well! Go. You can do no harm.'

'You have just come back,' said I, 'and it would be in vain to ask you to go with me?'

'Quite,' he returned. 'I am for Highgate to-night. I wanted you to come and stay a few days with us. Here I am, on purpose to bid you, and you fly off to Yarmouth!'

'You are a nice fellow to talk of flying off, Steerforth.'

'Say the next day, and pass as much of to-morrow as you can with us! I want you to stand between Rosa Dartle and me, and keep us asunder.'

'Would you love each other too much, without me?'

'Yes; or hate,' laughed Steerforth. 'Say the next day!'

I said the next day; and he put on his great-coat and lighted his cigar, and set off to walk home. I walked with him as far as the open road. He was in great spirits all the way; and when we parted, I thought of his saying. 'Ride on over all obstacles, and win the race!' and wished that he had some worthy race to run.

I was undressing in my own room, when Mr Micawber's letter tumbled on the floor. It was dated an hour and a half before dinner.

'Sir – for I dare not say my dear Copperfield,

'The present communication is penned within the personal range (I cannot call it the society) of an individual in legal possession of the premises under a distress for rent. His inventory includes, not only the chattels and effects of every description belonging to the undersigned, but also those appertaining to Mr Thomas Traddles.

'If any drop of gloom were wanting it would be found in the fact that a friendly acceptance granted to the undersigned, by the before-mentioned Mr Thomas Traddles, for the sum of £23 4s. 9d is over due, and is NOT provided for. Also, in the fact, that the living responsibilities clinging to the undersigned, will, in the course of nature, be increased by the sum of one more helpless victim; whose miserable appearance may be looked for – in round numbers – at the expiration of a period not exceeding six lunar months from the present date.

'After premising thus much, it would be a work of supererogation to add, that dust and ashes are for ever scattered

'On
'The
'Head
'Of
'WILKINS MICAWBER.'

Poor Traddles! I knew enough of Mr Micawber by this time, to foresee that *he* might be expected to recover the blow; but my night's rest was sorely distressed by thoughts of Traddles, and of the curate's daughter, who was one of ten, down in Devonshire, and who was such a dear girl, and who would wait for Traddles (ominous praise!) until she was sixty, or any age that could be mentioned.

CHAPTER 29

I visit Steerforth at his Home, again

Mrs Steerforth was pleased to see me, and so was Rosa Dartle. I was agreeably surprised to find that Littimer was not at Highgate. But what I particularly observed was the close and attentive watch Miss Dartle kept upon me; and the lurking manner in which she seemed to compare my face with Steerforth's. So surely as I looked towards her, did I see that eager visage, with its gaunt black eyes and searching brow, intent on mine; or passing suddenly from mine to Steerforth's.

When we all four went out walking in the afternoon, she closed her thin hand on my arm like a spring, to keep me back, while Steerforth and his mother went on out of hearing.

'You have been a long time,' she said, 'without coming here. Is your profession really so engaging and interesting as to absorb your whole attention? Is it really, though?'

I replied that I liked it well enough, but that I certainly could not claim so much for it.

'You mean it is a little dry, perhaps?'

'Well,' I replied; 'perhaps it *was* a little dry.'

'Oh! and that's a reason why you want change – excitement, and all that?' said she. 'Ah! very true! But isn't it a little – Eh? – for him?'

A quick glance of her eye towards the spot where Steerforth was walking showed me whom she meant; but beyond that, I was quite lost.

'Don't it make him, perhaps, a little more remiss than usual in his visits to his blindly-doting – eh?' With such a glance at me as seemed to look into my innermost thoughts.

'It certainly is not the fact,' said I, perplexed, 'that I am accountable for Steerforth's having been away from home longer than usual. I have not seen him until last night.'

'No?'

As she looked full at me, I saw her face grow sharper and paler, and the marks of the old wound lengthen.

'What is he doing?' she said, with an eagerness that seemed to consume her like a fire. 'In what is that man assisting him, who never looks at me without an inscrutable falsehood in his eyes? If you are honourable, I don't ask you to betray your friend. I ask you only to tell me, is it anger, is it hatred, is it love, *what is it,* that is leading him?'

'Miss Dartle,' I returned, 'how shall I tell you, so that you will believe me, that I know of nothing in Steerforth different from what there was when I first came here? I hardly understand even what you mean.'

As she stood looking fixedly at me, a throbbing came into that cruel mark and lifted up the corner of her lip as if with scorn. She put her hand upon it hurriedly, and saying, in a fierce, passionate way, 'I swear you to secrecy about this!' said not a word more.

Mrs Steerforth was particularly happy in her son's society, and Steerforth was particularly attentive and respectful to her. It was very interesting to me to see them together. I thought that it was well no serious cause of division had ever come between them; or two such shades of the same nature might have been harder to reconcile than the two extremest opposites in creation. The idea did not originate in my own discernment, I am bound to confess, but in a speech of Rosa Dartle's.

She said at dinner: 'Do tell me, somebody, because I have been thinking about it all day, and I want to know.'

'Pray, Rosa, do not be mysterious,' returned Mrs Steerforth.

'Mysterious!' she cried. 'Oh! really? Do you consider me so?'

'It has become a second nature,' said Mrs Steerfoth, without any displeasure; 'but I remember when your manner was not so guarded, and was more trustful.'

'Really! Less guarded and more trustful? How *can* I have changed, I wonder! I must study to regain my former self.'

'I wish you would,' said Mrs Steerforth, with a smile.

'I will learn frankness from – let me see – from James.'

'You cannot learn frankness, Rosa,' said Mrs Steerforth quickly – for there was always some effect of sarcasm in what Rosa Dartle said – 'in a better school.'

'That I am sure of,' she answered, with uncommon fervour.

Mrs Steerforth appeared to regret having been a little nettled; for she presently said, in a kind tone:

'My dear Rosa, we have not heard what it is that you want to be satisfied about?'

'Oh! It was only whether people, who are like each other in their moral constitution, are in greater danger than people not so circumstanced, supposing any serious variance to arise between them?'

'I should say yes,' said Steerforth.

'Should you?' she retorted. 'Dear me! Supposing then – any unlikely thing will do for a supposition – that you and your mother were to have a serious quarrel.'

'My dear Rosa,' interposed Mrs Steerforth, laughing good-naturedly, 'suggest some other supposition! James and I know our duty to each other better, I pray Heaven!'

'Oh!' said Miss Dartle, nodding her head thoughtfully. 'To be sure. *That* would prevent it? Why, of course it would. I am glad I have been so foolish as to put the case, for it is so very good to know that your duty to each other would prevent it!'

During the whole of this day, Steerforth exerted himself with his utmost skill to charm this singular creature into a pleasant companion. That he should succeed, was no matter of surprise to me. That she should struggle against the influence of his delightful art – delightful nature I thought it then – did not surprise me either; for I knew that she was sometimes jaundiced and perverse. I saw her features and her manner slowly change; I saw her look at him with growing admiration; I saw her try to resist the captivating power that he possessed; and finally, I saw her sharp glance soften, and we sat about the fire, talking and laughing together, with as little reserve as if we had been children.

We did not remain in the dining-room more than five minutes after her departure. 'She is playing her harp,' said Steerforth, softly, 'and nobody but my mother has heard her do that, I believe, these three years.' We went into the room and found her alone.

'My dear Rosa,' said Steerforth, 'be kind for once, and sing us an Irish song.'

'What do you care for an Irish song?' she returned.

'Much!' said Steerforth. 'Much more than for any other. Let me sit and listen as I used to do.'

He did not touch her, but sat himself near the harp. She stood beside it in a curious way, going through the motion of playing it with her right hand, but not sounding it. At length she drew it to her with one sudden action.

I don't know what it was, in her touch or voice, that made that song the most unearthly I have ever heard in my life. There was something fearful in the reality of it, as if it had never been written, or set to music, but sprang out of the passion within her.

A minute more, and this had roused me from my trance: – Steerforth had put his arm laughingly about her, and said, 'Come, Rosa, for the future we will love each other very much!' And she had struck him, and had thrown him off with the fury of a wild cat, and had burst out of the room.

'What is the matter with Rosa?' said Mrs Steerforth, coming in.

'She has been an angel, mother,' returned Steerforth, 'for a little while; and has run into the opposite extreme, since, by way of compensation.'

Rosa did not come back; and no other mention was made of her, until I went with Steerforth into his room to say good-night. Then he laughed about her, and asked me if I had ever seen such a fierce little piece of incomprehensibility.

I asked if he could guess what it was that she had taken so much amiss.

'Oh, Heaven knows,' said Steerforth. 'Anything you like – or nothing! I told you she took everything, herself included, to a grindstone, and sharpened it. She is always dangerous. Good-night!'

'Good-night!' said I. 'I shall be gone before you wake in the morning.'

He was unwilling to let me go. 'Daisy, if anything should ever separate us, you must think of me at my best. Come! Let us make that bargain!'

'You have no best to me, Steerforth,' said I, 'and no worst. You are always equally loved, and cherished in my heart.'

'God bless you, Daisy.' We shook hands and parted.

I was up with the dull dawn, and looked into his room. He was fast asleep; lying with his head upon his arm, as I had often seen him lie at school.

The time came very soon, when I almost wondered that nothing troubled his repose. But he slept – let me think of him so again – as I had often seen him sleep at school; and thus, in this silent hour, I left him.

Never more, oh God forgive you, Steerforth! to touch that passive hand in love and friendship. Never, never more!

CHAPTER 30

A Loss

I got down to Yarmouth in the evening, and went to the inn. I knew that Peggotty's spare room – my room – was likely to have occupation enough in a little while, if that great Visitor, before whose presence all the living must give place, were not already in the house.

It was ten o'clock when I went out. When I came to Omer and Joram's, I found the shutters up, but the shop-door standing open.

'Why, bless my life and soul!' said Mr Omer. 'Take a seat.'

'I am sorry to have heard bad news of Mr Barkis,' said I. 'Do you know how he is to-night?'

'The very question I should have put to you, sir,' returned Mr Omer, 'but on account of delicacy. It's one of the drawbacks of our line of business. When a party's ill, we *can't* ask how the party is. We dursn't do it. It would be a shock that the generality of parties mightn't recover, to say "Omer and Joram's compliments, and how do you find yourself this morning?" It's one of the things that cut the trade off from attentions they could wish to show.'

I felt it was rather hard on Mr Omer, and I told him so.

'It ain't that I complain of my line of business,' said Mr Omer. 'What I wish is, that parties was brought up stronger-minded. Accordingly we're obleeged, in ascertaining how Barkis goes on, to limit ourselves to Em'ly. Minnie and Joram have just stepped down to the house to ask her how he is to-night; and if you was to please to wait till they come back, they'd give you full partic'lers.'

I inquired how little Emily was.

'Well, sir,' said Omer, 'I tell you truly, I shall be glad when her marriage has taken place.'

'Why so?' I inquired.

'Well, she's unsettled at present,' said Mr Omer. 'It ain't that she's not as pretty as ever, for she's prettier. It ain't that she don't work as well as ever, for she does. But somehow she wants heart. If you understand,' said Mr Omer, after rubbing his chin again.

Mr Omer's face and manner went for so much, that I could

conscientiously nod my head, as divining his meaning. My quickness of apprehension seemed to please him, and he went on:

'Now, I consider this is principally on account of her being in an unsettled state, you see. We have talked it over a good deal, her uncle and myself, and her sweetheart and myself, after business. I said, "Now, don't consider Em'ly nailed down in point of time, at all. Her services have been more valuable than was supposed; her learning has been quicker than was supposed; Omer and Joram can run their pen through what remains; and she's free when you wish. We're no losers, anyhow." For – don't you see,' said Mr Omer, 'it ain't likely that a man so short of breath as myself, and a grandfather too, would go and strain points with a little bit of a blue-eyed blossom, like *her*?'

'Not at all, I am certain,' said I.

'You're right!' said Mr Omer. 'Well, sir, her cousin she's going to be married to went and took as comfortable a little house as you or I could wish to clap eyes on. That little house is now furnished, and but for Barkis's illness, they would have been man and wife, I dare say, by this time. As it is, there's a postponement.'

'And has she become more settled?'

'Em'ly's still a little fluttered; perhaps, upon the whole, she's more so than she was. Every day she seems to get fonder and fonder of her uncle, and more loth to part from all of us. A kind word from me brings the tears into her eyes; and if you was to see her with my daughter Minnie's little girl, you'd never forget it.'

Having so favourable an opportunity, it occurred to me to ask Mr Omer, whether he knew anything of Martha.

'Ah!' he rejoined, shaking his head. 'A sad story, sir, however you come to know it. I never thought there was harm in the girl. None of us ever did.'

Mr Omer, hearing his daughter's footstep before I heard it, shut up one eye, as a caution. She and her husband came in immediately afterwards. Their report was, that Mr Barkis was 'as bad as bad could be' and that he was quite unconscious.

Hearing this, I determined to go to the house at once and directed my steps thither. My low tap at the door was answered by Mr Peggotty. He was not so much surprised to see me as I had expected; I think, in the expectation of that dread surprise, all other changes and surprises dwindle to nothing.

I shook hands with Mr Peggotty, and passed into the kitchen. Little Emily was sitting by the fire, with her hands before her face. Ham was standing near her.

'Em'ly, my dear,' cried Mr Peggotty. 'See here! Here's Mas'r Davy come! What, cheer up, pretty!'

There was a trembling upon her, that I can see now. The coldness of her hand when I touched it, I can feel yet. Its only sign of animation was to shrink from mine.

'It's such a loving art,' said Mr Peggotty, smoothing her rich hair with his great hard hand, 'that it can't abear the sorrer of this.'

She clung the closer to him, but neither lifted up her face, nor spoke a word.

'It's getting late, my dear,' said Mr Peggotty, 'and here's Ham come fur to take you home. What, Em'ly? Eh, my pretty?'

The sound of her voice had not reached me, but he said: 'Let you stay with your uncle? When your husband that'll be so soon, is here fur to take you home?'

'Lookee here!' said Ham. 'As Em'ly wishes of it, I'll leave her till morning. Let me stay too!'

'No, no,' said Mr Peggotty. 'You doen't ought to watch and work both. You go home and turn in.'

Ham yielded to this persuasion, and took his hat to go. Even when he kissed her, she seemed to cling closer to her uncle, even to the avoidance of her chosen husband. I shut the door after him, and when I turned back, I found Mr Peggotty still talking to her.

'Now, I'm a going up-stairs to tell your aunt as Mas'r Davy's here, and that'll cheer her up a bit,' he said. 'What? You'll go along with me?'

Afterwards, when I went up-stairs, as I passed the door of my little chamber, which was dark, I had an indistinct impression of her being within it, cast down upon the floor.

Peggotty came down, and took me in her arms, and blessed and thanked me for being such a comfort to her (that was what she said) in her distress. She then entreated me to come up-stairs, sobbing that Mr Barkis had always liked me and would brighten up at sight of me, if he could brighten up at any earthly thing.

The probability of his ever doing so, appeared to me, when I saw him, to be very small. He was lying with his head and shoulders out of bed, in an uncomfortable attitude, half resting on the box which had cost him so much pain and trouble. Time and the world were slipping from beneath him, but the box was there; and the last words he had uttered were 'Old clothes!'

'Barkis, my dear!' said Peggotty, almost cheerfully, bending over him. 'Here's Master Davy, who brought us together, Barkis! That you sent messages by, you know!'

He was as senseless as the box, from which his form derived the only expression it had.

'He's a going out with the tide,' said Mr Peggotty to me.

I repeated in a whisper, 'With the tide?'

'People can't die along the coast,' said Mr Peggotty, 'except when the tide's pretty nigh out. He's a going out with the tide. It's ebb at half-arter three, slack water half-an-hour. If he lives 'till it turns, he'll hold his own till past the flood, and go out with the next tide.'

We remained there, watching him, a long time. What mysterious influence my presence had upon him in that state, I shall not pretend to say; but when he at last began to wander feebly, it is certain he was muttering about driving me to school.

'Barkis, my dear!' said Peggotty.

'C. P. Barkis,' he cried faintly. 'No better woman anywhere!'

'Look! Here's Master Davy!' said Peggotty. For he now opened his eyes.

I was on the point of asking him if he knew me, when he tried to stretch out his arm, and said to me, distinctly, with a pleasant smile: 'Barkis is willin'!'

And, it being low water, he went out with the tide.

CHAPTER 31

A greater Loss

It was not difficult for me, on Peggotty's solicitation, to resolve to stay where I was until after the remains of the poor carrier should have made their last journey to Blunderstone. She had long ago bought a little piece of ground in our old churchyard near the grave of my mother; and there they were to rest.

In keeping Peggotty company, I had a satisfaction, of a personal and professional nature, in taking charge of Mr Barkis's will, and expounding its contents.

It was found in the box, at the bottom of a horse's nose-bag. For years, Mr Barkis had carried this box, on all his journeys. He had hoarded all these years to good purpose. His property in money amounted to nearly three thousand pounds. Of this he bequeathed the interest of one thousand to Mr Peggotty for his life; on his decease, the principal to be divided between Peggotty, little Emily, and me, share and share alike. All the rest he bequeathed to Peggotty.

I felt myself quite a proctor when I read this document and set forth its provisions to those whom they concerned. I began to think there was more in the Commons than I had supposed. In making an account for Peggotty of all the property into which she had come; in arranging all the affairs in an orderly manner; and in being her referee and adviser on every point; I passed the week before the funeral.

I walked over to Blunderstone early in the morning, and was in the churchyard when it came, attended only by Peggotty and her brother. Mr Omer breathed short in the background; no one else was there; and it was very quiet. We walked about the churchyard for an hour, after all was over and pulled some young leaves from the tree above my mother's grave.

A dread falls on me here. A cloud is lowering on the distant town, towards which I retraced my solitary steps. I fear to approach it.

My old nurse was to go to London with me next day, on the business of the will. Little Emily was passing that day at Omer's. We were all to meet in the old boathouse that night. I walked back towards Yarmouth

and it was evening when I reached it. Rain was falling heavily and it was
a wild night.

I was soon within sight of Mr Peggotty's house, and I went in. The
fire was bright, the ashes were thrown up, the locker was ready for little
Emily in her old place. In her own old place sat Peggotty, once more,
looking (but for her dress) as if she had never left it. Mrs Gummidge appeared to be fretting a little, in her old corner; and consequently looked
quite natural, too.

'You're first of the lot, Mas'r Davy!' said Mr Peggotty, with a happy
face. 'It ain't o' no use saying welcome to you, but you're welcome, kind
and hearty.'

'Thank you, Mr Peggotty, I am sure of that. Well, Peggotty!' said I,
giving her a kiss. 'And how are you, old woman?'

'Ha, ha!' laughed Mr Peggotty, sitting down beside us, 'there's not
a woman in the wureld, sir – as I tell her – that need to feel more easy
in her mind than her! She has done her dooty by the departed, and the
departed know'd it; and the departed done what was right by her – and
– and it's *all* right!'

Mrs Gummidge groaned.

'Cheer up, my pretty mawther!' said Mr Peggotty. (But he shook his
head aside at us, evidently sensible of the tendency of the late occurrences to recall the memory of the old one.) 'Doen't be down!'

Mr Peggotty snuffed the candle, and put it in the window.

'Theer we are, Missis Gummidge,' said Mr Peggotty. 'Lighted up, accordin' to custom! You're a wonderin' what that's fur, sir! Well, it's fur
our little Em'ly. You see, the path ain't cheerful arter dark; and when I'm
here at the hour as she's a comin' home, I puts the light in the winder.
That meets two objects. She says, "Theer's home!" And likewise, says
Em'ly, "My uncle's theer!" Fur if I ain't theer, I never have no light
showed.'

'You're a baby!' said Peggotty; very fond of him for it, if she thought
so.

'Right for all that,' said Mr Peggotty, smiting his hands together; 'fur
here she is!'

It was only Ham. The night should have turned more wet since I came
in, for he had a large sou'wester hat on, slouched over his face.

'Wheer's Em'ly?' said Mr Peggotty.

Ham made a motion with his head, as if she were outside. Mr Peggotty
was busily stirring the fire, when Ham, who had not moved, said:

'Mas'r Davy, will you come out a minute?'

We went out. As I passed him at the door, I saw, to my astonishment, that he was deadly pale. He pushed me hastily into the open air, and closed the door upon us. Only upon us two.

'Ham! what's the matter?'

'My love, Mas'r Davy – her that I'd have died for, and would die for now – she's gone!'

'Gone!'

'Em'ly's run away! Oh, Mas'r Davy, think *how* she's run away, when I pray my good and gracious God to kill her sooner than let her come to ruin and disgrace!'

The face he turned up to the troubled sky, the quivering of his clasped hands, the agony of his figure, remain associated with that lonely waste, in my remembrance, to this hour.

'You're a scholar,' he said, hurriedly, 'and know what's right and best. What am I to say, indoors? How am I ever to break it to him, Mas'r Davy?'

I saw the door move, and instinctively tried to hold the latch on the outside, to gain a moment's time. It was too late. Mr Peggotty thrust forth his face; and never could I forget the change that came upon it when he saw us, if I were to live five hundred years.

I remember a great wail and cry, and the women hanging about him, and we all standing in the room; I with a paper in my hand, which Ham had given me; Mr Peggotty, his face and lips quite white, looking fixedly at me.

'Read it, sir,' he said, in a low shivering voice.

I read thus, from a blotted letter:

' "When you, who love me so much better than I ever have deserved, even when my mind was innocent, see this, I shall be far away." '

'I shall be fur away,' he repeated slowly. 'Stop! Em'ly fur away. Well!'

' "When I leave my dear home in the morning –" '

the letter bore date on the previous night:

' " – it will be never to come back, unless he brings me back a lady. Oh, if you knew how my heart is torn. If even you, that I have wronged so much, that never can forgive me, could only know what I suffer! For mercy's sake, tell uncle that I never loved him half so dear as now. Oh, don't remember how affectionate and kind you have all been to me – don't remember we were ever to be married – but try to think as if I died when I was little, and was buried somewhere. Love some good girl, that will be what I was once to uncle, and be true to you, and worthy of you, and know no shame but me. If he don't bring me back a lady, I'll pray for all. My last tears, and my last thanks, for uncle!" '

That was all.

He stood, long after I had ceased to read, still looking at me. At length I ventured to entreat him, as well as I could, to endeavour to get some command of himself. He replied, 'I thankee, sir!' without moving.

At last, as if he were waking from a vision, he said, in a low voice:

'Who's the man? I want to know his name.'

Ham glanced at me, and suddenly I felt a shock that struck me back.

'There's a man suspected,' said Mr Peggotty. 'Who is it?'

'Mas'r Davy!' implored Ham. 'Go out and let me tell him what I must. You doen't ought to hear it, sir.'

I sank down in a chair, and tried to utter some reply; but my tongue was fettered.

'For some time past,' Ham faltered, 'there's been a servant about here, at odd times. There's been a gen'lm'n too. Both of 'em belong to one another.'

Mr Peggotty stood fixed as before, but now looking at him.

'A strange chay and hosses was outside town, this morning, on the Norwich road, a'most afore the day broke,' Ham went on. 'The servant went to it, and Em'ly was nigh him. The t'other was inside. He's the man.'

'For the Lord's love,' said Mr Peggotty, falling back, and putting out his hand, as if to keep off what he dreaded. 'Doen't tell me his name's Steerforth!'

'Mas'r Davy,' exclaimed Ham, in a broken voice, 'it ain't no fault of yourn – and I am far from laying of it to you – but his name is Steerforth, and he's a damned villain!'

Mr Peggotty pulled down his rough coat from its peg in a corner.

Ham asked him whither he was going.

'I'm a going to seek my niece. I'm a going, first, to stave in that theer boat, and sink it where I would have drowned *him*, as I'm a livin' soul, if I had had one thought of what was in him! I'm a going to find my poor niece in her shame, and bring her back. No one stop me!'

'No, no!' cried Mrs Gummidge. 'No, Dan'l, not as you are now. Seek her in a little while. Sit ye down, and let us speak a word about them times when she was first an orphan, and when I was a poor widder woman, and you took me in. It'll soften your poor heart, Dan'l, and you'll bear your sorrow better.'

He was quite passive now; and when I heard him crying, my over-charged heart found the same relief, and I cried too.

CHAPTER 32

The Beginning of a long Journey

What is natural in me, is natural in many other men, and so I am not afraid to write that I never loved Steerforth better than when the ties that bound me to him were broken. In the keen distress of the discovery of his unworthiness, I did more justice to the qualities that might have made him a man of a noble nature than ever I had done in the height of my devotion to him. I believe that if I had been brought face to face with him, I should have been as weak as a spirit-wounded child, in all but the entertainment of a thought that we could ever be re-united. That thought I never had. I felt that all was at an end between us. What his remembrances of me were, I have never known, but mine of him were as the remembrances of a cherished friend, who was dead.

The news of what happened soon spread through the town. Many were hard upon her, some few were hard upon him, but towards her second father and her lover there was but one sentiment. Among all kinds of people a respect for them prevailed, which was full of gentleness and delicacy.

It was on the beach that I found them. They looked worn; and I thought Mr Peggotty's head was bowed in one night more than in all the years I had known him. But they were both as grave and steady as the sea itself.

'We have had a mort of talk, sir,' said Mr Peggotty to me, 'of what we ought and don't ought to do. But we see our course now.'

I happened to glance at Ham, and a frightful thought came into my mind – that if ever he encountered Steerforth he would kill him.

'My dooty here, sir,' said Mr Peggotty, 'is done. I'm a going to seek her. That's my dooty evermore.'

He inquired if I were going to London to-morrow? I told him I was ready to go when he would.

'I'll go along with you, sir,' he rejoined, 'if you're agreeable. Ham – he'll hold to his present work, and go and live along with my sister. The old boat yonder – my wishes is as it shall look, winter and summer, as it has always looked. Every night the candle must be stood in its old pane of glass, that if ever she should see it, it may seem to say "Come back, my child!"'

We approached the old boat, and entered. Mrs Gummidge, no longer moping in her especial corner, was busy preparing breakfast. She spoke so comfortably and softly, that I hardly knew her.

'Dan'l, my good man,' said she, 'you must eat and drink, and keep up your strength, for without it you'll do nowt. Try, that's a dear soul!'

When she had served us all, she withdrew to the window, where she sedulously employed herself in repairing some shirts belonging to Mr Peggotty, and packing them in an old oilskin bag.

'All times and seasons, you know, Dan'l,' said Mrs Gummidge, 'I shall be allus here, and everythink will look accordin' to your wishes. I'm a poor scholar, but I shall write to you, odd times, when you're away.'

What a change in Mrs Gummidge in a little time! She was another woman, so regardful of the sorrow about her, that I held her in a sort of veneration. In short, I left her, when I went away at night, the prop and staff of Mr Peggotty's affliction.

Strolling in a melancholy manner through the town, I stopped at Mr Omer's door. Mr Omer had taken it so much to heart, his daughter told me, that he had gone to bed.

'A deceitful, bad-hearted girl,' said Mrs Joram.

'Don't say so,' I returned. 'You don't think so.'

'Yes, I do!' cried Mrs Joram, endeavouring to be very stern and cross; but she could not command her softer self, and began to cry.

'What will become of her! Where will she go!' sobbed Minnie.

'My little Minnie,' said Mrs Joram, 'is sobbing for Em'ly. All day long, little Minnie has cried for her, and asked me, over and over again, whether Em'ly was wicked? What can I say to her, when Em'ly tied a ribbon off her own neck round little Minnie's the last night she was here! The ribbon's round her neck now. Em'ly is very bad, but they were fond of one another. And the child knows nothing!'

I went home to Peggotty's; more melancholy myself, if possible, than I had been yet. Peggotty was at her brother's where she meant to stay till morning. I sat down before the kitchen fire a little while, to think, when I was recalled from my wanderings by a knock.

I opened the door; and looked down to my amazement, on nothing but a great umbrella that appeared to be walking about of itself. But presently I discovered underneath it, Miss Mowcher.

I might not have been prepared to give the little creature a very kind reception but her face was so earnest that I rather inclined towards her.

'Miss Mowcher!' said I. 'What is the matter?'

She went into the kitchen. I followed and found her sitting on the corner of the fender, chafing her hands upon her knees like a person in pain.

Quite alarmed at being the only recipient of this untimely visit, I exclaimed again, 'Pray tell me, Miss Mowcher, are you ill?'

'My dear young soul,' returned Miss Mowcher, 'I am very ill. To think that it should come to this, when I might have known and perhaps prevented it.'

'I am surprised,' I began, 'to see you so distressed' – when she interrupted me.

'Yes, it's always so!' she said. 'They are all surprised, these inconsiderate full grown people, to see any natural feeling in a little thing like me! They make a plaything of me, use me for their amusement, throw me away when they are tired.'

'It may be, with others,' I returned, 'but I do assure you it is not with me. Perhaps I ought not to be at all surprised to see you as you are now. I know so little of you. I said, without consideration, what I thought.'

'What can I do?' returned the little woman, standing up, and holding out her arms to show herself. 'See! What I am, my father was; and my sister is; and my brother is. I have worked for sister and brother these many years – hard, Mr Copperfield – all day. I must live. If there are people so cruel, as to make a jest of me, what is left for me to do but to make a jest of myself? If I had shown myself a sensitive dwarf to your false friend,' pursued the little woman, 'how much of his help or goodwill do you think *I* should ever have had? If little Mowcher addressed herself to the like of him, because of her misfortunes, when do you suppose her small voice would have been heard? She might whistle for her bread and butter till she died of Air.'

Miss Mowcher sat down on the fender again. 'Be thankful for me, if you have a kind heart, as I think you have, that I can be cheerful and endure it all. I am thankful for myself, that I can find my tiny way through the world without being beholden to any one.

'Do you remember what Steerforth said to me about this unfortunate girl, that time when I saw you both at the inn?'

I remembered very well what she referred to, having had it in my thoughts many times that day. I told her so.

'May the Father of all Evil confound him,' said the little woman, holding up her forefinger between me and her sparkling eyes; 'and ten times more confound that wicked servant; but I believed it was *you* who had a boyish passion for her!'

'I?' I repeated.

'Child, child!' cried Miss Mowcher wringing her hands impatiently, 'why did you praise her so, and blush, and look disturbed?'

I could not conceal from myself that I had done this, though for a reason very different from her supposition.

'What did I know?' said Miss Mowcher. 'You were soft wax in his hands, I saw. Had I left the room a minute, when his man told me that "Young Innocence" (so he called you) had set his heart upon her? How could I *but* believe him? I saw Steerforth please you by his praise of her! You were the first to mention her name. You owned to an old admiration of her. You were hot and cold, and red and white, all at once when I spoke to you of her. What could I think – what *did* I think – but that you were a young libertine in everything but experience, and had fallen into hands that had experience enough, and could manage you for your own good? Oh! They were afraid of my finding out the truth,' exclaimed Miss Mowcher, 'because I am a sharp little thing – I need be, to get through the world at all! – and they deceived me altogether, and I gave the poor unfortunate girl a letter, which I fully believe was the beginning of her ever speaking to Littimer, who was left behind on purpose!'

I stood amazed at the revelation of all this perfidy. Without otherwise moving and without breaking silence.

'My country rounds,' she added, 'brought me to Norwich, the night before last. What I happened to find out there, about their secret way of coming and going, without you – which was strange – led to my suspecting something wrong. I got into the coach from London last night, and was here this morning. Oh, too late!'

I sat in a chair on the other side of the hearth, lost in unhappy reflections, and looking at the fire and sometimes at her.

'I must go,' she said at last, rising as she spoke. 'You don't mistrust me?'

Meeting her sharp glance, which was as sharp as ever when she asked me, I could not on that short challenge answer no, quite frankly.

'Come!' said she, looking wistfully up into my face, 'you know you wouldn't mistrust me, if I was a full-sized woman!'

I felt that there was much truth in this; and I felt rather ashamed of myself.

'You are a young man,' she said, nodding. 'Take a word of advice, even from three foot nothing. Try not to associate bodily defects with mental, my good friend, except for a solid reason.'

I told her that I believed she had given me a faithful account of herself, and that we had both been hapless instruments in designing hands. She thanked me, and said I was a good fellow.

'Now mind!' she exclaimed, turning back on her way to the door. 'I have some reason to suspect, from what I have heard, that they are gone abroad. But if ever one of them returns, I am more likely than another, going about as I do, to find it out. Whatever I know, you shall know. If ever I can do anything to serve the poor betrayed girl, I will do it faithfully, please Heaven! And Littimer had better have a bloodhound at his back, than little Mowcher!'

I placed implicit faith in this last statement, when I marked the look with which it was accompanied.

I gave Miss Mowcher my hand, with a very different opinion of her from that which I had hitherto entertained.

In the morning I was joined by Mr Peggotty and by my old nurse, and we went at an early hour to the coach-office, where Mrs Gummidge and Ham were waiting to take leave of us.

'Mas'r Davy,' Ham whispered, drawing me aside, while Mr Peggotty was stowing his bag among the luggage, 'he's bound upon a voyage that'll last, on and off, all the rest of his days, take my wured for't, unless he finds what he's a seeking of. I am sure you'll be a friend to him, Mas'r Davy?'

'Trust me, I will indeed,' said I, shaking hands with Ham earnestly.

'One thing furder. I'm in good employ, you know, and I han't no ways now of spending what I gets. Money's of no use to me no more, except to live. If you can lay it out for him, I shall do my work with a better art.'

I hinted that I hoped the time might even come, when he would cease to lead the lonely life he naturally contemplated now.

'No, sir,' he said, shaking his head. 'No one can never fill the place that's empty. But you'll bear in mind about the money?'

I promised to do so. We then took leave of each other. I cannot leave him even now, without remembering with a pang his modest fortitude and his great sorrow.

When we got to our journey's end, our first pursuit was to look about for a little lodging for Peggotty, where her brother could have a bed. We were so fortunate as to find one over a chandler's shop, only two streets removed from me.

Mr Peggotty had made a communication to me on the way to London for which I was not unprepared. It was, that he purposed first seeing Mrs Steerforth. As I felt bound to assist him in this, I wrote to her that night. I said he was a man in very common life, but of a most gentle and upright character; and that I ventured to express a hope that she would not refuse to see him in his heavy trouble. I mentioned two o'clock in the afternoon as the hour of our coming, and I sent the letter myself by the first coach in the morning.

At the appointed time, we stood in the drawing-room. Mrs Steerforth was sitting there. Rosa Dartle glided, as we went in, from another part of the room, and stood behind her chair.

I saw, directly, in his mother's face, that she knew from himself what he had done. It was very pale, and bore the traces of deeper emotion than my letter alone, weakened by the doubts her fondness would have raised upon it, would have been likely to create.

She sat upright in her arm-chair, with a stately air, that it seemed as if nothing could disturb. She looked very steadfastly at Mr Peggotty when he stood before her; and he looked quite as steadfastly at her. Rosa Dartle's keen glance comprehended all of us. For some moments not a word was spoken. She motioned to Mr Peggotty to be seated. He said, in a low voice, 'I shouldn't feel it nat'ral, ma'am, to sit down in this house. I'd sooner stand.' And this was succeeded by another silence, which she broke thus:

'I know, with deep regret, what has brought you here. What do you want of me?'

Feeling in his breast for Emily's letter, he gave it to her.

She read it, untouched by its contents, as far as I could see and returned it to him.

'"Unless he brings me back a lady,"' said Mr Peggotty, tracing out that part with his finger. 'I come to know, ma'am, whether he will keep his wured?'

'No,' she returned.

'Why not?' said Mr Peggotty.

'It is impossible. He would disgrace himself. You cannot fail to know that she is far below him.'

'Raise her up!' said Mr Peggotty.

'She is uneducated and ignorant.'

'Teach her better!'

'Since you oblige me to speak more plainly, her humble connexions would render such a thing impossible, if nothing else did.'

'Hark to this, ma'am,' he returned, slowly and quietly. 'You know what it is to love your child. So do I. If she was a hundred times my child, I couldn't love her more. You doen't know what it is to lose your child. I do. But save her from this disgrace, and she shall never be disgraced by us. Not one of us that she's growed up among, will ever look upon her pritty face again. We'll be content to let her be.'

She still preserved her proud manner, but there was a touch of softness in her voice, as she answered.

'I am sorry to repeat, it is impossible. Such a marriage would irretrievably blight my son's career and ruin his prospects. Nothing is more certain than that it never can take place, and never will. If there is any other compensation –'

'I am looking at the likeness of the face,' interrupted Mr Peggotty, 'that has looked at me, in my home, smiling and friendly, when it was so treacherous. If the likeness of that face don't turn to burning fire, at the thought of offering money to me for my child's ruin, it's as bad.'

She changed now, in a moment. An angry flush overspread her features; and she said, 'What compensation can you make to *me* for opening such a pit between me and my son? What is your love to mine? My son, who has been the object of my life, from whom I have had no separate existence since his birth – to take up in a moment with a miserable girl, and avoid me! To set this wretched fancy against his mother's claims upon his duty, love, respect, gratitude – is this no injury?

'Let him put away his whim now, and he is welcome back. Let him not put her away and he never shall come near me, living or dying. This is the separation that there is between us! And is this,' she added, looking at her visitor with the proud intolerant air with which she had begun, 'no injury?'

While I heard and saw the mother as she said these words, I seemed to hear and see the son. All that I had ever seen in him of an unyielding, wilful spirit, I saw in her.

She now observed to me that she begged to put an end to the interview. She rose with an air of dignity to leave the room, when Mr Peggotty signified that it was needless.

'Doen't fear me being any hindrance to you, I have no more to say, ma'am,' he remarked as he moved towards the door. 'I come heer with no hope, and I take away no hope. I have done what I thowt should be done, but I never looked fur any good to come of my stan'ning where I do. This has been too evil a house fur me and mine, fur me to be in my right senses and expect it.'

With this, we departed. We had, on our way out, to cross a paved hall. Rosa Dartle, entering this way with a noiseless step, addressed herself to me:

'You do well,' she said, 'to bring this fellow here!'

Such a concentration of rage and scorn as darkened her face, and flashed in her jet-black eyes, I could not have thought compressible even into that face. The scar made by the hammer was strongly marked.

'He is a deeply injured man, Miss Dartle,' I replied. 'You may not know it.'

'I know that James Steerforth,' she said, with her hand on her bosom, as if to prevent the storm that was raging there, 'has a false, corrupt heart, and is a traitor. But what need I know or care about this fellow, and his common niece?'

'Miss Dartle,' I returned, 'you deepen the injury. It is sufficient already. I will only say, at parting, that you do him a great wrong.'

'I do him no wrong,' she returned. 'They are a depraved, worthless set. I would have her whipped!'

'Oh, shame, Miss Dartle!' I said indignantly. 'How can you bear to trample on his undeserved affliction!'

'I would trample on them all,' she answered. 'I would have his house pulled down. I would have her branded on the face and cast out in the streets to starve. If I had the power to sit in judgment on her, I would see it done. If there was any word of comfort that would be a solace to her in her dying hour, and only I possessed it, I wouldn't part with it for Life itself.'

The mere vehemence of her words can convey, I am sensible, but a weak impression of the passion by which she was possessed, and which made itself articulate in her whole figure, though her voice, instead of being raised, was lower than usual. I have seen passion in many forms, but I have never seen it in such a form as that.

When I joined Mr Peggotty, he told me that having now discharged his mind of what he had purposed in London, he meant 'to set out on his travels,' that night.

We went back to the little lodging over the chandler's shop, and there I found an opportunity of repeating to Peggotty what he had said to me. She knew no more than I did, where he was going, but she thought he had some project shaped out in his mind.

I did not like to leave him under such circumstances, and we all three dined together off a beefsteak pie – which was one of the many good things for which Peggotty was famous. After dinner we sat for an hour or so near the window, without talking much; and then Mr Peggotty got up, and brought his oilskin bag and his stout stick, and laid them on the table.

He accepted, from his sister's stock of ready money, a small sum on account of his legacy. He promised to communicate with me, when anything befell him; and he slung his bag about him, took his hat and stick, and bade us both 'Good-bye!'

'All good attend you, dear old woman,' he said, embracing Peggotty, 'and you too, Mas'r Davy!' shaking hands with me. 'I'm a going to seek her, fur and wide. If she should come home while I'm away, or if I should bring her back, my meaning is, that she and me shall live where no one can reproach her. If any hurt should come to me, remember that the last words I left for her was, "My unchanged love is with my darling child, and I forgive her!"'

He said this solemnly, then he went down the stairs, and away. It was a warm, dusty evening, just the time when there was a temporary lull in the eternal tread of feet upon the pavement, and a strong red sunshine. He turned, at the corner of our shady street, into a glow of light, in which we lost him.

Rarely did that hour of the evening come, but I thought of his solitary figure toiling on.

CHAPTER 33

Blissful

All this time, I had gone on loving Dora, harder than ever. Her idea was my refuge in disappointment and distress, and made some amends to me even for the loss of my friend. The more I pitied myself, or pitied others, the more I sought for consolation in the image of Dora. The greater the accumulation of deceit and trouble in the world, the brighter and purer shone the star of Dora.

If I may so express it, I was steeped in Dora. I was not merely over head and ears in love with her, but I was saturated through and through.

My love was so much on my mind, and it was so natural to me to confide in Peggotty, that I imparted to her my great secret. Peggotty was strongly interested, but I could not get her into my view of the case at all. She was audaciously prejudiced in my favour, and quite unable to understand why I should have any misgivings. 'The young lady might think herself well off,' she observed, 'to have such a beau. And as to her Pa, what *did* the gentleman expect, for gracious sake!'

Taking the management of Peggotty's affairs into my own hands, with no little pride, I proved the will, and came to a settlement with the Legacy Duty-office, and took her to the Bank, and soon got everything into an orderly train.

Peggotty's business being settled, I took her down to the office one morning to pay her bill. Mr Spenlow had stepped out, old Tiffey said, to get a gentleman sworn for a marriage licence; but as I knew he would be back directly, I told Peggotty to wait.

We were a little like undertakers, in the Commons, generally making it a rule to look more or less cut up, when we had to deal with clients in mourning. In a similar feeling of delicacy, we were always blithe and light-hearted with the licence clients. Therefore I hinted to Peggotty that she would find Mr Spenlow much recovered from the shock of Mr Barkis's decease; and indeed he came in like a bridegroom.

But neither Peggotty nor I had eyes for him, when we saw, in company with him, Mr Murdstone. He was very little changed. His hair looked as thick, and was certainly as black, as ever; and his glance was as little to be trusted as of old.

'Ah, Copperfield?' said Mr Spenlow. 'You know this gentleman, I believe?'

I made a distant bow, and Peggotty barely recognised him. He was, at first, somewhat disconcerted to meet us two together; but came up to me.

'I hope,' he said, 'that you are doing well?'

'It can hardly be interesting to you,' said I. 'Yes, if you wish to know.'

We looked at each other, and he addressed himself to Peggotty.

'And you,' said he. 'I am sorry to observe that you have lost your husband.'

'It's not the first loss I have had in my life, Mr Murdstone,' replied Peggotty, trembling from head to foot. 'I am glad to hope that there is nobody to blame for this one.'

'Ha!' said he. 'You have done your duty?'

'I have not worn anybody's life away,' said Peggotty. 'No, Mr Murdstone, I have not worrited and frightened any sweet creetur to an early grave!'

He eyed her gloomily – remorsefully I thought – for an instant; and said, turning his head towards me, 'We are not likely to encounter soon again; a source of satisfaction to us both, no doubt. I do not expect that you, who always rebelled against my just authority, should owe me any good-will now. There is an antipathy between us –'

'An old one, I believe?' said I, interrupting him.

He smiled, and shot as evil a glance at me as could come from his dark eyes.

'It rankled in your baby breast,' he said. 'It embittered the life of your poor mother. You are right. I hope you may do better, yet; I hope you may correct yourself.'

Here he ended the dialogue, by passing into Mr Spenlow's room, and saying aloud, in his smoothest manner:

'Gentlemen of Mr Spenlow's profession are accustomed to family differences.' With that, he paid the money for his licence and went out of the office.

I might have had more difficulty in constraining myself to be silent under his words, if I had less difficulty in impressing upon Peggotty that we were not in a place for recrimination, and that I besought her to hold her peace.

Mr Spenlow did not appear to know what the connexion between Mr

Murdstone and myself was; which I was glad of, for I could not bear to acknowledge him, remembering what I did of the history of my poor mother.

'Rather a good marriage this, I believe?' said Mr Spenlow.

I explained that I knew nothing about it.

'Indeed!' he said. 'Speaking from the few words Mr Murdstone dropped and from what Miss Murdstone let fall, I should say it was rather a good marriage.'

'Do you mean that there is money, sir?' I asked.

'Yes,' said Mr Spenlow, 'I understand there's money. Beauty too, I am told.'

'Indeed! Is his new wife young?'

'Just of age,' said Mr Spenlow. 'So lately, that I should think they had been waiting for that.'

'Lord deliver her!' said Peggotty. So very emphatically and unexpectedly, that we were all three discomposed; until Tiffey came in with the bill.

Mr Spenlow went over the items with a deprecatory air – as if it were all Jorkins's doing – and handed it back to Tiffey with a bland sigh.

'I should have been extremely happy, Copperfield, to have limited these charges to the actual expenditure out of pocket, but it is an irksome incident in my professional life, that I am not at liberty to consult my own wishes. I have a partner – Mr Jorkins.'

I expressed my acknowledgment on Peggotty's behalf, and paid Tiffey in bank-notes. Peggotty then retired to her lodging, and Mr Spenlow and I fell into conversation. Mr Spenlow told me this day week was Dora's birthday, and he would be glad if I would come down and join a little picnic on the occasion.

I think I committed every possible absurdity, in the way of preparation for this blessed event. I turn hot when I remember the cravat I bought. My boots might be placed in any collection of instruments of torture. I sent down by the Norwood coach the night before a delicate little hamper, amounting in itself, I thought, almost to a declaration. At six in the morning, I was in Covent Garden Market, buying a bouquet for Dora. At ten I was on horseback (I hired a gallant grey, for the occasion), with the bouquet in my hat, to keep it fresh, trotting down to Norwood.

When I saw Dora in the garden sitting on a garden seat under a lilac tree, what a spectacle she was, upon that beautiful morning, among the butterflies, in a white chip bonnet and a dress of celestial blue!

There was a young lady with her – comparatively stricken in years

– almost twenty, I should say. Her name was Miss Mills, and Dora called her Julia. She was the bosom friend of Dora. Happy Miss Mills!

Jip was there, and Jip *would* bark at me again. When I presented my bouquet, he gnashed his teeth with jealousy. Well he might. If he had the least idea how I adored his mistress, well he might!

'Oh, thank you, Mr Copperfield! What dear flowers!' said Dora.

Then Dora held my flowers to Jip to smell. Then Jip growled, and wouldn't smell them. Then Dora laughed, and held them a little closer to Jip, to make him. Then Jip laid hold a bit of geranium with his teeth, and worried imaginary cats in it. Then Dora pouted, and said, 'My poor beautiful flowers!'

'You'll be so glad to hear, Mr Copperfield,' said Dora, 'that that cross Miss Murdstone is not here. She has gone to her brother's marriage, and will be away at least three weeks. Isn't that delightful?'

I said I was sure it must be delightful to her, and all that was delightful to her was delightful to me. Miss Mills, with an air of superior wisdom and benevolence, smiled upon us.

'You can't believe how ill-tempered and shocking she is, Julia,' said Dora.

'Yes, I can, my dear!' said Julia.

'*You* can, perhaps, love,' returned Dora, with her hand on Julia's.

I learnt, from this, that Miss Mills had had her trials in the course of a chequered existence, having been unhappy in a misplaced affection, and being understood to have retired from the world on her awful stock of experience, but still to take a calm interest in the unblighted hopes and loves of youth.

But now Mr Spenlow came out of the house, and Dora went to him saying, 'Look, papa, what beautiful flowers!' And Miss Mills smiled thoughtfully, as who should say, 'Ye May-flies, enjoy your brief existence in the bright morning of life!' And we all walked from the lawn towards the carriage, which was getting ready.

I shall never have such a ride again. I have never had such another. There were only those three, their hamper, my hamper, and the guitar-case, in the phaeton; and, of course, the phaeton was open; and I rode behind it, and Dora sat with her back to the horses, looking towards me. She kept the bouquet close to her on the cushion, and wouldn't allow Jip to sit on that side of her at all, for fear he should crush it. She often carried it in her hand, often refreshed herself with its fragrance. Our eyes at those times often met; and my great astonishment is that I didn't go over the head of my gallant grey into the carriage.

I don't know how long we were going, and to this hour I know as little where we went. Perhaps it was near Guildford, a green spot, on a hill, carpeted with soft turf. There were shady trees, and heather, and, as far as the eye could see, a rich landscape.

It was a trying thing to find people here, waiting for us; and my jealousy, even of the ladies, knew no bounds. But all of my own sex – especially one imposter, three or four years my elder, with a red whisker – were my mortal foes.

We unpacked our baskets and employed ourselves in getting dinner ready. Red Whisker pretended he could make a salad and obtruded himself on public notice. Some of the young ladies washed the lettuces for him, and Dora was among these. I felt that fate had pitted me against this man, and one of us must fall. By-and-by, I saw him, with the majority of a lobster on his plate, eating his dinner at the feet of Dora!

I have but an indistinct idea of what happened for some time after this baleful object presented itself to my view. I attached myself to a young creature in pink, with little eyes, and flirted with her desperately. She received my attentions with favour; but the young creature had a mother and I rather think the latter separated us from motives of policy. Howbeit, there was a general breaking up of the party, while the remnants of the dinner were being put away; and I strolled off by myself among the trees, in a raging and remorseful state. I was debating whether I should pretend that I was not well, and fly – I don't know where – upon my gallant grey, when Dora and Miss Mills met me.

'Mr Copperfield,' said Miss Mills, 'you are dull.'

I begged her pardon. Not at all.

'And Dora,' said Miss Mills, '*you* are dull.'

Oh dear no! Not in the least.

'Mr Copperfield and Dora,' said Miss Mills, with an almost venerable air. 'Enough of this. Do not allow a trivial misunderstanding to wither the blossoms of spring, which, once put forth and blighted, cannot be renewed. I speak,' said Miss Mills, 'from experience of the past – the remote irrevocable past. The gushing fountains which sparkle in the sun must not be stopped in mere caprice; the oasis in the desert of Sahara must not be plucked up idly.'

I hardly knew what I did, I was burning all over to that extraordinary extent; but I took Dora's little hand and kissed it – and she let me! I kissed Miss Mills's hand; and we all seemed, to my thinking, to go straight up to the seventh heaven.

Much too soon, we heard the others laughing and talking, and calling 'where's Dora?' So we went back, and they wanted Dora to sing. Red Whisker would have got the guitar-case out of the carriage, but Dora told him nobody knew where it was, but *I*. So Red Whisker was done for in a moment; and *I* got it, and *I* unlocked it, and *I* took the guitar out, and *I* sat by her, and *I* held her handkerchief and gloves, and *I* drank in every note of her dear voice, and she sang to *me* who loved her, and all the others might applaud as much as they liked, but they had nothing to do with it!

I was happier than ever when the party broke up, and the other people, defeated Red Whisker and all, went their several ways, and we went ours through the still evening and the dying light, with sweet scents arising up around us. Mr Spenlow being a little drowsy after the champagne and being fast asleep in a corner of the carriage, I rode by the side and talked to Dora. She admired my horse and patted him and her shawl would not keep right, and now and then I drew it round her with my arm; and I even fancied that Jip began to understand that he must make up his mind to be friends with me.

'Mr Copperfield,' said Miss Mills, 'come to this side of the carriage a moment – if you can spare a moment. I want to speak to you.'

Behold me, on my gallant grey, bending at the side of Miss Mills, with my hand upon the carriage door!

'Dora is coming to stay with me. She is coming home with me the day after to-morrow. If you would like to call, I am sure papa would be happy to see you.'

What could I do but invoke a silent blessing on Miss Mills's head, and store Miss Mills's address in the securest corner of my memory! What could I do but tell Miss Mills, with grateful looks and fervent words, how much I appreciated her good offices, and what an inestimable value I set upon her friendship!

Norwood was many miles too near, and we reached it many hours too soon; but Mr Spenlow came to himself a little short of it, and said, 'You must come in, Copperfield, and rest!' and I consenting, we had sandwiches and wine-and-water. In the light room, Dora blushing looked so lovely, that I could not tear myself away, but sat there staring, in a dream, until the snoring of Mr Spenlow inspired me with sufficient consciousness to take my leave. So we parted; I riding all the way to London, recalling every incident and word ten thousand times; lying down in my own bed at last, as enraptured a young noodle as ever was carried out of his five wits by love.

When I awoke next morning, I was resolute to declare my passion to Dora, and know my fate. Happiness or misery was now the question. I passed three days in a luxury of wretchedness, torturing myself by putting every conceivable variety of discouraging construction on all that ever had taken place between Dora and me. At last, arrayed for the purpose at a vast expense, I went to Miss Mills's, fraught with a declaration.

How many times I went up and down the street, and round the square, before I could persuade myself to go up the steps and knock, is no matter now.

Mr Mills was not at home. I did not expect he would be. Nobody wanted *him*. Miss Mills was at home. Miss Mills would do.

I was shown into a room up-stairs, where Miss Mills and Dora were. Jip was there. Miss Mills was copying music and Dora was painting flowers – my flowers.

Miss Mills was very glad to see me, and very sorry her papa was not at home: though I thought we all bore that with fortitude. Miss Mills was conversational for a few minutes, and then left the room.

'I hope your poor horse was not tired, when he got home at night,' said Dora, lifting up her beautiful eyes.

I began to think I would do it to-day.

'It was a long way for *him*,' said I, 'for *he* had nothing to uphold him on the journey.'

'Wasn't he fed, poor thing?' asked Dora.

I began to think I would put it off till to-morrow.

'I mean he had not the unutterable happiness that I had in being so near you.'

Dora bent her head over her drawing, and said, after a little while – I had sat, in the interval, in a burning fever – 'You didn't seem to be sensible of that happiness yourself, at one time of the day. You didn't care for that happiness in the least,' said Dora, 'when you were sitting by Miss Kitt.'

Kitt was the name of the creature in pink.

'Though certainly I don't know why you should call it a happiness at all,' said Dora. 'But of course you don't mean what you say. Jip, you naughty boy, come here!'

I don't know how I did it. I did it in a moment. I intercepted Jip. I had Dora in my arms. I told her how I loved her. I told her I should die without her. I told her that I idolised and worshipped her. Jip barked madly all the time.

When Dora hung her head and cried, my eloquence increased so much the more. I had loved her every minute, day and night, since I first saw her. I should always love her, every minute, to distraction. Lovers had loved before, and lovers would love again; but no lover had ever loved, might, could, would, or should ever love, as I loved Dora. The more I raved, the more Jip barked. Each of us, in his own way, got more mad every moment.

Well, well, Dora and I were sitting on the sofa by-and-by, quiet enough, and Jip was lying in her lap, winking peacefully at me. I was in a state of perfect rapture. Dora and I were engaged.

I suppose we had some notion that this was to end in marriage. We must have had some, because Dora stipulated that we were never to be married without her papa's consent. But, in our youthful ecstasy, I don't think that we had any aspiration beyond the ignorant present. We were to keep our secret from Mr Spenlow; but I am sure the idea never entered my head, then, that there was anything dishonourable in that.

Miss Mills was more than usually pensive when Dora, going to find her, brought her back; – I apprehend, because there was a tendency in what had passed to awaken the slumbering echoes in the caverns of Memory. But she gave us her blessing, and the assurance of her lasting friendship.

What an idle time it was! What an unsubstantial, happy, foolish time!

When I measured Dora's finger for a ring and when the jeweller laughed over his order-book, and charged me anything he liked for the pretty little toy – so associated in my remembrance with Dora's hand, that yesterday, when I saw such another, by chance on the finger of my own daughter, there was a momentary stirring in my heart, like pain!

When we had our first quarrel (within a week of our betrothal), and when Dora sent me back the ring, enclosed in a despairing cocked-hat note, wherein she used the terrible expression that 'our love had begun in folly, and ended in madness!' which dreadful words occasioned me to tear my hair, and cry that all was over!

When, under cover of the night, I flew to Miss Mills, whom I saw by stealth in a back kitchen, and implored her to interpose between us and avert insanity. When Miss Mills undertook the office and returned with Dora, exhorting us, from the pulpit of her own bitter youth, to mutual concession; and the avoidance of the desert of Sahara!

When we cried, and made it up, and were so blest again, that the back kitchen changed to Love's own temple, where we arranged a plan of correspondence through Miss Mills, always to comprehend at least one letter on each side every day!

What an idle time! What an unsubstantial, happy, foolish time! Of all the times of mine that Time has in his grip, there is none that I can smile at half so much, and think of half as tenderly.

CHAPTER 34

My Aunt astonishes me

I wrote to Agnes as soon as Dora and I were engaged. I entreated her not to regard this as a thoughtless passion which had the least resemblance to the boyish fancies that we used to joke about. I assured her that its profundity was quite unfathomable, and expressed my belief that nothing like it had ever been known.

Of Steerforth, I said nothing. I only told her there had been sad grief at Yarmouth, on account of Emily's flight; and that on me it made a double wound, by reason of the circumstances attending it. I knew how quick she always was to divine the truth, and that she would never be the first to breathe his name.

To this letter, I received an answer by return of post. As I read it, I seemed to hear Agnes speaking to me. What can I say more!

While I had been away from home lately, Traddles had called. Finding Peggotty within, he had established a good-humoured acquaintance with her, and had stayed to have a little chat with her about me. So Peggotty said; but I am afraid the chat was all on her own side, as she was very difficult to stop, God bless her! when she had me for her theme.

This reminds me that I expected Traddles on a certain afternoon.

'My dear Copperfield,' cried Traddles, punctually appearing at my door, 'how do you do?'

'My dear Traddles,' said I, 'I am very sorry I have not been at home before. But I have been so much engaged –'

'Yes, I know,' said Traddles. 'Yours lives in London, I think. Miss D, I believe?'

'Oh yes. Near London.'

'Mine, perhaps you recollect,' said Traddles, with a serious look, 'lives down in Devonshire – one of ten. Consequently, I am not so much engaged as you – in that sense.'

'Is she the eldest?' I inquired.

'Oh dear no,' said Traddles. 'The eldest is a Beauty. Not, of course, but that my Sophy is beautiful too in my eyes. But when I say the eldest is a

Beauty, I mean she really is a –' he seemed to be describing clouds about himself, with both hands: 'Splendid, you know.'

'Indeed!' said I.

'Then, you know, being formed for society and admiration, and not being able to enjoy much of it, she naturally gets a little irritable and exacting, sometimes. Sophy puts her in good humour!'

'Is Sophy the youngest?' I hazarded.

'Oh dear, no!' said Traddles, stroking his chin. 'The two youngest are only nine and ten. Sophy educates 'em.'

'The second daughter, perhaps?'

'Sarah's the second. Sarah has something the matter with her spine, poor girl. Sophy nurses her. Sophy's the fourth.'

'Is the mother living?' I inquired.

'Oh yes,' said Traddles, 'she is a very superior woman indeed, but the damp country is not adapted to her constitution, and – in fact, she has lost the use of her limbs. But in a merely domestic view it is not so bad as it might be, because Sophy takes her place. She is quite as much a mother to her mother, as she is to the other nine.'

I felt the greatest admiration for the virtues of this young lady; and inquired how Mr Micawber was.

'I am not living with him at present.' said Traddles. 'The truth is, he has changed his name to Mortimer, in consequence of his temporary embarrassments; and he don't come out till after dark – and then in spectacles. There was an execution put into our house for rent. Unfortunately, it broke up the establishment. I have been living in a furnished apartment since then, and the Mortimers have been very private indeed.'

I told him that he should make a solemn resolution to grant no more loans of his name, or anything else, to Mr Micawber.

'My dear Copperfield,' said Traddles, 'I have already done so. That first unlucky obligation, I have paid. I have no doubt Mr Micawber would have paid it if he could. I ought to mention the second obligation, which is not yet due. He won't tell me that it *is* provided for, but he says it *will be*. Now, I think there is something very fair and honest about that!'

I was unwilling to damp my good friend's confidence, and therefore assented. After a little further conversation, we went round to the chandler's shop, to Peggotty; Traddles, declining to pass the evening with me, went his way and Peggotty and I turned back towards my chambers. On our way up-stairs, we were both very much surprised to find my outer door standing open and to hear voices inside.

What was my amazement to find of all people upon earth, my aunt there, and Mr Dick! My aunt sitting on a quantity of luggage, with her two birds before her, and her cat on her knee, like a female Robinson Crusoe, drinking tea. Mr Dick with more luggage piled about him!

'My dear aunt!' cried I. 'Why, what an unexpected pleasure!'

We cordially embraced; and Mr Dick and I cordially shook hands.

'Holloa!' said my aunt to Peggotty, who quailed before her awful presence. 'How are *you*?'

'You remember my aunt, Peggotty?' said I.

'For the love of goodness, child,' exclaimed my aunt, 'don't call the woman by that South Sea Island name! If she married and got rid of it, which was the best thing she could do, why don't you give her the benefit of the change? What's your name now, – P?' said my aunt, as a compromise for the obnoxious appellation.

'Barkis, ma'am,' said Peggotty.

'Well! That's human,' said my aunt. 'How d'ye do, Barkis? I hope you're well?'

Encouraged by these gracious words, Barkis came forward, and curt-seyed her acknowledgments.

'We have only met each other once before,' said my aunt. 'A nice business we made of it then! Trot, my dear, another cup.'

I handed it dutifully to my aunt, who was in her usual inflexible state of figure; and ventured a remonstrance with her on the subject of her sitting on a box.

'Let me draw the sofa here, or the easy-chair, aunt,' said I. 'Why should you be so uncomfortable?'

'Thank you, Trot,' replied my aunt, 'I prefer to sit upon my property.'

I knew my aunt sufficiently well to know that she had something of importance on her mind, and that there was far more matter in this arrival than a stranger might have supposed. I noticed how her eye lighted on me, when she thought my attention otherwise occupied; and what a curious process of hesitation appeared to be going on within her. I began to reflect whether I had done anything to offend her; and my conscience whispered me that I had not yet told her about Dora. Could it by any means be that, I wondered!

'Trot,' said my aunt at last, when she had finished her tea, 'have you got to be firm and self-reliant?'

'I think so, aunt.'

'Then why, my love,' said my aunt, looking earnestly at me, 'why do you think I prefer to sit upon this property of mine to-night?'

I shook my head, unable to guess.

'Because,' said my aunt, 'it's all I have. Because I'm ruined, my dear!'

If the house, and every one of us, had tumbled out into the river together, I could hardly have received a greater shock.

'Dick knows it,' said my aunt, laying her hand calmly on my shoulder. 'All I have in the world is in this room, except the cottage; and that I have left Janet to let. Barkis, I want to get a bed for this gentleman to-night. To save expense, perhaps you can make up something here for myself. Anything will do. It's only for to-night. We'll talk about this, more, to-morrow.'

I was roused from my amazement and concern for her, by her falling on my neck for a moment, and crying that she only grieved for me. In another moment she suppressed this emotion; and said with an aspect more triumphant than dejected:

'We must meet reverses boldly, and not suffer them to frighten us, my dear. We must learn to act the play out. We must live misfortune down, Trot!'

CHAPTER 35

Depression

As soon as I could recover my presence of mind, which quite deserted me in the first overpowering shock of my aunt's intelligence, I proposed to Mr Dick to come round to the chandler's shop, and take possession of the bed which Mr Peggotty had lately vacated.

I tried to ascertain whether Mr Dick had any understanding of the causes of this great change in my aunt's affairs. As I might have expected, he had none at all. The only account he could give of it, was, that my aunt had said to him, the day before yesterday, 'Now, Dick, are you really and truly the philosopher I take you for?' That then he had said, Yes, he hoped so. That then my aunt had said, 'Dick, I am ruined.' That then he had said, 'Oh, indeed!' That then my aunt had praised him highly, which he was very glad of.

Mr Dick was so very complacent, telling me this, with his eyes wide open and a surprise smile, that I am sorry to say I was provoked into explaining to him that ruin meant distress, want, and starvation; but, I was soon bitterly reproved for this harshness, by seeing his face turn pale, and tears course down his lengthened cheeks.

'What can we do, Trotwood?'

'All we can do just now, Mr Dick, is to keep a cheerful countenance, and not let my aunt see that we are thinking about it.'

He assented to this in the most earnest manner. But I regret to state that the fright I had given him proved too much for his best attempts at concealment. All the evening his eyes wandered to my aunt's face, with an expression of the most dismal apprehension, as if he saw her growing thin on the spot.

My aunt, on the other hand, was in a composed frame of mind, which was a lesson to all of us. She was extremely gracious to Peggotty and, strange as I knew she felt in London, appeared quite at home. She was to have my bed, and I was to lie in the sitting-room.

'Trot,' said she, 'I rather like that Barkis of yours, do you know!'

'It's better than a hundred pounds to hear you say so!' said I.

'The poor fool has been begging and praying about handing over some of her money – because she has got too much of it. A simpleton!' Affecting to laugh, she got an opportunity of putting her hand to her eyes. Having availed herself of it, she resumed her discourse.

'I know all about it, Trot! Barkis and myself had quite a gossip. I didn't know where these wretched girls expect to go to, for my part.'

'Poor Emily!' said I.

'Oh, don't talk to me about poor,' returned my aunt. 'She should have thought of that, before she caused so much misery!'

Then my aunt said: 'And so you fancy yourself in love! Do you?'

'Fancy, aunt!' I exclaimed, as red as I could be. 'I adore her with my whole soul!'

'Dora, indeed!' returned my aunt. 'And you mean to say the little thing is very fascinating, I suppose?'

'My dear aunt,' I replied, 'no one can form the least idea what she is!'

'Ah! And not silly?' said my aunt. 'I only ask. I don't depreciate her. Poor little couple! And so you think you are to go through a party-supper-table kind of life, like two pretty pieces of confectionery, do you, Trot?'

'We are young and inexperienced, aunt, I know,' I replied. 'But we love one another truly, I am sure. If I thought Dora could ever love anybody else, or cease to love me; I don't know what I should do – go out of my mind, I think!'

'Ah, Trot!' said my aunt, shaking her head, and smiling gravely, 'blind, blind, blind! However, I don't want to put two young creatures out of conceit with themselves, or to make them unhappy; so we'll be serious about it, and hope for a prosperous issue one of these days.'

This was not upon the whole very comforting to a rapturous lover; but I was glad to have my aunt in my confidence. So I thanked her ardently for this mark of her affection, and after a tender good-night, she took her nightcap into my bedroom.

How miserable I was when I lay down! How I thought about my being poor, in Mr Spenlow's eyes; about my not being what I was when I proposed to Dora; about the chivalrous necessity of telling Dora what my worldly condition was, and releasing her from her engagement if she thought fit; about how I should contrive to live, during the long term of my articles, when I was earning nothing; about doing something to assist my aunt, and seeing no way of doing anything; about coming down to have no money in my pocket, and to wear a shabby coat, and to ride no gallant greys, and to show myself in no agreeable light! Sordid and selfish as I knew it was, I was so devoted to Dora that I could not help it. I knew that it was base in me not to think more of my aunt, and less of myself; but, so far, selfishness was inseparable from Dora, and I could not put Dora on one side for any mortal creature. How exceedingly miserable I was that night!

My aunt was restless, too, for I frequently heard her walking to and fro. Two or three times in the course of the night, I found that she sat down near me, whispering to herself 'Poor boy!' And then it made me twenty times more wretched, to know how unselfishly mindful she was of me, and how selfishly mindful I was of myself.

There was an old Roman bath in those days at the bottom of one of the streets out of the Strand in which I have had many a cold plunge. Leaving Peggotty to look after my aunt, I tumbled head foremost into it, and then went for a walk to Hampstead. I had a hope that this brisk treatment might freshen my wits a little; and I soon came to the conclusion that the first step I ought to take was to try if my articles could be cancelled and the premium recovered. I got some breakfast on the Heath, and walked back to Doctors' Commons.

I arrived at the office so soon that I had half an hour's loitering before old Tiffey appeared with his key. Then I sat down in my shady corner, thinking about Dora; until Mr Spenlow came in, crisp and curly.

'Fine morning!' said he.

'Beautiful morning, sir,' said I. 'I am sorry to say that I have some rather disheartening intelligence from my aunt.'

'No!' said he. 'Not paralysis, I hope?'

'It has no reference to her health, sir,' I replied. 'She has met with some large losses. In fact, she has very little left, indeed.'

'You as-tound me, Copperfield!' cried Mr Spenlow.

'Indeed, sir,' said I, 'her affairs are so changed, that I wished to ask whether it would be possible to cancel my articles?'

'To cancel your articles, Copperfield? Cancel?'

I explained with tolerable firmness, that I really did not know where my means of subsistence were to come from, unless I could earn them for myself. I had no fear for the future, I said – and I laid great emphasis on that, as if to imply that I should still be decidedly eligible for a son-in-law one of these days – but, for the present, I was thrown upon my own resources.

'I am extremely sorry to hear this, Copperfield,' said Mr Spenlow. 'It is not usual to cancel articles for any such reason. It is not a professional course of proceeding. At the same time – if I had not a partner – Mr Jorkins –'

My hopes were dashed but I made another effort.

'Do you think, sir,' said I, 'if I were to mention it to Mr Jorkins –'

Mr Spenlow shook his head discouragingly. 'I know my partner, Copperfield. Mr Jorkins is *not* a man to respond to a proposition of this peculiar nature. You know what he is!'

I am sure I knew nothing about him, except that he came very late of a day, and went away very early; that he never appeared to be consulted about anything; and that he had a dingy little black-hole of his own up-stairs, where no business was ever done.

'Would you object to my mentioning it to him, sir?' I asked.

'By no means,' said Mr Spenlow.

Availing myself of this permission, I sat thinking about Dora until Mr Jorkins came. I then went up to Mr Jorkins's room, and evidently astonished Mr Jorkins by making my appearance there.

'Come in, Mr Copperfield,' said Mr Jorkins who was not by any means the awful creature one might have expected, but a mild, smooth-faced man of sixty.

'You have mentioned this to Mr Spenlow, I suppose?' said Mr Jorkins; when he had heard me, very restlessly, to an end.

I answered Yes, and told him that Mr Spenlow had introduced his name.

'He said I should object?' asked Mr Jorkins.

I was obliged to admit that Mr Spenlow had considered it probable.

'I am sorry to say, Mr Copperfield, I can't advance your object,' said Mr Jorkins, nervously. 'The fact is – but I have an appointment at the Bank, if you'll have the goodness to excuse me.'

With that he rose in a great hurry, stopping at the door to shake his head. 'You must be aware, Mr Copperfield,' he added, 'if Mr Spenlow objects – hopeless!' With that he fairly ran away.

I was completely bewildered between Mr Spenlow and Mr Jorkins, as to which of them really was the objecting partner; but I saw with sufficient clearness that there was obduracy somewhere in the firm, and the recovery of my aunt's thousand pounds was out of the question. In a state of despondency, I left the office, and went homeward.

I was trying to present to myself the arrangements we should have to make for the future in their sternest aspect, when a hackney chariot coming after me occasioned me to look up. A fair hand was stretched forth to me from the window.

'Agnes!' I joyfully exclaimed.

She was going to my rooms to see my aunt. I dismissed the coachman, and she took my arm, and we walked on together. She was like Hope embodied, to me. How different I felt in one short minute, having Agnes at my side!

She was not alone, she said. Her papa was with her – and Uriah Heep.

'And now they are partners,' I said. 'Confound him!'

'Yes,' said Agnes. 'They have some business here; and I took advantage of their coming, to come too. You must not think my visit all friendly and disinterested, Trotwood, for I do not like to let papa go away alone, with him.'

'Does he exercise the same influence over Mr Wickfield still, Agnes?'

'There is such a change at home,' said she. 'Mr Heep and his mother live with us now. He sleeps in your old room.'

'I wish I had the ordering of his dreams,' said I. 'He wouldn't sleep there long.'

'I keep my own little room,' said Agnes, 'where I used to learn my lessons. But I cannot always desert Mrs Heep, you know. And so, I feel obliged to bear her company, when I might prefer to be alone. The chief evil of their presence in the house is that I cannot be as near papa as I would wish – Uriah Heep being so much between. But, if any fraud or treachery is practising against him, I hope that simple love and truth are stronger in the end than any evil or misfortune in the world.'

She asked me if I knew how the reverse in my aunt's circumstances had been brought about. On my replying no, Agnes became thoughtful, and I fancied I felt her arm tremble in mine.

We found my aunt alone and greatly pleased to see Agnes. We began to talk about my aunt's losses, and I told them what I had tried to do that morning.

'Which was injudicious, Trot,' said my aunt, 'but well meant. Now, let us look the case of Betsey Trotwood in the face, and see how it stands.'

I observed Agnes turn pale, as she looked very attentively at my aunt. My aunt looked very attentively at Agnes.

'Betsey Trotwood,' said my aunt, 'had a certain property. It don't matter how much; enough to live on. More; for she had saved a little, and added to it. By the advice of her man of business, she laid it out on landed security. That did very well, and returned very good interest, till Betsey was paid off. Then, Betsey had to look for a new investment. She thought she was wiser, now, than her man of business, who was not such a good man of business by this time, as he used to be – I am alluding to your father, Agnes – and she took it into her head to lay it out for herself. So she took her pigs,' said my aunt, 'to a foreign market; and a very bad market it turned out to be. It fell to pieces, and never will and never can pay sixpence; and Betsey's sixpences were all there, and there's an end of them. Least said, soonest mended!'

My aunt concluded this philosophical summary, by fixing her eyes with a kind of triumph on Agnes, whose colour was gradually returning.

'Dear Miss Trotwood, is that all the history?' said Agnes.

'I hope it's enough, child,' said my aunt.

Agnes breathed more freely. I thought she had had some fear that her unhappy father might be in some way to blame for what had happened.

My aunt took her hand in hers, and laughed. 'Now, Agnes, you have a wise head. So have you, Trot, in some things, though I can't compliment you always. What's to be done? Here's the cottage will produce, say seventy pounds a year. Well! – That's all we've got.

'Then, there's Dick. He's good for a hundred a year, but of course that must be expended on himself. How can Trot and I do best, upon our means? What do you say, Agnes?'

Agnes inquired if my rooms were held for any long term?

'You come to the point, my dear,' said my aunt. 'They are not to be got rid of, for six months at least. I have a little ready money; and I agree with you, the best thing we can do, is, to live the term out here, and get Dick a bedroom hard by.'

'I have been thinking, Trotwood,' said Agnes, diffidently, 'that if you had time –'

'I have a good deal of time, Agnes. I am always disengaged after four or five o'clock, and I have time early in the morning.'

'I know you would not mind,' said Agnes, 'the duties of a secretary. Because Doctor Strong has come to live in London, and he asked papa if he could recommend him one. Don't you think he would rather have his favourite old pupil near him, than anybody else?'

I was scarcely more delighted with the prospect of earning my own bread, than with the hope of earning it under my old master; in short, I sat down and wrote a letter to the Doctor, stating my object, and appointing to call on him next day. This I addressed to Highgate – for in that place, so memorable to me, he lived – and went and posted.

When I came back, I found my aunt's birds hanging, just as they had hung so long in the parlour window of the cottage: and the round green fan, which my aunt had brought away with her, screwed on to the window-sill. I knew who had done all this, by its seeming to have quietly done itself.

A knock came at the door.

'I think,' said Agnes, 'it's papa. He promised me that he would come.'

I admitted not only Mr Wickfield, but Uriah Heep. I had not seen Mr Wickfield for some time. I was prepared for a great change in him, after what I had heard from Agnes, but his appearance shocked me.

It was not that he looked many years older, or that his eyes were full and bloodshot; or that there was a nervous trembling in his hand; but the thing that struck me most was that he should submit himself to that crawling impersonation of meanness, Uriah Heep. The reversal of the two natures, in their relative positions, Uriah's power and Mr Wickfield's of dependence, was a sight more painful to me than I can express. If I had seen an Ape taking command of a Man, I should hardly have thought it a more degrading spectacle.

Agnes softly said to him, 'Papa! Here is Miss Trotwood – and Trotwood, whom you have not seen for a long while!' and then he approached, and constrainedly gave my aunt his hand, and shook hands more cordially with me. In the moment's pause I speak of, I saw Uriah's countenance form itself into a most ill-favoured smile. Agnes saw it too, I think, for she shrank from him.

'Well, Wickfield!' said my aunt; and he looked up at her for the first time. 'I have been telling your daughter how well I have been disposing of my money for myself, because I couldn't trust it to you. Agnes is worth the whole firm, in my opinion.'

'If I may umbly make the remark,' said Uriah Heep, with a writhe, 'I fully agree with Miss Betsey Trotwood, and should be only too appy if Miss Agnes was a partner.'

'You're a partner yourself, you know,' returned my aunt, 'and that's about enough for you, I expect. How do you find yourself, sir?'

In acknowledgment of this question, addressed to him with extraordinary curtness, Mr Heep replied that he was pretty well, and hoped she was the same.

'And you, Master – I should say, Mister Copperfield,' pursued Uriah. 'I am rejoiced to see you, even under present circumstances.'

I believed that; for he seemed to relish them very much.

'And how do you think we are looking?' fawned Uriah. 'Don't you find Mr Wickfield blooming, sir? Years don't tell much in our firm, Master Copperfield, except in raising up the umble, namely, mother and self – and in developing,' he added, as an after-thought, 'the beautiful, namely, Miss Agnes.'

He jerked himself about, after this compliment, in such an intolerable manner, that my aunt, who had sat looking straight at him, lost all patience.

'Deuce take the man!' said my aunt, sternly. 'Don't be galvanic, sir!'

'I ask your pardon, Miss Trotwood,' returned Uriah; 'I'm aware you're nervous.'

'Go along with you, sir!' said my aunt, anything but appeased. 'Control your limbs, sir!'

Mr Heep was rather abashed, but he said to me aside in a meek voice:

'I am well aware, Master Copperfield, that Miss Trotwood has a quick temper and it's only natural that it should be made quicker by present circumstances. I only called to say that if there was anything we could do, in present circumstances, mother, or self, or Wickfield and Heep, we should be really glad. I may go so far?' said Uriah, with a sickly smile at his partner.

'Uriah Heep,' said Mr Wickfield, in a monotonous forced way, 'is active in the business, Trotwood. What he says, I quite concur in.'

'Oh, what a reward it is,' said Uriah, 'to be so trusted in! But I hope I am able to do something to relieve him from the fatigues of business, Master Copperfield!'

'Uriah Heep is a great relief to me,' said Mr Wickfield, in the same dull voice. 'It's a load off my mind, Trotwood, to have such a partner.'

The red fox made him say all this, I knew, to exhibit him to me in the light he had indicated on the night when he poisoned my rest. I saw the same ill-favoured smile upon his face again.

'You are not going, papa?' said Agnes, anxiously. 'Will you not walk back with Trotwood and me?'

He would have looked to Uriah, I believe, before replying, if that worthy had not anticipated him.

'I am bespoke myself,' said Uriah, 'on business; otherwise I should have been appy to have kept with my friends. But I leave my partner to represent the firm. Miss Agnes, ever yours! I wish you good-day, Master Copperfield, and leave my umble respects for Miss Betsey Trotwood.'

With those words, he retired, kissing his great hand, and leering at us.

We sat there, talking about our pleasant old Canterbury days, an hour or two. Mr Wickfield, left to Agnes, soon became more like his former self; though there was a settled depression upon him, which he never shook off.

My aunt would not accompany us to the place where they were staying, but insisted on my going. We dined together. After dinner, Agnes sat beside him, as of old, and poured out his wine. When it was almost dark, he lay down on a sofa, Agnes pillowing his head. It was not so dark but I could see tears glittering in her eyes.

I pray Heaven that I never may forget the dear girl in her love and truth, at that time of my life. She filled my heart with such good resolutions, strengthened my weakness so, by her example, that all the little good I have done, and all the harm I have forborne, I solemnly believe I may refer to her.

And how she spoke to me of Dora; listened to my praises of her; and round the little fairy-figure shed some glimpses of her own pure light, that made it yet more precious and more innocent to me! Oh, Agnes, sister of my boyhood, if I had known then, what I knew long afterwards!

There was a beggar in the street, when I went down; and he made me start by muttering, as if he were an echo of the morning:

'Blind! Blind! Blind!'

CHAPTER 36

Enthusiasm

I began the next day with another dive into the Roman bath, and then started for Highgate. I was not dispirited now. I was not afraid of the shabby coat, and had no yearnings after gallant greys. What I had to do, was, to take my woodman's axe and clear my own way through the forest of difficulty, by cutting down the trees until I came to Dora. And I went on at a mighty rate, as if it could be done by walking.

I got into such a transport, that I felt quite sorry my coat was not a little shabby already. In this state, I went into a cottage that I saw was to let, and examined it narrowly – for I felt it necessary to be practical. It would do for me and Dora admirably; with a little front garden for Jip to run about in, and a capital room up-stairs for my aunt. I came out and dashed up to Highgate, at such a rate that I was there an hour too early.

My first care was to find the Doctor's house. It was not in that part of Highgate where Mrs Steerforth lived, but quite on the opposite side of the little town. When I had made this discovery, I went back to a lane by Mrs Steerforth's, and looked over the corner of the garden wall. His room was shut up close and Rosa Dartle was walking, with a quick impetuous step, up and down a gravel walk on one side of the lawn. She gave me the idea of some fierce thing that was dragging the length of its chain to and fro upon a beaten track, and wearing its heart out. I came softly away from my place of observation, wishing I had not gone near it.

When I approached the Doctor's cottage, I saw him walking in the garden at the side, as if he had never left off walking since the days of my pupilage. When he came towards me, his benevolent face expressed extraordinary pleasure, and he took me by both hands.

'Why, my dear Copperfield, how do you do?'

I hoped he was well, and Mrs Strong too.

'Oh dear, yes!' said the Doctor. 'She'll be delighted to see you. You were always her favourite. She said so, last night, when I showed her your letter. And Mr Jack Maldon, *he's* pretty well, too.'

'Has he come home, sir?' I inquired.

'From India?' said the Doctor. 'Yes. Mr Jack Maldon couldn't bear the climate. Mrs Markleham – you have not forgotten Mrs Markleham? – was quite vexed about him, poor thing; so we have got him at home again; and we have bought him a little Patent place, which agrees with him much better.'

I knew enough of Mr Jack Maldon to suspect from this account that it was a place where there was not much to do, and which was pretty well paid. The Doctor, his kind face turned encouragingly to mine, went on: 'Now, in reference to this proposal of yours. It's very gratifying and agreeable to me, I am sure; but don't you think you could do better? You achieved distinction, you know, when you were with us. You have laid a foundation that any edifice may be raised upon; and is it not a pity that you should devote the spring-time of your life to such a poor pursuit as I can offer?'

I urged my request strongly: reminding the Doctor that I had already a profession.

'Well, well,' said the Doctor, 'that's true. Certainly, your having a profession makes a difference. But, my good young friend, what's seventy pounds a year?'

'It doubles our income, Doctor Strong,' said I. 'If you will take such time as I have, and that is my mornings and evenings, and can think it worth seventy pounds a year, you will do me such a service as I cannot express.'

'Dear me!' said the Doctor, innocently. 'To think that so little should go for so much! And when you can do better, you will? On your word, now?'

'On my word, sir!' I returned, answering in our old school manner. 'And I shall be twenty times happier, if my employment is to be on the Dictionary.'

The Doctor exclaimed, as if I had penetrated to the profoundest depths of mortal sagacity, 'My dear young friend, you have hit it. It is the Dictionary!'

How could it be anything else! He told me that since his retirement from scholastic life, he had been advancing with it wonderfully. The Doctor was quite happy in the prospect of our going to work together and we settled to begin next morning at seven o'clock. We were to work two hours every morning, and two or three hours every night, except on Saturdays, when I was to rest. On Sundays, of course, I was to rest also, and I considered these very easy terms.

Our plans being thus arranged, the Doctor took me into the house to present me to Mrs Strong. They had postponed their breakfast on my account, and we sat down to table together. We had not been seated long, when I saw an approaching arrival in Mrs Strong's face, before I heard any sound of it. A gentleman came into the breakfast parlour, whip in hand. It was Mr Jack Maldon, not at all improved by India, I thought. I was in a state of ferocious virtue, however, as to young men who were not cutting down the trees in the forest of difficulty; and my impression must be received with due allowance.

Mr Jack shook hands with me; but with an air of languid patronage, at which I secretly took great umbrage. But his languor altogether was quite a wonderful sight; except when he addressed himself to his cousin Annie.

'Have you breakfasted this morning, Mr Jack?' said the Doctor.

'I hardly ever take breakfast, sir,' he replied, 'I find it bores me. I came out to inquire whether Annie would like to go to the opera to-night.'

The Doctor said: 'You must go, Annie.'

'I would rather not,' she said.

Without looking at her cousin, she then addressed me, and asked me about Agnes, and whether she was not likely to come that day; and was so much disturbed, that I wondered how even the Doctor could be blind to what was so obvious.

But he saw nothing. He told her that she was young and ought to be entertained. I was curious to find out next morning, whether she had been. She had not, but had gone out in the afternoon to see Agnes. I wondered then, whether Agnes had some good influence over her too!

I was pretty busy now; up at five in the morning, and home at nine or ten at night. But I felt enthusiastically that the more I tired myself, the more I was doing to deserve Dora. I had not revealed myself in my altered character to Dora yet, because she was coming to see Miss Mills in a few days, and I deferred all I had to tell her until then. In the mean-time, I wholly abandoned scented soap and sold off three waistcoats at a prodigious sacrifice, as being too luxurious for my stern career.

Burning with impatience to do something more, I went to see Traddles. I took Mr Dick with me, because, acutely sensitive to my aunt's reverses, he had begun to fret and worry himself as having nothing useful to do.

We found Traddles hard at work with his inkstand and papers. He received us cordially, and made friends with Mr Dick in a moment.

The first subject on which I had to consult Traddles was this – I had heard that many distinguished men had begun life by reporting the debates in Parliament. I had told Traddles that I wished to know how I could qualify myself for this pursuit. Traddles now informed me that the mere mechanical acquisition necessary for thorough excellence in short-hand writing and reading was about equal in difficulty to the mastery of six languages; and that it might perhaps be attained, by dint of perseverance, in the course of a few years. Traddles reasonably supposed that this would settle the business; but I, feeling that here indeed were a few tall trees to be hewn down, immediately resolved to work my way on to Dora through this thicket, axe in hand.

'I'll buy a book,' said I, 'with a good scheme of this art in it; I'll work at it at the Commons, where I haven't half enough to do; I'll take down the speeches in our court for practice – Traddles, my dear fellow, I'll master it!'

'Dear me,' said Traddles, opening his eyes, 'I had no idea you were such a determined character, Copperfield!'

I passed that off, and brought Mr Dick on the carpet.

'You see,' said Mr Dick, wistfully, 'if I could exert myself, Mr Traddles – if I could beat a drum – or blow anything!'

Poor fellow! I have little doubt he would have preferred such an employment in his heart to all others. Traddles replied composedly:

'But you are a very good penman, sir. You told me so, Copperfield?'

'Excellent!' said I. And indeed he was. He wrote with extraordinary neatness.

'Don't you think,' said Traddles, 'you could copy writings, sir, if I got them for you?'

I explained to Traddles that there was a difficulty in keeping King Charles the First out of Mr Dick's manuscripts.

'But these writings that I speak of, are already drawn up and finished,' said Traddles. 'Wouldn't that make a difference?'

This gave us new hope. We concocted a scheme in virtue of which we got him to work next day, with triumphant success.

On a table by the window in Buckingham Street, we set out the work Traddles procured for him and on another table we spread the great Memorial. Our instructions to Mr Dick were that he should copy exactly what he had before him, and that when he felt it necessary to make the slightest allusion to King Charles the First, he should fly to the Memorial. We left my aunt to observe him. She reported to us that, at first, he was like a man playing the kettle-drums, and constantly divided his attentions between the two; but that, finding this confuse and fatigue him, he soon sat at it in an orderly manner. In a word, he earned by the following Saturday night ten shillings and nine pence; and never, while I live, shall I forget his going about to all the shops in the neighbourhood to change this treasure into sixpences, or his bringing them to my aunt with tears of joy and pride in his eyes.

'No starving now,' said Mr Dick, 'I'll provide for her, sir!' and he flourished his fingers in the air, as if they were ten banks.

I hardly know which was the better pleased, Traddles or I. 'It really,' said Traddles, suddenly, taking a letter out of his pocket, and giving it to me, 'put Mr Micawber quite out of my head!'

The letter ran thus:

'MY DEAR COPPERFIELD
    'I am about to establish myself in one of the provincial towns of our favoured island in immediate connexion with one of the learned professions. Mrs Micawber and our offspring will accompany me in bidding adieu to the modern Babylon, where we have undergone many vicissitudes, I trust not ignobly. Mrs Micawber and myself cannot disguise from our minds that we part, it may be for years and it may be for ever, with an individual linked by strong associations to the altar of our domestic life. If, on the eve of such a departure, you will accompany our mutual friend, Mr Thomas Traddles, to our present abode, and there reciprocate the wishes natural to the occasion, you will confer a Boon

On
One
Who
Is
Ever yours,
'WILKINS MICAWBER.'

I was glad to find that something really had turned up at last. Learning from Traddles that the invitation referred to the evening then wearing away, we went off together to the lodging which Mr Micawber occupied as Mr Mortimer, near the top of the Gray's Inn Road.

'My dear Copperfield,' said Mr Micawber, 'yourself and Mr Traddles find us on the brink of migration, and will excuse any little discomforts incidental to that position.'

Glancing round as I made a suitable reply, I observed that the family effects were already packed, and that the amount of luggage was by no means overwhelming. I congratulated Mrs Micawber on the approaching change.

'My family may consider it banishment,' said Mrs Micawber, 'but I am a wife and mother, and I never will desert Mr Micawber. It may be a sacrifice, to immure one's-self in a Cathedral town; but surely, Mr Copperfield, if it is a sacrifice in me, it is much more a sacrifice in a man of Mr Micawber's abilities.'

'You are going to a Cathedral town?' said I.

Mr Micawber replied: 'To Canterbury. In fact, my dear Copperfield, I have entered into arrangements, by virtue of which I stand pledged and contracted to our friend Heep, to assist and serve him in the capacity of – and to be – his confidential clerk.'

I stared at Mr Micawber, who greatly enjoyed my surprise.

'I am bound to state to you,' he said, with an official air, 'that the prudent suggestions of Mrs Micawber have in a great measure conduced to this result. The gauntlet, being thrown down in the form of an advertisement, was taken up by my friend Heep, and led to a mutual recognition. Such address and intelligence as I chance to possess,' said Mr Micawber, boastfully disparaging himself, with the old genteel air, 'will be devoted to my friend Heep's service.'

'What I particularly request Mr Micawber to be careful of,' said Mrs Micawber, 'is that he does not in applying himself to this subordinate branch of the law, place it out of his power to rise, ultimately, to the top of the tree. I am convinced that Mr Micawber, giving his mind to a profession so adapted to his fertile resources, and his flow of language, *must* distinguish himself. Now, for example, Mr Traddles,' said Mrs Micawber, assuming a profound air, 'a Judge, or even say a Chancellor. Does an individual place himself beyond the pale of those preferments by entering on such an office as Mr Micawber has accepted?'

Mr Micawber drank his punch with an air of exceeding satisfaction – glancing at Traddles, as if he desired to have his opinion.

'Why, the plain state of the case, Mrs Micawber,' said Traddles, 'is that only a barrister is eligible for such preferments; and Mr Micawber could not be a barrister, without being entered at an inn of court as a student, for five years.'

'Do I understand,' said Mrs Micawber, 'that at the expiration of that period, Mr Micawber would be eligible as a Judge or Chancellor?'

'He would be *eligible*,' returned Traddles, with a strong emphasis on that word.

'Thank you,' said Mrs Micawber. 'That is quite sufficient. If such is the case, my anxiety is set at rest. I speak,' said Mrs Micawber, 'as a female, necessarily; but I have always been of opinion that Mr Micawber possesses what I have heard my papa call, when I lived at home, the judicial mind; and I hope Mr Micawber is now entering on a field where that mind will develop itself, and take a commanding station.'

When we were nearly come to the last round of the punch, I addressed myself to Traddles, and reminded him that we must not separate without wishing our friends health, happiness, and success in their new career. I begged Mr Micawber to fill us bumpers, and proposed the toast in due form.

'My dear Copperfield,' said Mr Micawber, rising with one of his thumbs in each of his waistcoat pockets, 'the companion of my youth, and my esteemed friend Traddles: allow me to thank them in the warmest and most uncompromising terms for their good wishes. It may be expected that on the eve of a migration which will consign us to a perfectly new existence,' Mr Micawber spoke as if they were going five hundred thousand miles, 'I should offer a few valedictory remarks to two such friends as I see before me. But all that I have to say in this way, I have said. I have been under the necessity of assuming a garb from which my natural instincts recoil – I allude to spectacles – and possessing myself of a cognomen, to which I can establish no legitimate pretensions. All I have to say on that score is, that the cloud has passed from the dreary scene, and the God of Day is once more high upon the mountain tops. On Monday next, on the arrival of the four o'clock afternoon coach at Canterbury, my foot will be on my native heath – my name, Micawber!'

Mr Micawber drank two glasses of punch in grave succession. He then said with much solemnity:

'One thing more I have to do, before this separation is complete, and that is to perform an act of justice. My friend Mr Thomas Traddles has, on two several occasions, "put his name" to bills of exchange for my accommodation. These sums, united, make a total, if my calculation is correct, amounting to forty-one, ten, eleven and a half. My friend Copperfield will perhaps do me the favour to check that total?'

I did so and found it correct.

'To leave this metropolis,' said Mr Micawber, 'without acquitting myself of the pecuniary part of this obligation, would weigh upon my mind to an insupportable extent. I have, therefore, prepared a document, which accomplishes the desired object. I beg to hand to my friend Mr Thomas Traddles my IOU for forty-one, ten, eleven and a half, and I am happy to recover my moral dignity, and to know that I can once more walk erect before my fellow man!'

With this introduction (which greatly affected him), Mr Micawber placed his IOU in the hands of Traddles, and said he wished him well in every relation of life. I am persuaded, not only that this was quite the same to Mr Micawber as paying the money, but that Traddles himself hardly knew the difference until he had time to think about it.

Mr Micawber walked so erect before his fellow man, on the strength of this virtuous action, that his chest looked half as broad again when he lighted us down-stairs. We parted with great heartiness on both sides; and when I had seen Traddles to his own door, and was going home alone, I thought that, slippery as Mr Micawber was, I was probably indebted to some compassionate recollection he retained of me as his boy-lodger, for never having been asked by him for money. I certainly should not have had the moral courage to refuse it; and I have no doubt he knew that quite as well as I did.

CHAPTER 37

A little Cold Water

My new life had lasted for more than a week, and I was stronger than ever in those tremendous practical resolutions that I felt the crisis required. As yet, Dora was quite unconscious of my desperate firmness, but, on Saturday evening she was to be at Miss Mills's; and I was to go there to tea.

By this time, we were quite settled down in Buckingham Street, where Mr Dick continued his copying in a state of absolute felicity. My aunt, being uncommonly neat and ingenious, made so many little improvements in our domestic arrangements, that I seemed to be richer instead of poorer.

Peggotty had considered herself highly privileged in being allowed to participate in these labours; and, although she still retained something of her old sentiment of awe in reference to my aunt, had received so many marks of encouragement and confidence, that they were the best friends possible. But the time had now come when it was necessary for her to return home. 'So good-bye, Barkis,' said my aunt, 'I am sure I never thought I could be sorry to lose you!'

I took Peggotty to the coach-office. She cried at parting, and confided her brother to my friendship as Ham had done. We had heard nothing of him since he went away.

'And now, my own dear Davy,' said Peggotty, 'if you should want any money, who has such a right to ask leave to lend it you, as me!'

I was not so savagely independent as to say anything in reply, but that if ever I borrowed money of any one, I would borrow it of her. Next to accepting a large sum on the spot, I believe this gave Peggotty more comfort than anything I could have done.

I fatigued myself as much as I possibly could in the Commons all day and at the appointed time in the evening repaired to Mr Mills's street.

Dora came to the drawing-room door to meet me; and Jip came scrambling out, tumbling over his own growls, under the impression that I was a Bandit; and we all three went in, as happy and loving as could be. I soon carried desolation into the bosom of our joys by asking

Dora, without the smallest preparation, if she could love a beggar?

'How can you ask me anything so foolish?' pouted Dora. 'Love a beggar!'

'Dora, my own dearest!' said I. 'I am a beggar!'

'How can you be such a silly thing,' replied Dora, slapping my hand, 'as to sit there, telling such stories? I'll make Jip bite you!'

But I looked so serious, that Dora began to cry. That was dreadful. At last, after an agony of supplication and protestation, I got Dora to look at me. Then I told her, with my arms clasped round her, how I loved her, so dearly; how I felt it right to offer to release her from her engagement, because now I was poor; how I had no fears of poverty, if she had none; how I had begun to be practical, and look into the future; how a crust well-earned was sweeter far than a feast inherited; and much more to the same purpose.

'Is your heart mine still, dear Dora?' said I rapturously, for I knew by her clinging to me that it was.

'Oh, yes!' cried Dora. 'Oh, yes, it's all yours. Oh, don't talk about being poor, and working hard!'

'My dearest love,' said I, 'the crust well-earned –'

'I don't want to hear any more about crusts!' said Dora. 'And Jip must have a mutton-chop every day at twelve, or he'll die!'

I was charmed with her childish, winning way. I fondly explained to Dora that Jip should have his mutton-chop with his accustomed regularity. I drew a picture of our frugal home, sketching in the little house I had seen at Highgate, and my aunt in her room up-stairs.

'But I hope your aunt will keep in her own room a good deal,' cried Dora. 'And I hope she's not a scolding old thing!'

If it were possible for me to love Dora more than ever, I am sure I did. But I felt she was a little impracticable. I made another trial.

'My own! May I mention something?'

'Oh, please don't be practical!' said Dora coaxingly. 'Because it frightens me so!'

'But, Dora, my beloved!' said I, 'if you will sometimes look about now and then at your papa's housekeeping, and endeavour to acquire a little habit – of accounts, for instance –'

Poor little Dora received this suggestion with something that was half a sob and half a scream.

'It would be so useful to us afterwards,' I went on. 'And if you would promise me to read a little Cookery Book that I would send you, it would be so excellent for both of us. For our path in life, my Dora,' said I, warming with the subject, 'is stony and rugged now, and it rests with us to smooth it. We must fight our way onward. There are obstacles to be met, and we must crush them!'

I was going on at a great rate, with a clenched hand, and a most enthusiastic countenance; but I had done it again. Oh, she was so frightened! Oh, take her to Julia Mills, and go away, please!

I thought I had killed her, this time. I sprinkled water on her face. I ravaged Miss Mills's work-box for a smelling-bottle, and dropped all the needles over Dora. I shook my fists at Jip, who was as frantic as myself, when Miss Mills came into the room.

'Who has done this?' exclaimed Miss Mills, succouring her friend.

At first Miss Mills thought it was a quarrel, and that we were verging on the Desert of Sahara, but she soon found out how matters stood, for my dear affectionate little Dora, embracing her, began exclaiming that I was 'a poor labourer'.

Miss Mills ascertained from me in a few words what it was all about, comforted Dora, and gradually convinced her that I was not a labourer – and so brought us together in peace. When we were quite composed, and Dora had gone up-stairs to put some rosewater to her eyes, Miss Mills rang for tea.

I then expounded to Miss Mills what I had endeavoured, so very unsuccessfully, to expound to Dora. Miss Mills replied, on general principles, that the Cottage of content was better than the Palace of cold splendour, and that where love was, all was.

I then put it to Miss Mills, to say whether she considered that there was any practical merit in the suggestion I had been anxious to make, concerning the accounts, the housekeeping, and the Cookery Book?

Miss Mills, after some consideration, thus replied:

'Mr Copperfield, I will be plain with you. The suggestion is not appropriate to our Dora. She is a thing of light, and airiness, and joy. I am free to confess that if it could be done, it might be well, but –' And Miss Mills shook her head.

I was encouraged to ask her if she had any opportunity of luring her attention to such preparations for an earnest life, she would avail herself of it? Miss Mills replied in the affirmative so readily, that I further asked her if she would take charge of the Cookery Book. Miss Mills accepted this trust, too; but was not sanguine.

And Dora returned, looking such a lovely little creature, that I really doubted whether she ought to be troubled with anything so ordinary. And she loved me so much, and was so captivating, that I felt like a sort of Monster, who had got into a Fairy's bower, when I thought of having frightened her, and made her cry.

After tea we had the guitar; and Dora sang those same dear old French songs about the impossibility of ever on any account leaving off dancing, La ra la, La ra la, until I felt a much greater Monster than before.

We had only one check to our pleasure. I unluckily let out that, being obliged to exert myself now, I got up at five o'clock. It made a great impression on her, and she neither played nor sang any more.

It was still on her mind when I bade her adieu; and she said, 'Now don't get up at five o'clock, you naughty boy.'

'My love,' said I, 'I have work to do.'

'Oh! How ridiculous!' cried Dora.

'How shall we live without, Dora?' said I.

'How? Any how!' said Dora.

Well! I loved her, and I went on loving her. But going on, too, working pretty hard, and busily keeping red-hot all the irons I now had in the fire, I would sit sometimes of a night, opposite my aunt, thinking how I had frightened Dora that time, and how I could best make my way with a guitar-case through the forest of difficulty, until I used to fancy that my head was turning quite grey.

CHAPTER 38

A Dissolution of Partnership

I did not allow my resolution with respect to the Parliamentary Debates to cool. It was one of the irons I hammered at with a perseverance I may honestly admire. I bought an approved scheme of the noble art of stenography and plunged into a sea of perplexity that brought me, in a few weeks, to the confines of distraction.

It might have been quite heart-breaking, but for Dora, who was the stay and anchor of my tempest-driven bark. Every scratch in the scheme was a gnarled oak in the forest of difficulty, and I went on cutting them down with such vigour, that in three or four months I was in a condition to make an experiment.

Traddles suggested that he should dictate speeches to me, at a pace and with occasional stoppages, adapted to my weakness. I accepted the proposal; and almost every night we had a sort of Private Parliament in Buckingham Street after I came home from the Doctor's.

Often we pursued these debates until the clock pointed to midnight. The result of so much good practice was, that by-and-by I began to keep pace with Traddles pretty well, and should have been quite triumphant if I had the least idea what my notes were about.

There was nothing for it but to begin all over again. It was very hard, but I turned back to plod over the same tedious ground at a snail's pace; stopping to know these elusive characters by sight wherever I met them. I was always punctual at the office; at the Doctor's too; and I really did work, as the common expression is, like a cart-horse.

One day, when I went to the Commons, I found Mr Spenlow in the doorway looking extremely grave.

He looked at me in a distant, ceremonious manner, and coldly requested me to accompany him to a certain coffee-house. My mind misgave me that he had found out about my darling Dora.

If I had not guessed this, on the way to the coffee-house, I could hardly have failed to know what was the matter when I found Miss Murdstone there.

'Have the goodness to show Mr Copperfield,' said Mr Spenlow, 'what you have in your reticule, Miss Murdstone.'

I believe it was the old identical steel-clasped reticule of my childhood that shut up like a bite. Miss Murdstone opened it and produced my last letter to Dora, teeming with expressions of devoted affection.

'I believe that is your writing, Mr Copperfield?' said Mr Spenlow.

I was very hot, and the voice I heard was very unlike mine, when I said, 'It is, sir!'

'If I am not mistaken,' said Mr Spenlow, as Miss Murdstone brought a parcel of letters out of her reticule, tied round with the dearest bit of blue ribbon, 'those are also from your pen, Mr Copperfield?'

I took them from her with a most desolate sensation; and, glancing at such phrases at the top, as 'My ever dearest and own Dora,' 'My best beloved angel' and the like, blushed deeply, and inclined my head.

'Miss Murdstone, be so good as to proceed!' said Mr Spenlow, coldly.

That gentle creature delivered herself as follows:

'I must confess to having entertained my suspicions of Miss Spenlow, in reference to David Copperfield, for some time. The depravity of the human heart is such –'

'You will oblige me, ma'am,' interrupted Mr Spenlow, 'by confining yourself to facts.'

Miss Murdstone with frowning dignity resumed:

'On my return to Norwood, after the period of absence occasioned by my brother's marriage, it appeared to me that Miss Spenlow received too many letters from her friend Miss Mills. Last evening after tea, I observed the little dog worrying something. I said to Miss Spenlow, "Dora, what is that the dog has in his mouth? It's paper." Miss Spenlow immediately put her hand to her frock, gave a sudden cry, and ran to the dog. I interposed, and said, "Dora my love, you must permit me."'

Oh Jip, miserable Spaniel, this wretchedness, then, was your work!

'Miss Spenlow endeavoured,' said Miss Murdstone, 'to bribe me with small articles of jewellery – that, of course, I pass over. The little dog still kept the letter in his mouth; and on my endeavouring to take it from him, he kept it between his teeth so pertinaciously as to suffer himself to be held suspended in the air by means of the document. At length I obtained possession of it. After perusing it, I taxed Miss Spenlow with having many such letters in her possession; and ultimately obtained from her the packet which is now in David Copperfield's hand.'

Here she ceased, snapping her reticule again.

'You have heard Miss Murdstone,' said Mr Spenlow, turning to me. 'I beg to ask, Mr Copperfield, if you have anything to say in reply?'

The picture I had before me of the beautiful little treasure of my heart sobbing and crying, of her having so piteously begged that stony-hearted woman to forgive her, of her being in such grievous distress and all for me – very much impaired the little dignity I had been able to muster.

'There is nothing I can say, sir,' I returned, 'except that all the blame is mine. Dora –'

'Miss Spenlow, if you please,' said her father, majestically.

' – was induced and persuaded by me,' I went on, 'to consent to this concealment, and I bitterly regret it.'

'You are very much to blame, sir,' said Mr Spenlow. 'When I take a gentleman to my house, I take him there in a spirit of confidence. If he abuses my confidence, he commits a dishonourable action, Mr Copperfield.'

'I feel it, sir, I assure you,' I returned. 'But I love Miss Spenlow to that extent –'

'Pooh! nonsense!' said Mr Spenlow, reddening. 'Pray don't tell me to my face that you love my daughter, Mr Copperfield!'

'Could I defend my conduct if I did not, sir?' I returned, with all humility.

'Can you defend your conduct if you do, sir?' said Mr Spenlow. 'Have you considered my daughter's station in life, the projects I may contemplate for her advancement, the testamentary intentions I may have with reference to her? Have you considered anything, Mr Copperfield?'

'Very little, sir, I am afraid,' I answered, speaking to him as respectfully and sorrowfully as I felt. 'When I explained my altered position to you, sir, this concealment, into which I am so unhappy as to have led Miss Spenlow, had begun. Since I have been in that altered position, I have exerted every energy, to improve it. I am sure I shall improve it in time. Will you grant me time? We are both so young, sir –'

'You are right,' interrupted Mr Spenlow, nodding his head a great many times, 'you are both very young. Take away those letters, and throw them in the fire; give me Miss Spenlow's letters to throw in the fire; and although our future intercourse must, you are aware, be restricted to the Commons here, we will agree to make no further mention of the past.'

No. I couldn't think of agreeing to it. I was very sorry, but there was a higher consideration than sense. Love was above all earthly considerations, and I loved Dora to idolatry, and Dora loved me. I didn't exactly say so; I softened it down as much as I could; but I implied it, and I was resolute upon it.

'Very well,' said Mr Spenlow, 'I must try my influence with my daughter.'

A silence succeeding, I was undecided whether to go or stay.

'You are probably aware, Mr Copperfield, that I am not altogether destitute of worldly possessions, and that my daughter is my nearest and dearest relative? And you can hardly think, having experience of what we see, in the Commons here, every day, of the negligent proceedings of men in respect of their testamentary arrangements but that mine are made?'

I inclined my head in acquiescence.

'I should not allow my suitable provision for my child to be influenced by a piece of youthful folly like the present. But I might, if this silly business were not completely relinquished altogether, be induced in some anxious moment to surround her with protections against the consequences of any foolish step in the way of marriage. Now, Mr Copperfield, I hope that you will not render it necessary for me to unsettle grave affairs long since composed.'

What could I do? I could not deny Dora and my own heart. When he told me I had better take a week to consider of what he had said, how could I fail to know that no amount of weeks could influence such love as mine?

'Confer with Miss Trotwood, or with any person with any knowledge of life,' said Mr Spenlow. 'Take a week, Mr Copperfield.'

I submitted; and, with a countenance as expressive as I was able to make it of dejected and despairing constancy, came out of the room.

When I got to the office and sat at my desk, in the bitterness of my spirit cursing Jip, I fell into such a state of torment about Dora, that I wonder I did not rush insanely to Norwood. The idea of their making her cry, and of my not being there to comfort her, was so excruciating, that it impelled me to write a wild letter to Mr Spenlow, beseeching him not to visit upon her the consequences of my awful destiny. I implored him to spare her gentle nature – not to crush a fragile flower – and addressed him generally as if he had been an Ogre. This letter I laid upon his desk.

He said nothing about it all the morning; but before he went away in the afternoon he called me in, and told me that I need not make myself at all uneasy about his daughter's happiness. He had assured her, he said, that it was all nonsense; and he had nothing more to say to her. He believed he was an indulgent father (as indeed he was), and I might spare myself any solicitude on her account.

'You may make it necessary, if you are foolish or obstinate, Mr

Copperfield,' he observed, 'for me to send my daughter abroad but I have a better opinion of you. I hope you will be wiser than that, in a few days. All I desire, is that it should be forgotten. All you have got to do, Mr Copperfield, is to forget it.'

All! In the note I wrote to Miss Mills, I bitterly quoted this sentiment. All I had to do, I said, with gloomy sarcasm, was to forget Dora. I entreated Miss Mills to see me that evening. I informed her that my reason was tottering on its throne, and only she, Miss Mills, could prevent its being deposed. I signed myself, hers distractedly; and I couldn't help feeling that it was something in the style of Mr Micawber.

However, I sent it. At night I repaired to Miss Mills's street, and walked up and down, until I was stealthily fetched in by Miss Mills's maid, and taken to the back kitchen. I have since seen reason to believe that there was nothing on earth to prevent my going in at the front door except Miss Mills's love of the romantic and mysterious.

In the back kitchen I raved as became me. I went there, I suppose, to make a fool of myself, and I am quite sure I did it.

Miss Mills had received a hasty note from Dora, telling her that all was discovered. Miss Mills had a wonderful flow of words, and liked to pour them out. I could not help feeling, though she mingled her tears with mine, that she had a dreadful luxury in our afflictions. She made me much more wretched than I was before, and I felt that she was indeed a friend. We resolved that she should go to Dora the first thing in the morning, and find some means of assuring her of my devotion and misery. We parted, overwhelmed with grief, and I think Miss Mills enjoyed herself completely.

I confided all to my aunt when I got home; and went to bed despairing. I got up despairing, and went out despairing straight to the Commons.

I was surprised, when I came within sight of our office-door, to see the ticket-porters standing outside talking together.

The clerks were there, but nobody was doing anything. Old Tiffey, for the first time in his life I should think, had not hung up his hat.

'This is a dreadful calamity, Mr Copperfield,' said he, as I entered.

'What is?' I exclaimed.

'Don't you know?' cried Tiffey. 'Mr Spenlow.'

'What about him?'

'Dead!'

One of the clerks caught hold of me. They sat me down in a chair, untied my neckcloth, and brought me some water.

'He dined in town yesterday, and drove down in the phaeton by himself,' said Tiffey, 'having sent his own groom home by the coach, as he sometimes did. The phaeton went home without him. The horses stopped at the stable gate. The man went out with a lantern. Nobody in the carriage. The house was roused up directly, and three of them went out along the road. They found him a mile off. Whether he fell out in a fit, or got out, feeling ill before the fit came on, no one appears to know. Medical assistance was got as soon as possible, but it was quite useless.'

I cannot describe the state of mind into which I was thrown by this intelligence. The shock of such an event happening so suddenly is easily intelligible to any one. What I cannot describe is how, in the innermost recesses of my own heart, I had a lurking jealousy even of Death. How I felt as if its might would push me from my ground in Dora's thoughts. How it made me restless to think of her being consoled by others.

In this state of mind, I went down to Norwood that night; and finding from one of the servants that Miss Mills was there, got my aunt to direct a letter to her, which I wrote. I deplored the untimely death of Mr Spenlow most sincerely, and shed tears in doing so. I entreated her to tell Dora, if Dora were in a state to hear it, that he had spoken to me with the utmost kindness and consideration; and had coupled nothing but tenderness with her name. I know I did this selfishly, to have my name brought before her; but I tried to believe it was an act of justice to his memory.

My aunt received a few lines next day in reply; addressed outside to her; within, to me. Dora was overcome by grief; and when her friend had asked her should she send her love to me, had only cried, as she was always crying, 'Oh, dear papa! oh, poor papa!' But she had not said No, and that I made the most of.

Mr Jorkins came to the office a few days afterwards. He and Tiffey were closeted together for some few moments, and then Tiffey beckoned me in.

'Mr Tiffey and myself,' said Mr Jorkins, 'are about to examine the desks, the drawers, and other such repositories of the deceased, with the view of sealing up his private papers, and searching for a Will. There is no trace of any, elsewhere. It may be as well for you to assist us, if you please.'

We began the search at once. The office papers we placed on one side, and the private papers on the other.

We had sealed up several packets when Mr Jorkins said to us, 'Mr Spenlow was very difficult to move from the beaten track. I am disposed to think he had made no will.'

'Oh, I know he had!' said I.

They both stopped and looked at me.

'On the very day when I last saw him, he told me that he had, and that his affairs were long since settled.'

Mr Jorkins and old Tiffey shook their heads with one accord.

'That looks unpromising,' said Tiffey.

'Surely you don't doubt –' I began.

'My good Mr Copperfield!' said Tiffey, laying his hand upon my arm, 'if you had been in the Commons as long as I have, you would know that there is no subject on which men are so inconsistent, and so little to be trusted. My opinion is – no will.'

It turned out that there *was* no will. What was scarcely less astonishing to me was that his affairs were in a most disordered state. It was extremely difficult, I heard, to make out what he owed, or what he had paid, or of what he died possessed. It came out that, in the competition on all points of appearance and gentility then running high in the Commons, he had spent more than his professional income, and had reduced his private means to a very low ebb indeed. There was a sale of the furniture and lease at Norwood; and Tiffey told me that, paying all the just debts of the deceased, and deducting his share of outstanding bad and doubtful debts due to the firm, he wouldn't give a thousand pounds for all the assets remaining.

This was at the expiration of about six weeks. I had suffered tortures all the time. Miss Mills reported to me that Dora had no other relations than two aunts, maiden sisters of Mr Spenlow. These two ladies now proposed to take Dora to live at Putney. Dora, clinging to them both, and weeping, exclaimed, 'O yes, aunts! Please take Julia Mills and me and Jip to Putney!' So they went, very soon after the funeral.

How I found time to haunt Putney, I am sure I don't know; but I contrived, by some means or other, to prowl about the neighbourhood pretty often. Miss Mills, for the more exact discharge of the duties of friendship, kept a journal; and she used to meet me sometimes, on the Common, and read it, or lend it to me. How I treasured up the entries, of which I subjoin a sample! –

'Monday. My sweet D. still much depressed. Headache. Called attention to J. as being beautifully sleek. D. fondled J. Associations thus awakened, opened floodgates of sorrow. Rush of grief admitted. (Are tears the dewdrops of the heart? J. M.)

'Tuesday. D. weak and nervous. Beautiful in pallor. (Do we not remark this in moon likewise? J. M.) D. J. M. and J. took airing in carriage. J. looking out of window, and barking violently at dustman, occasioned smile to overspread features of D. (Of such slight links is chain of life composed! J. M.)'

Miss Mills and her journal were my sole consolation at this period. To see her, who had seen Dora but a little while before – to be made more miserable by her – were my only comforts. I felt as if I had been living in a palace of cards, which had tumbled down, leaving only Miss Mills and me among the ruins!

CHAPTER 39

Wickfield and Heep

My aunt, beginning to be made uncomfortable by my prolonged dejection, made a pretence of being anxious that I should go to Dover to see that all was working well at the cottage. Janet was drafted into the service of Mrs Strong, where I saw her every day.

Although it required an effort to leave Miss Mills, I fell willingly into my aunt's pretence, as a means of enabling me to pass a few tranquil hours with Agnes.

I found everything in a satisfactory state at the cottage in Dover; and was enabled to gratify my aunt exceedingly by reporting that the tenant waged incessant war against donkeys. Having settled the business there, I walked on to Canterbury early in the morning.

Arrived at Mr Wickfield's house, I found, in the little lower room on the ground floor where Uriah Heep had been of old accustomed to sit, Mr Micawber plying his pen with great assiduity. He was dressed in a legal-looking suit of black, and loomed, burly and large, in that small office.

'How do you like the law, Mr Micawber?' said I.

'My dear Copperfield, to a man possessed of the higher imaginative powers, the objection to legal studies is the amount of detail which they involve. Even in our professional correspondence,' said Mr Micawber, glancing at some letters he was writing, 'the mind is not at liberty to soar to any exalted form of expression. Still, it is a great pursuit.'

He then told me that he had become the tenant of Uriah Heep's old house.

'It is humble,' said Mr Micawber, 'to quote a favourite expression of my friend Heep; but it may prove the stepping-stone to more ambitious domiciliary accommodation.'

I asked him whether he had reason, so far, to be satisfied with his friend Heep's treatment of him? He got up to ascertain if the door were close shut, before he replied, in a lower voice:

'My dear Copperfield, a man who labours under the pressure of pecuniary embarrassments is, with the generality of people, at a disadvantage.

That disadvantage is not diminished when that pressure necessitates the drawing of stipendiary emoluments before those emoluments are strictly due and payable. All I can say is that my friend Heep has responded in a manner calculated to redound equally to the honour of his head, and of his heart.'

'Do you see much of Mr Wickfield?' I asked, to change the subject.

'Not much,' said Mr Micawber, slightingly. 'Mr Wickfield is, I dare say, a man of very excellent intentions; but he is – in short, he is obsolete.'

'I am afraid his partner seeks to make him so,' said I.

'My dear Copperfield!' returned Mr Micawber, after some uneasy evolutions on his stool, 'I am here, in a capacity of confidence. I would therefore take the liberty of suggesting that in our friendly intercourse we draw a line. On one side of this line,' said Mr Micawber, representing it on the desk with the office ruler, 'is the whole range of the human intellect, with a trifling exception; on the other, *is* that exception; that is to say, the affairs of Messrs Wickfield and Heep. I trust I give no offence in submitting this proposition?'

Though I saw an uneasy change in Mr Micawber, I felt I had no right to be offended. My telling him so, appeared to relieve him.

'I am charmed, Copperfield,' said Mr Micawber, 'let me assure you, with Miss Wickfield. She is a very superior young lady. If you had not assured us that D was your favourite letter, I should unquestionably have supposed that A. had been so.'

We have all some experience of knowing perfectly what will be said next, as if we suddenly remembered it! I never had this mysterious impression more strongly in my life, than before he uttered those words.

I took my leave of Mr Micawber, for the time, charging him with my best remembrances to all at home. As I left him, I clearly perceived that there was something interposed between him and me since he had come into his new functions, which quite altered the character of our intercourse.

I looked into the room still belonging to Agnes, and saw her sitting by the fire. What a pleasure to be the cause of that bright change in her attentive face, and the object of that sweet regard and welcome!

'Ah, Agnes!' said I, when we were sitting together, side by side; 'I have missed you so much, lately!'

'Indeed?' she replied.

'Whenever I have not had you to advise, I have seemed to get into all sorts of difficulty. When I have come to you, I have come to peace and happiness. I come home, now, like a tired traveller, and find such a blessed sense of rest!'

In her placid sisterly manner she soon led me on to tell all that had happened since our last meeting.

'Now, my reliance is on you,' said I, when I had made an end of my confidence.

'But it must not be on me, Trotwood,' returned Agnes with a pleasant smile. 'It must be on Dora.'

'I have not mentioned,' said I, a little embarrassed, 'that Dora is easily disturbed and frightened.'

Accordingly, I told Agnes about my declaration of poverty, about the cookery-book, the housekeeping accounts, and all the rest of it.

'Oh, Trotwood!' she remonstrated. 'Just your old headlong way! You might have been in earnest in striving to get on in the world, without being so very sudden with a timid, loving, inexperienced girl. Poor Dora!'

'What ought I to do then, Agnes?'

'I think that the honourable course would be to write to those two ladies. I would relate all that has taken place; and I would ask their permission to visit sometimes, at their house. Considering that you are young, and striving for a place in life, I think it would be well to say that you would readily abide by any conditions they might impose upon you. I would entreat them not to dismiss your request without a reference to Dora; and to discuss it with her when they should think the time suitable. I would not be too vehement,' said Agnes, gently, 'or propose too much. I would trust to my fidelity and perseverance – and to Dora.'

'But if they were to frighten Dora again, Agnes, by speaking to her,' said I. 'And if Dora were to cry, and say nothing about me!'

'Is that likely?' inquired Agnes.

'God bless her, she is as easily scared as a bird,' said I. 'It might be! Or if the two Miss Spenlows should not be likely persons to address in that way!'

'I don't think, Trotwood,' returned Agnes, 'I would consider that. Perhaps it would be better only to consider whether it is right to do this; and, if it is, to do it.'

I had no longer any doubt on the subject. With a lightened heart I devoted the whole afternoon to the composition of the draft of this letter. But first I went down-stairs to see Mr Wickfield and Uriah Heep.

I found Uriah in possession of a new office, built out in the garden. He received me in his usual fawning way, and accompanied me into Mr Wickfield's room.

'You stay with us, Trotwood, while you remain in Canterbury?' said Mr Wickfield, not without a glance at Uriah for his approval.

'Is there room for me?' said I.

'I would turn out of your old room with pleasure, if it would be agreeable,' said Uriah.

'No, no,' said Mr Wickfield. 'Why should *you* be inconvenienced? There's another room.'

'Oh, but you know,' returned Uriah, with a grin. 'I should really be delighted!'

To cut the matter short, I said I would have the other room or none at all; and, taking my leave of the firm until dinner, I went up-stairs again.

I had hoped to have no other companion than Agnes. But Mrs Heep had asked permission to bring herself and her knitting near the fire, in that room; on pretence of its having an aspect more favourable for her rheumatics. Though I could almost have consigned her to the topmost pinnacle of the Cathedral, I gave her a friendly salutation.

'I'm umbly thankful to you, sir,' said Mrs Heep, in acknowledgment of my inquiries concerning her health, 'but I'm only pretty well. I haven't much to boast of. If I could see my Uriah well settled in life, I couldn't expect much more, I think.'

She never left us for a moment. I had arrived early in the day, and we had still three or four hours before dinner; but she sat there, plying her knitting-needles as monotonously as an hourglass might have poured out its sands. Whensoever I lifted up my eyes, and meeting the thoughtful face of Agnes, I was conscious of the evil eye passing me, and going on to her, and coming back to me again, and dropping furtively upon the knitting.

At dinner she maintained her watch, with the same unwinking eyes. After dinner, her son took his turn; and when Mr Wickfield, himself, and I were left alone together, leered at me, and writhed until I could hardly bear it. In the drawing-room, there was the mother knitting and watching again. All the time that Agnes sang and played, the mother sat at the piano.

This lasted until bedtime. Next day the knitting and watching began again, and lasted all day.

I had not an opportunity of speaking to Agnes for ten minutes. I could barely show her my letter. Towards the twilight I went out by myself, musing on what I ought to do, and whether I was justified in withholding from Agnes any longer what Uriah Heep had told me in London; for that began to trouble me again, very much.

I had not walked out far enough to be quite clear of the town, when I was hailed by somebody behind me. The shambling figure was not to be mistaken. I stopped, and Uriah Heep came up.

'Where are you going?' said I.

'I am coming with you, Master Copperfield, if you'll allow me the pleasure of a walk with an old acquaintance.' Saying this, he fell into step beside me.

'Uriah,' said I, as civilly as I could. 'To tell you the truth I came out to walk alone, because I have had so much company.'

He looked at me sideways, and said with his hardest grin, 'You mean mother.'

'Why yes, I do,' said I.

'Ah! But you know we're so very umble,' he returned. 'And having such a knowledge of our own umbleness, we must really take care that we're not pushed to the wall by them as isn't umble. All stratagems are fair in love, sir. You see, you're quite a dangerous rival, Master Copperfield. You always was, you know.'

'Do you suppose,' said I, constraining myself to be very temperate with him, on account of Agnes, 'that I regard Miss Wickfield otherwise than as a very dear sister?'

'Well, Master Copperfield,' he replied, 'you may not, you know. But then, you see, you may!'

'Come then!' said I. 'For the sake of Agnes Wickfield – I am engaged to another young lady. I hope that contents you.'

'Upon your soul?' said Uriah.

I was about indignantly to give my assertion the confirmation he required, when he caught hold of my hand, and gave it a squeeze.

'Oh, Master Copperfield,' he said. 'If you had only had the condescension to return my confidence when I poured out the fullness of my art, the night I put you so much out of the way by sleeping before your sitting-room fire, I never should have doubted you. As it is, I'm sure I'll take off mother directly, and only too appy. I know you'll excuse the precautions of affection, won't you?'

All this time he was squeezing my hand with his damp fishy fingers, while I made every effort I decently could to get it away. But I was quite unsuccessful.

'Before we leave the subject, you ought to understand,' said I, 'that I believe Agnes Wickfield to be as far above *you,* and as far removed from all *your* aspirations, as that moon itself!'

'Peaceful! Ain't she!' said Uriah. 'Now confess, Master Copperfield, that you haven't liked me quite as I have liked you. All along you've thought me too umble now, I shouldn't wonder?'

'I am not fond of professions of humility,' I returned, 'or professions of anything else.'

'There now!' said Uriah. 'Didn't I know it! But how little you think of the rightful umbleness of a person in my station, Master Copperfield! Father and me was both brought up at a foundation school for boys; and mother, she was likewise brought up at a public school, sort of charitable, establishment. They taught us all a deal of umbleness – not much else that I know of, from morning to night. We was to be umble to this person, and umble to that; and to pull off our caps here, and to make bows there; and always to know our place, and abase ourselves before our betters. And we had such a lot of betters! Father got the monitor-medal by being umble. So did I. Father got made a sexton by being umble. He had the character, among the gentlefolks, of being such a well-behaved man, that they were determined to bring him in. "Be umble, Uriah," says father to me, "and you'll get on. It was what was always being dinned into you and me at school; it's what goes down best. Be umble," says father, "and you'll do!" And really it ain't done bad!'

It was the first time it had ever occurred to me, that this detestable cant of false humility might have originated out of the Heep family. I had seen the harvest, but had never thought of the seed.

'When I was quite a young boy,' said Uriah, 'I got to know what umbleness did, and I took to it. I ate umble pie with an appetite. I stopped at the umble point of my learning, and says I, "Hold hard!" When you offered to teach me Latin I knew better. "People like to be above you," says father, "keep yourself down." I am very umble to the present moment, Master Copperfield, but I've got a little power!'

And he said all this – I knew, as I saw his face in the moonlight – that I might understand he was resolved to recompense himself by using his power. I had never doubted his meanness, his craft and malice; but I fully comprehended now, for the first time, what a base, unrelenting, and revengeful spirit, must have been engendered by this early suppression.

We walked back, side by side, saying very little more by the way.

Whether his spirits were elevated by the communication I had made to him, or by his having indulged in this retrospect, I don't know; but they were raised by some influence. He talked more at dinner than was usual with him.

When we three males were left alone after dinner, he got into a more adventurous state. I had observed yesterday that he tried to entice Mr Wickfield to drink; and had limited myself to one glass. I would have done so again to-day; but Uriah was too quick for me.

'We seldom see our present visitor, sir,' he said, addressing Mr Wickfield, sitting at the end of the table, 'and I should propose to give him welcome in another glass or two of wine, if you have no objections. Mr Copperfield, your elth and appiness.'

I was obliged to make a show of taking the hand he stretched across to me.

'Come, fellow-partner,' said Uriah, 'now, suppose you give us something appropriate to Copperfield!'

I pass over Mr Wickfield's proposing my aunt, his proposing Mr Dick, his proposing Doctors' Commons, his proposing Uriah, his drinking everything twice; his consciousness of his own weakness, the ineffectual effort that he made against it; the manifest exultation with which Uriah twisted and turned, and held him up before me. It made me sick at heart to see.

'Come, fellow-partner!' said Uriah at last, 'I'll give you another one, and I umbly ask for bumpers, seeing I intend to make it the divinest of her sex.'

Her father had his empty glass in his hand. I saw him set it down, put his hand to his forehead, and shrink back in his elbow-chair.

'I'm an umble individual to give you her elth,' proceeded Uriah, 'but I admire – adore her.'

No physical pain that her father's grey head could have borne, I think, could have been more terrible to me, than the mental endurance I saw compressed now within both his hands.

'Agnes Wickfield,' said Uriah, 'is the divinest of her sex. May I speak out, among friends? To be her father is a proud distinction, but to be her usband –'

Spare me from ever again hearing such a cry, as that with which her father rose up from the table!

'What's the matter?' said Uriah, turning of a deadly colour. 'You are not gone mad, after all, Mr Wickfield, I hope? If I say I've an ambition to make your Agnes my Agnes, I have as good a right to it as another man. I have a better right to it than any other man!'

I had my arms round Mr Wickfield, imploring him by everything that I could think of to calm himself a little.

He pointed to Uriah, pale and glowering in a corner, evidently very much out in his calculations, and taken by surprise.

'Look at my torturer,' he replied. 'Before him I have step by step abandoned name and reputation, peace and quiet, house and home.'

'I have kept your name and reputation for you, and your peace and quiet,' said Uriah. 'Don't be foolish, Mr Wickfield. There's no harm done.'

'I looked for single motives in every one,' said Mr Wickfield, 'and I was satisfied I had bound him to me by motives of interest. But see what he is!'

'You had better stop him, Copperfield, if you can,' cried Uriah, with his long forefinger pointing towards me. 'He'll say something he'll be sorry to have said afterwards, and you'll be sorry to have heard!'

'Oh, Trotwood!' exclaimed Mr Wickfield, wringing his hands. 'What I have come down to be, since I first saw you in this house! I have preyed on my own morbid coward heart, and it has preyed on me. Oh see the ruin I am, and hate me, shun me!'

He dropped into a chair, and weakly sobbed. The excitement into which he had been roused was leaving him. Uriah came out of his corner.

'I don't know all I have done,' said Mr Wickfield. '*He* knows best,' meaning Uriah Heep, 'for he has always been at my elbow, whispering me. You see the millstone that he is about my neck. You find him in my house, you find him in my business. What need have I to say more!'

'You haven't need to say anything at all,' observed Uriah. 'You wouldn't have took it up so, if it hadn't been for the wine. You'll think better of it to-morrow, sir.'

The door opened, and Agnes, gliding in, put her arm round his neck, and said, 'Papa, you are not well. Come with me!' He laid his head upon her shoulder and went out with her. Her eyes met mine for but an instant, yet I saw how much she knew of what had passed.

'I didn't expect he'd cut up so rough, Master Copperfield,' said Uriah. 'But it's nothing. I'll be friends with him to-morrow.'

I gave him no answer, and went up-stairs. I took up a book and tried to read. I heard the clocks strike twelve, and was still reading, without knowing what I read, when Agnes touched me.

'You will be going early in the morning, Trotwood. Let us say good-bye, now!'

She had been weeping, but her face was calm and beautiful.

'Dearest Agnes!' I returned, 'I see you ask me not to speak of to-night – but is there nothing to be done?'

'There is God to trust in!' she replied.

'Can *I* do nothing – *I*, who come to you with *my* poor sorrows?'

'And make mine so much lighter,' she replied. 'Dear Trotwood, no!'

'Agnes,' I said, 'it is presumptuous for me, who am so poor in all in which you are so rich, to doubt or direct you; but you know how much I love you, and how much I owe you. You will never sacrifice yourself to a mistaken sense of duty?'

More agitated for a moment than I had ever seen her, she took her hand from me, and moved a step back.

'Say you have no such thought, dear Agnes!'

Oh! long, long afterwards, I saw that face rise up before me, with its momentary look, not wondering, not accusing, not regretting. I saw that look subside, as it did now, into the lovely smile with which she told me she had no fear for herself – I need have none for her – and parted from me by the name of Brother.

It was dark in the morning when I got upon the coach at the inn door. As I sat thinking of her, came struggling up the coach side Uriah's head.

'Copperfield!' said he, in a croaking whisper, 'I thought you'd be glad to hear, before you went off, that there are no squares broke between us. I've been into his room already, and we've made it all smooth. Why, though I'm umble, I'm useful to him, you know; and he understands his interest when he isn't in liquor!'

I obliged myself to say that I was glad he had made his apology.

'Oh, to be sure!' said Uriah. 'When a person's umble, what's an apology? So easy! I suppose you have sometimes plucked a pear before it was ripe, Master Copperfield?'

'I suppose I have,' I replied.

'*I* did that last night,' said Uriah; 'but it'll ripen yet! I can wait!'

Profuse in his farewells, he got down again as the coachman got up. For anything I know, he was eating something to keep the raw morning air out; but he made motions with his mouth as if the pear were ripe already, and he were smacking his lips over it.

CHAPTER 40

The Wanderer

We had a very serious conversation in Buckingham Street that night, about the domestic occurrences I have detailed in the last chapter. My aunt was deeply interested in them, and walked up and down the room with her arms folded, for more than two hours afterwards. Whenever she was particularly discomposed, she always performed one of these pedestrian feats.

She read my letter to the two old ladies, in the morning, and approved of it. I posted it, and had nothing to do then, but wait for the reply. I was still in this state of expectation, and had been, for nearly a week; when I left the Doctor's one snowy night, to walk home.

My shortest way home was through Saint Martin's Lane. As I passed the steps of the portico, I encountered, at the corner, a woman's face. It looked in mine, passed across the narrow lane, and disappeared. I had seen it somewhere. But I could not remember where.

On the steps of the church, there was the stooping figure of a man, who had put down some burden on the smooth snow, to adjust it; my seeing the face, and my seeing him, were simultaneous. I stood face to face with Mr Peggotty!

Then I remembered the woman. It was Martha, to whom Emily had given the money that night in the kitchen. Martha Endell – side by side with whom, he would not have seen his dear niece, Ham had told me, for all the treasures wrecked in the sea.

We shook hands heartily.

'Mas'r Davy!' he said, gripping me tight, 'it do my art good to see you, sir.'

'Well met, my dear old friend!' said I.

'I had my thowts o' coming to make inquiration for you, sir, to-night,' he said, 'but I was afeerd it was too late. I should have come early in the morning, sir, afore going away.'

'Again?' said I.

'Yes, sir,' he replied, patiently shaking his head, 'I'm away to-morrow.'

In those days there was a side-entrance to the stable-yard of the Golden Cross. Two or three public-rooms opened out of the stable-yard; and looking into one of them, and finding it empty, and a good fire burning, I took him in there.

When I saw him in the light, I observed that his face was burnt dark by the sun. He had every appearance of having wandered through all varieties of weather; but he looked very strong, and like a man upheld by steadfastness of purpose, whom nothing could tire out. He sat down opposite to me at a table, with his back to the door.

'I'll tell you, Mas'r Davy,' he said, – 'I've been fur, and we've heerd little; but I'll tell you!'

I rang the bell for something hot to drink.

'When she was a child,' he said, lifting up his head soon after we were left alone, 'she used to talk to me a deal about them coasts where the sea got to be dark blue, and to lay a-shining and a-shining in the sun. When she was lost, I know'd in my mind, as he would take her to them countries. I know'd in my mind, as he'd have told her wonders of 'em, and how she was to be a lady theer. I went across-channel to France.'

I saw the door move, and the snow drift in. I saw it move a little more, and a hand softly interpose to keep it open.

'I found out an English gen'leman as was in authority,' said Mr Peggotty, 'and told him I was a going to seek my niece. He got me them papers as I wanted fur to carry me through. I told him, best as I was able, what my gratitoode was, and went away.'

'On foot?' said I.

'Mostly a-foot,' he rejoined; 'sometimes in carts along with people going to market; sometimes in empty coaches. When I come to any town, I found the inn, and waited about the yard till some one turned up as know'd English. Then they told me what manner of gentlefolks was in the house, and I waited to see any as seemed like her, going in or out. Little and little, when I come to a new village I found they know'd about me. They would set me down at their cottage doors, and give me what-not fur to eat and drink, and show me where to sleep. Some has had daughters as was dead. And God only knows how good them mothers was to me!'

It was Martha at the door. I saw her face distinctly. My dread was lest he should turn his head and see her too.

'It warn't hard, you may suppose, for a seafaring man like me to work his way over to Italy. When I got theer, I got news of her being seen among them Swiss mountains yonder. One as know'd his sarvant see 'em there, all three, and told me where they was. I made for them mountains, Mas'r Davy, day and night. When I got nigh the place as I had been told of, I began to think within my own self, "What shall I do when I see her?"'

The listening face still drooped at the door, and the hands begged me – prayed me – not to cast it forth.

'I never doubted her,' said Mr Peggotty. 'On'y let her see my face – on'y let my stanning still afore her bring to her thoughts the home she had fled away from, and the child she had been – and if she had growed to be a royal lady, she'd have fell down at my feet! I know'd it well!'

He shook his head.

'But it warn't to be. I was too late, and they was gone. Wheer, I couldn't learn and I travelled home.'

'How long ago?' I asked.

'A matter o' fower days,' said Mr Peggotty. 'I sighted the old boat arter dark and I see the faithful creetur Missis Gummidge sittin' by the fire, as we had fixed upon.'

From some pocket in his breast he took out a small paper bundle containing two or three packets, which he laid upon the table.

'This fust one come,' he said, 'afore I had been gone a week. A fifty-pound bank-note, in a sheet of paper, directed to me, and put underneath the door in the night.'

He folded up the note again.

'This come to Missis Gummidge,' he said, opening another, 'two or three months ago.'

I read as follows:

'Oh what will you feel when you see this writing, and know it comes from my wicked hand! But try – not for my sake, but for uncle's goodness, try to let your heart soften to me, only for a little time! Pray relent towards a miserable girl, and write down on a bit of paper whether he is well, and what he said about me before you left off ever naming me among yourselves. Oh, my heart is breaking when I think about it! I am kneeling down to you, begging and praying you not to be as hard with me as I deserve but to be so good, as to write down something of him, and to send it to me. You need not call me Little, you need not call me by the name I have disgraced; but oh, listen to my agony, and have mercy on me so far as to write me some word of uncle, never, never to be seen in this world by my eyes again!'

Some money was enclosed in this letter also. Five pounds. It was untouched like the previous sum, and he refolded it in the same way. Detailed instructions were added relative to the address of a reply, which, although they betrayed the intervention of several hands, made it at least not unlikely that she had written from that spot where she was stated to have been seen.

'What answer was sent?' I inquired of Mr Peggotty.

'They told her I was gone to seek her, and what my parting words was.'

'Is that another letter in your hand?' said I.

'It's money, sir,' said Mr Peggotty, unfolding it a little way. 'Ten pound, you see. And wrote inside, "From a true friend," like the fust. But the fust was put underneath the door, and this come by the post, day afore yesterday. I'm a-going to seek her at the postmark.'

He showed it to me. It was a town on the Upper Rhine. He had found out, at Yarmouth, some foreign dealers who knew that country, and they had drawn him a rude map on paper.

I asked him how Ham was. He shook his head.

'He works,' he said, 'as bold as a man can. He's never been heerd fur to complain. But my sister's belief is as it has cut him deep.'

'Poor fellow, I can believe it!'

He gathered up the letters; put them into their little bundle; and placed it tenderly in his breast again. The face was gone from the door. I still saw the snow drifting in; but nothing else was there.

'Well!' he said, looking to his bag, 'having seen you to-night, Mas'r Davy, I shall away betimes to-morrow morning. You have seen what I've got heer,' putting his hand on where the little packet lay; 'all that troubles me is, to think that any harm might come to me, afore that money was give back.'

He rose, and we grasped each other by the hand again, before going out.

'I'd go ten thousand mile,' he said, 'to lay that money down afore him. If I do that, and find my Em'ly, I'm content.'

As he went out into the rigorous night, I saw the lonely figure flit away before us. I turned him hastily on some pretence, and held him in conversation until it was gone.

He spoke of a traveller's house on the Dover Road, where he knew he could find a clean, plain lodging for the night. I went with him over Westminster Bridge, and parted from him on the Surrey shore.

I returned to the inn yard, and, impressed by my remembrance of the face, looked around for it. It was not there. The snow had covered our late footprints; my new track was the only one to be seen; and even that began to die away (it snowed so fast) as I looked back over my shoulder.

CHAPTER 41

Dora's Aunts

At last, an answer came from the two old ladies. They presented their compliments to Mr Copperfield, and informed him that they had given his letter their best consideration. They begged to forbear expressing, 'through the medium of correspondence,' an opinion on the subject of Mr Copperfield's communication; but that if Mr Copperfield would do them the favour to call, upon a certain day (accompanied, if he thought proper, by a confidential friend), they would be happy to hold some conversation on the subject.

To this favour, Mr Copperfield immediately replied, that he would have the honour of waiting on the Misses Spenlow, at the time appointed; accompanied by his friend Mr Thomas Traddles of the Inner Temple. Having despatched which missive, Mr Copperfield fell into a condition of strong nervous agitation; and so remained until the day arrived.

It was a great augmentation of my uneasiness to be bereaved, at this eventful crisis, of the inestimable services of Miss Mills. But Mr Mills was bound for India and Julia with him; and Julia went into the country to take leave of her relations.

I was in several minds how to dress myself on the important day; being divided between my desire to appear to advantage, and my apprehensions of putting on anything that might impair my severely practical character in the eyes of the Misses Spenlow. I endeavoured to hit a happy medium.

Excellent fellow as I knew Traddles to be, I could not help wishing that he had never contracted the habit of brushing his hair so very upright. It gave him a hearth-broomy kind of expression which might be fatal to us.

I took the liberty of mentioning it to Traddles, as we were walking to Putney; and saying that if he *would* smooth it down a little –

'My dear Copperfield,' said Traddles, 'nothing would give me greater pleasure. But it won't be smoothed down. It's quite an old story, my unfortunate hair. It stood very much in my way when I first fell in love with Sophy. In fact, all the sisters laugh at it.'

'By-the-by,' said I, 'when you became engaged, was there anything like what we are going through to-day?'

'It was rather a painful transaction, Copperfield, in my case. You see, Sophy being of so much use in the family, none of them could endure the thought of her ever being married. Indeed, they had quite settled among themselves that she never was to be married, and they called her the old maid. The fact is, my unsettled prospects and indifferent circumstances are a great consolation to them. There will be a deplorable scene, whenever we are married. It will be much more like a funeral than a wedding. And they'll all hate me for taking her away!'

On our approaching the house where the Misses Spenlow lived, I was at such a discount in respect of my personal looks and presence of mind, that Traddles proposed a gentle stimulant in the form of a glass of ale. This having been administered at a neighbouring public-house, he conducted me, with tottering steps, to the Misses Spenlow's door.

I had a vague sensation of wavering, somehow, across a hall with a weather-glass in it, into a quiet little drawing-room on the ground-floor, commanding a neat garden. Also of seeing Traddles's hair start up, now his hat was removed, like one of those obtrusive little figures made of springs, that fly out of fictitious snuff-boxes when the lid is taken off. Also of thinking that Jip once barked in the distance, and was instantly choked by somebody. Ultimately I found myself backing Traddles into the fireplace, and bowing in great confusion to two dry little elderly ladies, dressed in black, and each looking wonderfully like a preparation in chip or tan of the late Mr Spenlow.

'Pray,' said one of the two little ladies, 'be seated.'

When I had sat upon something which was not a cat – my first seat was – I so far recovered as to perceive that there was a disparity of six or eight years between the two sisters; and that the younger appeared to be the manager of the conference, inasmuch as she had my letter in her hand. They were both upright in their carriage, formal and composed. The sister who had not my letter, had her arms crossed on her breast.

'Mr Copperfield, I believe,' said the sister who had got my letter, addressing herself to Traddles.

This was a frightful beginning. Traddles had to indicate that I was Mr Copperfield, and I had to lay claim to myself. We all distinctly heard Jip give two short barks, and receive another choke.

'Mr Copperfield!' said the sister with the letter.

I did something – bowed, I suppose – and was all attention, when the other sister struck in.

'My sister Lavinia,' said she, 'being conversant with matters of this nature, will state what we consider most calculated to promote the happiness of both parties.'

I discovered afterwards that Miss Lavinia was an authority in affairs of the heart, by reason of there having anciently existed a certain Mr Pidger, who played short whist, and was supposed to have been enamoured of her.

'We will not,' said Miss Lavinia, 'enter on the past history of this matter. Our poor brother Francis's death has cancelled that.'

'We had not,' said Miss Clarissa, 'been in the habit of frequent association with our brother Francis; but there was no decided division or disunion between us. Francis took his road; we took ours.'

'Our niece's position is much changed by our brother's death,' said Miss Lavinia; 'and therefore we consider our brother's opinions as regarded her position as being changed too. We have no reason to doubt, Mr Copperfield, that you are a young gentleman possessed of good qualities and honourable character; or that you have an affection for our niece.'

I replied, as I usually did whenever I had a chance, that nobody had ever loved anybody else as I loved Dora. Traddles came to my assistance with a confirmatory murmur.

'Mr Copperfield, my sister Clarissa and I have been very careful indeed in considering this letter; and we have not considered it without discussing it with our niece. We have no doubt that you think you like her very much.'

'Think, ma'am,' I rapturously began, 'oh! –'

But Miss Clarissa giving me a look (just like a sharp canary), as requesting that I would not interrupt the oracle, I begged pardon.

'Affection,' said Miss Lavinia, glancing at her sister for corroboration, 'mature affection, homage, devotion, does not easily express itself. Its voice is low. It is modest and retiring, it lies in ambush, waits and waits. Such is the mature fruit. Sometimes a life glides away, and finds it still ripening in the shade.'

I saw, from the gravity with which Miss Clarissa nodded her head, that great weight was attached to these words.

'The light inclinations of very young people,' pursued Miss Lavinia, 'are dust, compared to rocks. It is owing to the difficulty of knowing whether they are likely to endure that my sister Clarissa and myself have been undecided how to act.'

Now, although I had not received any express encouragement as yet, I fancied that I saw in the two little sisters an enjoyment of this new and fruitful subject of domestic interest in which there was a bright ray of hope. I thought that Miss Lavinia would have uncommon satisfaction in superintending two young lovers and that Miss Clarissa would have hardly less satisfaction in chiming in whenever that impulse was strong upon her. This gave me courage to protest most vehemently that I loved Dora better than I could tell, every one who knew me, knew how I loved her. For the truth of this, I appealed to Traddles. And Traddles really did come out nobly: confirming me in good round terms that evidently made a favourable impression.

'I speak as one who has some experience of such things,' said Traddles, 'being myself engaged to a young lady and seeing no probability, at present, of our engagement coming to a termination.'

'You may be able to confirm what I have said, Mr Traddles,' observed Miss Lavinia, evidently taking a new interest in him, 'of the affection that is modest and retiring; that waits and waits?'

'Entirely, ma'am,' said Traddles.

Miss Lavinia referred through her eye-glass to some notes she had made.

'It seems to us,' said she, 'prudent, Mr Traddles, to bring these feelings to the test of our own observation. Therefore we are inclined so far to accede to Mr Copperfield's proposal, as to admit his visits here.'

'I shall never, dear ladies,' I exclaimed, relieved of an immense load of apprehension, 'forget your kindness!'

'But,' pursued Miss Lavinia, – 'but, we would prefer to regard those visits, Mr Traddles, as made, at present, to us. We must guard ourselves from recognising any positive engagement between Mr Copperfield and our niece, until we have had an opportunity of observing them.'

'Copperfield,' said Traddles, turning to me, 'you feel, I am sure, that nothing could be more reasonable or considerate.'

'Nothing!' cried I, 'I am deeply sensible of it.'

'In this position of affairs,' said Miss Lavinia, again referring to her notes, 'and admitting his visits on this understanding only, we must require from Mr Copperfield a distinct assurance, on his word of honour, that no communication of any kind shall take place between him and our niece, without our knowledge. That no project whatever shall be entertained with regard to our niece, without being first submitted to us and receiving our concurrence. We must make this a most express and serious stipulation, not to be broken on any account.'

I bound myself to the prescribed conditions.

'Sister Clarissa,' said Miss Lavinia, 'the rest is with you.'

Miss Clarissa, unfolding her arms for the first time, took the notes. 'We shall be happy to see Mr Copperfield to dinner, every Sunday, if it should suit his convenience. Our hour is three. In the course of the week, we shall be happy to see Mr Copperfield to tea. Our hour is half-past six. Twice in the week, but, as a rule, not oftener. Miss Trotwood, mentioned in Mr Copperfield's letter, will perhaps call upon us.'

I intimated that my aunt would be proud and delighted to make their acquaintance. The conditions being now closed, I expressed my acknowledgments in the warmest manner; and, taking the hand, first of Miss Clarissa, and then of Miss Lavinia, pressed it, in each case, to my lips.

Miss Lavinia then arose and, begging Mr Traddles to excuse us for a minute, requested me to follow her. I was conducted into another room. There, I found my blessed darling stopping her ears behind the door and Jip in the plate-warmer with his head tied up in a towel.

Oh! How beautiful she was in her black frock, and how she sobbed and cried at first, and wouldn't come out from behind the door! How fond we were of one another, when she did come out at last; and what a state of bliss I was in, when we took Jip out of the plate-warmer and were all three reunited!

'My dearest Dora! Now, indeed, my own for ever!'

'Oh DON'T !' pleaded Dora. 'Please!'

'Are you not my own for ever, Dora?'

'Oh yes, of course I am!' cried Dora, 'but I am so frightened! Why don't he go?'

'Who, my life?'

'Your friend,' said Dora. 'It isn't any business of his. What a stupid he must be!'

'My love! He is the best creature! You will soon know him well, and like him of all things. And here is my aunt coming soon: and you'll like her, too, when you know her.'

'No, please don't bring her!' said Dora, giving me a horrified little kiss. 'I know she's a naughty, mischief-making old thing! Don't let her come here, Doady!' which was a corruption of David.

Remonstrance was of no use, then; so I laughed, and admired, and was very much in love and very happy – and I don't know how long I should have stayed there, if Miss Lavinia had not come in to take me away. Miss Lavinia was very fond of Dora and she treated Dora just as if she had been a toy. I wanted Dora to come and see Traddles, but on my proposing it she ran off to her own room, and locked herself in; so I went to Traddles without her, and walked away with him on air.

'Nothing could be more satisfactory,' said Traddles; 'I shouldn't be at all surprised if you were to be married years before me, Copperfield.'

Of course my aunt was immediately made acquainted with the successful issue of the conference. She was happy to see me so happy, and promised to call on Dora's aunts without loss of time. But she took such a long walk up and down our rooms that night, while I was writing to Agnes, that I began to think she meant to walk till morning.

My letter to Agnes was a grateful one, narrating all the good effects that had resulted from my following her advice. She wrote, by return of post. Her letter was hopeful, earnest, and cheerful. She was always cheerful from that time.

I had my hands more full than ever, now. My daily journeys to Highgate considered, Putney was a long way off. The proposed tea-drinkings being quite impracticable, I compounded with Miss Lavinia for permission to visit every Saturday afternoon, without detriment to my privileged Sundays. So, the close of every week was a delicious time for me; and I got through the rest of the week by looking forward to it.

I was wonderfully relieved to find that my aunt and Dora's aunts rubbed on more smoothly than I could have expected. My aunt made her promised visit within a few days of the conference; and within a few more days, Dora's aunts called upon her. Similar but more friendly exchanges took place afterwards, at intervals of three or four weeks. Dora's aunts soon agreed to regard my aunt as an eccentric lady, with a strong understanding; and although my aunt occasionally ruffled the feathers of Dora's aunts, by expressing heretical opinions on various points of ceremony, she loved me too well not to sacrifice some of her little peculiarities to the general harmony.

The only member of our small society, who positively refused to adapt himself to circumstances, was Jip. He never saw my aunt without immediately displaying every tooth in his head and growling incessantly. All kinds of treatment were tried with him but he never could prevail upon himself to bear my aunt's society, to the extent that there was nothing for it but to blind him and put him in the plate-warmer.

One thing troubled me – that Dora seemed by one consent to be regarded like a pretty toy. My aunt, with whom she gradually became familiar, always called her Little Blossom; and the pleasure of Miss Lavinia's life was to curl her hair and treat her like a pet child. What Miss Lavinia did, her sister did as a matter of course. It was very odd to me; but they all seemed to treat Dora, in her degree, much as Dora treated Jip in his.

I made up my mind to speak to Dora about this; and one day I said to her that I wished she could get them to behave towards her differently.

'I am sure they're very kind to me,' said Dora, 'and I am very happy.'

'But, my dearest life!' said I, 'you might be very happy, and yet be treated rationally.'

Dora gave me a reproachful look, saying if I didn't like her, why had I ever wanted so much to be engaged to her? And why didn't I go away now, if I couldn't bear her?

What could I do, but kiss away her tears, and tell her how I doted on her!

'I am sure I am very affectionate,' said Dora; 'you oughtn't to be cruel to me, Doady!'

'Cruel, my precious love! As if I would be cruel to you, for the world!'

'Then don't find fault with me,' said Dora, making a rosebud of her mouth; 'and I'll be good.'

I was charmed by her presently asking me, of her own accord, to give her that cookery-book I had once spoken of, and to show her how to keep accounts, as I had once promised I would. I brought the volume with me on my next visit and as we strolled about the Common, I showed her an old housekeeping-book of my aunt's.

But the cookery-book made Dora's head ache, and the figures made her cry. They wouldn't add up, she said. So she rubbed them out, and drew little nosegays, and likenesses of me and Jip.

Then I tried verbal instruction in domestic matters. Sometimes, for example, I would say:

'Now suppose that we were married, and you were going to buy a shoulder of mutton for dinner, would you know how to buy it?'

Dora would think a little, and then reply, perhaps, with great triumph:

'Why, the butcher would know how to sell it, and what need *I* know? Oh, you silly Boy!'

So, when I once asked Dora, with an eye to the cookery-book, what she would do, if I were to say I should like a nice Irish stew, she replied that she would tell the servant to make it; and then clapped her little hands together and laughed in such a charming manner that she was more delightful than ever.

Consequently, the principal use to which the cookery-book was devoted, was being put down in the corner for Jip to stand upon. But Dora was so pleased when she had trained him to stand upon it and at the same time to hold the pencil-case in his mouth, that I was very glad I had bought it.

And we fell back on the guitar and the songs about never leaving off dancing, Ta ra la! and were as happy as the week was long. I occasionally wished I could venture to hint to Miss Lavinia, that she treated the darling of my heart a little too much like a plaything; and I sometimes awoke, wondering to find that I had fallen into the general fault, and treated her like a plaything too – but not often.

CHAPTER 42

Mischief

I feel as if it were not for me to record how hard I worked at that tremendous shorthand in my sense of responsibility to Dora. I will only add, to what I have already written, of a patient and continuous energy which then began to be matured within me, and which I find the source of my success. I have been very fortunate in worldly matters; many men have worked much harder, and not succeeded half so well; but I never could have done what I have done, without the habits of punctuality, order, and diligence, without the determination to concentrate myself on one object at a time, which I then formed.

How much of the practice I have just reduced to precept, I owe to Agnes, I will not repeat here. She came on a visit of a fortnight to the Doctor's with her father. I was not much surprised to hear that she had engaged a lodging in the neighbourhood for Mrs Heep. Neither was I surprised when, on the very next day, Uriah, like a dutiful son, brought his worthy mother to take possession.

'You see, Master Copperfield,' said he, 'where a person loves, a person is a little jealous – leastways, anxious to keep an eye on the beloved one.'

'Of whom are you jealous, now?' said I.

'Thanks to you, Master Copperfield,' he returned, 'no male person, at least.'

'Do you mean that you are jealous of a female person?'

He laughed. 'I don't mind telling you, I'm not a lady's man in general, sir, and I never was, with Mrs Strong.'

'What do you mean?'

'When I was but an umble clerk, she always looked down upon me. She was for ever having my Agnes backwards and forwards at her ouse, but I was too far beneath her, myself, to be noticed. And beneath him too.'

'Don't you know the Doctor better?' said I.

'Oh dear, I am not referring to the Doctor! I mean Mr Maldon!'

My heart quite died within me. All the Doctor's happiness and peace, I saw, in a moment, at the mercy of this fellow's twisting.

'He never could come into the office, without ordering and shoving me about,' said Uriah. 'She is one of your lovely women, she is, and ready to be no friend to such as me, *I* know. She's just the person as would put my Agnes up to higher sort of game. I've had eyes in my ed, a pretty long time back. We umble ones have got eyes, mostly speaking – and we look out of 'em.'

I endeavoured to appear unconscious and not disquieted, but with poor success.

'Now, I'm not a going to let myself be run down, Copperfield,' he continued, 'and I shall do what I can to put a stop to this friendship. I don't approve of it. I ain't a going, if I know it, to run the risk of being plotted against.'

'You are always plotting, and delude yourself into the belief that everybody else is doing the like, I think,' said I.

'Perhaps so, Master Copperfield,' he replied. 'But I've got a motive, as my fellow-partner used to say; and I go at it tooth and nail. I mustn't be put upon, as a numble person, too much. I can't allow people in my way.'

It was on the next evening but one that I took Agnes to see Dora. I was in a flutter of pride and anxiety; pride in my dear little betrothed, and anxiety that Agnes should like her.

Dora was afraid of Agnes. She had told me that she knew Agnes was 'too clever.' But when she saw her looking at once so cheerful and so earnest, she gave a little cry of pleased surprise, and put her arms round Agnes's neck.

I never was so happy as when I saw those two sit down together, side by side.

Miss Lavinia and Miss Clarissa partook, in their way, of my joy. It was the pleasantest tea-table in the world. The gentle cheerfulness of Agnes went to all their hearts. Her quiet interest in everything that interested Dora; her manner of making acquaintance with Jip (who responded instantly); her modest grace and ease, eliciting a crowd of blushing little marks of confidence from Dora; seemed to make our circle quite complete.

We made merry about Dora's wanting to be liked, and Dora said I was a goose, and she didn't like me at any rate, and the short evening flew away on gossamer-wings. The time was at hand when the coach was to call for us. I was standing alone before the fire, when Dora came stealing softly in, to give me that usual precious little kiss before I went.

'Don't you think, if I had had her for a friend a long time ago, Doady,' said Dora, 'I might have been more clever perhaps?'

'My love!' said I, 'what nonsense!'

'I have forgotten,' said Dora, 'what relation Agnes is to you, you dear bad boy.'

'No blood-relation,' I replied; 'but we were brought up together, like brother and sister.'

'I wonder why you ever fell in love with me?'

'Perhaps because I couldn't see you, and not love you, Dora!'

'Suppose you had never seen me at all.'

'Suppose we had never been born!' said I, gaily.

At length her eyes were lifted up to mine, and she stood on tiptoe to give me, more thoughtfully than usual, that precious little kiss – once, twice, three times – and went out of the room.

They all came back together within five minutes and Dora's unusual thoughtfulness was quite gone then. She was laughingly resolved to put Jip through the whole of his performances, before the coach came. They were still unfinished when it was heard at the door. There was a hurried but affectionate parting between Agnes and herself; and Dora was to write to Agnes (who was not to mind her letters being foolish, she said), and Agnes was to write to Dora.

The stage-coach was to put us down near Covent Garden, where we were to take another for Highgate. I was impatient for the short walk in the interval, that Agnes might praise Dora to me. Ah! what praise it was! How lovingly and fervently did it commend the pretty creature I had won, with all her artless graces best displayed, to my most gentle care!

Never, never, had I loved Dora so deeply and truly, as I loved her that night. When we were walking in the starlight along the quiet road that led to the Doctor's house, I told Agnes it was her doing.

'When you were sitting by her,' said I, 'you seemed to be no less *her* guardian angel than mine; and you seem so now, Agnes.'

'A poor angel,' she returned, 'but faithful.'

The clear tone of her voice, going straight to my heart, made it natural to say:

'The cheerfulness that belongs to you, Agnes, is so restored that I have begun to hope you are happier at home?'

'I am happier in myself,' she said. 'There has been no change at home.'

'No fresh reference,' said I, 'to what we spoke of, when we parted last?'

'None,' she answered. 'Have no apprehensions for me, Trotwood; the step you dread my taking, I shall never take.'

We were now within the little court-yard of the Doctor's cottage. It was growing late and Agnes bade me good-night.

'Do not be troubled,' she said, giving me her hand. 'If you can ever give me help, rely upon it I will ask you for it.'

I stood awhile, looking at the stars, with a heart full of love and gratitude, and then I saw a light in the Doctor's study. With the view of bidding him good-night I looked in.

The first person I saw was Uriah. He was standing with one of his skeleton hands over his mouth. The Doctor sat in his study chair, covering his face with his hands. Mr Wickfield was leaning forward, touching the Doctor's arm.

For an instant, I supposed that the Doctor was ill, when I met Uriah's eye, and saw what was the matter. I would have withdrawn, but the Doctor made a gesture to detain me.

'I have felt it incumbent upon me, Master Copperfield,' said Uriah, 'to point out to Doctor Strong what you and me have already talked about.'

I gave him a look, but no other answer; and, going to my good old master, said a few words that I meant to be words of comfort and encouragement. He put his hand upon my shoulder but did not lift his grey head.

Uriah resumed in the same officious manner, 'I have called Doctor Strong's attention to the goings-on of Mrs Strong. I have mentioned to Doctor Strong that any one may see that Mr Maldon, and the lovely and agreeable lady as is Doctor Strong's wife, are too sweet on one another. Really the time is come when Doctor Strong must be told that this was full as plain to everybody as the sun, before Mr Maldon went to India; that Mr Maldon made excuses to come back, for nothing else; and that he's always here, for nothing else. When you come in, sir, I was just putting it to my fellow-partner,' towards whom he turned, 'to say to Doctor Strong upon his word and honour, whether he'd ever been of this opinion long ago, or not. Come, Mr Wickfield, sir! Would you be so good as tell us?'

'For God's sake, my dear Doctor,' said Mr Wickfield, 'don't attach too much weight to any suspicions I may have entertained.'

'There!' cried Uriah, shaking his head. 'What a melancholy confirmation: ain't it? Him! Such an old friend! When I was nothing but a clerk in his office, I've seen him twenty times, if I've seen him once, quite put out to think that Miss Agnes was mixing herself up with what oughtn't to be.'

'My dear Strong,' said Mr Wickfield in a tremulous voice, 'I needn't tell you that it has been my vice to look for some one master motive in everybody, and to try all actions by one narrow test. I may have fallen into such doubts as I have had, through this mistake.'

'You have had doubts, Wickfield,' said the Doctor, without lifting up his head.

'I had, at one time, certainly,' said Mr Wickfield. 'I thought *you* had.'

'No, no, no!' returned the Doctor, in a tone of most pathetic grief.

'I thought,' said Mr Wickfield, 'that you wished to send Maldon abroad to effect a desirable separation.'

'No, no, no!' returned the Doctor. 'To give Annie pleasure, by making some provision for the companion of her childhood. Nothing else.'

'But I thought that, in a case where there was so much disparity in point of years – a lady of such youth, and such attractions, however real her respect for you, might have been influenced in marrying, by worldly considerations only.'

'How kind he puts it!' said Uriah, shaking his head.

'I am forced to confess now,' said Mr Wickfield, 'that I did doubt her, and think her wanting in her duty to you; and that I did sometimes feel averse to Agnes being in such a familiar relation towards her. And though it is terrible to you to hear,' said Mr Wickfield, quite subdued, 'if you knew how terrible it is for me to tell, you would feel compassion for me!'

The Doctor, in the perfect goodness of his nature, put out his hand.

'I am sure,' said Uriah, 'that this is a subject full of unpleasantness to everybody. But I ought to take the liberty of mentioning that Copperfield has noticed it too.'

I turned upon him, and asked him how he dared refer to me!

'Oh! it's very kind of you, Copperfield,' returned Uriah, undulating all over, 'but you know that the moment I spoke to you the other night, you knew what I meant. Don't deny it!'

I saw the mild eye of the good old Doctor turned upon me for a moment, and I felt that the confession of my old misgivings was too plainly written in my face to be overlooked.

We were silent until the Doctor rose and walked twice or thrice across the room. Presently he returned to his chair and, occasionally putting his handkerchief to his eyes, said:

'I have been much to blame. I have exposed one whom I hold in my heart, to trials and aspersions of which she never, but for me, could have been the object. Gentlemen, I am old now; I do not feel, to-night, that I have much to live for. But my life upon the truth and honour of the dear lady who has been the subject of this conversation!

'But I am not prepared,' he went on, 'to deny that I may have unwittingly ensnared that lady into an unhappy marriage. I married that lady when she was extremely young. I took her to myself when her character was scarcely formed. So far as it was developed, it had been my happiness to form it. I regarded myself as a refuge, for her, from the dangers and vicissitudes of life. I persuaded myself that, unequal though we were in years, she would live tranquilly and contentedly with me. I did not shut out of my consideration the time when I should leave her free, and still young and beautiful, but with her judgment more matured.'

His homely figure seemed to be lightened up by his fidelity and generosity. Every word he uttered had a force that no other grace could have imparted to it.

'My life with this lady has been very happy. Until to-night, I have had uninterrupted occasion to bless the day on which I did her great injustice. Once awakened from my dream I see how natural it is that she should have some regretful feeling towards her old companion and her equal. That she does regard him with some blameless thoughts of what might have been, but for me, is, I fear, too true. Much that I have seen has come back upon me with new meaning, during this last trying hour. But, beyond this, gentlemen, the dear lady's name never must be coupled with a word of doubt. It is she who should reproach; not I. To save her from cruel misconstruction, that even my friends have not been able to avoid, becomes my duty. The more retired we live, the better I shall discharge it. And when the time comes when my death shall release her from constraint, I shall leave her to happier and brighter days.'

I could not see him for the tears which his goodness, so adorned, brought into my eyes. He added:

'Gentlemen, I have shown you my heart. I am sure you will respect it. What we have said to-night is never to be said more. Wickfield, give me an old friend's arm up-stairs!'

Without interchanging a word they went slowly out of the room together, Uriah looking after them.

'You villain,' said I, 'what do you mean by entrapping me into your schemes? How dare you appeal to me just now, you false rascal, as if we had been in discussion together?'

As we stood, front to front, I saw so plainly that he had set a deliberate trap for me in this very matter, that I couldn't bear it. The whole of his lank cheek was invitingly before me, and I struck it with my open hand with that force that my fingers tingled as if I had burnt them.

He caught the hand in his, and we stood in that connexion, looking at each other. We stood long enough for me to see the white marks of my

'You will doubtless be surprised, my dear Mr Copperfield, to receive this communication. But my feelings as a wife and mother require relief; and I know no one of whom I can better ask advice than my friend and former lodger.

'You may be aware that between myself and Mr Micawber (whom I will never desert), there has always been preserved a spirit of mutual confidence. Mr Micawber has had no secrets from the bosom of affection – I allude to his wife – and has invariably, on our retirement to rest, recalled the events of the day.

'You will picture to yourself, my dear Mr Copperfield, what the poignancy of my feelings must be, when I inform you that Mr Micawber is entirely changed. He is reserved. He is secret. His life is a mystery to the partner of his joys and sorrows – I again allude to his wife. But this is not all. Mr Micawber is morose. He is severe. He is estranged from our eldest son and daughter, he has no pride in his twins. The pecuniary means of meeting our expenses, kept down to the utmost farthing, are obtained from him with great difficulty, and he inexorably refuses to give any explanation whatever of this distracting policy.

'This is hard to bear. This is heart-breaking. If you will advise me, knowing my feeble powers such as they are, how you think it will be best to exert them in a dilemma so unwonted, you will add another friendly obligation to the many you have already rendered me. I remain, dear Mr Copperfield,

'Your afflicted,
'EMMA MICAWBER.'

I did not feel justified in giving a wife of Mrs Micawber's experience any other recommendation, than that she should try to reclaim Mr Micawber by patience and kindness (as I knew she would in any case); but the letter set me thinking about him very much.

CHAPTER 43

Another Retrospect

Once again, let me pause upon a memorable period of my life. Let me stand aside, to see the phantoms of those days go by in dim procession.

Weeks, months, seasons, pass along. I have attained the dignity of twenty-one. Let me think what I have achieved.

I have tamed that savage stenographic mystery. I make a respectable income by it. I am joined with eleven others in reporting the debates in Parliament for a Morning Newspaper. Night after night, I record predictions that never come to pass, professions that are never fulfilled, explanations that are only meant to mystify. I wallow in words.

My dear old Traddles is called to the Bar. A great deal of very hot port wine was consumed at his call; and, considering the figure, I should think the Inner Temple must have made a profit by it.

I have come out in another way. I wrote a little something, in secret, and sent it to a magazine, and it was published. Since then, I have taken heart to write a good many trifling pieces. Now, I am regularly paid for them.

We have removed from Buckingham Street, to a pleasant little cottage very near the one I looked at, when my enthusiasm first came on. My aunt, however (who has sold the house at Dover, to good advantage), intends removing herself to a still more tiny cottage close at hand. What does this portend? My marriage?

Yes! I am going to be married to Dora! Miss Lavinia and Miss Clarissa have given their consent; and if ever canary birds were in a flutter, they are. Miss Lavinia is self-charged with the superintendence of my darling's wardrobe. A dressmaker boards and lodges in the house; and seems to me never to take her thimble off. Miss Clarissa and my aunt roam all over London, to find out articles of furniture for Dora and me to look at.

Peggotty comes up to make herself useful, and falls to work immediately. Her department appears to be, to clean everything over and over again. And now I begin to see her solitary brother passing through the dark streets at night, and looking among the wandering faces. I never speak to him at such an hour. I know too well what he seeks, and what he dreads.

Why does Traddles look so important when he calls upon me this afternoon in the Commons – where I still occasionally attend? The realisation of my boyish daydreams is at hand. I am going to take out the licence.

'I hope the next time you come here, my dear fellow,' I say to Traddles, 'it will be on the same errand for yourself. And I hope it will be soon.'

'I hope so too,' he replies. 'It's a satisfaction to know that she'll wait for me any length of time.'

'When are you to meet her at the coach?'

'At seven,' says Traddles. 'The great friendship and consideration of personally associating Sophy with the joyful occasion, and inviting her to be a bridesmaid in conjunction with Miss Wickfield, demands my warmest thanks. I am extremely sensible of it.'

Sophy arrives in due course. She is one of the most engaging creatures I have ever seen. Traddles presents her to us with great pride. I have brought Agnes from the Canterbury coach. It is capital to see them meet, and to observe the glory of Traddles as he commends the dearest girl in the world to her acquaintance.

I don't believe it. I feel in a misty and unsettled kind of state; as if I had got up very early in the morning a week or two ago, and had never been to bed since.

I have never seen my aunt in such state. She is dressed in lavender-coloured silk, and has a white bonnet on. Peggotty is ready to go to church, intending to behold the ceremony from the gallery. Mr Dick, who is to give my darling to me at the altar, has had his hair curled. Traddles, whom I have taken up by appointment at the turnpike, presents a dazzling combination of cream colour and light blue; and both he and Mr Dick have a general effect about them of being all gloves.

The church is calm enough, I am sure; but it might be a steampower loom in full action, for any sedative effect it has on me. I am too far gone for that.

The rest is all a more or less incoherent dream.

A dream of their coming in with Dora. Of the clergyman and clerk appearing. Of Miss Lavinia being the first to cry, and of her doing homage (as I take it) to the memory of Pidger, in sobs. Of my aunt endeavouring to represent herself as a model of sternness, with tears rolling down her face. Of our kneeling down together, side by side. Of Dora's clasping Agnes by the hand. Of my young wife being hysterical in the vestry, and crying for her poor dear papa.

Of her soon cheering up again, and our signing the register all round. Of my going into the gallery for Peggotty to bring *her* to sign it; of Peggotty's hugging me in a corner, and telling me she saw my own dear mother married; of its being over, and our going away.

Of there being a breakfast, with abundance of things, pretty and substantial, to eat and drink. Of my making a speech without having an idea of that I want to say, beyond the full conviction that I haven't said it. Of our being very sociably happy; and of Jip's having wedding cake, and its not agreeing with him afterwards.

Of the pair of hired post-horses being ready, and of Dora's going away to change her dress. Of Dora's being ready, and of Miss Lavinia's hovering about her, loth to lose the pretty toy that has given her so much pleasant occupation.

Of my wanting to carry Jip (who is to go along with us), and Dora's saying, No, that she must carry him, or else he'll think she don't like him any more, now she is married, and will break his heart. Of our going, arm in arm, and Dora stopping and looking back, and saying, 'If I have ever been cross or ungrateful to anybody, don't remember it!' and bursting into tears.

We drive away together, and I awake from the dream. I believe it at last. It is my dear, dear, little wife beside me, whom I love so well!

'Are you happy now, you foolish boy?' says Dora, 'and sure you don't repent?'

I have stood aside to see the phantoms of those days go by me. They are gone, and I resume the journey of my story.

CHAPTER 44

Our Housekeeping

It was a strange condition of things, the honeymoon being over, when I found myself, sitting down in my own small house with Dora; quite thrown out of employment, as I may say, in respect of the delicious old occupation of making love.

It seemed such an extraordinary thing to have Dora always there. It was so unaccountable not to have any occasion to be tormenting myself about her, not to have to write to her, not to be scheming and devising opportunities of being alone with her.

I doubt whether two young birds could have known less about keeping house, than I and my pretty Dora did. We had a servant, of course. She kept house for us. I have still a latent belief that she must have been Mrs Crupp's daughter in disguise, we had such an awful time of it with Mary Anne.

We should have been at her mercy, if she had had any; but she was a remorseless woman, and had none. She was the cause of our first little quarrel.

'My dearest life,' I said one day to Dora, 'do you think Mary Anne has any idea of time? It's five, and we were to have dined at four.'

Dora glanced wistfully at the clock, and hinted that she thought it was too fast.

'On the contrary, my love,' said I, referring to my watch, 'it's a few minutes too slow. Don't you think, it would be better for you to remonstrate with Mary Anne?'

'Oh no! I couldn't, Doady!' said Dora. 'I am such a little goose, and she knows I am!'

I thought this sentiment so incompatible with the establishment of any check on Mary Anne, that I frowned.

'My precious wife,' said I, 'we must be serious sometimes. You must remember, I am sure, that I was obliged to go out yesterday when dinner was half over, and that, the day before, I was made quite unwell by being obliged to eat underdone veal; to-day, I don't dine at all. I am not blaming you, Dora. We have both a great deal to learn. I am only trying to show you that you must – you really must – accustom yourself to look after Mary Anne.'

But I had wounded Dora's soft little heart, and she was not to be comforted. I was obliged to hurry away; I was kept out late; and I felt all night such pangs of remorse as made me miserable. I had the conscience of an assassin, and was haunted by a vague sense of enormous wickedness.

It was two or three hours past midnight when I got home. I found my aunt, in our house, sitting up for me.

'Is anything the matter, aunt?' said I, alarmed.

'Nothing, Trot,' she replied. 'Little Blossom has been rather out of spirits, and I have been keeping her company. That's all.'

I leaned my head upon my hand; and felt more sorry and downcast than I could have supposed possible so soon after the fulfilment of my brightest hopes.

'I assure you, aunt,' said I, 'I have been quite unhappy myself all night, to think of Dora's being so. But I had no other intention than to speak to her tenderly and lovingly about our home affairs.'

My aunt nodded encouragement.

'You must have patience, Trot,' she said.

'Don't you think, aunt,' said I, after some further contemplation of the fire, 'that you could advise Dora a little, for our mutual advantage, now and then?'

'Trot,' returned my aunt, with some emotion, 'no! Don't ask me such a thing.'

Her tone was so very earnest that I raised my eyes in surprise.

'I look back on my life, child,' said my aunt, 'and I think of some who are in their graves, with whom I might have been on kinder terms. But you and I have done one another some good, Trot, and division must not come between us, at this time of day.'

'Division between *us*!' cried I.

'Child, child!' said my aunt, smoothing her dress, 'how soon it might come between us, or how unhappy I might make our Little Blossom, if I meddled in anything, a prophet couldn't say. I want our pet to like me, and be as gay as a butterfly. Remember your own home, in that second marriage; and never do both me and her the injury you have hinted at!'

I comprehended, at once, that my aunt was right.

'These are early days, Trot,' she pursued. 'You have chosen freely for yourself; and you have chosen a very pretty and a very affectionate creature. It will be your duty, and it will be your pleasure too, to estimate her by the qualities she has, and not by the qualities she may not have. Your future is between you two. No one can assist you; you are to work it out for yourselves. This is marriage, Trot; and Heaven bless you both in it, for a pair of babes in the wood as you are!'

With this my aunt tied her head up in a handkerchief, and I escorted her home.

Dora came stealing down in her little slippers now that I was alone; and cried upon my shoulder, and said I had been hard-hearted and she had been naughty; and I said much the same thing; and we agreed that our first little difference was to be our last, and that we were never to have another if we lived a hundred years.

The next domestic trial we went through, was the Ordeal of Servants. Mary Anne's cousin deserted into our coal-hole. This nerved me to get rid of Mary Anne, who went so mildly that I was surprised, until I found out about little sums she had borrowed in my name of the tradespeople without authority. She was succeeded by a long line of Incapables, terminating in a young person of genteel appearance who went to Greenwich Fair in Dora's bonnet. After whom I remember nothing but an average equality of failure.

Everybody we had anything to do with seemed to cheat us. Our appearance in a shop was a signal for the damaged goods to be brought out immediately. If we bought a lobster, it was full of water. All our meat turned out to be tough, and there was hardly any crust to our loaves.

One of our first feats in the housekeeping way was a little dinner to Traddles. I could not have wished for a prettier little wife at the opposite end of the table, but I certainly could have wished, when we sat down, for a little more room. Traddles was so hemmed in by the guitar-case and my writing-table, that I had serious doubts of the possibility of his using his knife and fork; but he protested, with his own good-humour, 'Oceans of room, Copperfield! I assure you, Oceans!'

There was another thing I could have wished; namely, that Jip had never been encouraged to walk about the table-cloth during dinner. I began to think there was something disorderly in his being there at all, even if he had not been in the habit of putting his foot in the butter.

However, as I knew how sensitive Dora would be to any slight upon her favourite, I hinted no objection. For similar reasons I made no allusion to the skirmishing plates upon the floor; or to the further blockade of Traddles by wandering vegetable dishes and jugs. I could not help wondering, as I contemplated the leg of mutton before me, how it came to pass that our joints of meat were of such extraordinary shapes – and whether our butcher contracted for all the deformed sheep that came into the world; but I kept my reflections to myself.

When Traddles went away, my wife sat down by my side.

'I am very sorry,' she said. 'Will you try to teach me, Doady?'

'I must teach myself first, Dora,' said I. 'I am as bad as you, love.'

'Will you call me a name I want you to call me?' inquired Dora.

'What is it?' I asked with a smile.

'It's a stupid name,' she said, shaking her curls for a moment. 'Child-wife. I don't mean you should use the name instead of Dora. I only mean that you should think of me that way. When you are going to be angry with me, say to yourself, "it's only my child-wife!" When you miss what I should like to be, and I think can never be, say, "still my foolish child-wife loves me!" For indeed I do.'

This appeal of Dora's made a strong impression on me. I look back on the time I write of; I invoke the innocent figure that I dearly loved, to come out from the mists of the past, and turn its gentle head towards me once again; and I can still declare that this one little speech was constantly in my memory.

Sometimes, of an evening, when I was at home and at work – for I was beginning in a small way to be known as a writer – I would lay down my pen, and watch my child-wife trying to be good. She would sit down with the tablets, and a little basket of bills, and endeavour to get some result out of them. After severely comparing one with another, and making entries on the tablets, and blotting them out, and counting all the fingers of her left hand over and over again, she would look so unhappy, that it gave me pain to see her bright face clouded.

Then I would commence a practical demonstration, to which Dora would pay profound attention, perhaps for five minutes; when she would begin to be dreadfully tired, and would lighten the subject by curling my hair, or trying the effect of my face with my shirt-collar turned down. If I tacitly checked this playfulness, and persisted, she would look so scared and disconsolate that the remembrance of her being my child-wife would come reproachfully upon me; and I would lay the pencil down, and call for the guitar.

I had a great deal of work to do, and had many anxieties, but the same considerations made me keep them to myself. I am far from sure, now, that it was right to do this, but I did it for my child-wife's sake. I did feel, sometimes, that I could have wished my wife had been my counsellor, had had more character and purpose, to sustain me, and improve me by; had been endowed with power to fill up the void which somewhere seemed to be about me; but I felt as if this were an unearthly consummation of my happiness, that never had been meant to be.

I was a boyish husband as to years. I had known the softening influence of no other sorrows or experiences than those recorded in these leaves. If I did any wrong, as I may have done much, I did it in mistaken love, and in my want of wisdom.

Thus it was that I took upon myself the toils and cares of our life, and had no partner in them. We lived much as before, in reference to our scrambling household arrangements; but I had got used to those, and Dora, I was pleased to see, was seldom vexed now. She was bright and cheerful in the old childish way.

When the debates were heavy and I went home late, Dora would always come downstairs to meet me. When I was engaged in writing at home, she would sit quietly near me, however late the hour, and be so mute, that I would often think she had dropped asleep. But generally, when I raised my head, I saw her blue eyes looking at me with quiet attention.

'Oh, what a weary boy!' said Dora one night, when I met her eyes as I was shutting up my desk.

'What a weary girl!' said I. 'That's more to the purpose. You must go to bed another time, my love. It's far too late for you.'

'No, don't send me to bed!' pleaded Dora. 'Let me stop and see you write. You'll not forget me then, while you are full of silent fancies. Will you mind it, if I say something very, very silly?'

'What wonderful thing is that?' said I.

'Please let me hold the pens,' said Dora. 'I want to have something to do with all those many hours when you are so industrious.'

The remembrance of her pretty joy when I said Yes, brings tears into my eyes. The next time I sat down to write, and regularly afterwards, she sat in her old place, with a spare bundle of pens at her side.

She took possession of the keys soon after this, and went jingling about the house with the whole bunch tied to her slender waist. I seldom found that the places to which they belonged were locked, or that they were of any use except as a plaything for Jip – but Dora was pleased, and that pleased me. She was quite satisfied that a good deal was effected by this make-belief of house-keeping; and was as merry as if we had been keeping a baby-house, for a joke.

So we went on. Dora was hardly less affectionate to my aunt than to me, and I never saw my aunt unbend more systematically to any one. She courted Jip, though Jip never responded; listened, day after day, to the guitar, though I am afraid she had no taste for music; never attacked the Incapables, though the temptation must have been severe; and never came in by the garden, but she would call out, at the foot of the stairs, in a voice that sounded cheerfully all over the house:

'Where's Little Blossom?'

CHAPTER 45

Mr Dick fulfils my Aunt's Prediction

It was some time now, since I had left the Doctor but, living in his neighbourhood, I saw him frequently. The Old Soldier was in permanent quarters under the Doctor's roof. Mrs Markleham was far more fond of pleasure than her daughter. The Doctor's desire that Annie should be entertained, was therefore particularly acceptable to this excellent parent; who expressed unqualified approval of his discretion.

'My dear Doctor,' said the Soldier, 'you may command me, at all times and seasons. Now, do understand that I am entirely at your service. I am ready to go with Annie to operas, concerts, exhibitions, all kinds of places; and you shall never find that I am tired. Duty, my dear Doctor, before every consideration in the universe!'

She was as good as her word. She was one of those people who can bear a great deal of pleasure, and she never flinched in her perseverance in the cause.

It rarely happened now that Mr Maldon accompanied them. Sometimes my aunt and Dora were invited to do so, and accepted the invitation. My aunt rubbed her nose sometimes when she happened to be alone with me, and said she couldn't make it out; she wished they were happier, she didn't think our military friend (so she always called the Old Soldier) mended the matter at all.

But her abiding reliance was on Mr Dick. That man had evidently an idea in his head, she said; and if he could only once pen it up into a corner, which was his great difficulty, he would distinguish himself in some extraordinary manner.

One night, when I had been married some months, Mr Dick put his head into the parlour, where I was writing, and said, with a significant cough:

'You couldn't speak to me without inconveniencing yourself, Trotwood, I am afraid?'

'Certainly, Mr Dick,' said I; 'come in!'

Mr Dick sat down with greater gravity than usual, and looked at me.

'Now, boy, I am going to put a question to you. What do you consider me, sir?'

'A dear old friend,' said I.

'Thank you, Trotwood,' returned Mr Dick, laughing, and reaching across in high glee to shake hands. 'But what do you consider me in this respect?' touching his forehead. 'Weak?'

'Well,' I replied, dubiously. 'Rather so.'

'Exactly!' cried Mr Dick, who seemed quite enchanted by my reply. 'That is, Trotwood, when they took some of the trouble out of you-know-who's head, and put it you know where, there was a –' Mr Dick made his two hands revolve very fast about each other to express confusion. I nodded at him, and he nodded back again.

'In short, boy,' said Mr Dick, dropping his voice, 'I am simple. She pretends I am not. I know I am. If she hadn't stood my friend, sir, I should have been shut up, to lead a dismal life these many years. Your aunt is the most wonderful woman in the world, sir. But I'll provide for her! I never spend the copying money. I have made a will. I'll leave it all to her. She shall be rich!

'Now you are a scholar, Trotwood. You know what a learned man, the Doctor is. You know what honour he has always done me. Condescending even to poor Dick, who is simple and knows nothing. And his beautiful wife is a shining star, sir. But,' laying one hand upon my knee – 'clouds, sir – clouds.'

'There is some unfortunate division between them,' I replied. 'It may be inseparable from the discrepancy in their years. It may have grown up out of almost nothing.'

Mr Dick sat considering. 'Doctor not angry with her, Trotwood?' he said, after some time.

'No. Devoted to her.'

'Most wonderful woman in the world, Trotwood. Why has *she* done nothing to set things right?'

'Too delicate and difficult a subject for such interference,' I replied.

'Fine scholar,' said Mr Dick, touching me with his finger. 'Why has *he* done nothing?'

'For the same reason,' I returned.

'Then, I have got it, boy!' said Mr Dick. 'A simpleton, a weak-minded person – present company, you know,' striking himself again, 'may do what wonderful people may not do. I'll bring them together, boy. They'll not mind what I do, if it's wrong. I'm only Mr Dick.' He blew a slight, contemptuous breath, as if he blew himself away.

One fair evening, my aunt and I strolled up to the Doctor's cottage. Mrs Strong was just coming out of the garden, where Mr Dick yet lingered. The Doctor was engaged with some one in his study; but the visitor would be gone directly, Mrs Strong said. We went into the drawing-room with her, and sat down by the darkening window.

We had not sat here many minutes, when Mrs Markleham came bustling in, with her newspaper in her hand, and said, 'My goodness gracious, Annie, why didn't you tell me there was some one in the Study! I never had such a turn in all my life!'

'Have you been to the Study, then, mama?' asked Annie.

'Indeed I have! I came upon the amiable creature in the act of making his will.'

Her daughter looked round from the window quickly.

'Perhaps you know, Miss Trotwood,' said Mrs Markleham, 'that there is never a candle lighted in this house, until one's eyes are literally falling out of one's head with being stretched to read the paper. This took me to the Study, where I saw a light. I opened the door. In company with the dear Doctor were two professional people, evidently connected with the law, and they were all three standing at the table. "This simply expresses then," said the Doctor, "the confidence I have in Mrs Strong, and gives her all unconditionally!" One of the professional people replied, "And gives her all unconditionally." Upon that, I said, "Good God, I beg your pardon!" and came away.'

Here the bell rang, and we heard the sound of the visitors' feet as they went out.

'It's all over, no doubt,' said the Old Soldier, after listening; 'the dear creature has signed, sealed, and delivered, and his mind's at rest. Well it may be! Miss Trotwood, David, pray come and see the Doctor.'

We saw the Doctor before he saw us, sitting at his table, resting his head calmly on his hand. In the same moment, we saw Mrs Strong glide in, pale and trembling. Mr Dick supported her on his arm. He laid his other hand upon the Doctor's arm, causing him to look up with an abstracted air. As the Doctor moved his head, his wife dropped down on one knee at his feet, and fixed upon his face the memorable look I had never forgotten.

The gentleness of the Doctor's manner and surprise, the dignity that mingled with the supplicating attitude of his wife, the amiable concern of Mr Dick, and the earnestness with which my aunt said to herself, '*That* man mad!' I see and hear, rather than remember, as I write about it.

'Doctor!' said Mr Dick. 'What is it that's amiss? Look here!'

'Annie!' cried the Doctor. 'Not at my feet, my dear!'

'Yes!' she said. 'I beg and pray that no one will leave the room! Oh, my husband and father, break this long silence. Let us both know what it is that has come between us!'

'Annie!' said the Doctor, tenderly taking her in his hands. 'My dear! If any unavoidable change has come, in the sequence of time, upon our married life, you are not to blame. The fault is mine, and only mine. Rise, Annie, pray!'

But she did not rise. She laid her arm across his knee, and dropping her head upon it, said: 'If I have any friend here, who has anything within his knowledge, that may help to mediate between us – I implore that friend to speak!'

After a few moments of painful hesitation, I broke the silence.

'Mrs Strong,' I said, 'there is something which I have been earnestly entreated by Doctor Strong to conceal, but your appeal absolves me from his injunction.'

She turned her face towards me for a moment, and I knew that I was right. Without any other compromise of the truth than a little softening of the coarseness of Uriah Heep, I related plainly what had passed in that same room that night.

When I had finished, Annie took the Doctor's hand and pressed it to her breast, and kissed it. Mr Dick softly raised her; and she stood, looking down upon her husband – from whom she never turned her eyes.

'When I was very young,' said Annie, 'my first associations with knowledge of any kind were inseparable from a patient friend and teacher who was always dear to me. I can remember nothing that I know, without remembering him. He stored my mind with its first treasures, and stamped his character upon them all.'

'Makes her mother nothing!' exclaimed Mrs Markleham.

'Not so, mama,' said Annie; 'but I make him what he was. I must do that. As I grew up, he occupied the same place still. I was proud of his interest: deeply, fondly, gratefully attached to him. You know, mama, how young and inexperienced I was, when you presented him before me, of a sudden, as a lover.'

'I have mentioned the fact, fifty times at least, to everybody here!' said Mrs Markleham.

('Then don't mention it any more!' muttered my aunt.)

'I never thought,' proceeded Annie, 'of any worldly gain that my husband would bring me. My young heart had no room in its homage for any such poor reference. Mama, forgive me when I say that it was *you* who first presented to my mind the thought that any one could wrong me, and wrong him, by such a cruel suspicion.'

'Me!' cried Mrs Markleham.

('Ah! You, to be sure!' observed my aunt, 'and you can't fan it away, my military friend!')

'It was the first unhappiness of my new life,' said Annie. 'It was the first occasion of every unhappy moment I have known. Mama is blameless of having ever urged you for herself, and she is blameless in intention every way, I am sure, – but when I saw how many importunate claims were pressed upon you in my name; how generous you were, and how Mr Wickfield, who had your welfare very much at heart, resented it; the first sense of my exposure to the mean suspicion that my tenderness was bought – and sold to you, of all men, on earth – fell upon me, like unmerited disgrace.'

'A specimen of the thanks one gets,' cried Mrs Markleham, 'for taking care of one's family! I wish I was a Turk!'

('I wish you were, with all my heart – and in your native country!' said my aunt.)

'It was at that time that mama was most solicitous about my Cousin Maldon. I had liked him:' she spoke softly, but without any hesitation: 'very much. We had been little lovers once. If circumstances had not happened otherwise, I might have married him, and been most wretched. There can be no disparity in marriage like unsuitability of mind and purpose. There is nothing,' said Annie, 'that we have in common. I should be thankful to my husband for having saved me from the mistaken impulse of my undisciplined heart.

'When he was waiting to be the object of your munificence, so freely bestowed for my sake, I thought it would have become him better to have worked his own way on. I thought that if I had been he, I would have tried to do it, at the cost of almost any hardship. But I thought no worse of him, until the night of his departure for India. That night I knew he had a false and thankless heart. I saw a double meaning, then, in Mr Wickfield's scrutiny of me. I perceived, for the first time, the dark suspicion that shadowed my life.'

'Suspicion, Annie!' said the Doctor. 'No, no, no!'

'In your mind there was none, I know, my husband!' she returned. 'And when I came to you, that night, to tell you that one of my own kindred, to whom you had been a benefactor, had spoken to me words that should have found no utterance, my mind revolted from the taint the very tale conveyed. I have never, but in your presence, interchanged a word with him from that time; then, only when it has been necessary for the avoidance of this explanation.

'I used to think there were so many whom you might have married, who would not have brought such trouble on you, and who would have made your home a worthier home. I used to be afraid that I had better have remained your pupil. I used to fear that I was so unsuited to your learning and wisdom. If all this made me shrink within myself when I had that to tell, it was still because I honoured you so much, and hoped that you might one day honour me.'

'That day has shone this long time, Annie,' said the Doctor.

'The cause of the late change in you, which I have seen with so much pain, has been made clear to-night; and by an accident I have also come to know, to-night, the full measure of your noble trust in me. I do not hope that any love and duty I may render in return, will ever make me worthy of your priceless confidence; but I can lift my eyes to this dear face, revered as a father's, loved as a husband's, sacred to me in my childhood as a friend's, and solemnly declare that I had never wronged you; never wavered in the love and the fidelity I owe you!'

She had her arms around the Doctor's neck, and he leant his head down over her, mingling his grey hair with her dark brown tresses.

'Oh, hold me to your heart, my husband! Never cast me out! Do not think or speak of disparity between us, for there is none. Oh, take me to your heart, my husband, for my love was founded on a rock, and it endures!'

In the silence that ensued, my aunt walked gravely up to Mr Dick, without at all hurrying herself, and gave him a hug and a sounding kiss.

'You are a very remarkable man, Dick!' said my aunt, with an air of unqualified approbation; 'and never pretend to be anything else, for I know better!'

With that, we three stole quietly out of the room, and came away.

'That's a settler for our military friend, at any rate,' said my aunt, on the way home. 'There never would have been anything the matter, if it hadn't been for that old Animal. It's very much to be wished that some mothers would leave their daughters alone after marriage. What are you thinking of, Trot?'

I was thinking of all that had been said. My mind was still running on some of the expressions used. 'There can be no disparity in marriage like unsuitability of mind and purpose.' 'The first mistaken impulse of an undisciplined heart.' 'My love was founded on a rock.' But we were at home; and the trodden leaves were lying under-foot, and the autumn wind was blowing.

CHAPTER 46

Intelligence

I must have been married about a year, when one evening, as I was returning from a solitary walk, thinking of the book I was then writing – I was engaged at that time upon my first work of fiction – I came past Mrs Steerforth's house. As I went by, a voice at my side made me start.

It was Mrs Steerforth's parlour-maid. 'If you please, sir, would you have the goodness to walk in, and speak to Miss Dartle? She saw you pass a night or two ago; and when I saw you again, I was to ask you to step in.'

I was directed to Miss Dartle in the garden. Our meeting was not cordial. We had parted angrily on the last occasion; and there was an air of disdain about her, which she took no pains to conceal.

'I am told you wish to speak to me,' said I, declining her invitation to sit down.

'If you please,' said she. 'Has this girl been found?'

'No.'

'And yet she has run away!'

'Run away?' I repeated.

'Yes! From him,' she said, with a laugh. 'If she is not found, perhaps she never will be found. She may be dead!'

The vaunting cruelty with which she met my glance, I never saw expressed in any other face.

'I am glad that time has softened you so much, Miss Dartle.'

With another scornful laugh, she said: 'Do you wish to know what is known of her?'

'Yes.'

Taking a few steps towards a wall of holly that divided the lawn from a kitchen-garden, she said, 'Come here!' – as if she were calling to some beast and returned, followed by Mr Littimer who, with undiminished respectability, made me a bow and took up his position behind her. The air of triumph with which she reclined upon the seat between us was worthy of a cruel Princess in a Legend.

Mr Littimer began. 'Mr James and myself have been abroad with the young woman, ever since she left Yarmouth under Mr James's protection. We have been in France, Switzerland, Italy – in fact, almost all parts.

'Mr James took quite uncommonly to the young woman; and was more settled, for a length of time, than I have known him to be since I have been in his service. The young woman was very improvable, and spoke the languages; and wouldn't have been known for the same country-person. I noticed that she was much admired wherever we went.

'The young woman went on in this manner for some time, until she began to weary Mr James by giving way to her low spirits and tempers of that kind; and things were not so comfortable. Mr James began to be restless. The more restless he got, the worse she got; and I must say, for myself, that I had a very difficult time of it indeed between the two. Still, matters lasted, I am sure, for longer than anybody could have expected.

'At last, Mr James set off one morning from Naples, where we had a villa and, under pretence of coming back in a day or so, left me to break it, that, for the general happiness of all concerned, he was' – here an interruption of the short cough – 'gone. But Mr James, I must say, certainly did behave extremely honourable; for he proposed that the young woman should marry a very respectable person, who was fully prepared to overlook the past, and who was, at least, as good as anybody the young woman could have aspired to in a regular way: her connexions being very common.'

He wetted his lips. I was convinced that the scoundrel spoke of himself, and I saw my conviction reflected in Miss Dartle's face.

'I was willing to do anything to relieve Mr James from his difficulty, and to restore harmony between himself and an affectionate parent, who has undergone so much on his account. Therefore I undertook the commission. The young woman's violence, when I broke the fact of his departure, was beyond all expectations. She was quite mad, and had to be held by force.'

Miss Dartle, leaning back upon the seat, with a light of exultation in her face, seemed almost to caress the sounds this fellow had uttered.

'But when I came to the second part of what had been entrusted to me,' said Mr Littimer, 'then the young woman came out in her true colours. If I hadn't been upon my guard, I am convinced she would have had my blood.'

'I think the better of her for it,' said I, indignantly.

Mr Littimer bent his head, as much as to say, 'Indeed, sir? But you're young!' and resumed his narrative.

'It was necessary to take away everything nigh her, that she could do herself, or anybody else, an injury with, and to shut her up close. Notwithstanding which, she got out in the night; forced the lattice of a window, and never has been seen or heard of since.'

'She is dead, perhaps,' said Miss Dartle, with a smile.

'She may have drowned herself, miss,' returned Mr Littimer. 'Or, she may have had assistance from the boatmen, and the boatmen's wives and children. Being given to low company, she was very much in the habit of talking to them on the beach.'

Oh, Emily! Unhappy beauty! What a picture rose before me of her sitting on the far-off shore, among the children like herself when she was innocent.

'When it was clear,' he said, 'that she was not to be found, I went to Mr James and informed him of what had occurred. Words passed between us in consequence, and I felt it due to my character to leave him. I could bear, and I have borne, a great deal from Mr James; but he insulted me too far. Knowing the unfortunate difference between himself and his mother, and what her anxiety of mind was likely to be, I took the liberty of coming home to England, and relating –'

'For money which I paid him,' said Miss Dartle to me.

'Just so, ma'am – and relating what I knew. I am not aware,' said Mr Littimer, 'that there is anything else.'

Miss Dartle glanced at me, as though she would inquire if there were anything that I desired to ask. I said:

'I could wish to know whether they intercepted a letter that was written to her from home.'

'Sir,' he rejoined, 'it is not probable that Mr James would encourage the receipt of letters likely to increase low spirits and unpleasantness; but further than that, sir, I should wish to avoid going.'

'Is that all?' inquired Miss Dartle of me.

I indicated that I had nothing more to say. 'Except,' I added, 'that I understand this fellow's part in the wicked story and that, as I shall make it known to the honest man who has been her father from her childhood, I would recommend him to avoid going too much into public.'

He listened with his usual repose of manner.

'Thank you, sir. But you'll excuse me if I say that people are not allowed to take the law into their own hands. If they do, it is more to their own peril, I believe, than to other people's. Consequently speaking, I am not at all afraid of going wherever I may wish, sir.'

With that, he went away through the arch in the wall of holly by which he had come.

'He says besides,' she observed, with a slow curling of her lip, 'that his master is coasting Spain. But this is of no interest to you. Between these two proud persons, mother and son, there is a wider breach than before, and little hope of its healing, for time makes each more obstinate. This low girl whom he picked out of the tide-mud may be alive. If she is, you will desire to have a pearl of such price found and taken care of. We desire that, too; that he may not by any chance be made her prey again. So far, we are united in one interest; and that is why I have sent for you to hear what you have heard.'

I saw, by the change in her face, that some one was advancing behind me. It was Mrs Steerforth, who gave me her hand more coldly than of yore. She was greatly altered.

'Is Mr Copperfield informed of everything, Rosa?'

'Yes; I have told him why you wished it.'

'You are a good girl. I have had some slight correspondence with your former friend, sir,' addressing me, 'but it has not restored his sense of duty. Therefore I have no other object in this, than what Rosa has mentioned. If, by the course which may relieve the mind of the decent man you brought here (for whom I am sorry – I can say no more), my son may be saved from again falling into the snares of a designing enemy, well!'

She drew herself up, and sat looking straight before her, far away.

'Madam,' I said respectfully, 'I understand. But I must say, having known this injured family from childhood, that if you suppose the girl has not been cruelly deluded, and would not rather die a hundred deaths than take a cup of water from your son's hand now, you cherish a terrible mistake.'

'Well,' said Mrs Steerforth, 'it is no matter. Let it be. You are married, sir, I am told? And are doing well?'

'I have been very fortunate,' I said.

'You have no mother?' – in a softened voice.

'No.'

'It is a pity,' she returned. 'She would have been proud of you. Good-night!'

I took the hand she held out with a dignified, unbending air.

As I moved away from them along the terrace, I could not help observing how steadily they both sat gazing on the prospect, and how it thickened and closed around them. A mist was rising like a sea, which, mingling with the darkness, made it seem as if the gathering waters would encompass them. I have reason to remember this; for before I looked upon those two again, a stormy sea had risen to their feet.

Reflecting on what had been thus told me, I felt it right that it should be communicated to Mr Peggotty. On the following evening I went in quest of him. He kept a lodging over the little chandler's shop in Hungerford Market, from which he first went forth upon his errand of mercy.

He was sitting reading by a window in which he kept a few plants. The room was very neat and orderly. I saw in a moment that it was always kept prepared for her reception.

'Mas'r Davy! You're kindly welcome, sir!'

'Mr Peggotty,' said I, taking the chair he handed me, 'I have heard some news.'

He listened in profound silence to all I had to tell. When I had done, he put his hand down firmly on the table, and set his sunburnt face into a resolute expression.

'My niece, Em'ly, is alive, sir!' he said, stedfastly.

He looked almost like a man inspired, as he said it. I waited for a few moments, until he could give me his undivided attention.

'Now, my dear friend, if she should make her way to London, which is likely if she does not go home –'

'And she won't go home,' he interposed, shaking his head mournfully. 'If she had left of her own accord, she might; not as 't was, sir.'

'If she should come here,' said I, 'I believe there is one person more likely to discover her than any other in the world. Do you remember Martha?'

'Of our town?' I needed no other answer than his face. 'I have seen her in the streets.'

'But you don't know,' said I, 'that Emily was charitable to her, with Ham's help, before she fled from home. Nor, that, when we met one night, and spoke together in the room over the way, she listened at the door.'

'Mas'r Davy!' he replied in astonishment. 'That night when it snew so hard?'

'That night. I have never seen her since. I went back, after parting from you, to speak to her, but she was gone. She is the person of whom I speak, and with whom I think we should communicate.'

'I think, Mas'r Davy, I know wheer to look.'

'Shall we go out now, and try to find her?'

'The time was, Mas'r Davy,' he said, as we came downstairs, 'when I thowt this girl, Martha, a'most like the dirt underneath my Em'ly's feet. God forgive me, there's a difference now!'

As we went along, I asked him about Ham. He said that Ham was 'wearing away his life with kiender no care nohow for 't; but never murmuring, and liked by all.'

I asked him what he thought Ham's state of mind was. What he supposed Ham would do, if he and Steerforth ever should encounter?

'I doen't know, sir,' he replied. 'I have thowt of it often times, but I can't arrize myself of it, no matters. I doen't know as he'd do violence under any circumstances, but I hope as them two may be kep asunders.'

We had come, through Temple Bar, into the city. We were not far from Blackfriars Bridge, when he turned his head and pointed to a solitary female figure flitting along the opposite side of the street. I knew it, readily, to be the figure that we sought.

We were pressing on towards her, when it occurred to me that she might be more disposed to feel a woman's interest in the lost girl, if we spoke to her in a quieter place, where we should be less observed. I advised my companion, therefore, that we should not address her yet, but follow her.

She went on a long way. It was evident, from the manner in which she held her course, that she was going to some fixed destination. At length she turned into a dull, dark street, where the noise and crowd were lost; and I said, 'We may speak to her now;' and we went after her.

CHAPTER 47

Martha

We were in a narrow water-side street by Millbank before we came up with her. At that moment she crossed the road, as if to avoid the footsteps that she heard so close behind; and, without looking back, passed on even more rapidly.

There was at the end of that low-lying street, a dilapidated little wooden building, probably an obsolete old ferry-house. Its position is just at that point where the street ceases, and the road begins to lie between a row of houses and the river. As soon as she came here, and saw the water, she stopped as if she had come to her destination.

The neighbourhood was a dreary one at that time; as oppressive, sad, and solitary by night, as any about London. The girl we had followed strayed down to the river's brink, and, lonely and still, looked at the water.

There were some boats and barges astrand in the mud, and these enabled us to come within a few yards of her without being seen. I then signed to Mr Peggotty to remain where he was, and emerged from their shade to speak to her.

I think she was talking to herself. There was that in her wild manner which gave me no assurance but that she would sink before my eyes, until I had her arm within my grasp.

At the same moment I said, 'Martha!'

She uttered a terrified scream, and struggled with me with such strength that I doubt if I could have held her alone. But a stronger hand than mine was laid upon her; and when she raised her frightened eyes and saw whose it was, she made but one more effort and dropped down between us. We carried her away from the water to where there were some dry stones, and there laid her down.

'Oh, the river!' she cried passionately. 'I know that I belong to it. It comes from country places, where there was once no harm in it – and it creeps through the dismal streets, defiled and miserable – and it goes away, like my life, to a great sea, that is always troubled – and I feel that I must go with it!'

I have never known what despair was, except in the tone of those words. The thought passed through my mind that in the face of my companion, as he looked upon her without speech or motion, I might have read his niece's history, if I had known nothing of it.

'Martha,' said I. 'Do you know who this is, who is with me?'

She said faintly, 'Yes.'

'Are you composed enough,' said I, 'to speak on the subject which so interested you that snowy night?'

Her sobs broke out afresh, and she murmured some inarticulate thanks to me for not having driven her away from the door.

'It was you, if I don't deceive myself,' she said in a broken voice, 'that came into the kitchen, the night she took such pity on me; didn't shrink away from me like all the rest, and gave me such kind help! Was it you, sir?'

'It was,' said I.

'I should have been in the river long ago,' she said, glancing at it with a terrible expression, 'if any wrong to her had been upon my mind. I never could have kept out of it a single winter's night, if I had not been free of any share in that!'

'The cause of her flight is too well understood,' I said. 'You are innocent of any part in it.'

'When I heard what had happened before that snowy night, from some belonging to our town,' cried Martha, 'the bitterest thought in all my mind was, that the people would remember she once kept company with me, and would say I had corrupted her! When, Heaven knows, I would have died to have brought back her good name!'

Long unused to any self-control, the piercing agony of her remorse and grief was terrible.

'What shall I ever do!' she said, fighting thus with her despair. 'How can I go on as I am, a living disgrace to every one I come near!' Suddenly she turned to my companion. 'Stamp upon me, kill me! When she was your pride, you would have thought I had done her harm if I had brushed against her in the street. I know there is a long, long way between us. I only say, with all my guilt and wretchedness upon my head, that I am grateful to her from my soul, and love her. Oh, don't think that all the power I had of loving anything, is quite worn out! Kill me for being what I am; but don't think that of me!'

'Martha,' said Mr Peggotty, 'God forbid as I should judge you. You doesn't know half the change that's come, in course of time, upon me, when you think it likely. Well!' he paused a moment, then went on. 'You doesn't understand how 'tis that this here gentleman and me has wished to speak to you. If you heerd owt of what passed between Mas'r Davy and me, th' night when it snew so hard, you know as I have been fur to seek my dear niece. Fur she's more dear to me now, Martha, than ever she was dear afore.'

She put her hands before her face; but otherwise remained quiet.

'Whereby,' said he, 'I know, both as she would go to the wureld's furdest end with me, if she could once see me again; and that she would fly to the wureld's furdest end to keep off seeing me. For though she ain't no call to doubt my love, there's shame steps in, and keeps betwixt us.

'According to our reckoning, she is like, one day, to make her own poor solitary course to London. Help us all you can to find her, and may Heaven reward you!'

She looked at him hastily, and for the first time, as if she were doubtful of what he had said.

'Will you trust me to speak to her, if I should ever find her? Shelter her, if I have any shelter to divide with her? And then, bring you to her?' she asked.

We both replied together, 'Yes!'

She lifted up her eyes, and solemnly declared that she would devote herself to this task, fervently and faithfully. That she would never waver in it while there was any chance of hope.

We judged it expedient, now, to tell her all we knew; which I recounted at length. She listened with great attention. Her eyes occasionally filled with tears, but those she repressed. It seemed as if her spirit were quite altered.

Under a dull lamp in the road, I wrote out two addresses on a leaf of my pocket-book, which I gave to her. I asked her where she lived herself. She said, after a pause, in no place long. It was better not to know.

I could not prevail upon her to accept any money. I represented to her that the idea of her engaging in this search, while depending on her own resources, shocked us both. She continued stedfast.

'I could not do what I have promised, for money,' she replied. 'I could not take it, if I was starving. It has been put into your hearts to save a wretched creature for repentance. If any good should come of me, I might begin to hope. I am to be trusted, for the first time in a long while. I can say no more.'

Again she repressed the tears that had begun to flow; and, putting out her trembling hand, and touching Mr Peggotty, as if there was some healing virtue in him, went away along the desolate road.

It was midnight when I arrived at home. I had reached my own gate, when I was surprised to see that the door of my aunt's cottage was open.

I went to speak to her. It was with very great surprise that I saw a man standing in her little garden.

He had a glass and bottle in his hand, and was in the act of drinking. I stopped short and recognised the man whom I had once encountered with my aunt in the streets of the city.

He was eating as well as drinking with a hungry appetite. He seemed curious regarding the cottage, too, as if it were the first time he had seen it; he looked up at the windows.

My aunt came out and told some money into his hand. I heard it chink.

'What's the use of this?' he demanded. 'Is this all you mean to give me?'

'It is all I *can* give you,' said my aunt. 'You know I am poorer than I used to be. I have told you so. Having got it, why do you give me the pain of looking at you for another moment, and seeing what you have become?'

'I have become shabby enough, if you mean that,' he said.

'You stripped me of the greatest part of all I ever had,' said my aunt. 'You closed my heart against the whole world, years and years. You treated me falsely, ungratefully, and cruelly. Go, and repent of it. Don't add new injuries to the long, long list of injuries you have done me!'

'Aye!' he returned. 'It's all very fine! – Well! I must do the best I can, I suppose.'

In spite of himself, he appeared abashed by my aunt's indignant tears, and came slouching out of the garden. I met him at the gate, and went in as he came out. We eyed one another narrowly in passing, and with no favour.

'Aunt,' said I, hurriedly. 'This man alarming you again! Let me speak to him. Who is he?'

'Child,' returned my aunt, taking my arm, 'come in, and don't speak to me.'

My aunt retired behind the round green fan of former days, for about a quarter of an hour. Then she came out, and took a seat beside me.

'Trot,' said my aunt, calmly, 'it's my husband.'

'Your husband, aunt? I thought he had been dead!'

'Dead to me,' returned my aunt, 'but living.'

I sat in silent amazement.

'Betsey Trotwood don't look a likely subject for the tender passion,' said my aunt, composedly, 'but the time was, Trot, when she believed in that man most entirely. When she loved him, Trot, right well. He repaid her by breaking her fortune, and nearly breaking her heart. So she put all that sort of sentiment, once and for ever, in a grave, and filled it up, and flattened it down.'

'My dear good aunt!'

'I left him,' my aunt proceeded, 'generously. He had been so cruel to me, that I might have effected a separation on easy terms for myself; but I did not. He sank lower and lower, married another woman, I believe, became an adventurer, a gambler, and a cheat. What he is now, you see. But he was a fine-looking man when I married him and I believed him to be the soul of honour!'

She gave my hand a squeeze, and shook her head.

'He is nothing to me now, Trot. But, sooner than have him punished for his offences (as he would be if he prowled about in this country), I give him more money than I can afford, when he reappears, to go away.'

My aunt dismissed the matter with a heavy sigh and smoothed her dress.

'There, my dear!' she said. 'We won't mention the subject to one another any more; neither, of course, will you mention it to anybody else. This is my grumpy, frumpy story, and we'll keep it to ourselves, Trot!'

CHAPTER 48

Domestic

I laboured hard at my book and it came out and was very successful. It is not my purpose to pursue the history of my own fictions. When I refer to them, incidentally, it is only as part of my progress. Having some foundation for believing, by this time, that nature and accident had made me an author, I pursued my vocation with confidence.

I now write of the time when I had been married about a year and a half. After several varieties of experiment, we had given up the housekeeping as a bad job. The house kept itself, and we kept a page. This unlucky page, engaged in an evil hour at six pounds ten per annum, was a source of continual trouble to me. I watched him as he grew – and he grew like scarlet beans – with painful apprehensions of the time when he would begin to shave; even of the days when he would be bald or grey. I saw no prospect of ever getting rid of him.

I never expected anything less, than this unfortunate's manner of getting me out of my difficulty. He stole Dora's watch and, converting it into money, spent the produce in incessantly riding up and down between London and Uxbridge outside the coach. He was taken to Bow Street, as well as I remember, on the completion of his fifteenth journey.

The consequences would have been much less disagreeable to me if he had not been penitent. But he was very penitent indeed, by instalments. For example: the day after that on which I was obliged to appear against him, he made certain revelations touching a hamper in the cellar, which we believed to be full of wine, but which had nothing in it except bottles and corks. We supposed he had now told the worst he knew of the cook; but, a day or two afterwards, he disclosed how she had a little girl, who, early every morning, took away our bread; and also how he himself had been suborned to maintain the milkman in coals. In two or three days more, he confessed to a knowledge of burglarious intentions on the part of the pot-boy. I got so ashamed of being such a victim, that I would have given him any money to hold his tongue.

At last I ran away myself, whenever I saw an emissary of the police approaching with some new intelligence; and lived a stealthy life until he was transported.

All this presented our mistakes in a new aspect; as I could not help communicating to Dora one evening.

'My love,' said I, 'it is very painful to me to think that our want of system and management, involves not only ourselves but other people.'

'Now you are going to be cross!' said Dora.

'No, my dear, indeed! Let me explain. It is not merely that we lose money and comfort by not learning to be more careful; but that we incur the serious responsibility of spoiling every one who comes into our service. I begin to be afraid that the fault is not entirely on one side, but that these people all turn out ill because we don't turn out very well ourselves.'

'Oh, what an accusation,' exclaimed Dora, opening her eyes wide; 'to say that you ever saw me take gold watches!'

'My dearest,' I remonstrated, 'don't talk preposterous nonsense! Who made the least allusion to gold watches?'

'You did. You said I hadn't turned out well, and compared me to the page,' sobbed Dora. 'Oh, you cruel fellow, to compare your affectionate wife to a transported page! Why didn't you tell me your opinion of me before we married?'

'My darling girl,' I retorted, 'I really must entreat you to be reasonable, and listen to what I did say. Unless we learn to do our duty to those whom we employ, they will never learn to do their duty to us. I am afraid we present opportunities to people to do wrong, that never ought to be presented. We are positively corrupting people. It is a reflection I am unable to dismiss, and it sometimes makes me very uneasy. Come now. Don't be foolish!'

Dora sat sobbing and murmuring that, if I was uneasy, why had I ever been married? In short, Dora was so afflicted, that I felt I must take some other course.

What other course was left to take? I resolved to form Dora's mind.

I began immediately. When Dora was very childish, I tried to be grave. I talked to her on the subjects which occupied my thoughts; and I read Shakespeare to her – and fatigued her to the last degree. I accustomed myself to giving her, as it were quite casually, little scraps of useful information, or sound opinion – and she started from them when I let them off, as if they had been crackers. No matter how naturally I endeavoured to form my little wife's mind, I could not help seeing that she always had an instinctive perception of what I was about, and became a prey to the keenest apprehension. In particular, it was clear to me, that she thought

Shakespeare a terrible fellow. The formation went on very slowly.

I persevered for months. Finding at last, however, that I had effected nothing, it began to occur to me that perhaps Dora's mind was already formed.

On further consideration this appeared so likely, that I abandoned my scheme, resolving henceforth to be satisfied with my child-wife. I was heartily tired of being sagacious and prudent by myself, and of seeing my darling under restraint; so, I bought a pretty pair of ear-rings for her, and a collar for Jip, and went home one day to make myself agreeable.

Dora was delighted with the little presents, and kissed me joyfully; but, there was a shadow between us, and I had made up my mind that it should not be there. If there must be such a shadow anywhere, I would keep it for the future in my own breast.

I sat down by my wife and told her that I feared we had not been quite as good company lately, as we used to be, and that the fault was mine.

'The truth is, Dora, my life,' I said, 'I have been trying to be wise.'

'And to make me wise too,' said Dora, timidly. 'Haven't you, Doady? It's of not a bit of use, you know what a little thing I am. Are you sure you don't think, sometimes, it would have been better to have –'

'Done what, my dear?'

'Nothing!' said Dora.

'Don't I think it would have been better to have done nothing, than to have tried to form my little wife's mind?' said I, laughing at myself, 'Is that the question? But I shall never try any more, for I love her dearly as she is.'

'Really?' inquired Dora, creeping closer to me.

'Why should I seek to change,' said I, 'what has been so precious to me for so long? You never can show better than as your own natural self, my sweet Dora.'

'And you won't mind things going a tiny morsel wrong, sometimes?'

'No, no,' said I.

So ended my last attempt to make any change in Dora. And the shadow I have mentioned, that was not to be between us any more, but was to rest wholly on my own heart. How did that fall?

The old unhappy feeling pervaded my life. It addressed me like a strain of sorrowful music faintly heard in the night. I loved my wife dearly, and I was happy; but the happiness I had vaguely anticipated, once, was not the happiness I enjoyed, and there was always something wanting.

Sometimes, the speculation came into my thoughts. What would have happened, if Dora and I had never known each other? But I always loved her. What I am describing, slumbered in the innermost recesses of my mind. I know of no influence it had in anything I said or did. I bore the weight of all our little cares, and all my projects; Dora held the pens. She was truly fond of me, and proud of me; and when Agnes wrote a few earnest words in her letters to Dora, of the pride with which my old friends heard of my growing reputation, Dora read them out to me with tears of joy, and said I was a dear clever, famous boy.

'The first mistaken impulse of an undisciplined heart.' Those words of Mrs Strong's were constantly recurring to me, at this time. For I knew, now, that my own heart was undisciplined when it first loved Dora.

'There can be no disparity in marriage, like unsuitability of mind and purpose.' Those words I remembered too. I had endeavoured to adapt myself to Dora; to share with her what I could, and be happy; to bear on my own shoulders what I must, and be still happy. It made my second year much happier than my first; and, what was better still, made Dora's life all sunshine.

But, as that year wore on, Dora was not strong. I had hoped that lighter hands than mine would help to mould her character, and that a baby-smile upon her breast might change my child-wife to a woman. It was not to be.

'When I can run about again, as I used to do, aunt,' said Dora, 'I shall make Jip race. He is getting quite slow and lazy.'

'I suspect, my dear,' said my aunt, 'he has a worse disorder than that. Age, Dora.'

'Do you think he is old?' said Dora, astonished. 'Oh, how strange it seems that Jip should be old!'

'It's a complaint we are all liable to, Little One, as we get on in life,' said my aunt, cheerfully; 'I don't feel more free from it than I used to be, I assure you.'

'But Jip,' said Dora, looking at him with compassion, 'even little Jip!'

Dora made him lie down by her, with a good deal of persuasion; and when he was quiet, drew one of his long ears through her hand, repeating thoughtfully, 'Even little Jip ! Oh, poor fellow!'

'His lungs are good enough,' said my aunt, gaily, 'and his dislikes are not at all feeble. He has a good many years before him, no doubt. But if you want a dog to race with, Little Blossom, I'll give you one.'

'Thank you, aunt,' said Dora, faintly. 'But don't, please! I couldn't be such friends with any other dog but Jip; because he wouldn't have known me before I was married, and wouldn't have barked at Doady when he first came to our house. I couldn't care for any other dog but Jip, I am afraid, aunt.'

'To be sure!' said my aunt, patting her cheek again. 'You are right.'

Jip nestled closer to his mistress, and lazily licked her hand.

'You are not so old, Jip, are you, that you'll leave your mistress yet?' said Dora. 'We may keep one another company, a little longer!'

My pretty Dora! When she came down to dinner on the ensuing Sunday, and was so glad to see old Traddles (who always dined with us on Sunday), we thought she would be 'running about as she used to do,' in a few days. But they said, wait a few days more, and then, wait a few days more; and still she neither ran nor walked. She looked very pretty, and was very merry; but the little feet that used to be so nimble were dull and motionless.

I began to carry her downstairs every morning, and up-stairs every night. She would clasp me round the neck and laugh, the while, as if I did it for a wager. Jip would bark and caper round us. My aunt, the best and most cheerful of nurses, would trudge after us, a moving mass of shawls and pillows. Mr Dick would not have relinquished his post of candle-bearer to any one alive. We made quite a gay procession of it, and my child-wife was the gayest there.

But, sometimes, when I took her up, and felt that she was lighter in my arms, a dead blank feeling came upon me, as if I were approaching some frozen region yet unseen, that numbed my life. I avoided the recognition of this feeling until one night my aunt had left her with a parting cry of 'Good-night, Little Blossom,' I sat down at my desk alone, and cried to think, Oh what a fatal name it was, and how the blossom withered in its bloom upon the tree!

CHAPTER 49

I am involved in Mystery

I received one morning the following letter, dated Canterbury, which I read with some surprise:

'MY DEAR SIR,

'Circumstances beyond my individual control have, for a considerable lapse of time, effected a severance of that intimacy which, tinged by the prismatic hues of memory, has ever afforded me gratifying emotions of no common description. This fact, my dear sir, combined with the distinguished elevation to which your talents have raised you, deters me from presuming to aspire to the liberty of addressing the companion of my youth, by the familiar appellation of Copperfield! It is sufficient to know that the name to which I do myself the honour to refer, will ever be treasured among the muniments of our house with sentiments of personal esteem amounting to affection.

'If your more important avocations should admit of your ever tracing these imperfect characters thus far, you will naturally inquire by what object am I influenced, then, in inditing the present missive? Allow me to say that it is *not* an object of a pecuniary nature.

'Placed in a mental position of peculiar painfulness, beyond the assuaging reach even of Mrs Micawber's influence, it is my intention to fly from myself for a short period, and devote a respite of eight-and-forty hours to revisiting some metropolitan scenes of past enjoyment. Among other havens of domestic tranquillity, my feet will naturally tend towards the King's Bench Prison. In stating that I shall be on the outside of the south wall of that place of incarceration the day after to-morrow, at seven in the evening, precisely, my object in this epistolary communication is accomplished.

'I do not feel warranted in soliciting my former friend Mr Copperfield, or my former friend Mr Thomas Traddles of the

Inner Temple to condescend to meet me, and renew our past relations of the olden time. I confine myself to throwing out the observation, that, at the hour and place I have indicated, may be found such ruined vestiges as yet

Remain,

Of

A

Fallen Tower,

WILKINS MICAWBER

'p.s. It may be advisable to superadd that Mrs Micawber is *not* in confidential possession of my intentions.'

Making due allowance for Mr Micawber's lofty style, I believed that something important lay hidden at the bottom of this roundabout communication. I was still pursuing it, when Traddles found me.

'My dear fellow,' said I, 'I have received a very singular letter from Mr Micawber.'

'And I have received one from Mrs Micawber!'

With that, Traddles made an exchange with me. Mrs Micawber's epistle ran thus:

'My best regards to Mr Thomas Traddles, and may I beg a few moments of his leisure time? Though harrowing to myself to mention, the alienation of Mr Micawber from his wife and family is the cause of my unhappy appeal.

'Mr T. can form no adequate idea of the change in Mr Micawber's conduct. It has gradually augmented, until it assumes the appearance of aberration of intellect. The slightest provocation, even being asked if there is anything he would prefer for dinner, causes him to express a wish for a separation. Last night, on being childishly solicited for twopence, to buy "lemon-stunners" – a local sweetmeat – he presented an oyster-knife at the twins!

'May I now venture to confide to Mr T. the purport of my letter? Mr Micawber is going to London. Though he studiously concealed his hand in writing the direction-card which he attached to the little brown valise of happier days, the eagle-glance of matrimonial anxiety detected the West-End destination of the coach. Dare I fervently implore Mr T. to see my misguided husband, and to reason with him?

'If Mr Copperfield should yet remember one unknown to fame,

will Mr T. take charge of my similar entreaties? In any case, he
will have the benevolence *to consider this communication strictly
private, and on no account to be alluded to in the presence of Mr
Micawber.*

'Mr Thomas Traddles's respectful suppliant,

EMMA MICAWBER.'

'What do you think of that letter?' said Traddles, when I had read it
twice.

'What do you think of the other?' said I.

'I think that the two together,' replied Traddles, 'mean more than Mr
and Mrs Micawber usually mean in their correspondence – but I don't
know what.'

I now wrote a comforting letter to Mrs Micawber, in our joint names,
and we both signed it. We took my aunt into our counsels in the afternoon; but our only decided conclusion was, that we would be very
punctual in keeping Mr Micawber's appointment.

Although we appeared at the stipulated place a quarter of an hour
before the time, we found Mr Micawber already there.

When we accosted him, his manner was something more confused
than of yore. His very eye-glass seemed to hang less easily, and his shirt-
collar, though still of the old formidable dimensions, rather drooped.

'Gentlemen!' said Mr Micawber, after the first salutations, 'you are
friends in need, and friends indeed. Your cordiality overpowers me.
This reception of a shattered fragment of the Temple once called Man
bespeaks a heart that is an honour to our common nature. I was about
to observe that I again behold the serene spot where some of the happiest hours of my existence fleeted by.'

'Made so, I am sure, by Mrs Micawber,' said I. 'I hope she is well?'

'Thank you,' returned Mr Micawber, whose face clouded at this reference, 'she is but so-so. And this,' said Mr Micawber, nodding his head
sorrowfully, 'is the Bench! Where, for the first time in many revolving years, the overwhelming pressure of pecuniary liabilities was not
proclaimed; where there was no knocker on the door for any creditor
to appeal to; where personal service of process was not required, and
detainers were merely lodged at the gate!'

'We have all got on in life since then, Mr Micawber,' said I.

'Mr Copperfield,' returned Mr Micawber, bitterly, 'when I was an
inmate of that retreat I could look my fellow-man in the face, and punch
his head if he offended me. My fellow-man and myself are no longer on
those glorious terms!'

'Oh, you are in low spirits, Mr Micawber,' said Traddles.

'I am, sir,' interposed Mr Micawber.

'How is our friend Heep, Mr Micawber?' said I, after a silence.

'My dear Copperfield,' returned Mr Micawber, bursting into a state of much excitement, and turning pale, 'if you ask after my employer as *your* friend, I am sorry for it; if you ask after him as *my* friend, I sardonic-ally smile at it. In whatever capacity you ask after my employer, I beg, without offence to you, to limit my reply to this – that whatever his state of health may be, his appearance is foxy: not to say diabolical.'

I expressed my regret for having touched upon a theme that roused him so much. 'May I ask,' said I, 'how my old friends Mr and Miss Wickfield are?'

'Miss Wickfield,' said Mr Micawber, now turning red, 'is the only starry spot in a miserable existence. My respect for that young lady, my admiration of her character – upon my soul, in my present state of mind I am not equal to this!'

He took out his pocket-handkerchief, and stood with his back to the wall.

'It is my fate, gentlemen, that the finer feelings of our nature have become reproaches to me. My homage to Miss Wickfield is a flight of arrows in my bosom.'

I then mentioned that it would give me great pleasure to introduce him to my aunt, if he would ride out to Highgate.

'You shall make us a glass of your own punch, Mr Micawber,' said I, 'and forget whatever you have on your mind, in pleasanter reminis-cences.'

'Gentlemen,' returned Mr Micawber, 'do with me as you will! I am a straw upon the surface of the deep, and am tossed in all directions by the elephants – I beg your pardon; I should have said the elements.'

We went to my aunt's house rather than to mine, because of Dora's not being well. My aunt welcomed Mr Micawber with gracious cordial-ity. Mr Micawber kissed her hand, retired to the window, and had a mental wrestle with himself.

Mr Dick was by nature so exceedingly compassionate of any one who seemed to be ill at ease, that he shook hands with Mr Micawber, at least half-a-dozen times in five minutes.

'How do you find yourself?' said Mr Dick, with an anxious look.

'Indifferent, my dear sir,' returned Mr Micawber, sighing.

'You must keep up your spirits,' said Mr Dick.

Mr Micawber was quite overcome by these friendly words. At another time I should have been amused by this; but I felt that we were all constrained and uneasy, and I watched Mr Micawber so anxiously, in his vacillations between an evident disposition to reveal something, and a counter-disposition to reveal nothing, that I was in a perfect fever. My aunt had more useful possession of her wits than either of us; for she held him in conversation.

'I hope Mrs Micawber and your family are well, sir,' said my aunt.

Mr Micawber inclined his head. 'They are as well, ma'am, as Aliens and Outcasts can ever hope to be.'

'Lord bless you, sir!' exclaimed my aunt in her abrupt way. 'What are you talking about?'

'The subsistence of my family, ma'am,' returned Mr Micawber, 'trembles in the balance. My employer –'

Here Mr Micawber provokingly left off; and began to peel the lemons that had been under my directions set before him, together with all the other appliances he used in making punch.

'My employer, ma'am – Mr Heep – once did the favour to observe to me, that if I were not in the receipt of the stipendiary emoluments appertaining to my engagement with him, I should probably be a mountebank about the country. For anything that I can perceive to the contrary, it is still probable that my children may be reduced to seek a livelihood by personal contortion, while Mrs Micawber abets their unnatural feats, by playing the barrel-organ.'

Mr Micawber, with a random but expressive flourish of his knife, signified that these performances might be expected to take place after he was no more.

Notwithstanding the aversion with which I regarded the idea of entrapping him into any disclosure he was not prepared to make voluntarily, I should have taken him up at this point, but for the strange proceedings in which I saw him engaged; whereof his putting the lemon-peel into the kettle, the spirit into the empty jug, and confidently attempting to pour boiling water out of a candlestick, were among the most remarkable. I saw that a crisis was at hand, and it came. He rose from his chair and burst into tears.

'My dear Copperfield,' said Mr Micawber, 'this is an occupation, of all others, requiring an untroubled mind, and self-respect. I cannot perform it.'

'Mr Micawber,' said I, 'what is the matter? Pray speak out. You are among friends.'

'Good heavens, it is principally because I *am* among friends that my state of mind is what it is. What is the matter, gentlemen? Villainy is the matter; deception, fraud, conspiracy, are the matter; and the name of the whole atrocious mass is – HEEP!'

My aunt clapped her hands, and we all started up as if we were possessed.

'The struggle is over!' said Mr Micawber, violently gesticulating. 'I will lead this life no longer. I have been under a Taboo in that infernal scoundrel's service. Give me back my wife, give me back my family, substitute Micawber for the petty wretch who walks about in the boots at present on my feet!'

I never saw a man so hot in my life. I tried to calm him, but he got hotter.

'I'll put my hand in no man's hand,' said Mr Micawber, gasping, puffing, and sobbing, 'until I have – blown to fragments – the – a – detestable – serpent – HEEP! I'll partake of no one's hospitality, until I have – a – moved Mount Vesuvius – to eruption – on – the abandoned rascal – HEEP! Refreshment – a – underneath this roof – particularly punch – would – a – choke me – unless – I had previously – choked the eyes – out of the head – a – of – interminable cheat, and liar – HEEP!'

I had some fear of Mr Micawber's dying on the spot. The manner in which he struggled through these inarticulate sentences was frightful; but now, when he sank into a chair, steaming, and looked at us, with every possible colour in his face that had no business there, he had the appearance of being in the last extremity. I would have gone to his assistance, but he waved me off.

'No, Copperfield! – No communication – a – until – redress from wrongs inflicted by consummate scoundrel – HEEP! Inviolable secret – a – from the whole world – a – no exceptions – this day week – a – at breakfast time – a – everybody present – including aunt – a – and extremely friendly gentleman – to be at the hotel at Canterbury – a – where – Mrs Micawber and myself – Auld Lang Syne in chorus – and – a – will expose intolerable ruffian, HEEP!'

With this Mr Micawber rushed out of the house; leaving us in a condition little better than his own. But even then his passion for writing letters was too strong to be resisted; for while we were yet in the height of our excitement, the following note was brought to me: —

'Most secret and confidential.

'MY DEAR SIR,

'I beg to be allowed to convey, through you, my apologies to your excellent aunt for my late excitement. I trust I rendered tolerably intelligible my appointment for the morning of this day week, at the house of public entertainment at Canterbury,

where Mrs Micawber and myself had once the honour of uniting
our voices to yours, in the well-known strain of the Immortal
exciseman, nurtured beyond the Tweed.

'The duty done, I shall be known no more. I shall simply require
to be deposited in that place of universal resort, where

> 'Each in his narrow cell for ever laid,
> 'The rude forefathers of the hamlet sleep.'

' – With the plain Inscription,
'WILKINS MICAWBER'

CHAPTER 50

Mr Peggotty's Dream comes true

By this time, some months had passed since our interview on the bank of the river with Martha. I had never seen her, but she had communicated with Mr Peggotty on several occasions. Nothing had come of her zealous intervention; nor could I infer from what he told me, that any clue had ever been obtained to Emily's fate. I confess that I began to despair of her recovery, and gradually to sink deeper and deeper into the belief that she was dead.

His conviction remained unchanged. So far as I know – and I believe his honest heart was transparent to me – he never wavered again, in his solemn certainty of finding her.

Dora had often seen him since our marriage, and was quite fond of him. I fancy his figure before me now, standing near her sofa, with his rough cap in his hand, and the blue eyes of my child-wife raised, with a timid wonder, to his face. Sometimes of an evening, I would induce him to smoke his pipe in the garden.

One evening, at this hour, he told me that he had found Martha waiting near his lodgings on the preceding night when he came out, and that she had asked him not to leave London on any account.

'Did she tell you why?' I inquired.

'I asked her, Mas'r Davy,' he replied, 'but it is few words as she ever says, and she on'y got my promise and so went away.'

I was walking alone in the garden, one evening, about a fortnight afterwards. I remember that evening well. It was the second in Mr Micawber's week of suspense.

There was a little green perspective of trellis-work at the side of our cottage, through which I could see into the road. I happened to turn my eyes towards this place, and I saw a figure beyond, dressed in a plain cloak. It was beckoning.

'Martha!' said I.

'Can you come with me?' she inquired, in an agitated whisper. 'I have been to him, and he is not at home. I wrote down where he was to come, and left it on his table with my own hand. They said he would not be out long. I have tidings for him. Can you come directly?'

My answer was to pass out at the gate immediately. She turned towards London, whence she had come on foot.

I asked her if that were not our destination? On her motioning Yes, I stopped an empty coach that was coming by, and we got into it. When I asked her where the coachman was to drive, she answered, 'Anywhere near Golden Square! And quick!'

We alighted at one of the entrances to the Square. She laid her hand on my arm, and hurried me on to one of the sombre streets, where the houses were once fair dwellings of single families, but had long degenerated into poor lodgings let off in rooms. Entering one of these, and releasing my arm, she beckoned me to follow her up the common staircase.

The house swarmed with inmates. As we went up, doors of rooms were opened and people's heads put out; and we passed other people on the stairs, who were coming down.

We proceeded to the top-story of the house. Two or three times, I thought I observed in the indistinct light the skirts of a female figure going up before us. As we turned to ascend the last flight we caught a full view of this figure pausing for a moment, at a door. Then it turned the handle, and went in.

'She has gone into my room,' said Martha. 'I don't know her!'

I knew her. I had recognised with amazement Miss Dartle.

I said it was a lady whom I had seen before; and had scarcely done so when we heard her voice in the room, though not what she was saying. Martha softly led me up the stairs; and then, by a little back door into a small garret with a low sloping roof. Between this, and the room she had called hers, there was a small door standing partly open. Here we stopped. I could only see, of the room beyond, that it was pretty large; that there was a bed in it. I could not see Miss Dartle, or the person whom we had heard her address.

Martha kept one hand on my lips, and raised the other in a listening attitude.

'It matters little to me her not being at home,' said Rosa Dartle, haughtily, 'it is you I come to see.'

'Me?' replied a soft voice.

At the sound of it, a thrill went through my frame. For it was Emily's!

'Yes,' returned Miss Dartle, 'I have come to look at you.'

The unrelenting hatred of her tone presented her before me, as if I had seen her standing in the light. I saw the flashing black eyes, and the passion-wasted figure; and I saw the scar, with its white track cutting through her lips, quivering and throbbing as she spoke.

'I have come to see,' she said, 'James Steerforth's fancy; the girl who ran away with him, and is the town-talk of the commonest people of her native place. I want to know what such a thing is like.'

There was a rustle, as if the unhappy girl on whom she heaped these taunts, ran towards the door, and the speaker swiftly interposed herself before it.

When Miss Dartle spoke again, it was through her set teeth. 'Stay there! If you try to evade *me*, I'll stop you, if it's by the hair, and raise the very stones against you!'

I did not know what to do. Much as I desired to put an end to the interview, I felt that it was for Mr Peggotty alone to see her and recover her. Would he never come?

'So!' said Rosa Dartle, with a contemptuous laugh, 'I see her at last! Why, he was a poor creature to be taken by that delicate mock-modesty, and that hanging head!'

'I have deserved this,' cried Emily, 'but it's dreadful! Dear, dear lady, think what I have suffered, and how I am fallen! Oh, Martha, come back!'

Miss Dartle placed herself in a chair, within view of the door, and looked downward, as if Emily were crouching on the floor before her. I could see her curled lip, and her cruel eyes intently fixed on one place, with a greedy triumph.

'Listen to what I say!' she said; 'and reserve your false arts for your dupes. Do you hope to move *me* by your tears? Do you know what you have done? Do you ever think of the home you have laid waste?'

'Oh, is there ever night or day, when I don't think of it!' cried Emily; and now I could see her, on her knees, with her head thrown back, her pale face looking upward, her hands held out. 'Has there ever been a single minute, waking or sleeping, when it hasn't been before me, just as it used to be in the lost days when I turned my back upon it for ever and for ever!'

Rosa Dartle sat looking down upon her, as inflexible as a figure of brass.

'The miserable vanity of these earth-worms!' she said. '*Your* home! Do you imagine that I bestow a thought on it? You were a part of the trade of your home, and were bought and sold like any other vendible thing your people deal in.'

'Oh not that!' cried Emily. 'Don't visit my disgrace and shame on folks who are as honourable as you!'

'I speak,' she said, not deigning to take any heed of this appeal, 'of *his* home – where I live. Here,' she said, looking down upon the prostrate girl, 'is a worthy cause of division between lady-mother and gentleman-son. This piece of pollution to be made much of for an hour, and then tossed back to her original place!'

'No! no!' cried Emily. 'When he first came into my way I had been brought up as virtuous as you and was going to be the wife of as good a man as any lady in the world can ever marry. If you live in his home, you know, perhaps, what his power with a weak, vain girl might be. I don't defend myself but I know well, and he knows well, that he used all his power to deceive me, and that I believed him, trusted him, and loved him!'

Rosa Dartle sprang up from her seat with a face of such malignity that I had almost thrown myself between them.

'*You* love him? *You?*' she cried, with her clenched hand, quivering as if it only wanted a weapon to stab the object of her wrath. '*She* love! And he ever cared for her, she'd tell me. Ha, ha! The liars that these traders are!'

Her mockery was worse than her undisguised rage but she chained it up again. 'I came here, you pure fountain of love,' she said, 'to see what such a thing as you was like. I was curious. I am satisfied. Also to tell you, that you had best hide yourself. If not at home, somewhere beyond reach; in some obscure life – or, better still, in some obscure death. If you live here to-morrow, I'll have your story and your character proclaimed on the common stair. There are decent women in the house, I am told; and it is a pity such a light as you should be among them. If you seek refuge in this town in any character but your true one the same service shall be done you. Being assisted by a gentleman who not long ago aspired to the favour of your hand, I am sanguine as to that.'

Would he never come?

'What, what, shall I do!' exclaimed the wretched Emily.

'Do?' returned the other. 'Consecrate your existence to the recollection of James Steerforth's tenderness – he would have made you this serving-man's wife, would he not? Or, if those proud remembrances will not sustain you, marry that good man, and be happy in his condescension. If this will not do either, die! There are doorways and dust-heaps for such deaths – find one, and take your flight to Heaven!'

I heard a distant foot upon the stairs. I knew it, I was certain. It was his, thank God!

She moved slowly from before the door when she said this, and passed out of my sight.

'But mark!' she added, 'I am resolved to cast you out, unless you withdraw from my reach altogether. This is what I had to say; and what I say, I mean to do!'

The foot upon the stairs came nearer – nearer – passed her as she went down – rushed into the room!

'Uncle!'

A fearful cry followed the word. I paused a moment, and, looking in, saw him supporting her insensible figure in his arms. He gazed for a few seconds in the face; then stooped to kiss it – oh, how tenderly!

'Mas'r Davy,' he said, in a low tremulous voice. 'I thank my Heav'nly Father as my dream's come true! I thank Him hearty for having guided of me, in His own ways, to my darling!'

With those words he took her up in his arms; and carried her, motionless and unconscious, down the stairs.

CHAPTER 51

The Beginning of a longer Journey

It was early in the morning of the following day, as I was walking in my garden with my aunt, I was told that Mr Peggotty desired to speak with me. He came to meet me and bared his head when he saw my aunt, for whom he had a high respect. I had been telling her all that had happened overnight. She shook hands with him and patted him on the arm. It was so expressively done, that she had no need to say a word. Mr Peggotty understood her quite as well as if she had said a thousand.

'I'll go in now, Trot,' said my aunt, 'and look after Little Blossom.'

'By your leave, ma'am,' returned Mr Peggotty, 'I should take it kind, if you'd bide heer.'

So, she drew her arm through Mr Peggotty's, and walked with him to a little summer-house at the bottom of the garden, where she sat down on a bench, and I beside her. There was a seat for Mr Peggotty too, but he preferred to stand.

'I took my dear child away last night,' Mr Peggotty began, as he raised his eyes to ours, 'to my lodging, wheer I have a long time been expecting of her. It was hours afore she knowed me right: and when she did, she kneeled down at my feet, and kiender said to me, as if it was her prayers, how it all come to be.

'When my Em'ly took flight, from the house wheer she was made a pris'ner by that theer spotted snake as Ms'r Davy see, it was a dark night, with many stars a shining. She ran along the beach, believing the old boat was theer; and calling out to us. Even so far she ran, and there was fire afore her eyes, and roarings in her ears. Of a sudden – or so she thowt, you unnerstand – the day broke, and she was lying upon the shore, and a woman was speaking to her, saying, in the language of that country, what was it as had gone so much amiss? Em'ly told her, and she took her home.

'It was a little cottage, but she found space for Em'ly in it – her husband was away at sea – and she kep it secret, and prevailed upon such neighbours as she had to keep it secret too. Em'ly was took bad with fever, and the language of that country went out of her head, and

333

she could only speak her own, that no one unnerstood. She recollects believing as the old boat was round the next pint in the bay, and begging and imploring of 'em to send theer and tell how she was dying, and bring back a message of forgiveness, if it was on'y a wured. How long this lasted, I doen't know; but then there come a sleep; and in that sleep, she fell into the weakness of the littlest child.'

Here he stopped, as if for relief from the terrors of his own description. After a few moments, he pursued his story.

'It was a pleasant arternoon when she awoke and saw the vine leaves at the winder and the hills beyond, then she know'd as the old boat warn't round that next pint in the bay no more, and know'd where she was, and why; and broke out a crying on that good young woman's bosom. That done my Em'ly good and she begun to mend. One evening come, when she was looking at a little girl upon the beach. And of a sudden this child held out her hand, and said, "Fisherman's daughter, here's a shell!" – Then Em'ly unnerstands her language and it all comes back!

'When Em'ly got strong again, she casts about to leave that good young creetur, and get to her own country. The husband was come home, then; and the two together put her aboard a small trader bound to Leghorn, and from that to France. She had a little money, but it was less than little as they would take for all they done. I'm a'most glad on it, though they was so poor. What they done, is laid up wheer neither moth nor rust doth corrupt, and wheer thieves do not break through nor steal. Mas'r Davy, it'll outlast all the treasure in the wureld.

'Em'ly took service to wait on travelling ladies at a inn in the port. Theer come, one day, that snake. – Let him never come nigh me. I doen't know what hurt I might do him! – Soon as she see him, without him seeing her, all her fear returned and she fled to England, and was set ashore at Dover.

'All the way to England she had thowt to come to her dear home. But, fear of not being forgiv, fear of being pinted at, fear of many things, turned her from it upon the road. She come to London – alone – without a penny – young – so pretty. A'most the moment as she lighted heer, she found a friend; a decent woman as spoke to her about a lodging for the night, and making secret inquiration concerning of me. Martha, trew to her promise, saved her.'

I could not repress a cry of joy.

'Mas'r Davy!' said he, gripping my hand in that strong hand of his, 'it was you as first made mention of her to me. I thankee, sir! She was arnest. She had know'd of her bitter knowledge wheer to watch and what to do. She had done it. She told Emily she had seen me, and know'd I loved her, and forgive her. She wrapped her in her clothes. She took her, faint and trembling, on her arm. She brought her safe out, in the dead of the night, from that black pit of ruin!

'Then she went in search of me; then in search of you, Mas'r Davy. She didn't tell Em'ly what she come out fur, lest she should think of hiding of herself. How the cruel lady know'd of her being theer, I doen't greatly ask myself. My niece is found.

'All night long,' said Mr Peggotty, 'we have been together, Em'ly and me. All night long, her arms has been about my neck; and we knows full well, as we can put our trust in one another ever more.'

We all remained silent, and occupied with our own reflections until I spoke.

'You have quite made up your mind,' said I to Mr Peggotty, 'as to the future, good friend?'

'Quite, Mas'r Davy,' he returned; 'Our future life lays over the sea.'

'They will emigrate together, aunt,' said I.

'Yes!' said Mr Peggotty, with a hopeful smile. 'No one can't reproach my darling in Australia. I was down at the Docks early this morning, to get information concerning of them ships. In about six weeks or two months from now, there'll be one sailing and we shall take our passage in her.'

'Quite alone?' I asked.

'Aye, Mas'r Davy!' he returned. 'My sister, you see, she's that fond of you and yourn, that it wouldn't be hardly fair to let her go. Besides which, theer's one she has in charge, Mas'r Davy, as doen't ought to be forgot.'

'Poor Ham!' said I.

'My good sister takes care of his house, you see, ma'am, and he takes kindly to her,' Mr Peggotty explained for my aunt's better information.

'And Mrs Gummidge?' said I.

'Well, I've had a mort of con-sideration, I do tell you, concerning of Missis Gummidge. I means to make her a 'lowance afore I go, as'll leave her pretty comfort'ble. 'Tan't to be expected at her time of life as the good old Mawther is to be knocked about aboardship, and in the woods and wilds of a fur-away country.'

He forgot nobody. He thought of everybody's claims and strivings, but his own.

'Theer's one thing furder, Mas'r Davy,' said he, putting his hand in his breast-pocket, and gravely taking out the little paper bundle I had seen before. 'Theer's these heer bank-notes – fifty pound, and ten. To them I wish to add the money as she come away with. This money, if you doen't see objections, Mas'r Davy, I shall put up jest afore I go, in a cover d'rected to him; and put that up in another, d'rected to his mother. I shall tell her, in no more wureds than I speak to you, what it's the price on; and that I'm gone, and past receiving of it back.'

I told him that I thought it would be right to do so.

'I said that theer was on'y one thing furder,' he proceeded 'but theer was two. I warn't sure in my mind, wen I come out this morning, as I could go and break to Ham, of my own self, what had happened. So I writ a letter while I was out, and put it in the post-office, telling of 'em how all was as 'tis, and that I should come down to-morrow and take my farewell leave of Yarmouth.'

'And do you wish me to go with you?' said I, seeing that he left something unsaid.

'If you could do me that kind favour, Mas'r Davy,' he replied, 'I know the sight on you would cheer 'em up a bit.'

I readily pledged myself to accompany him in accordance with his wish. Next morning, consequently, we were on the Yarmouth coach.

As we passed along the familiar street at night, I glanced into Omer and Joram's shop, and saw my old friend Mr Omer there, smoking his pipe. I felt reluctant to be present, when Mr Peggotty first met his sister and Ham; and made Mr Omer my excuse for lingering behind.

'How is Mr Omer after this long time?' said I, going in.

He recognised me with great delight.

'I should get up, sir, to acknowledge such an honour as this visit,' said he, 'only my limbs are rather out of sorts, and I am wheeled about. With the exception of my limbs and my breath, hows'ever, I am as hearty as a man can be, I'm thankful to say.'

I saw, now, that his easy-chair went on wheels.

'It's an ingenious thing, ain't it?' he inquired. 'It runs as light as a feather, and tracks as true as a mail-coach. My grand-daughter gives it a shove, and away we go, as clever and merry as ever you see anything! And it's a most uncommon chair to smoke a pipe in.'

I never saw such a good old fellow to make the best of a thing, and find out the enjoyment of it, as Mr Omer. He was as radiant, as if his chair, his asthma, and the failure of his limbs, were the various branches of a great invention for enhancing the luxury of a pipe.

'I see more of the world, I can assure you,' said Mr Omer, 'in this chair, than ever I see out of it. You'd be surprised at the number of people that looks in of a day to have a chat. You really would! There's twice as much in the newspaper, since I've taken to this chair, as there used to be. As to general reading, dear me, what a lot of it I do get through! And since I've took to general reading, you've took to general writing, eh, sir?' said Mr Omer, surveying me admiringly. 'What a lovely work that was of yours! I read it every word. And as to feeling sleepy! Not at all!'

I laughingly expressed my satisfaction, but I must confess that I thought this association of ideas significant. I changed the subject by referring to Emily. I gave him a general account of her restoration to her uncle by the aid of Martha; which I knew would please the old man.

'I am rejoiced at it, sir! It's the best news I have heard for many a day. And what's going to be undertook for that unfortunate young woman, Martha, now?'

'You touch a point that my thoughts have been dwelling on but I can give you no information yet.'

'Because,' said Mr Omer, 'whatever *is* done, I should wish to be a member of. Put me down for anything you may consider right, and let me know. I never could think the girl all bad, and I am glad to find she's not. So will my daughter Minnie be.'

I shook hands with him, and wished him good-night.

'Half a minute, sir,' said Mr Omer. 'If you was to go without seeing my little elephant, you'd lose the best of sights. Minnie!'

A musical little voice answered, from somewhere up-stairs, 'I am coming, grandfather!' and a pretty little girl with flaxen hair came running into the shop.

'This is my little elephant, sir,' said Mr Omer, fondling the child. 'Now, little elephant!'

The little elephant set the door of the parlour open, enabling me to see that, in these latter days, it was converted into a bedroom for Mr Omer and then hid her pretty forehead against the back of Mr Omer's chair.

'The elephant butts, you know, sir,' said Mr Omer, winking, 'when he goes at a object. Once, elephant. Twice. Three times!'

At this signal, the little elephant, with a dexterity that was next to marvellous in so small an animal, whisked the chair round with Mr Omer in it, and rattled it off, pell-mell, into the parlour, without touching the doorpost: Mr Omer indescribably enjoying the performance, and looking back at me on the road as if it were the triumphant issue of his life's exertions.

After a stroll about the town, I went to Ham's house. Peggotty had now removed here for good; and had let her own house to the successor of Mr Barkis in the carrying business, who had paid her very well for the goodwill, cart, and horse. I believe the very same slow horse that Mr Barkis drove, was still at work.

I found them in the kitchen, accompanied by Mrs Gummidge, who had been fetched from the old boat by Mr Peggotty. He had evidently told them all. Both Peggotty and Mrs Gummidge had their aprons to their eyes, and Ham had just stepped out 'to take a turn on the beach.' He presently came home, very glad to see me; and I hope they were all the better for my being there. We spoke, with some approach to cheerfulness, of Mr Peggotty's growing rich in a new country, and of the wonders he would describe in his letters. We said nothing of Emily by name, but distantly referred to her more than once. Ham was the serenest of the party.

But, Peggotty told me, she believed that he was broken-hearted. I thought I had read in his face that he would like to speak to me alone. I therefore resolved to put myself in his way next evening, as he came home from his work. So I arranged that I met him at a retired part of the sands, which I knew he would cross, and turned back with him. We had walked but a little way together, when he said, 'Mas'r Davy, have you seen her?'

'Only for a moment,' I softly answered.

We walked a little farther, and he said: 'Shall you see her, d'ye think?'

'It would be too painful to her, perhaps,' said I. 'But if there is anything that I could write to her, for you, I should consider it a sacred trust.'

'I thankee, sir, most kind! I think theer is something I could wish said or wrote.'

'What is it?'

We walked a little farther in silence, and then he spoke.

''Tan't that I forgive her. 'Tis more as I beg of her to forgive me, for having pressed my affections upon her. Odd times, I think that if I hadn't had her promise fur to marry me, she'd have told me what was struggling in her mind, and I might have saved her.'

I pressed his hand. 'Is that all?'

'Theer's yet a something else,' he returned. 'I loved too deep to be able to lead her to believe of my own self as I'm a happy man. But if you could think of anything to say as might bring her to believe I wasn't greatly hurt – anything as would ease her sorrowful mind, and yet not make her think 'twas possible that any one could ever be to me what she was – I should ask of you to say that – with my prayers for her – that was so dear.'

I told him I would charge myself to do this as well as I could.

'I thankee, sir,' he answered. ''Twas kind of you to bear him company down. Mas'r Davy, I unnerstan' very well that I am not like to see him agen. The last you see on him will you give him the lovingest duty and thanks of the orphan, as he was ever more than a father to?'

This I also promised, faithfully, and he turned away.

The door of the boat-house stood open when I approached; and, on entering, I found it emptied of all its furniture, saving one of the old lockers, on which Mrs Gummidge was seated, looking at Mr Peggotty.

'Come to bid farewell to't, eh, Mas'r Davy?' he said, taking up the candle. 'Bare enough, now, ain't it?'

'Indeed you have made good use of the time,' said I.

'Why, we have not been idle, sir. Theer's the very locker that you used to sit on, 'long with Em'ly!' said Mr Peggotty, in a whisper. 'I'm a going to carry it away with me, last of all. And heer's your old bedroom, see, Mas'r Davy? A'most as bleak to-night, as 'art could wish!'

In truth, the wind crept around the deserted house with a wailing that was very mournful. I thought of myself, lying here, when that first great change was being wrought at home. I thought of the blue-eyed child who had enchanted me. I thought of Steerforth: and a foolish, fearful fancy came upon me of his being near at hand, and liable to be met at any turn.

We came back to Mrs Gummidge, sitting on the locker.

'Dan'l,' said Mrs Gummidge, suddenly clinging to his arm, 'the parting words I speak in this house is, I mustn't be left behind. Take me 'long with you and Em'ly! I'll be your servant, constant and trew.'

'My good soul,' said Mr Peggotty, shaking his head, 'you doen't know what a long voyage, and what a hard life 'tis!'

'Yes I do, Dan'l! I can guess!' cried Mrs Gummidge. 'But my parting words under this roof is, I shall go into the house and die, if I am not took. I can dig, Dan'l. I can work. I can live hard. I can be loving and patient now – more than you think, Dan'l, if you'll on'y try me. Dan'l, deary Dan'l, let me go 'long with you!'

And Mrs Gummidge took his hand, and kissed it in a homely rapture of devotion and gratitude, that he well deserved.

We brought the locker out, extinguished the candle, and left the old boat close shut up, a dark speck in the cloudy night. Next day, when we were returning to London outside the coach, Mrs Gummidge and her basket were on the seat behind, and Mrs Gummidge was happy.

CHAPTER 52

I assist at an Explosion

When the time Mr Micawber had appointed so mysteriously, was within four-and-twenty hours of being come, my aunt and I consulted how we should proceed; for my aunt was very unwilling to leave Dora. Ah! how easily I carried Dora up and down stairs, now!

We were disposed, notwithstanding Mr Micawber's stipulation for my aunt's attendance, to arrange that she should stay at home, and be represented by Mr Dick and me, when Dora declared that she never would forgive her bad boy, if my aunt remained behind.

'I won't speak to you,' said Dora. 'You'll only be gone one night, and Jip will take care of me while you are gone. Doady will carry me up-stairs before you go, and I won't come down again till you come back.'

We agreed that we would both go, and that Dora was a little Impostor, who feigned to be rather unwell, because she liked to be petted. She was greatly pleased, and very merry; and we four, that is to say, my aunt, Mr Dick, Traddles, and I, went down to Canterbury by the Dover mail that night.

We all became very anxious and impatient, when we sat down to breakfast at the hotel. As it approached nearer and nearer to half-past nine o'clock, our restless expectation of Mr Micawber increased. At last he appeared.

'Gentlemen, and madam,' said Mr Micawber, 'good morning!'

'Now, sir,' said my aunt to Mr Micawber, 'we are ready for Mount Vesuvius as soon as *you* please.'

'Madam,' returned Mr Micawber, 'I trust you will shortly witness an eruption. Mr Traddles, I have your permission to mention here that we have been in communication?'

'It is undoubtedly the fact, Copperfield,' said Traddles, to whom I looked in surprise. 'Mr Micawber has consulted me, and I have advised him to the best of my judgment.'

'Perhaps, under such circumstances, madam and gentlemen,' said Mr Micawber, 'you will do me the favour to submit yourselves for the moment, to the direction of one who is still your fellow-man, though crushed out of his original form by individual errors. I would beg to be allowed a start of five minutes by the clock; and then to receive the present company at the office of Wickfield and Heep, whose Stipendiary I am.'

With which, he included us all in a comprehensive bow, and disappeared; his manner being extremely distant, and his face extremely pale.

Traddles only smiled, and shook his head when I looked to him for an explanation. When the time was expired, we all went together to the old house, without saying one word on the way.

We found Mr Micawber at his desk. The large office-ruler was stuck into his waistcoat, and was not so well concealed but that a foot or more of that instrument protruded from his bosom.

'Mr Copperfield,' said Mr Micawber, gravely. 'Will you walk in, sir?'

He preceded us to the dining-room and flinging open the door of Mr Wickfield's former office, said, in a sonorous voice:

'Miss Trotwood, Mr David Copperfield, Mr Thomas Traddles, and Mr Dixon!'

I had not seen Uriah Heep since the time of the blow. Our visit astonished him, evidently. He frowned to that degree that he almost closed his small eyes, while the hurried raising of his gristly hand to his chin betrayed some trepidation. A moment afterwards, he was as fawning and as humble as ever.

'This is indeed an unexpected pleasure!' he said. 'Mr Copperfield; I hope I see you well, and Mrs Copperfield, sir, I hope she's getting on. We have been made quite uneasy by the poor accounts we have had of her state, lately, I do assure you.'

I felt ashamed to let him take my hand, but I did not know yet what else to do.

'Things are changed in this office, Miss Trotwood, since I was an umble clerk, and held your pony; ain't they?' said Uriah, with his sickliest smile. 'But *I* am not changed, Miss Trotwood.'

'Well, sir,' returned my aunt, 'to tell you the truth, I think you are pretty constant to the promise of your youth; if that's any satisfaction to you.'

'Thank you, Miss Trotwood,' said Uriah, writhing in his ungainly manner, 'for your good opinion! Micawber, tell 'em to let Miss Agnes know – and mother. Mother will be quite in a state, when she sees the present company!' said Uriah, setting chairs.

'You are not busy, Mr Heep?' said Traddles.

'No, Mr Traddles,' replied Uriah, resuming his official seat. 'Not but what myself and Micawber have our hands pretty full in general, on account of Mr Wickfield's being hardly fit for any occupation, sir. You've not been intimate with Mr Wickfield, I think, Mr Traddles?'

'No, I have not been intimate with Mr Wickfield,' returned Traddles; 'or I might perhaps have waited on you long ago, Mr Heep.'

There was something in the tone of this reply, which made Uriah look at the speaker again, with a very suspicious expression. But, seeing only Traddles, with his good-natured face, simple manner, and hair on end, he dismissed it as he replied, 'I am sorry for that, Mr Traddles. You would have admired him as much as we all do. His little failings would only have endeared him to you the more.'

Agnes was now ushered in by Mr Micawber. She was not quite so self-possessed as usual, I thought; and I saw Uriah watch her while she greeted us; he reminded me of an ugly genie watching a good spirit. In the meanwhile, some slight sign passed between Mr Micawber and Traddles; and Traddles, unobserved except by me, went out.

'Don't wait, Micawber,' said Uriah.

Mr Micawber, with his hand upon the ruler in his breast, stood erect before the door, most unmistakably contemplating one of his fellow-men, and that man his employer.

'What are you waiting for?' said Uriah. 'Micawber! did you hear me tell you not to wait?'

'Yes!' replied the immovable Mr Micawber.

'Then why *do* you wait?' said Uriah.

'Because I – in short, choose,' replied Mr Micawber, with a burst.

Uriah's cheeks lost colour. 'You are a dissipated fellow, as all the world knows and I am afraid you'll oblige me to get rid of you. Go along!'

'If there is a scoundrel on this earth,' said Mr Micawber, suddenly breaking out with the utmost vehemence, 'with whom I have already talked too much, that scoundrel's name is – HEEP !'

Uriah fell back, as if he had been struck. Looking upon us with the darkest expression that his face could wear, he said:

'This is a conspiracy! You have met here, by appointment! Now, take care, Copperfield. You were always a puppy with a proud stomach, from your first coming here; and you envy me my rise, do you? None of your plots against me; I'll counterplot you! Miss Trotwood, you had better stop this; or I'll stop your husband shorter than will be pleasant to you. I won't know your story professionally, for nothing, old lady! Miss Wickfield, if you have any love for your father, you had better not join that gang. I'll ruin him, if you do. Now, come! I have got some of you under the harrow. Think twice, before it goes over you. Where's mother?'

'Mrs Heep is here, sir,' said Traddles, returning with that worthy mother of a worthy son. 'I have taken the liberty of making myself known to her.'

'Who are you to make yourself known?' retorted Uriah.

'I am the agent and friend of Mr Wickfield, sir,' said Traddles, in a composed business-like way. 'And I have a power of attorney from him in my pocket, to act for him in all matters.'

'It has been got from him by fraud!'

'Something has been got from him by fraud, I know,' returned Traddles quietly; 'and so do you, Mr Heep. We will refer that question, if you please, to Mr Micawber.'

'Ury – !' Mrs Heep began, with an anxious gesture.

'You hold your tongue, Mother,' he returned; 'least said, soonest mended.'

Though I had long known that his servility was false, I had had no adequate conception of the extent of his hypocrisy, until I now saw him with his mask off.

Mr Micawber, whose impetuosity I had restrained thus far with the greatest difficulty, now drew the ruler from his breast and produced from his pocket a foolscap document, folded in the form of a large letter. Opening this packet, with his old flourish, he began to read as follows:

' "In appearing before you to denounce probably the most consummate Villain that has ever existed," ' Mr Micawber pointed the ruler, like a ghostly truncheon, at Uriah Heep, ' "I ask no consideration for myself. In an accumulation of Ignominy, Want, Despair, and Madness, I entered the office – or, as our lively neighbour the Gaul would term it, the Bureau – of the Firm, nominally conducted under the appellation of Wickfield and HEEP, but, in reality, wielded by HEEP alone." '

Uriah made a dart at the letter, as if to tear it in pieces. Mr Micawber, with a perfect miracle of dexterity or luck, caught his advancing knuckles with the ruler and disabled his right hand.

'The Devil take you!' said Uriah, writhing with pain.

'Approach me again, you HEEP of infamy,' gasped Mr Micawber, 'and if your head is human, I'll break it. Come on, come on!'

I think I never saw anything more ridiculous than Mr Micawber making broad-sword guards with the ruler, and crying, 'Come on!' while Traddles and I pushed him back into a corner. When he was sufficiently cool, he proceeded with his letter.

' "The stipendiary emoluments in consideration of which I entered into the service of HEEP, were not defined, beyond the pittance of twenty-two shillings and six per week. Need I say, that it soon became necessary for me to solicit from HEEP pecuniary advances towards the support of Mrs Micawber, and our blighted family? Need I say that those advances were secured by IOU's and other similar acknowledgments and thus I became immeshed in the web he had spun for my reception?

"'Then it was that HEEP began to favour me with just so much of his confidence, as was necessary to the discharge of his infernal business. I found that my services were constantly called into requisition for the falsification of business, and the mystification of an individual whom I will designate as Mr W. That Mr W was imposed upon, kept in ignorance, and deluded, in every possible way; yet, that all this while, the ruffian HEEP was professing unbounded friendship for that much-abused gentleman. This was bad enough but worse remains behind!

"'My charges against HEEP,'" he read on, "'are as follows.'"

We all held our breath, I think. I am sure Uriah held his.

"'First,'" said Mr Micawber. "'When Mr W's faculties for business became weakened and confused, HEEP designedly complicated the whole of the official transactions. When Mr W was least fit to enter on business, HEEP was always at hand to force him to enter on it. He obtained Mr W's signature under such circumstances to documents of importance, representing them to be other documents of no importance. He induced Mr W to empower him to draw out, thus, one particular sum of trust-money, amounting to twelve six fourteen, two and nine, and employed it to meet pretended business. He gave this proceeding, throughout, the appearance of having originated in Mr W's own dishonest act; and has used it, ever since, to torture and constrain him.'"

'You shall prove this, you Copperfield!' said Uriah, with a threatening shake of the head.

'Ask HEEP, Mr Traddles, who lived in his house after him,' said Mr Micawber.

'The fool himself – and lives there now,' said Uriah, disdainfully.

'Ask HEEP if he ever kept a pocket-book in that house,' said Mr Micawber. 'Or ask him, if he ever burnt one there. If he says Yes, and asks you where the ashes are, refer him to Wilkins Micawber, and he will hear of something not at all to his advantage!'

These words had a powerful effect in alarming the mother, who cried out in much agitation;

'Ury, Ury! Be umble, and make terms, my dear!'

'Mother!' he retorted, 'will you keep quiet?'

Mr Micawber proceeded.

"'Second. HEEP has, on several occasions, to the best of my knowledge, information, and belief, systematically forged, to various entries, books, and documents, the signature of Mr W; and has distinctly done so in one instance, capable of proof by me. I have, in my possession, in his hand and pocket-book, several similar imitations of Mr W's signature, here and there defaced by fire, but legible to any one. I never attested any such document. And I have the document itself, in my possession" – that is to say, I had, early, this morning, but have since relinquished it to Mr Traddles.'

'It is quite true,' assented Traddles.

'Ury, Ury!' cried the mother, 'be umble and make terms.'

It was singular to see how the mother still held to the old trick, when the son had abandoned it as useless.

'Mother,' he said, with an impatient bite at the handkerchief in which his hand was wrapped, 'you had better fire a loaded gun at me.'

'But I love you, Ury,' cried Mrs Heep. 'And I can't bear to hear you provoking the gentleman, and endangering of yourself more. I told the gentleman at first, when he told me up-stairs it was come to light, that I would answer for your making amends. Oh, see how umble *I* am, gentlemen, and don't mind him!'

'Why, there's Copperfield, mother,' he angrily retorted, 'would have given you a hundred pound to say less than you've blurted out!'

'I can't help it, Ury,' cried his mother. 'I can't see you running into danger, through carrying your head so high.'

He said to me with a scowl: 'What more have you got to bring forward? Go on with it.'

Mr Micawber promptly resumed. "'Third. And last. I am now in a condition to show, by Heep's false books, and Heep's memoranda, that Mr W has been for years deluded and plundered, in every conceivable manner, to the pecuniary aggrandisement of the avaricious, false, and grasping Heep. That the engrossing object of Heep was to subdue Mr and Miss W entirely to himself. That his last act, completed but a few months since, was to induce Mr W to execute a relinquishment of his share in the partnership, and even a bill of sale on the very furniture of his house. That these meshes gradually thickened until the unhappy Mr W could see no world beyond. Bankrupt, as he believed, his sole reliance was upon the monster in the garb of man who, by making himself necessary to him, had achieved his destruction. All this I undertake to show. Probably much more!"'

I whispered a few words to Agnes, who was weeping, half joyfully, half sorrowfully, at my side.

Mr Micawber proceeded, with a mixture of the lowest spirits and the most intense enjoyment, to the peroration of his letter.

"'I have now concluded. It merely remains for me to substantiate these accusations; and then, with my ill-starred family, to disappear from the landscape on which we appear to be an incumbrance. I trust that the labour and hazard of an investigation, when completed, may be as the sprinkling of a few drops of sweet water on my funereal pyre. I ask no more. Let it be, in justice, merely said of me, as of a gallant and eminent naval Hero with whom I have no pretensions to cope, that what I have done, I did, in despite of mercenary and selfish objects.

"'For England, home, and Beauty.'"
"'Remaining always, WILKINS MICAWBER.'"

Much affected, but still intensely enjoying himself, Mr Micawber folded up his letter, and handed it with a bow to my aunt.

There was an iron safe in the room. A hasty suspicion seemed to strike Uriah; and, with a glance at Mr Micawber, he threw the doors open. It was empty.

'Some thief has stolen the books!' he cried, with a frightful face.

Mr Micawber tapped himself with the ruler. 'I did, when I got the key from you as usual this morning.'

'Don't be uneasy,' said Traddles. 'They have come into my possession. I will take care of them, under the authority I mentioned.'

'You receive stolen goods, do you?' cried Uriah.

'Under such circumstances,' answered Traddles, 'yes.'

What was my astonishment when I beheld my aunt, who had been profoundly quiet and attentive, make a dart at Uriah Heep, and seize him by the collar with both hands!

'You know what *I* want?' said my aunt. 'My property! Agnes, my dear, as long as I believed it had been really made away with by your father, I wouldn't breathe a syllable of its having been placed here for investment. But now I know this fellow's answerable for it, I'll have it!'

Whether my aunt supposed, for the moment, that he kept her property in his neck-kerchief, I am sure I don't know; but she certainly pulled at it as if she thought so. I hastened to assure her that we would all take care that he should make the utmost restitution of everything he had wrongly got. This pacified her; but she was not at all disconcerted by what she had done.

'My Uriah means to be umble!' cried his mother. 'Don't mind what he says, good gentlemen!'

'What must be done,' said Traddles, 'is this. First, the deed of relinquishment must be given over to me now – here.'

'Suppose I haven't got it,' Uriah interrupted.

'But you have,' said Traddles; 'therefore, you know, we won't suppose so.' And I cannot help avowing that this was the first occasion on which I really did justice to the practical good sense of my old schoolfellow. 'Then,' said Traddles, 'you must prepare to disgorge all that your rapacity has become possessed of, and to make restoration to the last farthing. All the partnership books and papers must remain in our possession; all your books and papers; all money accounts and securities, of both kinds. In short, everything here.'

'I must have time to think about that,' said Uriah.

'Certainly,' replied Traddles; 'but, in the meanwhile, we shall maintain possession of these things; and compel you to keep your own room, and hold no communication with any one.'

'I won't do it!' said Uriah, with an oath.

'Maidstone Jail is a safer place of detention,' observed Traddles; 'Copperfield, will you go round to the Guildhall, and bring a couple of officers?'

Here, Mrs Heep broke out again, crying on her knees to Agnes to interfere in their behalf, exclaiming that he was very humble, and it was all true, and if he didn't do what we wanted, she would, and much more to the same purpose.

'Stop!' he growled. 'Mother, hold your noise. Let 'em have that deed. Go and fetch it!'

Mrs Heep returned with the deed and with a box in which we found a banker's book and some other papers.

Uriah shuffled across the room and, pausing at the door, said: 'Copperfield, I have always hated you. You've always been an upstart, and you've always been against me. Micawber, you old bully, I'll pay *you*!'

Mr Micawber, making a great deal of his chest until he had slunk out at the door, then addressed himself to the company generally.

'The veil that has long been interposed between Mrs Micawber and myself, is now withdrawn,' said Mr Micawber; 'and my children and the Author of their Being can once more come in contact on equal terms.'

Mr Dick, my aunt, and I went home with Mr Micawber. His house was not far off; and as the street-door opened into the sitting-room, we found ourselves at once in the bosom of the family. Mr Micawber exclaiming, 'Emma! my life!' rushed into Mrs Micawber's arms. Mrs Micawber shrieked, and folded Mr Micawber in her embrace.

'Emma!' said Mr Micawber. 'The cloud is past from my mind. Mutual confidence, so long preserved between us once, is restored, to know no further interruption. Now, welcome poverty!' cried Mr Micawber, shedding tears. 'Welcome misery, welcome houseless-ness, welcome hunger, rags, tempest, and beggary! Mutual confidence will sustain us to the end!'

With these expressions, Mr Micawber placed Mrs Micawber in a chair, and embraced the family all round.

'Is this all your family, ma'am?' said my aunt.

'There are no more at present,' returned Mrs Micawber.

My aunt mused a little while, and then said:

'Mr Micawber, I wonder you have never turned your thoughts to emigration.'

'Madam,' returned Mr Micawber, 'it was the dream of my youth.' I am thoroughly persuaded, by-the-by, that he had never thought of it in his life.

'Aye?' said my aunt, with a glance at me. 'Why, what a thing it would be for yourselves and your family, Mr and Mrs Micawber, if you were to emigrate now.'

'Capital, madam, capital,' urged Mr Micawber, gloomily.

'That is the principal, I may say the only difficulty, my dear Mr Copperfield,' assented his wife.

'Capital?' cried my aunt. 'But you have done us a great service, I may say, for surely much will come out of the fire – and what could we do for you, that would be half so good as to find the capital?'

'I could not receive it as a gift,' said Mr Micawber, 'but if a sufficient sum could be advanced, say at five per cent interest per annum, upon my personal liability – to allow time for something to turn up –'

'Could be? Shall be, on your own terms,' returned my aunt, 'if you say the word. Think of this now, both of you. Here are some people David knows, going out to Australia shortly. If you decide to go, why shouldn't you go in the same ship? You may help each other.'

'There is but one question, my dear ma'am, I could wish to ask,' said Mrs Micawber. 'Are the circumstances of the country such, that a man of Mr Micawber's abilities would have a fair chance of rising in the social scale? I will not say, at present, might he aspire to be Governor, or anything of that sort; but would there be a reasonable opening for his talents to develop themselves?'

'No better opening anywhere,' said my aunt, 'for a man who conducts himself well, and is industrious.'

'For a man who conducts himself well,' repeated Mrs Micawber, with her clearest business manner, 'and is industrious. Precisely. It is evident to me that Australia is the legitimate sphere of action for Mr Micawber!'

'I entertain the conviction, my dear madam,' said Mr Micawber, 'that it is, under existing circumstances, the only land, for myself and family; and that something of an extraordinary nature will turn up on that shore.'

Shall I ever forget how, in a moment, he was the most sanguine of men, looking on to fortune; or how Mrs Micawber presently discoursed about the habits of the kangaroo! Shall I ever recall that street of Canterbury on a market day, without recalling him looking at the bullocks, as they came by, with the eye of an Australian farmer!

CHAPTER 53

Another Retrospect

I must pause once again. Oh, my child-wife, there is a figure in the moving crowd before my memory, quiet and still, saying in its innocent love and childish beauty, Stop to think of me – turn to look upon the Little Blossom, as it flutters to the ground!

I do. I am again with Dora, in our cottage. I do not know how long she has been ill. It is not really long, in weeks or months; but it is a weary, weary while.

I have begun to fear that the day may never shine, when I shall see my child-wife running in the sunlight with her old friend Jip. He mopes, and his sight is weak, and his limbs are feeble, and my aunt is sorry that he objects to her no more, but creeps near her as he lies on Dora's bed and licks her hand.

Dora lies smiling and utters no complaining word. What a strange pause in my life there seems to be when I sit in the quiet room, with her little fingers twining round my hand! Many an hour I sit thus but, of all those times, three come the freshest on my mind.

It is morning; and Dora, made so trim by my aunt's hands, shows me how her pretty hair *will* curl upon the pillow yet.

'Not that I am vain of it, now,' she says, 'but because you used to say you thought it so beautiful; and because when I first began to think about you, I used to wonder whether you would like very much to have a lock of it. Oh what a foolish fellow you were, Doady, when I gave you one!'

'That was on the day when you were painting the flowers I had given you, Dora, and when I told you how much in love I was.'

'Ah! but I didn't like to tell *you*,' says Dora, '*then,* how I had cried over them, because I believed you really liked me! When I can run about again as I used to do, Doady, let us go and see those places where we were such a silly couple, shall we?'

'Yes, we will. So you must make haste to get well, my dear.'

'Oh, I shall soon do that! I am so much better, you don't know!'

*

It is evening; and I sit in the same chair, by the same bed. I have ceased to carry my light burden up and down stairs now. She lies here all the day.

'Doady! I want to see Agnes.'

'I will write to her, my dear.'

'What a good, kind boy! It's not a foolish fancy. I want, very much indeed, to see her!'

'I have only to tell her so, and she is sure to come.'

'You are very lonely when you go down-stairs, now?' Dora whispers, with her arm about my neck.

'How can I be otherwise, my own love, when I see your empty chair?'

'And you really miss me? Even poor, giddy, stupid me?'

'My heart, who is there upon earth that I could miss so much?'

'Oh, husband! I am so glad, yet so sorry!' Only give Agnes my dear love, and tell her that I want very, very much to see her; and I have nothing left to wish for.'

'Except to get well again, Dora.'

'Ah, Doady! Sometimes I think that that will never be!'

'Don't say so, Dora!'

'I won't if I can help it, Doady. But I am very happy; though my dear boy is so lonely by himself, before his child-wife's empty chair!'

It is night; and I am with her still. Agnes has arrived; has been among us, for a whole day and an evening.

Do I know, now, that my child-wife will soon leave me? They have told me so; but what I cannot firmly settle in my mind is, that the end will absolutely come. I hold her hand in mine, I see her love for me, alive in all its strength. I cannot shut out a pale lingering shadow of belief that she will be spared.

'I am going to speak to you, Doady. I am going to say something I have often thought of saying. I am afraid I was too young.'

I lay my face upon the pillow by her, and she looks into my eyes, and speaks very softly. Gradually, as she goes on, I feel, with a stricken heart, that she is speaking of herself as past.

'I am afraid, dear, I was too young, in experience, and thoughts, and everything. I was such a silly creature! It would have been better if we had only loved each other as a boy and girl, and forgotten it. I have begun to think I was not fit to be a wife.'

I try to stay my tears, and to reply, 'Oh, Dora, love, as fit as I to be a husband!'

'I don't know,' with the old shake of her curls. 'Perhaps!'

'We have been very happy, my sweet Dora.'

'I was very happy, very. But, as years went on, my dear boy would have wearied of his child-wife. It is better as it is.'

'Oh, Dora, dearest, do not speak to me so. Every word seems a reproach!'

'No, not a syllable!' she answers, kissing me. 'Oh, how my poor boy cries! Hush, hush! Now, I want to speak to Agnes and while I speak to her, let no one come – not even aunt. I want to speak to Agnes, quite alone.'

I promise that she shall, immediately; but I cannot leave her, for my grief.

Agnes is down-stairs, when I go into the parlour; and I give her the message. She disappears, leaving me alone with Jip.

I sit down by the fire, thinking with a blind remorse of all those secret feelings I have nourished since my marriage. I think of every little trifle between me and Dora, and feel the truth, that trifles make the sum of life. Ever rising from the sea of my remembrance, is the image of the dear child as I knew her first, graced by my young love, and by her own, with every fascination wherein such love is rich. Would it, indeed, have been better if we had loved each other as a boy and girl, and forgotten it? Undisciplined heart, reply!

How the time wears, I know not; until I am recalled by my child-wife's old companion. More restless than he was, he wanders to the door, and whines to go up-stairs.

'Not to-night, Jip!'

He comes very slowly back to me and lifts his dim eyes to my face.

'Oh, Jip! It may be, never again!'

He lies down at my feet, stretches himself out as if to sleep, and with a plaintive cry, is dead.

'Oh, Agnes! Look, look here!'

That face, so full of pity, and of grief, that rain of tears, that awful mute appeal to me, that solemn hand upraised towards Heaven!

'Agnes?'

It is over. Darkness comes before my eyes; and, for a time, all things are blotted out of my remembrance.

CHAPTER 54

Mr Micawber's Transactions

I was to go abroad. That seemed to have been determined among us from the first. The ground now covering all that could perish of my departed wife, I waited only for what Mr Micawber called the 'final pulverisation of Heep,' and for the departure of the emigrants.

At the request of Traddles, we returned to Canterbury: my aunt, Agnes, and I. We proceeded straight to Mr Micawber's house; where, and at Mr Wickfield's, my friend had been labouring ever since our explosive meeting.

'Well, Mr and Mrs Micawber,' was my aunt's first salutation after we were seated, 'pray, have you thought about that emigration proposal of mine?'

'My dear madam,' returned Mr Micawber, 'our Boat is on the shore, and our Bark is on the sea.' He then referred to a memorandum. 'With respect to the pecuniary assistance enabling us to launch our frail canoe on the ocean of enterprise, I would beg to propose my notes of hand – drawn, it is needless to stipulate, on stamps of the amounts respectively required by the various Acts of Parliament applying to such securities – at eighteen, twenty-four, and thirty months.'

'Arrange it in any way you please, sir,' said my aunt.

'In reference to our domestic preparations, madam,' said Mr Micawber, with some pride, 'for meeting the destiny to which we are now understood to be self-devoted, I beg to report them. My eldest daughter attends at five every morning to acquire the process of milking cows. My younger children are instructed to observe the habits of the pigs and poultry maintained in the poorer parts of the city. I have myself directed some attention, during the past week, to the art of baking; and my son Wilkins has driven cattle, when permitted, by the rugged hirelings who had them in charge – which I regret to say was not often; he being generally warned, with imprecations, to desist.'

'Mrs Micawber has been busy, too, I have no doubt,' said my aunt, encouragingly.

'My dear madam,' returned Mrs Micawber, 'such opportunities as I have been enabled to alienate from my domestic duties, I have devoted to corresponding at some length with my family. For I own it seems to me, that the time is come when my family should take Mr Micawber by the hand, and be on terms with Mr Micawber.'

I said I thought so too. She continued:

'My individual impression is that the gulf between my family and Mr Micawber may be traced to an apprehension, on the part of my family, that Mr Micawber would require pecuniary accommodation. Mr Micawber being now on the eve of casting off the pecuniary shackles that have so long enthralled him, and of commencing a new career in a country where there is sufficient range for his abilities, it seems to me that my family should signalise the occasion by coming forward. What I could wish to see, would be a meeting between Mr Micawber and my family at a festive entertainment where Mr Micawber's health and prosperity are proposed by some leading member of my family.'

'All I would say,' said Mr Micawber with some heat, 'is that I can go abroad without your family coming forward to favour me – in short, with a parting shove of their cold shoulders; and that, upon the whole, I would rather leave England with such impetus as I possess, than derive any acceleration of it from that quarter. At the same time, my dear, if they should condescend to reply to your communications – which our joint experience renders most improbable – far be it from me to be a barrier to your wishes.'

The matter being thus settled, Mr Micawber, glancing at the heap of books and papers lying before Traddles on the table, said they would leave us to ourselves; which they ceremoniously did.

'My dear Copperfield,' said Traddles, looking at me with an affection that made his hair all kinds of shapes, 'I don't make any excuse for troubling you with business, because I know you are deeply interested in it, and it may divert your thoughts. I hope you are not worn out?'

'I am quite myself,' said I. 'We have more cause to think of my aunt than of any one. During the last fortnight, some new trouble has vexed her; and she has been in and out of London every day. Last night, with this journey before her, it was almost midnight before she came home. She will not tell me what has happened to distress her.'

My aunt, very pale, and with deep lines in her face, sat immovable. 'It's nothing, Trot. You shall know by-and-by. Now, let us attend to these affairs.'

'I must do Mr Micawber the justice to say,' Traddles began, 'that although he would appear not to have worked to any good account for himself, he is a most untiring man when he works for other people. The heat into which he has been continually putting himself; and the manner in which he has been diving, day and night, among papers and books; to say nothing of the immense number of letters he has written me is quite extraordinary.'

'Letters!' cried my aunt. 'I believe he dreams in letters!'

'I am happy to say, Miss Wickfield,' pursued Traddles, 'that in your absence Mr Wickfield has considerably improved. He has been able to assist us in making some things clear, that we should have found very difficult indeed without him.'

His natural manner made it transparent that he said this to put us in good heart, and to enable Agnes to hear her father mentioned with greater confidence; but it was not the less pleasant for that.

'Now, let me see,' said Traddles, looking among the papers on the table. 'Having counted our funds, and reduced to order a great mass of confusion, we take it to be clear that Mr Wickfield might now wind up his business and exhibit no deficiency whatever.'

'Oh, thank Heaven!' cried Agnes, fervently.

'But,' said Traddles, 'that surplus that would be left as his means of support – and I suppose the house to be sold, even in saying this – would be so small that perhaps, Miss Wickfield, it would be best to consider whether he might not retain his agency of the estate to which he has so long been receiver. His friends might advise him, you know.'

'I have considered it,' said Agnes, 'and I feel that it ought not to be. To take our future on myself will be the next great happiness that I can know.'

'Have you thought how, Agnes?'

'Our wants are not many. If I rent the dear old house, and keep a school, I shall be useful and happy.'

'Next, Miss Trotwood,' said Traddles, 'that property of yours.'

'Well, sir,' sighed my aunt. 'If it's gone, I can bear it; and if it's not gone, I shall be glad to get it back.'

'It was originally, I think, eight thousand pounds, Consols?' said Traddles. 'I can't account for more than five.'

' – thousand, do you mean?' inquired my aunt, 'or pounds?'

'Five thousand pounds,' said Traddles.

'It was all there was,' returned my aunt. 'I sold three, myself. One, I paid for your articles, Trot, my dear; and the other two I have by me. When I lost the rest, I thought it wise to say nothing about that sum, but to keep it secretly for a rainy day. I wanted to see how you would come out of the trial, Trot; and you came out nobly – persevering, self-reliant, self-denying! So did Dick. Don't speak to me, for I find my nerves a little shaken!'

Nobody would have thought so, to see her sitting upright, with her arms folded; but she had wonderful self-command.

'Then I am delighted to say,' cried Traddles, beaming with joy, 'that we have recovered the whole money!'

'How so, sir?' exclaimed my aunt.

'You believed it had been misappropriated by Mr Wickfield?' said Traddles.

'Of course I did,' said my aunt, 'and was therefore easily silenced. Agnes, not a word.'

'And indeed,' said Traddles, 'it was sold, by virtue of the power of management he held from you; but I needn't say by whom sold, or on whose actual signature. It was afterwards pretended to Mr Wickfield, by that rascal, that he had possessed himself of the money to keep other deficiencies and difficulties from the light. Mr Wickfield, being so weak and helpless in his hands as to pay you, afterwards, several sums of interest on a pretended principal which he knew did not exist, made himself, unhappily, a party to the fraud.'

'And at last took the blame upon himself,' added my aunt; 'and wrote me a mad letter, charging himself with robbery, and wrong unheard of. Upon which I paid him a visit early one morning, called for a candle, burnt the letter, and told him if he ever could right me and himself, to do it; and if he couldn't, to keep his own counsel for his daughter's sake. – If anybody speaks to me, I'll leave the house!'

We all remained quiet; Agnes covering her face.

'Well, my dear friend,' said my aunt, after a pause, 'and you have really extorted the money back from Heep?'

'The fact is,' returned Traddles, 'Mr Micawber had so completely hemmed him in that he could not escape from us. A most remarkable circumstance is, that I really don't think he grasped this sum even so much for the gratification of his avarice, as in the hatred he felt for Copperfield. He said so to me, plainly. He said he would even have spent as much, to baulk or injure Copperfield.'

'Ha!' said my aunt. 'And what's become of him?'

'I don't know. He left here,' said Traddles, 'with his mother by one of the London night coaches, and I know no more about him; except that his malevolence to me at parting was audacious. He seemed to consider himself hardly less indebted to me, than to Mr Micawber; which I consider (as I told him) quite a compliment.'

'Do you suppose he has any money, Traddles?' I asked.

'I should think so,' he replied. 'He must have pocketed a good deal, in one way or other. But, I think that money would never keep that man out of mischief. He is such an incarnate hypocrite, that whatever object he pursues, he must pursue crookedly.'

'He's a monster of meanness!' said my aunt. 'And now, touching Mr Micawber – what would you give him?'

'Before you come to that,' said Traddles, a little disconcerted, 'I am afraid I thought it discreet to omit two points in making this adjustment of a difficult affair. Those IOU's and so forth, which Mr Micawber gave Heep for the advances he had –'

'Well! They must be paid,' said my aunt.

'Yes, but I don't know where they are,' rejoined Traddles, 'and I anticipate, that, between this time and his departure, Mr Micawber will be constantly arrested, or taken in execution.'

'Then he must be constantly set free again, and taken out of execution,' said my aunt. 'What's the amount altogether?'

'Mr Micawber makes the amount a hundred and three pounds, five.'

'Now, what shall we give him, that sum included?' said my aunt. 'Five hundred pounds?'

Upon this, Traddles and I both struck in at once. We both recommended a small sum in money, and the payment, without stipulation to Mr Micawber, of the Uriah claims as they came in. We proposed that the family should have their passage and their outfit, and a hundred pounds; and that Mr Micawber's arrangement for the repayment of the advances should be gravely entered into, as it might be wholesome for him to suppose himself under the responsibility. To this, I added the suggestion, that Mr Peggotty should be quietly entrusted with the discretion of advancing another hundred. I further proposed to interest Mr Micawber in Mr Peggotty, by confiding Mr Peggotty's story to him. We all entered warmly into these views; and I may mention at once, that the principals themselves did so, shortly afterwards, with perfect good will and harmony.

Seeing that Traddles now glanced anxiously at my aunt, I reminded him of the second point to which he had adverted.

'You will excuse me, if I touch upon a painful theme,' said Traddles, hesitating. 'On the day of Mr Micawber's memorable denunciation, a threatening allusion was made by Uriah Heep to your aunt's – husband. Perhaps it was mere purposeless impertinence?'

'No,' returned my aunt.

'Can I – or Copperfield – do anything?' asked Traddles, gently.

'Nothing,' said my aunt. 'I thank you, Trot, my dear. Let us have Mr and Mrs Micawber back. And don't any of you speak to me!' With that she sat looking at the door.

'Well, Mr and Mrs Micawber!' said my aunt, when they entered. 'We have been discussing your emigration.'

These she explained to the unbounded satisfaction of the family, – children and all being then present – and so much to the awakening of Mr Micawber's punctual habits in the opening stage of all bill transactions, that he could not be dissuaded from immediately rushing out, in the highest spirits, to buy the stamps for his notes of hand. But, his joy received a sudden check; for within five minutes, he returned in the custody of a sheriff's officer, informing us, in a flood of tears, that all was lost. We being quite prepared for this proceeding of Uriah Heep's, soon paid the money; and in five minutes more Mr Micawber was seated at the table, filling up the stamps with an expression of perfect joy.

This closed the proceedings of the evening. We were weary with sorrow and fatigue, and my aunt and I passed the night at the old house, which, freed from the presence of the Heeps, seemed purged of a disease; and I lay in my old room, like a shipwrecked wanderer come home.

We went back next day to my aunt's house – not to mine; and when she and I sat alone, she said:

'Trot, do you really wish to know what I have had upon my mind lately? You have had sorrow enough, without the addition of *my* little miseries. I could have no other motive in keeping anything from you.'

'I know that well,' said I. 'But tell me now.'

'Would you ride with me a little way to-morrow morning?' asked my aunt. 'At nine. I'll tell you then.'

At nine, accordingly, we drove to London until we came to one of the large hospitals. Standing hard by the building was a plain hearse. The driver recognised my aunt, and in obedience to a motion of her hand at the window, drove slowly off; we following.

'You understand it now, Trot,' said my aunt. 'He is gone!'

'Did he die in the hospital?'

'Yes.' She sat immovable beside me; but, again I saw the stray tears on her face. 'He was ailing a long time – a shattered, broken man, these many years. He asked them to send for me. He was sorry then. Very sorry. I was with him a good deal afterwards.'

'He died the night before we went to Canterbury?' said I.

My aunt nodded. 'No one can harm him now,' she said. 'It was a vain threat.'

We drove away, out of the town, to the churchyard at Hornsey. We alighted; and followed the plain coffin.

'Six-and-thirty years ago, this day, my dear,' said my aunt, as we walked back to the chariot, 'I was married. God forgive us all!'

She sat beside me for a long time holding my hand. At length she suddenly burst into tears, and said: 'He was a fine-looking man when I married him – and he was sadly changed!'

So we rode back to her little cottage at Highgate, where we found the following short note, which had arrived by that morning's post from Mr Micawber:

'My dear Madam, and Copperfield,

'The fair land of promise lately looming on the horizon is again enveloped in impenetrable mists. Another writ has been issued in another cause of HEEP *v* MICAWBER, and the defendant in that cause is the prey of the sheriff.

'Some future traveller, visiting from motives of curiosity not unmingled, let us hope, with sympathy, the place of confinement allotted to debtors in this city, may ponder, as he traces on its wall, inscribed with a rusty nail,

'The obscure initials

'W.M.

'P.S. I re-open this to say that our common friend, Mr Thomas Traddles, has paid the debt in the noble name of Miss Trotwood; and that myself and family are at the height of earthly bliss.'

CHAPTER 55

Tempest

I now approach an event in my life so indelible that, from the beginning of my narrative, I have seen it throwing its fore-cast shadow even on the incidents of my childish days.

The time drawing on for the sailing of the emigrant-ship, my good old nurse came up to London. One evening I was alone with Peggotty and her brother. Our conversation turned on Ham. It was a subject of which the affectionate creature never tired.

My aunt and I were at that time vacating the two cottages at Highgate; I intending to go abroad, and she to return to her house at Dover. We had a temporary lodging in Covent Garden. As I walked home to it, after this evening's conversation, I wavered in the original purpose I had formed of leaving a letter for Emily when I should take leave of her uncle on board the ship, and thought it would be better to write to her now. She might desire, I thought, to send some parting word by me to her unhappy lover. I ought to give her the opportunity.

I therefore wrote to her. I told her that I had seen Ham, and that he had requested me to tell her what I have already written in its place in these sheets. I faithfully repeated it. Its deep fidelity and goodness were not to be adorned by me or any man. I left it out, to be sent round in the morning; and went to bed at day-break.

I was roused by the presence of my aunt at my bedside.

'Trot, my dear,' she said, 'Mr Peggotty is here.'

'Mas'r Davy,' he said, when we had shaken hands, 'I giv Em'ly your letter, sir, and she writ this heer; and begged of me fur to ask you to read it, and if you see no hurt in't, to be so kind as take charge on't.'

I read as follows:

'I have got your message. Oh, what can I write, to thank you for your good and blessed kindness to me!

'I have put the words close to my heart. I shall keep them till I die. They are sharp thorns, but they are such comfort. I have prayed over them. When I find what you are, and what uncle is, I think what God must be, and can cry to him.

'Now, my dear, my friend, good-bye for ever in this world. In another world, if I am forgiven, I may wake a child and come to you. All thanks and blessings. Farewell, evermore.'

'May I tell her as you doen't see no hurt in't, Mas'r Davy?' said Mr Peggotty when I had read it.

'Unquestionably,' said I. 'I'll go down to Yarmouth to put this letter in his hand to enable you to tell her that he has got it. I'll go down to-night.'

Though he endeavoured to dissuade me, I saw that he was of my mind; and he went round to the coach-office and took the box-seat for me on the mail. In the evening I started down the road I had traversed under so many vicissitudes.

'Don't you think that,' I asked the coachman, in the first stage out of London, 'a very remarkable sky? I don't remember to have seen one like it.'

'Nor I,' he replied. 'That's wind, sir. There'll be mischief done at sea, I expect, before long.'

As the night advanced, it came on to blow, harder and harder, until our horses could scarcely face the wind. We were often in serious apprehension that the coach would be blown over. We came to Ipswich – very late, having had to fight every inch of ground since we were ten miles out of London – and found a cluster of people in the market-place, who had risen from their beds in the night, fearful of falling chimneys. Some of these told us of great sheets of lead having been ripped off a high church-tower; country people from neighbouring villages had seen great trees torn out of the earth, and whole ricks scattered about the roads. Still, there was no abatement in the storm.

As we struggled on, its force became more and more terrific. Long before we saw the sea, its spray was on our lips. When we came within sight, the waves on the horizon were like glimpses of another shore with towers and buildings. When at last we got into Yarmouth, the people came out to their doors, all aslant, making a wonder of the mail that had come through such a night.

I put up at the old inn, and went down to look at the sea; staggering along the street, which was strewn with sand and seaweed, and with flying blotches of sea-foam. I found bewailing women whose husbands were away in herring or oyster boats, which there was too much reason to think might have foundered before they could run in anywhere for safety. Grizzled old sailors were shaking their heads; ship-owners, excited and uneasy; even stout mariners levelling their glasses at the sea from behind places of shelter, as if they were surveying an enemy.

The tremendous sea itself confounded me. As the high watery walls came rolling in, they looked as if the least would engulf the town. As the receding wave swept back with a hoarse roar, it seemed to scoop out deep caves in the beach, as if its purpose were to undermine the earth. Undulating hills were changed to valleys, undulating valleys were lifted up to hills; masses of water shivered and shook the beach with a booming sound. I seemed to see a rending and upheaving of all nature.

Not finding Ham among the people whom this memorable wind had brought together, I made my way to his house. As no one answered my knocking, I went to the yard where he worked. I learned he had gone to Lowestoft, but that he would be back to-morrow morning.

I went back to the inn. I had not sat five minutes by the coffee-room fire, when the waiter told me that two colliers had gone down, with all hands, and that some other ships had been seen labouring hard in the Roads. Mercy on them, and on all poor sailors, said he, if we had another night like the last!

I was very much depressed in spirits and felt an uneasiness in Ham's not being there. In this state, the waiter's dismal intelligence about the ships immediately connected itself with my uneasiness about Ham. This grew so strong with me, that I resolved to go back to the yard and ask the boat-builder if he thought his attempting to return by sea at all likely? The boat-builder quite laughed when I asked him the question, and said no man in his senses would put off in such a gale of wind, least of all Ham Peggotty, who had been born to seafaring.

I went back to the inn. If such a wind could rise, I think it was rising. The rattling of the doors and windows, the rumbling in the chimneys, the apparent rocking of the very house that sheltered me were more fearful than in the morning. But there was now a great darkness besides; and that invested the storm with new terrors, real and fanciful.

I could not eat, I could not sit still, I could not continue stedfast to anything. At length, the steady ticking of the clock on the wall, tormented me to that degree that I resolved to go to bed. I went exceedingly weary but, on my lying down, I was broad awake, with every sense refined.

For hours I lay there, listening to the wind and water; imagining, now, that I heard shrieks out at sea; now, that I distinctly heard the firing of signal guns; and now, the fall of houses in the town. At length, I fell – off a tower and down a precipice – into the depths of sleep.

The thunder of the cannon was so loud and incessant, that I could not hear something I much desired to hear, until I made a great exertion and awoke. It was broad day – eight or nine o'clock; the storm raging, in lieu of the batteries; and some one knocking and calling at my door.

'A wreck! Close by!'

I sprung out of bed, and asked, what wreck?

'A schooner, from Spain or Portugal. Make haste, sir, if you want to see her! It's thought she'll go to pieces every moment.'

Numbers of people were there before me, all running in one direction, to the beach. I soon came facing the wild sea.

The wind might by this time have lulled a little, but, the sea was infinitely more terrific than when I had seen it last. The height to which the breakers rose, and, looking over one another, bore one another down, and rolled in, in interminable hosts, was most appalling.

In the difficulty of hearing anything but wind and waves, I looked out to sea for the wreck, and saw nothing but the foaming heads of the great waves. A half-dressed boatman, standing next me, pointed to the left. Then, O great Heaven, I saw it, close in upon us!

One mast was broken short off, six or eight feet from the deck, and lay over the side, entangled in a maze of sail and rigging; and all that ruin, as the ship rolled, beat the side as if it would stave it in. Some efforts were being made to cut this portion of the wreck away, for I plainly descried her people at work with axes, especially one active figure with long curling hair, conspicuous among the rest. But the sea, sweeping over the rolling wreck, made a clean breach, and carried men, spars, planks into the boiling surge.

The second mast was yet standing, with the rags of a rent sail. The ship had struck once, the same boatman hoarsely said in my ear, and then lifted in and struck again. I understood him to add that she was parting amidships. As he spoke, four men arose with the wreck out of the deep, clinging to the rigging of the remaining mast; uppermost, the active figure with the curling hair.

As the ship rolled we lost her, and again she rose. Two men were gone. The agony on shore increased. Men groaned and clasped their hands; women shrieked, and turned away their faces. I found myself frantically imploring a knot of sailors whom I knew, not to let those two lost creatures perish before our eyes.

They were making out to me that the lifeboat had been bravely manned an hour ago, and could do nothing; and as no man would be so desperate as to attempt to wade off with a rope there was nothing left to try. Then I noticed some new sensation moved the people on the beach, and Ham come breaking through them to the front.

I ran to him but the determination in his face awoke me to a knowledge of his danger. I held him back with both arms; and implored the men with whom I had been speaking, not to let him stir from off that sand!

Another cry arose; looking to the wreck we saw the sail beat off the lower of the two men.

'Mas'r Davy,' said Ham, cheerily grasping me by both hands, 'if my time is come, 'tis come. If 'tan't, I'll bide it. Lord above bless you, and bless all! Mates, make me ready! I'm a going off!'

I was swept away to some distance, where the people around me made me stay; urging, as I confusedly perceived, that he was bent on going and that I should endanger the precautions for his safety by troubling those with whom they rested. I saw men running with ropes from a capstan that was there, and penetrating into a circle of figures that hid him from me. Then, I saw him standing alone, a rope in his hand, another round his body: and several of the best men holding the latter, which he laid out himself, slack upon the shore, at his feet.

The wreck, even to my unpractised eye, was breaking up. I saw that the life of the solitary man upon the mast hung by a thread. Still, he clung to it. He had a singular red cap on – not like a sailor's cap, but of a finer colour; and as the few yielding planks between him and destruction rolled and bulged, he was seen by all of us to wave. I saw him do it now, and thought I was going distracted when his action brought an old remembrance to my mind of a once dear friend.

Ham watched the sea, until there was a great retiring wave, when, with a backward glance at those who held the rope which was made fast round his body, he dashed in after it, and in a moment was buffeting with the water.

And now he made for the wreck, rising with the hills, falling with the valleys, lost beneath the rugged foam, borne in towards the shore, borne on towards the ship, striving hard and valiantly. The distance was nothing, but the power of the sea and wind made the strife deadly. At length he neared the wreck. He was so near, that with one more of his vigorous strokes he would be clinging to it – when, a high, green, vast hill-side of water, moving on shoreward, from beyond the ship, he seemed to leap up into it with a mighty bound, and the ship was gone!

Consternation was in every face. They drew him to my very feet – insensible – dead. He was carried to the nearest house, while every means of restoration were tried; but he had been beaten to death by the great wave, and his generous heart was stilled for ever.

As I sat beside the bed, a fisherman, who had known me when Emily and I were children, whispered my name at the door.

'Sir,' said he, 'will you come over yonder?'

The old remembrance that had been recalled to me was in his look. I asked him, terror-stricken, leaning on the arm he held out to support me: 'Has a body come ashore?'

He said, 'Yes.'

'Do I know it?' I asked then.

He answered nothing.

But, he led me to the shore. And on the part of it where she and I had looked for shells – on that part of it where some fragments of the old boat, blown down last night, had been scattered by the wind – among the ruins of the home he had wronged, I saw him lying with his head upon his arm, as I had often seen him lie at school.

CHAPTER 56

The New Wound, and the Old

No need, O Steerforth, to have said, when we last spoke together, 'Think of me at my best!' I had done that ever; and could I change now, looking on this sight!

They brought a hand-bier, and laid him on it, and covered him with a flag, and took him to the inn. So soon as I could collect my thoughts, I sent for Joram, and begged him to provide me a conveyance in which it could be got to London in the night. I knew that the care of it, and the hard duty of preparing his mother to receive it, could only rest with me.

Upon a mellow autumn day, about noon, I arrived at Highgate. I walked the last mile and left the carriage awaiting order to advance.

I had not, at first, the courage to ring at the gate; and when I did ring, my errand seemed to me to be expressed in the very sound of the bell. The little parlour-maid came out and, looking earnestly at me as she unlocked the gate, said: 'I beg your pardon, sir. Is anything the matter?'

'Hush!' said I. 'Yes, something has happened, that I have to break to Mrs Steerforth. She is at home?'

The girl replied that her mistress was up and Miss Dartle was with her. What message should she take up-stairs?

Giving her a strict charge only to carry in my card, I sat down in the drawing-room. Its former pleasant air of occupation was gone, and the shutters were half closed. The harp had not been used for many a day.

The house was so still that I heard the girl's light step up-stairs. On her return, she brought a message, to the effect that Mrs Steerforth was an invalid and could not come down; but, that if I would excuse her being in her chamber, she would be glad to see me. In a few moments I stood before her.

At her chair, as usual, was Rosa Dartle. From the first moment of her dark eyes resting on me, I saw she knew I was the bearer of evil tidings. The scar sprung into view that instant. She withdrew herself a step behind the chair, to keep her own face out of Mrs Steerforth's observation; and scrutinised me with a piercing gaze that never faltered.

'I am sorry to observe you are in mourning, sir,' said Mrs Steerforth.

'I am unhappily a widower,' said I.

'You are very young to know so great a loss,' she returned. 'I hope Time will be good to you.'

'I hope Time,' said I, 'will be good to all of us. Dear Mrs Steerforth, we must all trust to that, in our heaviest misfortunes.'

The earnestness of my manner, and the tears in my eyes, alarmed her. The whole course of her thoughts appeared to change.

She said, with enforced calmness: 'My son is ill.'

'Very ill.'

'You have seen him?'

'I have.'

'Are you reconciled?'

I could not say Yes, I could not say No. She slightly turned her head and in that moment I said, by the motion of my lips, to Rosa, 'Dead!'

I had seen Rosa Dartle throw her hands up in the air with vehemence of despair and horror, and then clasp them on her face.

The handsome lady put her hand to her forehead. I besought her to be calm but I should rather have entreated her to weep, for she sat like a stone figure.

'When I was last here,' I faltered, 'Miss Dartle told me he was sailing. The night before last was a dreadful one at sea. If he were at sea that night –'

'Rosa!' said Mrs Steerforth, 'come to me!'

She came, but with no sympathy or gentleness. Her eyes gleamed like fire and broke into a frightful laugh.

'Now,' she said, 'is your pride appeased, you madwoman? *Now* has he made atonement to you – with his life! Do you hear? His life!'

Mrs Steerforth, fallen back stiffly in her chair, and making no sound but a moan, cast her eyes upon her with a wide stare.

'Aye!' cried Rosa, smiting herself passionately on the breast, 'look at me! Look here!' striking her scar, 'at your dead child's handiwork!'

The moan the other uttered, from time to time, went to my heart.

'Do you remember when he did this?' she proceeded. 'Do you remember when, in his inheritance of your nature, and in your pampering of his pride and passion, he did this, and disfigured me for life?'

'Miss Dartle,' I entreated her. 'For Heaven's sake –'

'I *will* speak!' she said, turning on me with her lightning eyes. 'Look at me, I say, proud mother of a proud false son! Moan for your corruption of him, moan for your loss of him, moan for mine! Are you rewarded, *now*, for your years of trouble?'

'Oh Miss Dartle, shame!'

'Have I been silent all these years, and shall I not speak now? I loved him better than you ever loved him!' turning on her fiercely. 'I could have loved him, and asked no return. If I had been his wife, I could have been the slave of his caprices for a word of love a year. You were exacting, proud, selfish. My love would have trod your paltry whimpering under foot! When he was freshest and truest, he loved *me*. Yes, he did! Many a time, when you were put off with a slight word, he has taken Me to his heart!'

She said it with a taunting pride in the midst of her frenzy yet with an eager remembrance of it.

'I descended into a trifle for the occupation of an idle hour, to be dropped, and taken up, and trifled with, as the inconstant humour took him. We fell away from one another without a word. Perhaps you saw it, and were not sorry. Since then, I have been a mere disfigured piece of furniture between you both. Moan for what you made him; not for your love. I tell you that the time was when I loved him better than you ever did!'

'Miss Dartle,' said I, 'if you can be so obdurate as not to feel for this afflicted mother –'

'Who feels for me?' she retorted. 'She has sown this. Let her moan for the harvest that she reaps to-day!'

'And if his faults –' I began.

'Faults!' she cried, bursting into passionate tears. 'He had a soul worth millions of the friends to whom he stooped!'

'I meant to say, if you have no compassion for his mother; or if his faults – you have been bitter on them –'

'It's false,' she cried, tearing her hair; 'I loved him! It was an evil hour that you ever came here! A curse upon you! Go!'

After passing out of the room, I hurried back to ring the bell, the sooner to alarm the servants. She had then taken the impassive figure in her arms and was rocking it to and fro upon her bosom like a child, and trying every tender means to rouse the dormant senses.

Later in the day, I returned, and we laid him in his mother's room. She was just the same, they told me; Miss Dartle never left her; doctors were in attendance, but she lay like a statue, except for the low sound now and then.

I went through the dreary house, and darkened the windows. The windows of the chamber where he lay, I darkened last. I lifted up the leaden hand, and held it to my heart; and all the world seemed death and silence, broken only by his mother's moaning.

CHAPTER 57

The Emigrants

One thing more I had to do, before yielding myself to the shock of these emotions, was to conceal what had occurred from those who were going away; and to dismiss them on their voyage in happy ignorance.

I took Mr Micawber aside that same night, and confided to him the task of standing between Mr Peggotty and intelligence of the late catastrophe. He zealously undertook to do so.

'If it penetrates to him, sir,' said Mr Micawber, striking himself on the breast, 'it shall first pass through this body!'

Mr Micawber had acquired a bold buccaneering air. One might have supposed him a child of the wilderness, about to return to his native wilds. With a common mariner's telescope under his arm, and a shrewd trick of casting up his eye at the sky as looking out for dirty weather, he was far more nautical, after his manner, than Mr Peggotty. His whole family, if I may express it, were cleared for action.

Thus Traddles and I found them at nightfall, assembled on Hungerford Stairs, watching the departure of a boat with some of their property on board. I had told Traddles of the terrible event, and it had greatly shocked him; but there could be no doubt of the kindness of keeping it a secret, and he had come to help me in this last service. It was here that I took Mr Micawber aside, and received his promise.

The Micawber family were lodged in a tumble-down public-house close to the stairs. My aunt and Agnes were there, busily making some little extra comforts, in the way of dress, for the children. Peggotty was quietly assisting.

It was not easy to answer inquiries; still less to whisper Mr Peggotty, when Mr Micawber brought him in, that I had given the letter, and all was well. But I did both, and made them happy. If I showed any trace of what I felt, my own sorrows were sufficient to account for it.

'And when does the ship sail, Mr Micawber?' asked my aunt.

'Madam, I am informed that we must positively be on board before seven to-morrow morning.'

'Heyday!' said my aunt, 'that's soon. Is it a sea-going fact, Mr Peggotty?'

''Tis so, ma'am. She'll drop down the river with that theer tide. If Mas'r Davy and my sister comes aboard at Gravesen', arternoon o' next day, they'll see the last on us.'

'And that we shall do,' said I, 'be sure!'

'Emma, my love,' said Mr Micawber, clearing his throat in his magnificent way, 'my friend Mr Traddles is so obliging as to order the ingredients necessary to the composition of that Beverage which is peculiarly associated, in our minds, with the Roast Beef of Old England. I allude to – in short, Punch. Under ordinary circumstances, I should scruple to entreat Miss Trotwood and Miss Wickfield, but –'

'I can only say for myself,' said my aunt, 'that I will drink all happiness and success to you, Mr Micawber, with the utmost pleasure.'

'And I too!' said Agnes, with a smile.

Mr Micawber immediately descended to the bar, where he appeared to be quite at home, and in due time returned with a steaming jug. I could not but observe that he had been peeling the lemons with his own clasp-knife, which, as became the knife of a practical settler, was about a foot long. In a similar anticipation of life afloat and in the Bush, Mr Micawber, instead of helping Mrs Micawber and his eldest son and daughter to punch in wine-glasses, served it out to them in a series of villainous little tin pots; and I never saw him enjoy anything so much as drinking out of his own particular pint pot, and putting it in his pocket at the close of the evening.

'The luxuries of the old country,' said Mr Micawber, with intense satisfaction, 'we abandon. The denizens of the forest cannot, of course, expect to participate in the refinements of the land of the Free.'

Here, a boy came in to say that Mr Micawber was wanted downstairs.

'I have a presentiment,' said Mrs Micawber, setting down her tin pot, 'that it is a member of my family!'

'If so, my dear,' observed Mr Micawber, with his usual suddenness of warmth on that subject, 'as the member of your family has kept *us* waiting for a considerable period, perhaps the Member may now wait *my* convenience.'

'Micawber,' said the wife, in a low tone, 'at such a time as this –'

'Emma, I stand reproved,' said Mr Micawber, rising. 'I cannot, even now, distinctly pledge myself to fall upon your family's neck but the member of your family, who is now in attendance, shall have no genial warmth frozen by me.'

Mr Micawber withdrew, and was absent some little time; in the course of which Mrs Micawber was not wholly free from an apprehension that words might have arisen between him and the Member. At length the same boy re-appeared, and presented me with a note written in pencil, and headed 'Heep *v*. Micawber.' From this document, I learned that Mr Micawber being again arrested, begged me to send him his knife and pint pot as they might prove serviceable during the brief remainder of his existence in jail. He also requested, as a last act of friendship, that I would see his family to the Parish Workhouse.

Of course I answered this note by going down to pay the money. On his release, Mr Micawber embraced me with the utmost fervour; and made an entry of the transaction in his pocket-book. This momentous pocket-book was a timely reminder to him of another transaction. On our return to the room up-stairs he took out of it a large sheet of paper which he handed over to Traddles on the spot, a discharge of his debt in full (as between man and man), with many acknowledgements.

'I have still a presentiment,' said Mrs Micawber, 'that my family will appear on board, before we finally depart.'

Mr Micawber evidently had his presentiment of the subject too, but he put it in his tin pot and swallowed it.

'If you have any opportunity of sending letters home, on your passage,' said my aunt, 'you must let us hear from you.'

'Please Heaven, there will be many such opportunities,' said Mr Micawber. 'The ocean, in these times, is a perfect fleet of ships; and we can hardly fail to encounter many, in running over. It is merely crossing,' said Mr Micawber, trifling with his eye-glass. 'The distance is quite imaginary.'

I think, now, how wonderfully like Mr Micawber, that, when he went from London to Canterbury, he should have talked as if he were going to the farthest limits of the earth; and, when he went from England to Australia, as if he were going for a little trip across the channel.

'On the voyage, porpoises and dolphins, I believe, will be frequently observed athwart our Bows, and, wither on the Starboard or the Larboard Quarter, objects of interest will be continually descried. In short,' said Mr Micawber, with the old genteel air, 'the probability is, all will be found so exciting that when the look-out cries Land-oh! we shall be very considerably astonished!'

With that he flourished off the contents of his little tin pot as if he had made the voyage and had passed a first-class examination before the highest naval authorities.

'What *I* chiefly hope,' said Mrs Micawber, 'is, that in some branches of our family we may live again in the old country. Do not frown, Micawber! I do not now refer to my own family, but to our children's children. However vigorous the sapling, I cannot forget the parent-tree; and when our race attains to eminence and fortune, I own I should wish that fortune to flow into the coffers of Britannia.'

'My dear,' said Mr Micawber, 'Britannia must take her chance. I am bound to say that she has never done much for me.'

'Micawber,' returned Mrs Micawber, 'there you are wrong. You are going out, to this distant clime, to strengthen, not to weaken, the connexion between yourself and Albion. My dear Mr Copperfield, Mr Micawber is going to a distant country expressly in order that he may be fully appreciated for the first time. I wish Mr Micawber to take his stand upon that vessel's prow, and firmly say, "This country I am come to conquer! Have you honours? Have you riches? Have you posts of profitable pecuniary emolument? Let them be brought forward. They are mine!"'

Mr Micawber, glancing at us all, seemed to think there was a good deal in this idea.

'I wish Mr Micawber, if I make myself understood,' said Mrs Micawber, 'to be the Caesar of his own fortunes. From the first moment of this voyage, I wish Mr Micawber to say, "Enough of delay: enough of disappointment: enough of limited means. That was in the old country. This is the new. Produce your reparation. Bring it forward!"'

Mr Micawber folded his arms in a resolute manner, as if he were then stationed on the figure-head.

'And doing that,' said Mrs Micawber, 'am I not right in saying that Mr Micawber will strengthen, and not weaken, his connexion with Britain? An important public character arising in that hemisphere, shall I be told that its influence will not be felt at home? Can I be so weak as to imagine that Mr Micawber, wielding the rod of talent and of power in Australia, will be nothing in England?

'And therefore the probability is that Mr Micawber will be a page of History; and he ought then to be represented in the country which gave him birth, and did *not* give him employment!'

'Heaven forbid,' observed Mr Micawber, 'that I should grudge my native country any portion of the wealth that may be accumulated by our descendants!'

'That's well,' said my aunt, 'and I drink to you all, and every blessing and success attend you!'

Mr Peggotty put down the two children he had been nursing on each knee, to join Mr and Mrs Micawber in drinking to all of us in return, and when he and the Micawbers cordially shook hands as comrades, and his brown face brightened with a smile, I felt that he would make his way, establish a good name, and be beloved, go where he would.

It was a sorrowful farewell. They were all crying; the children hung about Agnes to the last; and we left poor Mrs Micawber in a very distressed condition.

In the afternoon the next day, my old nurse and I went down to Gravesend. We found the ship in the river and went on board. Mr Peggotty was waiting for us on deck. He told me that Mr Micawber had been arrested again and that he had paid the money: which I repaid him. He then took us down between decks.

Among the great beams, bulks, and ringbolts of the ship, and the emigrant-berths, and chests, and bundles, and barrels, and heaps of miscellaneous baggage, were groups of people, making new friendships, taking leave of one another, talking, laughing, crying, eating and drinking.

As my eye glanced round this place, I thought I saw a figure like Emily's; it first attracted my attention, by another figure parting from it with a kiss; and as it glided calmly away through the disorder, reminding me of – Agnes! But in the confusion, I lost it again, and only knew that the time was come when all visitors were being warned to leave the ship; that my nurse was crying on a chest beside me; and that Mrs Gummidge, assisted by some younger stooping woman in black, was busily arranging Mr Peggotty's goods.

'Is there any last wured, Mas'r Davy?' said he. 'Is there any one forgotten thing afore we parts?'

'One thing!' said I. 'Martha!'

He touched the younger woman on the shoulder, and Martha stood before me.

'Heaven bless you, you good man!' cried I. 'You take her with you!'

She answered for him, with a burst of tears. I could speak no more, at that time, but I wrung his hand; and if ever I have loved and honoured any man, I loved and honoured that man in my soul.

The ship was clearing fast of strangers. The greatest trial that I had, remained. I told him what the noble spirit that was gone, had given me in charge to say at parting. It moved him deeply. But when he charged me, in return, with many messages of affection and regret for those deaf ears, he moved me more.

The time was come. I embraced him, took my weeping nurse upon my arm, and hurried away. On deck, I took leave of poor Mrs Micawber. She was looking distractedly about for her family, even then; and her last words to me were, that she never would desert Mr Micawber.

We went over the side into our boat, and lay at a little distance to see the ship wafted on her course. As the sails rose to the wind, and the ship began to move, there broke from all the boats three resounding cheers, which those on board took up. My heart burst out when I heard the sound, and beheld the waving of the hats and handkerchiefs – and then I saw her! At her uncle's side, and trembling on his shoulder. He pointed to us, with an eager hand; and she saw us, and waved her last good-bye to me. Aye, Emily, beautiful and drooping, cling to him with the utmost trust of thy bruised heart; for he has clung to thee, with all the might of his great love!

Surrounded by the rosy light, and standing high upon the deck, apart together, she clinging to him, and he holding her, they solemnly passed away. The night had fallen on the Kentish hills when we were rowed ashore – and fallen darkly upon me.

CHAPTER 58

Absence

I went away from England; not knowing, even then, how great the shock was, that I had to bear. As a man upon a field of battle will receive a mortal hurt, and scarcely know that he is struck, so I, when I was left alone with my undisciplined heart, had no conception of the wound with which it had to strive.

The knowledge came upon me, not quickly, but little by little. The disconsolate feeling deepened and widened hourly. By imperceptible degrees, it became a hopeless consciousness of all that I had lost – love, friendship, interest; of all that had been shattered – my first trust, my first affection, the whole airy castle of my life; of all that remained – a ruined blank and waste, unbroken to the dark horizon.

If my grief were selfish, I did not know it to be so. I mourned for my child-wife. I mourned for him who might have won the love and admiration of thousands, as he had won mine long ago. I mourned for the broken heart that had found rest in the stormy sea; and for the wandering remnants of the simple home, where I had heard the night-wind blowing, when I was a child.

When this despondency was at its worst, I believed that I should die. Sometimes, I thought that I would like to die at home; and actually turned back on my road, that I might get there soon. At other times, I passed on farther away, from city to city, seeking I know not what, and trying to leave I know not what behind.

When I oblige myself to look back on this time, I see myself passing on among the novelties of foreign towns, palaces, cathedrals, castles, tombs, fantastic streets, as a dreamer might; bearing my painful load through all. For many months I travelled with this ever-darkening cloud upon my mind. I had had no purpose, no sustaining soul within me, anywhere.

I was in Switzerland. I came, one evening before sunset, down into a valley, where I was to rest. In the course of my descent, by the winding track along the mountain-side, I remember hoping that some better change was possible within me.

I came into the little village as the evening sun was shining on the remote heights of snow. The bases of the mountains were richly green; and high above this gentler vegetation, grew forests of dark fir, gradually blending with the crowning snow. In the quiet air, there was a sound of distant singing – shepherd voices; but I could almost have believed it was not earthly music. All at once, in this serenity, great Nature spoke to me; and soothed me to lay down my weary head upon the grass, and weep as I had not wept since Dora died!

I found a packet of letters awaiting me. I opened it, and read the writing of Agnes.

She was happy and useful, was prospering as she had hoped. That was all she told me of herself. The rest referred to me.

She gave me no advice; she only told me what her trust in me was. She knew (she said) how such a nature as mine would turn affliction to good. She knew that in me, sorrow could not be weakness, but must be strength. As the endurance of my childish days had done its part to make me what I was, so greater calamities would nerve me on, to be yet better than I was; and so, as they had taught me, would I teach others. She commended me to God, who had taken my innocent darling to His rest; and in her sisterly affection cherished me always, and was always at my side go where I would; proud of what I had done, but infinitely prouder yet of what I was reserved to do.

I put the letter in my breast, and thought what had I been an hour ago! There was no name for the love I bore her, dearer to me, henceforward, than ever until then.

I wrote to her before I slept. I told her that I had been in sore need of her help; that without her I was not what she thought me; but that she inspired me to be that, and I would try.

I resolved to remain away from home for some time longer; to settle myself for the present in Switzerland; to resume my pen; to work. I admitted to my breast the human interest I had lately shrunk from. It was not long before I had almost as many friends in the valley as in Yarmouth; and when I left it, before the winter set in, and came back in the spring, their cordial greetings had a homely sound to me.

I worked early and late, patiently and hard. I wrote a Story not remotely, out of my experience, and sent it to Traddles, and he arranged for its publication very advantageously for me; and the tidings of my growing reputation began to reach me. After some rest, I fell to work on a new fancy which took strong possession of me. This was my third work of fiction. It was not half written, when I thought of returning home.

My health, severely impaired when I left England, was quite restored. I had seen much. I had been in many countries, and I hope I had improved my store of knowledge.

I have now recalled all that I think it needful to recall of this term of absence – with one reservation.

I cannot so completely penetrate the mystery of my own heart, as to know when I began to think that I might have set its earliest and brightest hopes on Agnes.

I could not forget that the feeling with which she now regarded me had grown up in my own free choice. That if she had ever loved me with another love – and I sometimes thought the time was when she might have done so – I had cast it away. I had bestowed my passionate tenderness upon another object; and what I might have done, I had not done; and what Agnes was to me, I and her own noble heart had made her.

In the beginning of the change that gradually worked in me, when I tried to get a better understanding of myself, I did glance to a period when I might possibly hope to cancel the mistaken past, and to be so blessed as to marry her. But, as time wore on, this prospect faded. If she had ever loved me, then I should hold her the more sacred, remembering the sacrifice she must have made to be my friend and sister. If she had never loved me, could I believe that she would love me now?

I had always felt my weakness in comparison with her constancy; and now I felt it more. Whatever I might have been to her, or she to me, if I had been more worthy of her long ago, I was not now. The time was past and I had deservedly lost her. I made no effort to conceal from myself that I loved her; but it was now too late.

I endeavoured to convert what might have been between myself and Agnes, into a means of making me more self-denying, more resolved, more conscious of my defects. Thus, through the reflection that it might have been, I arrived at the conviction that it could never be.

These, with their perplexities and inconsistencies, were the shifting quicksands of my mind, from the time of my departure to the time of my return home, three years afterwards. Three years had elapsed since the sailing of the emigrant ship; when, at that same hour of sunset, and in the same place, I stood on the deck of the packet vessel that brought me home.

Three years. Long in the aggregate, though short as they went by. And home was very dear to me, and Agnes too – but she was not mine – she was never to be mine. She might have been, but that was past!

CHAPTER 59

Return

I landed in London on a wintry autumn evening. I saw more fog and mud in a minute than I had seen in a year. I walked from the Custom House to Monument before I found a coach; and although the house fronts were like old friends to me, I could not but admit that they were very dingy friends.

For some changes in the fortunes of my friends, I was prepared. My aunt had long been re-established at Dover, and Traddles had chambers in Gray's Inn now.

They expected me home before Christmas; but had no idea of my returning so soon. I had purposely misled them, that I might have the pleasure of taking them by surprise. And yet, I was perverse enough to feel a disappointment in receiving no welcome, and rattling, alone and silent, through the misty streets.

When I alighted at the door of the Gray's Inn Coffee-house, I had recovered my spirits.

'Do you know where Mr Traddles lives in the Inn?' I asked the waiter, as I warmed myself by the coffee-room fire.

'Holborn Court, sir. Number two.'

Being very anxious to see the dear old fellow, I despatched my dinner and hurried out. Number two in the Court was soon reached; and an inscription on the door-post informing me that Mr Traddles occupied a set of chambers on the top story, I ascended the crazy old staircase.

In the course of my stumbling up-stairs, I fancied I heard a pleasant sound of laughter of two or three merry girls. Happening, however, as I stopped to listen, to put my foot in a hole where the Honourable Society of Gray's Inn had left a plank deficient, I fell down with some noise, and when I recovered my footing all was silent.

Groping my way more carefully, for the rest of the journey, my heart beat high when I found the outer door, which had MR TRADDLES painted on it, open. I knocked. A considerable scuffling within ensued, but nothing else. I therefore knocked again and admitted myself.

In a little sitting-room I came into the presence of my old friend, seated at a table and bending over papers.

'Good God!' cried Traddles, looking up. 'It's Copperfield!' and rushed into my arms, where I held him tight.

We cried with pleasure, both of us.

'My dear fellow,' said Traddles, rumpling his hair in his excitement, which was a most unnecessary operation, 'how glad I am to see you! Good gracious me, *when* did you come, *where* have you come from, *what* have you been doing?'

Never pausing for an answer to anything he said, Traddles, who had clapped me into an easy-chair by the fire, all this time impetuously stirred the fire with one hand, and pulled at my neck-kerchief with the other, under some wild delusion that it was a great-coat. Both laughing and both wiping our eyes, we shook hands across the hearth.

'To think,' said Traddles, 'that you should have been so nearly coming home and not at the ceremony!'

'What ceremony, my dear Traddles?'

'Good gracious me!' cried Traddles, opening his eyes in his old way. 'Didn't you get my last letter? I am married!'

'Married!' I cried joyfully.

'Lord bless me, yes!' said Traddles – 'to Sophy – down in Devonshire. Why, my dear boy, she's behind the window curtain! Look here!'

To my amazement, the dearest girl in the world came at that same instant, laughing and blushing, from her place of concealment. I kissed her as an old acquaintance should, and wished them joy with all my might of heart.

'Dear me,' said Traddles, 'what a delightful reunion this is! God bless my soul, how happy I am!'

'And so am I,' said I.

'And I am sure I am!' said the blushing and laughing Sophy.

'We are all as happy as possible!' said Traddles. 'Even the girls are happy. Dear me, I declare I forgot them!'

'Forgot?' said I.

'The girls,' said Traddles. 'Sophy's sisters. They are staying with us. They have come to have a peep at London. The fact is, was it you that tumbled up-stairs, Copperfield?'

'It was,' said I, laughing.

'Well then, when you tumbled up-stairs,' said Traddles, 'I was romping with the girls, playing at Puss in the Corner. But as that wouldn't look quite professional if they were seen by a client, they decamped. And they are now – listening, I have no doubt,' said Traddles, glancing at the door of another room. 'My love, will you fetch the girls?'

Sophy tripped away, and we heard her received in the adjoining room with a peal of laughter.

'Really musical, isn't it, my dear Copperfield?' said Traddles. 'It's very agreeable to hear. It quite lights up these old rooms. The society of girls is a very delightful thing, Copperfield. It's not professional, but it's very delightful.'

'But then,' said Traddles, 'our domestic arrangements are quite unprofessional altogether, my dear Copperfield. Even Sophy's being here, is unprofessional. And we have no other place of abode. We have put to sea in a cockboat, but we are quite prepared to rough it. And Sophy's an extraordinary manager! You'll be surprised how those girls are stowed away. I am sure I hardly know how it's done.'

'Are many of the young ladies with you?' I inquired.

'The eldest, the Beauty is here,' said Traddles, in a low confidential voice, 'Caroline. And Sarah's here – the one I mentioned to you as having something the matter with her spine, you know. Immensely better! And the two youngest that Sophy educated are with us. And Louisa's here.'

'Indeed!' cried I.

'Yes,' said Traddles. 'Now the chambers is only three rooms; but Sophy arranges for the girls in the most wonderful way, and they sleep as comfortably as possible. Three in that room,' said Traddles, pointing. 'Two in that.'

I could not help glancing round, in search of the accommodation remaining for Mr and Mrs Traddles. Traddles understood me.

'Well!' said Traddles, 'there's a little room in the roof – a capital little gipsy sort of place. There's quite a view from it.'

'And you are happily married at last, my dear Traddles!' said I. 'How rejoiced I am!'

'Indeed, I am in a most enviable state. I work hard, and read Law insatiably. I get up at five every morning, and don't mind it at all. I hide the girls in the day-time, and make merry with them in the evening. And I assure you I am quite sorry that they are going home on Tuesday. But here,' said Traddles, breaking off in his confidence, and speaking aloud, '*are* the girls! Mr Copperfield, Miss Crewler – Miss Sarah – Miss Louisa – Margaret and Lucy!'

They were a perfect nest of roses; they looked so wholesome and fresh. They were all pretty, and Miss Caroline was very handsome; but there was a loving, cheerful, fireside quality in Sophy's bright looks, which was better than that, and which assured me that my friend had chosen well.

Mrs Traddles, with perfect pleasure and composure beaming from her household eyes, made the tea, then quietly sat in a corner by the fire.

She had seen Agnes, she told me. 'Tom' had taken her down into Kent for a wedding trip, and there she had seen my aunt, too; and both my aunt and Agnes were well, and they had all talked of nothing but me, 'Tom' had never had me out of his thoughts, she really believed, all the time I had been away. 'Tom' was evidently the idol of her life; never to be shaken on his pedestal by any commotion; always to be believed in, and done homage to with the whole faith of her heart, come what might.

Their self-forgetfulness charmed me. Their pride in these girls, and their submission of themselves to all their whims, was the pleasantest little testimony to their own worth I could have desired to see. If Traddles were addressed as 'a darling,' once in the course of that evening; and besought to bring something here, or carry something there, he was so addressed by his sisters-in-law at least twelve times in an hour. Neither could they do anything without Sophy. Somebody's hair fell down, and nobody but Sophy could put it up. Somebody forgot how a particular tune went, and nobody but Sophy could hum that tune right. Somebody wanted to recall the name of a place in Devonshire, and only Sophy knew it. They were entire mistresses of the place, and Sophy and Traddles waited on them. The best of all was that all the sisters had a great tenderness and respect both for Sophy and Traddles. When I took my leave, and Traddles was coming out to walk with me to the coffee-house, I thought I had never seen an obstinate head of hair, rolling about in such a shower of kisses.

Altogether, it was a scene I could not help dwelling on with pleasure, for a long time after I got back. Drawing a chair before one of the coffee-room fires to think about him at my leisure, I gradually fell from the consideration of his happiness to tracing prospects in the live-coals, and to thinking of the principal vicissitudes and separations that had marked my life.

I could think of the past now, gravely, but not bitterly; and could contemplate the future in a brave spirit. Home, in its best sense, was for me no more. She in whom I might have inspired a dearer love, I had taught to be my sister. She would marry, and would have new claimants on her tenderness; and in doing it, would never know the love for her that had grown up in my heart. It was right that I should pay the forfeit of my headlong passion. What I reaped, I had sown.

I was thinking – when I found my eyes resting on a countenance that might have arisen out of the fire, in its association with my early remembrances.

Little Mr Chillip the Doctor, to whose good offices I was indebted in the very first chapter of this history, sat reading a newspaper in the shadow of an opposite corner. He was tolerably stricken in years by this time; but, being a meek, calm little man, had worn so easily that I thought he looked at that moment just as he might have looked when he sat in our parlour, waiting for me to be born.

Mr Chillip had left Blunderstone six or seven years ago, and I had never seen him since. He sat placidly perusing the newspaper, with his little head on one side, and a glass of warm sherry negus at his elbow. He was so extremely conciliatory in his manner that he seemed to apologise to the very newspaper for taking the liberty of reading it.

I said, 'How do you do, Mr Chillip?'

He was greatly fluttered by this unexpected address and replied, in his slow way, 'I thank you, sir, you are very good.'

'You don't remember me?' said I.

'Well, sir,' returned Mr Chillip, shaking his head, 'I have an impression that something in your countenance is familiar to me, sir; but I couldn't lay my hand upon your name.'

'And yet you knew it, long before I knew it myself,' I returned.

'Is it possible that I had the honour, sir, of officiating when – ?'

'Yes,' said I.

On my telling him my name, he was really moved.

'Dear me, sir!' said Mr Chillip, surveying me with his head on one side. 'I think I should have known you, if I had taken the liberty of looking more closely at you. There's a strong resemblance between you and your poor father, sir.'

'I never had the happiness of seeing my father,' I observed.

'And very much to be deplored it was, on all accounts! We are not ignorant, sir,' said Mr Chillip, slowly shaking his little head, 'down in our part of the country, of your fame.'

'What is your part of the country now?' I asked, seating myself near him.

'I am established within a few miles of Bury St Edmund's,' said Mr Chillip. 'Mrs Chillip coming into a little property in that neighbourhood, under her father's will, I bought a practice down there.'

As the little man put his now empty glass to his lips, I proposed to him to have it refilled, and I would keep him company. 'Well, sir,' he returned, 'it's more than I am accustomed to; but I can't deny myself the pleasure of your conversation. It seems but yesterday that I had the honour of attending you in the measles. You came through them charmingly, sir!'

I acknowledged this compliment, and ordered the negus, which was soon produced. 'Quite an uncommon dissipation!' said Mr Chillip, stirring it, 'but I can't resist so extraordinary an occasion. I was aware that you sustained a bereavement, sir, some time ago. I heard it from your father-in-law's sister.'

'Where did you see her, Mr Chillip?'

'Are you not aware, that your father-in-law is again a neighbour of mine?'

'No,' said I.

'He is indeed, sir!' said Mr Chillip. 'Married a young lady of that part, with a good little property, poor thing.'

'Do you attend the family?' I asked.

'I have been called in,' he replied. 'Strong phrenological development of the organ of firmness, in Mr Murdstone and his sister, sir.'

I replied with such an expressive look, that Mr Chillip was emboldened by that, and the negus together, to give his head several short shakes, and thoughtfully exclaim, 'Ah, dear me! We remember old times, Mr Copperfield!'

'And the brother and sister are pursuing their old course, are they?' said I.

'I must say, they are very severe: both as to this life and the next. She was a charming woman, sir!' he observed in a plaintive manner.

'The present Mrs Murdstone?'

'A charming woman indeed. As amiable, I am sure, as it was possible to be! Mrs Chillip's opinion is, that her spirit has been entirely broken since her marriage, and that she is all but melancholy mad. And the ladies,' observed Mr Chillip, timorously, 'are great observers, sir.'

'I suppose she was to be subdued and broken to their detestable mould, Heaven help her!' said I. 'And she has been.'

'Well, sir, there were violent quarrels at first, I assure you,' said Mr Chillip; 'but she is quite a shadow now. Would it be considered forward if I was to say to you, sir, in confidence, that since the sister came to help, the brother and sister between them have nearly reduced her to a state of imbecility?'

I told him I could easily believe it.

'I have no hesitation in saying,' said Mr Chillip, fortifying himself with another sip of negus, 'between you and me, sir, that tyranny, gloom, and worry have made Mrs Murdstone nearly imbecile. She was a lively young woman, sir, before marriage, and their gloom and austerity destroyed her. They go about with her, now, more like her keepers than her husband and sister-in-law. That was Mrs Chillip's remark to me, only last week. And I assure you, sir, Mrs Chillip is a *great* observer!'

'Does he profess to be religious still?' I inquired.

'Mrs Chillip quite electrified me by pointing out that Mr Murdstone sets up an image of himself, and calls it the Divine Nature. Mrs Chillip goes so far as to say, that what such people miscall their religion, is a vent for their bad humours and arrogance. And I must say, sir,' he continued, laying his head on one side, 'that I *don't* find authority for Mr and Miss Murdstone in the New Testament.'

'I never found it either!' said I.

'In the meantime, sir,' said Mr Chillip, 'they are much disliked; and they are very free in consigning everybody who dislikes them to perdition! However, as Mrs Chillip says, they undergo a continual punishment; for they are turned inward, to feed upon their own hearts, and their own hearts are very bad feeding.'

Thoroughly tired, I went to bed at midnight; passed the next day on the Dover coach; burst safe and sound into my aunt's old parlour while she was at tea and was received by her, and Mr Dick, and dear old Peggotty, who acted as housekeeper, with open arms and tears of joy. My aunt was mightily amused by my account of my meeting with Mr Chillip and both she and Peggotty had a great deal to say about my poor mother's second husband, and 'that murdering woman of a sister,' – on whom I think no pain or penalty would have induced my aunt to bestow any Christian or Proper Name, or any other designation.

CHAPTER 60

Agnes

My aunt and I talked far into the night. How the emigrants never wrote home, otherwise than cheerfully; how Mr Micawber had actually remitted divers small sums of money; how Janet had finally carried out her renunciation of mankind by entering into wedlock with a thriving tavern-keeper, were among our topics. Mr Dick was not forgotten. My aunt informed me how he occupied himself in copying everything he could lay his hands on, and kept King Charles the First at a respectful distance by that semblance of employment.

'And when, Trot,' said my aunt, patting the back of my hand, 'are you going over to Canterbury?'

'I shall ride over to-morrow morning.'

I said I could not have come through Canterbury to-day without stopping, if I had been coming to any one but her.

She was pleased, but answered, '*My* old bones would have kept till to-morrow!' and softly patted my hand again, as I sat looking thoughtfully at the fire.

Thoughtfully, for I could not be so near Agnes, without the revival of those regrets with which I had so long been occupied. 'Oh, Trot,' I seemed to hear my aunt say once more; and I understood her better now – 'Blind, blind, blind!'

When I raised my eyes, I found that she was steadily observant of me. Perhaps she had followed the current of my mind.

'You will find her father a white-haired old man,' said my aunt, 'though a better man in all other respects. Neither will you find him measuring all human interests, with his poor little inch-rule now.

'You will find her,' pursued my aunt, 'as good, as beautiful, as earnest, as she has always been. If I knew higher praise, Trot, I would bestow it on her.'

There was no higher praise for her; no higher reproach for me. Oh, how had I strayed so far away!

'Has Agnes any –' I was thinking aloud, rather than speaking.

'Any what?' said my aunt, sharply.

'Any lover,' said I.

'A score. She might have married twenty times, my dear, since you have been gone!'

'No doubt,' said I. 'But has she any lover who is worthy of her?'

Slowly raising her eyes to mine, she said: 'I suspect she has an attachment.'

'A prosperous one?' said I.

'I can't say,' returned my aunt, gravely. 'She has never confided it to me, but I suspect it. You must not be ruled by my suspicions. You must keep them secret. I have no right to speak.'

'If it should be so,' I repeated, 'Agnes will tell me at her own good time. A sister to whom I have confided so much, aunt, will not be reluctant to confide in me.'

We both sat, looking into the past, without saying another word, until we parted for the night.

I rode away early in the morning for the scene of my old school days. The well-remembered ground was soon traversed, and I came into the quiet streets, where every stone was a boy's book to me. I went on foot to the old house and I was shown into the unchanged drawing-room. All the little changes that had crept in when the Heeps were there, were changed again. Everything was as it used to be.

The opening of the little door in the panelled wall made me start and turn. Her beautiful serene eyes met mine as she came towards me. She stopped and laid her hand upon her bosom, and I caught her in my arms.

'I am so rejoiced to see you, Trotwood!'

'Dear Agnes!'

We sat down, side by side; and her angel-face was turned upon me with the welcome I had dreamed of.

She led me back to the time of our parting; spoke to me of Emily, whom she had visited in secret many times; spoke to me tenderly of Dora's grave. With the unerring instinct of her noble heart, she touched the chords of my memory so softly and harmoniously, that not one jarred within me; I could listen to the sorrowful, distant music, and desire to shrink from nothing it awoke. How could I when, blended with it all, was her dear self, the better angel of my life?

'And you, Agnes,' I said, by-and-by. 'Tell me of yourself.'

'What should I tell?' she answered, with her radiant smile. 'Papa is well. You see us here, quiet in our own home; our anxieties set at rest, our home restored to us; and knowing that, dear Trotwood, you know all.'

'Is there nothing else, sister?' I said.

She smiled; with a quiet sadness, I thought; and shook her head.

I had sought to lead her to what my aunt had hinted at; for, sharply painful to me as it must be to receive that confidence, I was to discipline my heart, and do my duty to her. I saw, however, that she was uneasy, and I let it pass.

'You have much to do, dear Agnes?'

'With my school?' said she, looking up again, in all her bright composure.

'Yes. It is laborious, is it not?'

'The labour is so pleasant,' she returned, 'that it is scarcely grateful in me to call it by that name.'

'Nothing good is difficult to you,' said I.

Once more, as she bent her head, I saw the same sad smile.

'Even the old flowers are here,' said I, looking round; 'or the old kinds.'

'I have found a pleasure in keeping everything as it used to be when we were children. For we were very happy then, I think.'

'Heaven knows we were!' said I.

'And every little thing that has reminded me of my brother,' said Agnes, with her eyes turned cheerfully upon me, 'has been a welcome companion.'

It was for me to guard this sisterly affection with religious care. It was all that I had left myself, and it was a treasure. If I once shook the foundations of the sacred confidence, it was lost, and could never be recovered. I set this steadily before myself. The better I loved her, the more it behoved me never to forget it.

I walked through the streets; and there meditated on Miss Shepherd and the eldest Miss Larkins, and all the idle loves and likings of that time. Nothing seemed to have survived but Agnes; and she, ever a star above me, was brighter and higher.

When I returned, Mr Wickfield had come home. I found him as my aunt had described him. We sat down to dinner and he seemed but the shadow of his handsome picture on the wall.

When dinner was done, Mr Wickfield taking no wine, and I desiring none, we went up-stairs; where Agnes and her little charges sang and played. After tea the children left us; and we three sat together, talking of the bygone days.

'My part in them,' said Mr Wickfield, shaking his white head, 'has much matter for regret. But I would not cancel it, if it were in my power.'

I could readily believe that, looking at the face beside him.

'I should cancel with it,' he pursued, 'such a child's love as I must not forget. No one knows, how much she has done, how much she has undergone, how hard she has striven. Dear Agnes!'

She had put her hand entreatingly on his arm, to stop him.

'Well, well!' he said with a sigh. 'I have never told you, Trotwood, of her mother. She married me in opposition to her father's wish, and he renounced her. He was a very hard man, and her mother had long been dead. He repulsed her.'

Agnes leaned upon his shoulder, and stole her arm about his neck.

'She had an affectionate and gentle heart and it was broken. She loved me dearly, but was never happy. She being delicate and downcast at the time of his last repulse – for it was not the first, by many – pined away and died. She left me Agnes, two weeks old.'

He kissed Agnes on her cheek.

'My love for my dear child was a diseased love, but my mind was all unhealthy then. I say no more of that. What Agnes is, I need not say. I have always read something of her poor mother's story in her character; and so I tell it you to-night, when we three are again together, after such great changes.'

His bowed head, and her angel-face derived a more pathetic meaning from it than they had had before. If I had wanted anything by which to mark this night of our reunion, I should have found it in this.

Going softly to her piano, Agnes played some of the old airs.

'Have you any intention of going away again?' she asked me, as I was standing by.

'What does my sister say to that?'

'I think you ought not,' she said. 'Your growing reputation and success enlarge your power of doing good; and if *I* could spare my brother,' with her eyes upon me, 'perhaps the time could not.'

'What I am, you have made me, Agnes. You should know best.'

'I made you, Trotwood?'

'Yes! Agnes, my dear girl!' I said, bending over her. 'I tried to tell you, when we met to-day, something that has been in my thoughts since Dora died. You remember, when you came down to me in our little room – pointing upward, Agnes?'

'Oh, Trotwood!' she returned, her eyes filled with tears. 'Can I ever forget?'

'As you were then, you have ever been to me. Ever pointing upward, Agnes; ever directing me to higher things. I want you to know, that all my life long I shall be guided by you. Whatever changes may come between us, I shall always look to you, and love you as I do now. I shall see you always before me, pointing upward!'

She put her hand in mine, and told me she was proud of me, and of what I said; although I praised her very far beyond her worth. Then she went on softly playing.

'Do you know, what I have heard to-night, Agnes,' said I, 'seems to be a part of the feeling with which I regarded you when I saw you first.'

'You knew I had no mother,' she replied, 'and felt kindly towards me.'

'More than that, Agnes, I knew that there was something that might have been sorrowful in some one else but was not so in you. Will you laugh at my cherishing such fancies, Agnes?'

'No!'

'Or at my saying that I really believe I felt that you could be faithfully affectionate against all discouragement, and never cease to be so, until you ceased to live? – Will you laugh at such a dream?'

'Oh, no! Oh, no!'

For an instant, a distressful shadow crossed her face; but, even in the start it gave me, it was gone; and she was playing on, and looking at me with her own calm smile.

As I rode back in the lonely night, I thought of this, and feared she was not happy. *I* was not happy; but, thus far, I had faithfully set the seal upon the Past, and, thinking of her, pointing upward, thought of her as pointing to that sky above me, where, in the mystery to come, I might yet love her with a love unknown on earth, and tell her what the strife had been within me when I loved her here.

CHAPTER 61

I am shown Two Interesting Penitents

For a time – until my book should be completed – I took up my abode in my aunt's house at Dover. Occasionally I went to London to consult Traddles on some business point. He had managed for me, in my absence, with the soundest judgment; and my worldly affairs were prospering. As my notoriety began to bring upon me an enormous quantity of letters from people of whom I had no knowledge – chiefly about nothing, and extremely difficult to answer – I agreed with Traddles to have my name painted up on his door. There, the postman delivered bushels of letters for me; and there, at intervals, I laboured through them.

There I always found Sophy, the same bright housewife, humming her Devonshire ballads. I wondered, at first, why I so often found Sophy writing in a copybook; and why she always shut it up when I appeared. But the secret soon came out. One day, Traddles took a paper out of his desk, and asked me what I thought of that handwriting?

'Oh, *don't*, Tom!' cried Sophy.

'Why not?' returned Tom. 'What do you say to that, Copperfield?'

'It's extraordinarily legal and formal,' said I. 'I don't think I ever saw such a stiff hand.'

Traddles broke into a rapturous laugh, and informed me that it was Sophy's writing; that Sophy had declared he would need a copying-clerk soon, and she would be that clerk; that she had acquired this hand from a pattern. Sophy said that when Tom was made a judge he wouldn't be so ready to proclaim it. Which Tom denied; averring that he should always be equally proud of it, under all circumstances.

'What a thoroughly charming wife she is, Traddles!' said I, when she had gone away, laughing. 'I believe you make yourselves two of the happiest people in the world.'

'I am sure we *are* two of the happiest people,' returned Traddles. 'Bless my soul, when I see her getting up by candle-light on these dark mornings, going out to market before the clerks come into the Inn, sweet-tempered and encouraging always, and all for me, I positively sometimes can't believe it, Copperfield!

'Then, our pleasures! Dear me, they are inexpensive, but they are quite wonderful! When we are at home of an evening, and shut the outer door, where could we be more snug? When it's fine, and we go out for a walk, we look into the windows of the jewellers' shops; and I show Sophy which of the diamond-eyed serpents I would give her if I could afford it; and Sophy shows me which of the gold watches she would buy for me if *she* could afford it; and we pick out the spoons and forks, fish-slices and sugar-tongs, we should both prefer and we go away as if we had got them! Then, when we stroll into the streets and see a house to let, we say, how would *that* do, if I was made a judge? In walking home, perhaps we buy a little bit of something at a cook's-shop, and make a splendid supper, chatting about what we have seen. Now, you know, Copperfield, if I was Lord Chancellor, we couldn't do this!'

'You would do something, whatever you were, my dear Traddles,' thought I, 'that would be pleasant and amiable. By the way,' I said aloud, 'I suppose you never draw any skeletons now?'

'Really,' replied Traddles, reddening, 'I can't wholly deny that I do. In one of the back rows of the King's Bench the other day, the fancy came into my head. And I am afraid there's a skeleton – in a wig – on the ledge of the desk.'

After we had both laughed heartily, Traddles wound up by saying, in his forgiving way, 'Old Creakle!'

'I have a letter from that old Rascal here,' said I, looking over my letters. 'Among the persons who discover that they were always much attached to me is the self-same Creakle. He is not a schoolmaster now. He is a Middlesex Magistrate.'

I thought Traddles might be surprised to hear it, but he was not so at all.

'Perhaps he voted for somebody, or lent money to somebody, or knew somebody who got the lieutenant of the county to nominate him for the commission.'

'On the commission he is, at any rate,' said I. 'And he writes that he will be glad to show me, in operation, the only true system of making prisoners sincere and lasting penitents – which, you know, is by solitary confinement. What do you say to my accepting the offer, and your going with me?'

'I don't object,' said Traddles.

'Then I'll write to say so. If you'll read his letter, you'll find he is the tenderest of men to prisoners convicted of the whole calendar of felonies, though I can't find that his tenderness extends to any other class of created beings.'

On the appointed day, Traddles and I repaired to the prison where Mr Creakle was powerful. It was an immense building, erected at a vast expense. I could not help thinking what an uproar would have been made if any deluded man had proposed to spend one half the money on the erection of an industrial school for the young, or a house of refuge for the deserving old.

We were presented to our old schoolmaster, who was one of a group composed of two or three of the busier magistrates and some visitors. He received me like a man who had always loved me tenderly. On my introducing Traddles, Mr Creakle expressed, in like manner, but in an inferior degree, that he had always been Traddles's guide, philosopher, and friend. His face was as fiery as ever.

After some conversation among these gentlemen, from which I might have supposed that there was nothing in the world to be legitimately taken into account but the supreme comfort of prisoners, we began our inspection.

As we were going through some of the magnificent passages, I inquired what were supposed to be the main advantages of this system? I found them to be the perfect isolation of prisoners – so that no one man knew anything about another; and the reduction of prisoners to a wholesome state of mind, leading to sincere repentance.

Now, it struck me, when we began to visit individuals in their cells, that there was a strong probability of the prisoners knowing a good deal about each other, but it would have been flat blasphemy against the system to have hinted such a doubt. I looked out for the penitence as diligently as I could.

And here again, I had great misgivings. I found a vast amount of profession, varying very little in character: varying very little even in words. I found a great many foxes disparaging whole vineyards of inaccessible grapes; but I found very few foxes whom I would have trusted within reach of a bunch.

I found that the most professing men were the greatest objects of interest and heard repeatedly of a certain Number Twenty-Seven, who really appeared to be a Model Prisoner. Twenty-Eight was also a bright star; but it was his misfortune to have his glory a little dimmed by the extraordinary lustre of Twenty-Seven.

At last, we came to the door of his cell; and Mr Creakle, looking through a little hole, reported to us in a state of the greatest admiration, that he was reading a Hymn Book. To give us an opportunity of conversing with Twenty-Seven in all his purity, Mr Creakle directed Twenty-Seven to be invited out into the passage. Whom should Traddles and I then behold, to our amazement, but Uriah Heep!

He knew us directly; and said, as he came out – with the old writhe – 'How do you do, Mr Copperfield? How do you do, Mr Traddles?'

This recognition caused a general admiration in the party. I rather thought that every one was struck by his taking notice of us.

'Well, Twenty-Seven,' said Mr Creakle, mournfully admiring him. 'How do you find yourself to-day?'

'I am very umble, sir!' replied Uriah Heep.

'You are always so, Twenty-Seven,' said Mr Creakle.

Here, another gentleman asked, with extreme anxiety: 'Are you quite comfortable?'

'Far more comfortable here,' said Uriah Heep, 'than ever I was outside. I see my follies now, sir. That's what makes me comfortable.'

A third questioner inquired with extreme feeling: 'How do you find the beef?'

'It was tougher yesterday than I could wish,' replied Uriah, 'but it's my duty to bear.'

A murmur, partly of gratification at Twenty-Seven's celestial state of mind, and partly of indignation against the Contractor who had given him any cause of complaint, having subsided, Twenty-Seven stood in the midst of us, as if he felt himself the principal object of merit in a highly meritorious museum. That we might have an excess of light shining upon us all at once, orders were given to let out Twenty-Eight.

I had been so much astonished already, that I only felt a kind of resigned wonder when Mr Littimer walked forth!

'Twenty-Eight,' said a gentleman in spectacles, who it appeared to me backed his Twenty-Eight against Mr Creakle's Twenty-Seven, 'what is your state of mind?'

'I thank you, sir,' returned Mr Littimer; 'I see my follies now, sir. I am a good deal troubled when I think of the sins of my former companions, sir; but I trust they may find forgiveness.'

'Is there anything at all on your mind, now?' said the questioner.

'Sir,' said Mr Littimer, 'there is a gentleman present who was acquainted with me in my former life. It may be profitable to that gentleman to know that I attribute my past follies, entirely to having lived in the service of young men; and to having allowed myself to be led by them into weaknesses, which I had not the strength to resist. I hope that gentleman will take warning, sir, and may repent of all the wickedness and sin, to which he has been a party.'

'This does you credit, Twenty-Eight,' returned the questioner. 'Is there anything else?'

'Sir, there was a young woman who fell into dissolute courses that I endeavoured to save, sir. I beg that gentleman, if he has it in his power, to inform that young woman from me that I forgive her her bad conduct towards myself; and that I call her to repentance.'

With this, Number Twenty-Eight retired, after a glance between him and Uriah; as if they were not altogether unknown to each other, and a murmur went round the group, that he was a most respectable man, and a beautiful case.

'Now, Twenty-Seven,' said Mr Creakle, entering on a clear stage with *his* man, 'is there anything that any one can do for you?'

'I would umbly ask, sir,' returned Uriah, 'for leave to write again to mother. I should wish mother to be got into my state. I wish mother had come here. It would be better for everybody, if they was brought here.'

This sentiment gave greater satisfaction, I think, than anything that had passed yet.

'You are quite changed?' said Mr Creakle.

'Oh dear, yes, sir!' cried this hopeful penitent.

'You wouldn't relapse, if you were going out?' asked somebody else.

'Oh dear no, sir!'

'Well!' said Mr Creakle, 'this is very gratifying. You have addressed Mr Copperfield, Twenty-Seven. Do you wish to say anything further to him?'

'You knew me a long time before I was changed, Mr Copperfield,' said Uriah, looking at me; and a more villainous look I never saw, even on his visage. 'You knew me when I was umble among them that was proud, and meek among them that was violent – you was violent to me yourself, Mr Copperfield. Once, you struck me a blow in the face, you know.'

Several indignant glances directed at me.

'But I forgive you, Mr Copperfield,' said Uriah, 'I forgive everybody. I hope you'll curb your passions in future. I hope Mr W will repent, and Miss W, and all of that sinful lot. The best wish I could give you, Mr Copperfield, and give all of you gentlemen, is that you could be took up and brought here!'

He sneaked back into his cell, amidst a little chorus of approbation; and both Traddles and I experienced a great relief when he was locked in.

I was fain to ask what these two men had done to be there at all. That appeared to be the last thing about which they had anything to say. I addressed myself to one of the two warders who, I suspected from their faces, knew pretty well what all this stir was worth.

'Do you know,' said I, 'what felony was Number Twenty-Seven's last "folly?"'

It was a Bank case. 'Fraud, forgery, and conspiracy. He and some others. He set the others on. It was a deep plot for a large sum. Twenty-Seven was the knowingest bird of the lot, and had very nearly kept himself safe; but not quite. The Bank was just able to put salt upon his tail.'

'Do you know Twenty-Eight's offence?'

'Twenty-Eight,' returned my informant, speaking throughout in a low tone to guard himself from being overheard in such an unlawful reference to these Immaculates by Creakle and the rest; 'Twenty-Eight robbed a young master of two hundred and fifty pounds in money and valuables, the night before they were going abroad. I particularly recollect his case, from his being took by a dwarf. A little woman. I have forgot her name.'

'Not Mowcher?'

'That's it! He had eluded pursuit, and was going to America in a flaxen wig and whiskers, and such a complete disguise as never you see in all your born days; when the little woman picked him out with her sharp eye in a moment – ran betwixt his legs to unset him – and held on to him like grim Death.'

'Excellent Miss Mowcher!' cried I.

'He pounded her in the most brutal manner when she took him; but she never loosed her hold till he was locked up. She gave her evidence in the gamest way, and was highly complimented by the Bench, and cheered right home to her lodgings. She said in Court that she'd have took him single-handed, if he had been Samson. And it's my belief she would!'

It was mine too, and I highly respected Miss Mowcher for it.

We had now seen all there was to see. It would have been in vain to represent to such a man as the worshipful Mr Creakle, that Twenty-Seven and Twenty-Eight were the hypocritical knaves that they had always been. We left them to their system and themselves, and went home wondering.

CHAPTER 62

A Light shines on my Way

The year came round to Christmastime, and I had been at home above two months. I had seen Agnes frequently. At least once a week, and sometimes oftener, I rode over there and passed the evening. I usually rode back at night; for the old unhappy sense was always hovering about me now and I was glad to be up and out, rather than wandering over the past in weary wakefulness or miserable dreams. I wore away the longest part of many wild sad nights, in those rides; reviving, as I went, the thoughts that had occupied me in my long absence.

When I read to Agnes what I wrote; when I saw her listening face; moved her to smiles or tears; and heard her voice so earnest on the shadowy events of that imaginative world in which I lived; I thought what a fate mine might have been – but only thought so, as I had thought after I was married to Dora, what I could have wished my wife to be.

My duty to Agnes, who loved me with a love, which, if I disquieted, I wronged most selfishly and poorly, and could never restore; my matured assurance that I, who had worked out my own destiny, and won what I had impetuously set my heart on, had no right to murmur and must bear; comprised what I felt and what I had learned. But I loved her: and now it even became some consolation to me, vaguely to conceive a distant day when I might blamelessly avow it; when all this should be over; when I could say, 'Agnes, so it was when I came home; and now I am old, and I never have loved since!'

She did not once show me any change in herself. What she always had been to me, she still was; wholly unaltered.

Between my aunt and me there had been something, in this con-nexion, since the night of my return, which I cannot call an avoidance of the subject, so much as an implied understanding that we thought of it together, but did not shape our thoughts into words. We preserved an unbroken silence. I believed that she had read, or partly read, my thoughts that night; and that she fully comprehended why I gave mine no more distinct expression.

This Christmastime being come, and Agnes having reposed no new confidence in me, a doubt that had several times arisen in my mind – whether she could have that perception of the true state of my breast, which restrained her with the apprehension of giving me pain – began to oppress me heavily. I resolved to set this right beyond all doubt; – if such a barrier were between us, to break it down at once.

It was a cold, harsh, winter day. There had been snow some hours before; and it lay, not deep, but hard-frozen on the ground.

'Riding to-day, Trot?'

'I am going over to Canterbury. It's a good day for a ride.'

'I hope your horse may think so, too,' said my aunt; 'at present he is standing before the door as if he thought his stable preferable.'

My aunt, I may observe, allowed my horse on the forbidden ground, but had not at all relented toward the donkeys.

'Do you know anything more,' said I, 'of that attachment of Agnes?'

She looked up in my face a little while, before replying: 'I think I do, Trot.'

'Are you confirmed in your impression?' I inquired.

'I think I am, Trot.'

She looked so steadfastly at me: with a kind of doubt, or pity in her affection: that I summoned the determination to show her a perfectly cheerful face.

'And what is more, Trot,' said my aunt, 'I think Agnes is going to be married.'

'God bless her!' said I, cheerfully.

'God bless her!' said my aunt, 'and her husband too!'

I parted from my aunt and rode away. There was greater reason than before to do what I had resolved to do.

I found Agnes alone. The little girls had gone to their own homes now, and she was alone by the fire, reading. I sat beside her on the window-seat, and we talked of what I was doing, and the progress I had made since my last visit. Agnes was very cheerful; and laughingly predicted that I should soon become too famous to be talked to on such subjects.

'So I make the most of the present time, you see,' said Agnes, 'and talk to you while I may.'

As I looked at her beautiful face, she raised her eyes and saw that I was looking at her.

'You are thoughtful to-day, Trotwood!'

'My dear Agnes, do you doubt my being true to you?'

'No!' she answered, with a look of astonishment.

'Do you remember that I tried to tell you, when I came home, what a debt of gratitude I owed you, and how fervently I felt towards you?'

'I remember it,' she said, gently, 'very well.'

'You have a secret,' said I. 'Let me share it, Agnes.'

She cast down her eyes, and trembled.

'I could hardly fail to know – even if I had not heard from other lips than yours, Agnes, which seems strange – that there is some one upon whom you have bestowed your love. Do not shut me out of what concerns your happiness! If you can trust me as you say you can, let me be your friend, your brother, in this matter, of all others!'

With an appealing, almost a reproachful, glance, she rose from the window; and hurrying across the room as if without knowing where, put her hands before her face, and burst into such tears as smote me to the heart.

And yet they awakened something in me, bringing promise to my heart. Without my knowing why, these tears allied themselves with the quietly sad smile which was so fixed in my remembrance, and shook me more with hope than fear of sorrow.

'Agnes! Sister! Dearest! What have I done?'

'Let me go away, Trotwood. I am not myself. I will speak to you another time. Don't speak to me now. Don't, don't!'

I sought to recollect what she had said, when I had spoken to her on that former night, of her affection needing no return. It seemed a very world that I must search through in a moment.

'Agnes, I cannot bear to see you so, and think that I have been the cause. My dearest girl, dearer to me than anything in life, if you are unhappy, let me share your unhappiness. If you are in need of help, let me try to give it to you. If you have indeed a burden on your heart, let me try to lighten it. For whom do I live now, Agnes, if it is not for you?'

'Oh, spare me! I am not myself! Another time!' was all I could distinguish.

Was it a selfish error that was leading me away? Or, having once a clue to hope, was there something opening to me that I had not dared to think of?

'I must say more. For Heaven's sake, Agnes, let us not mistake each other after all these years! I must speak plainly. If you have any thought that I could envy the happiness you will confer; that I could not resign you to a protector of your own choosing; that I could not be a contented witness of your joy; dismiss it. There is no alloy of self in what I feel for you.'

She was quiet now. In a little time, she said in a low voice, 'I owe it to your pure friendship for me, Trotwood – which I do not doubt – I tell you, you are mistaken. I can do no more. If I have any secret, it is no new one; and is not what you suppose. I cannot reveal it. It has long been mine and must remain mine.'

'Agnes! Stay!'

She was going away, but I detained her. I clasped my arm about her waist. New thoughts and hopes were whirling through my mind, and all the colours of my life were changing.

'Dearest Agnes! Whom I so devotedly love! When I came here to-day, I thought that nothing could have wrested this confession from me. I thought I could have kept it in my bosom all our lives, till we were old. But Agnes, if I have indeed any new-born hope that I may ever call you something more than Sister –'

Her tears fell fast; but they were not like those she had lately shed, and I saw my hope brighten in them.

'Agnes! If you had been more mindful of yourself, and less of me, when we grew up here together, I think my heedless fancy never would have wandered from you. But you were so much better than I, so necessary to me in every boyish hope and disappointment, that to have you to confide in, and rely upon in everything, became a second nature, supplanting the greater one of loving you as I do!'

Still weeping, but not sadly – joyfully! And clasped in my arms as she had never been, as I had thought she never was to be!

'When I loved Dora – fondly, Agnes, as you know –'

'Yes!' she cried, earnestly.

'When I loved her – even then, my love would have been incomplete without your sympathy. I had it, and it was perfected. And when I lost her, Agnes, what should I have been without you!'

Closer in my arms, nearer to my heart, her trembling hand upon my shoulder, her sweet eyes shining through her tears, on mine!

'I went away, dear Agnes, loving you. I stayed away, loving you. I returned home, loving you!'

And now, I tried to tell her of the struggle I had had, and the conclusion I had come to. I tried to lay my mind before her, truly and entirely. I tried to show her how I had hoped I had come into the better knowledge of myself and of her; how I had resigned myself to what that better knowledge brought; and how I had come there, even that day, in my fidelity to this. If she did so love me (I said) that she could take me for her husband, she could do so, on no deserving of mine, except upon the truth of my love for her, and the trouble in which it had ripened to be what it was; and hence it was that I revealed it. And O, Agnes, even out of thy true eyes, in that same time, the spirit of my child-wife looked upon me, saying it was well; and winning me, through thee, to tenderest recollections of the Blossom that had withered in its bloom!

'I am so blest, Trotwood – my heart is so overcharged – but there is one thing I must say.'

'Dearest, what?'

'I have loved you all my life!'

Oh, we were happy! Our tears were not for the trials through which we had come, but for the rapture of being thus, never to be divided more!

We stood together in the same old-fashioned window at night, when the moon was shining; Agnes with her quiet eyes raised up to it; I following her glance. Long miles of road then opened out before my mind; and, toiling on, I saw a ragged way-worn boy forsaken and neglected, who should come to call even the heart now beating against mine, his own.

It was nearly dinner-time next day when we appeared before my aunt.

'Goodness me! Who's this you're bringing home?'

'Agnes,' said I.

As we had arranged to say nothing at first, my aunt was not a little discomfited. She darted a hopeful glance at me, when I said 'Agnes;' but seeing that I looked as usual she took off her spectacles and rubbed her nose with them.

She greeted Agnes heartily, nevertheless; and we were soon in the parlour. My aunt put on her spectacles twice or thrice, to take another look at me, but as often took them off again. Much to the discomfiture of Mr Dick, who knew this to be a bad symptom.

'By-the-by, aunt,' said I, after dinner; 'I have been speaking to Agnes about what you told me.'

'Then, Trot,' said my aunt, turning scarlet, 'you did wrong, and broke your promise.'

'You are not angry, aunt, I trust? I am sure you won't be, when you learn that Agnes is not unhappy in any attachment.'

'Stuff and nonsense!' said my aunt.

As my aunt appeared to be annoyed, I thought the best way was to cut her annoyance short. I took Agnes in my arm to the back of her chair, and we both leaned over her. My aunt with one clap of her hands, and one look through her spectacles, immediately went into hysterics, for the first and only time in all my knowledge of her.

The hysterics called up Peggotty. The moment my aunt was restored, she flew at Peggotty, and called her a silly old creature, hugged her with all her might. After that, she hugged Mr Dick (who was a good deal surprised); and after that, told them why. Then we were all happy together.

We were married within a fortnight. Traddles and Sophy, and Doctor and Mrs Strong, were the only guests at our quiet wedding. We left them full of joy; and drove away together. Clasped in my embrace, I held the source of every worthy aspiration I had ever had; the centre of myself, the circle of my life, my own, my wife; my love of whom was founded on a rock!

'Dearest husband!' said Agnes. 'Now that I may call you by that name, I have one thing more to tell you.'

'Let me hear it, love.'

'It grows out of the night when Dora died. She sent you for me.'

'She did.'

'She told me that she left me something. Can you think what it was?'

I believed I could. I drew the wife who had so long loved me, closer to my side.

'She told me that she made a last request to me, and left me a last charge.'

'And it was –'

'That only I would occupy this vacant place.'

And Agnes laid her head upon my breast, and wept; and I wept with her, though we were so happy.

CHAPTER 63

A Visitor

I had advanced in fame and fortune, my domestic joy was perfect, I had been married ten happy years. Agnes and I were sitting by the fire, in our house in London, one night in spring, and three of our children were playing in the room, when I was told that a stranger wished to see me.

He was an old man, my servant said, and looked like a farmer.

'Let him come in here!' said I.

There soon appeared, pausing in the dark doorway as he entered, a hale, grey-haired old man. Little Agnes, attracted by his looks, had run to bring him in, and I had not yet clearly seen his face, when my wife, starting up, cried out to me, in a pleased and agitated voice, that it was Mr Peggotty!

It *was* Mr Peggotty, in hearty old age. When our first emotion was over, and he sat before the fire with the children on his knees, and the blaze shining on his face, he looked to me as vigorous and robust, withal as handsome, an old man, as ever I had seen.

'Mas'r Davy,' said he. And the old name in the old tone fell so naturally on my ear! 'Mas'r Davy, 'tis a joyful hour as I see you, once more, 'long with your own trew wife!'

'A joyful hour indeed, old friend!' cried I.

'And these heer pretty ones,' said Mr Peggotty. 'Why, Mas'r Davy, you was but the height of the littlest of these, when I first see you! When Em'ly warn't no bigger, and our poor lad were *but* a lad!'

'Time has changed me more than it had changed you since then,' said I. 'But let these dear rogues go to bed; and as no house in England but this must hold you, tell me where to send for your luggage.'

'Are you alone?' asked Agnes.

'Yes, ma'am,' he said, 'quite alone. It's a mort of water to come across, and on'y stay a matter of fower weeks. But water ('specially when 'tis salt) comes nat'ral to me.'

'Are you going back those many thousand miles, so soon?' asked Agnes.

'Yes, ma'am, I giv the promise to Em'ly, afore I come away. You see, it's allus been on my mind, as I *must* come and see Mas'r Davy and your own sweet self in your wedded happiness, afore I got to be too old.'

He looked at us, as if he could never feast his eyes on us sufficiently.

'And now tell us,' said I, 'everything relating to your fortunes.'

'Our fortuns, Mas'r Davy,' he rejoined, 'is soon told. We've allus thrived. We've worked as we ought to't, and maybe we lived a leetle hard at first or so, but what with sheep-farming and stock-farming, and one thing with t'other, we are as well to do, as well could be.'

'And Emily?' said Agnes and I, both together.

'Em'ly,' said he, 'arter you left her, ma'am – and arter she and me lost sight of Mas'r Davy, that theer shining sundown – was that low at first, that if she had know'd then what Mas'r Davy kep from us so thowtful, 'tis my opinion she'd have drooped away. But theer was some poor folks aboard as had illness among 'em, and she took care of *them*; and theer was the children in our company, and she took care of *them*; and so she got to be busy and that helped her.'

'When did she first hear of it?' I asked.

'I kep it from her arter I heerd on 't, going on nigh a year. Theer come along one day, a traveller from our own Suffolk and of course we made him welcome. He'd got an old newspaper with him, and some other account in print of the storm. That's how she know'd it.'

He dropped his voice as he said these words, and the gravity I so well remembered overspread his face.

'Did it change her much?' we asked.

'Aye, for a good long time,' he said, shaking his head; 'I wonder, if you could see my Em'ly now, Mas'r Davy, whether you'd know her!'

'Is she so altered?' I inquired.

'I doen't know, I see her ev'ry day; but, odd times, I have thowt so. A slight figure,' said Mr Peggotty, looking at the fire, 'kiender worn; soft, sorrowful, blue eyes; a quiet voice – timid a'most. That's Em'ly! Some thinks as her affection was ill-bestowed; some, as her marriage was broke off by death. No one knows how 'tis. She might have married well a mort of times, "but, uncle," she says to me, "that's gone for ever." Fond of going any distance fur to teach a child, or fur to tend a sick person; liked by young and old; sowt out by all that has any trouble. That's Em'ly!'

'Is Martha with you yet?' I asked.

'Martha,' he replied, 'got married, Mas'r Davy, in the second year. A young man, a farm-labourer, made offers fur to take her fur his wife (wives is very scarce theer), and then to set up in the Bush. She spoke to me fur to tell him her trew story. I did. They was married, and they live fower hundred miles away from any voices but their own and the singing birds.'

'Mrs Gummidge?' I suggested.

'Would you believe it!' he said. 'Why, someun even made offers fur to marry *her*! If a ship's cook that was turning settler, Mas'r Davy, didn't make offers fur to marry Missis Gummidge, I'm Gormed – and I can't say no fairer than that!'

'And what did Mrs Gummidge say?'

'Missis Gummidge up'd with a bucket as was standing by, and laid it over that theer ship's cook's head 'till he sung out fur help, and I reskied of him.'

Mr Peggotty burst into a great roar of laughter, and Agnes and I both kept him company.

'But I must say this for the good creetur,' he resumed, 'she has been all she said she'd be to us, and more. I have never know'd her to be lone and lorn, for a single minute. And thinking of the old 'un is a thing she never done since she left England!'

'Now, Mr Micawber,' said I. 'He has paid off every obligation he incurred here – even to Traddles's bill – and therefore we may take it for granted that he is doing well. But what is the latest news of him?'

Mr Peggotty, with a smile, put his hand in his breast-pocket, and produced a little odd-looking newspaper.

'You are to understan', Mas'r Davy,' said he, 'as we have left the Bush now, being so well to do; and have gone right away round to Port Middlebay Harbour, wheer theer's what *we* call a town.'

'Mr Micawber was in the Bush near you?' said I.

'Bless you, yes,' said Mr Peggotty, 'and turned to with a will. I've seen that theer bald head of his, a perspiring in the sun, Mas'r Davy, 'till I a'most thowt it would have melted away. And now he's a Magistrate.'

'A Magistrate, eh?' said I.

Mr Peggotty pointed to a certain paragraph in the newspaper, where I read aloud as follows, from the 'Port Middlebay Times:'

'The public dinner to our distinguished fellow-colonist and townsman, WILKINS MICAWBER, ESQUIRE, Port Middlebay District Magistrate, came off yesterday in the large room of the Hotel, which was crowded to suffocation. The beauty, fashion, and exclusiveness of Port Middlebay, flocked to do honour to one so deservedly esteemed, so highly talented, and so widely popular. Doctor Mell (of Colonial Salem House Grammar school) presided, and on his right sat the distinguished guest. After the usual loyal and patriotic toasts were given, Dr Mell, in a speech replete with feeling, then proposed our distinguished guest. The cheering with which the toast was received defies description, it rose and fell like the waves of ocean. At length WILKINS MICAWBER, ESQUIRE, presented himself to return thanks. Far be it from us to endeavour to follow our distinguished townsman through the smoothly-flowing periods of his polished and highly-ornate address! Suffice it to observe, that it was a masterpiece of eloquence; and that those passages in which he more particularly traced his own successful career to its source, and warned the younger portion of his auditory from the shoals of ever incurring pecuniary liabilities which they were unable to liquidate, brought a tear into the manliest eye present. At the conclusion of the proceedings the tables were cleared as if by art-magic for dancing. Among the votaries of TERPSICHORE, who disported themselves until Sol gave warning for departure, Wilkins Micawber, Esquire, Junior, and the lovely Miss Helena, fourth daughter of Doctor Mell, were particularly remarkable.'

I was looking back to the name of Doctor Mell, pleased to have discovered, in these happier circumstances, Mr Mell, formerly poor pinched usher to my Middlesex magistrate, when Mr Peggotty pointed to another part of the paper and I read thus:

'TO DAVID COPPERFIELD, ESQUIRE.
THE EMINENT AUTHOR.

'MY DEAR SIR,

'Years have elapsed, since I had an opportunity of ocularly perusing the lineaments, now familiar to the imaginations of a considerable portion of the civilised world.

'But, my dear sir, though estranged from the personal society of the friend and companion of my youth, I have not been unmindful of his soaring flight. Nor have I been debarred.

        Though seas between us braid ha' roared,

(BURNS) from participating in the intellectual feast he has spread before us.

'I cannot, therefore, allow of the departure from this place of an individual whom we mutually respect and esteem, without, my dear sir, taking this public opportunity of thanking you, on my own behalf, and, I may undertake to add, on that of the whole of the Inhabitants of Port Middlebay, for the gratification of which you are the ministering agent.

'Go on, my dear sir! You are not unknown here, you are not unappreciated. Though "remote," we are neither "unfriended," "melancholy," nor (I may add) "slow." Go on, my dear sir, in your Eagle course! The inhabitants of Port Middlebay may at least aspire to watch it, with delight, with entertainment, with instruction!

'Among the eyes elevated towards you from this portion of the globe, will ever be found, while it has light and life,

The

Eye

Appertaining

to

WILKINS MICAWBER

Magistrate.'

I found, on glancing at the remaining contents of the newspaper, that Mr Micawber was a diligent and esteemed correspondent. There was an advertisement of a collection of letters by him, to be shortly republished, in a neat volume, 'with considerable additions;' and, unless I am very much mistaken, the Leading Article was his also.

We talked much of Mr Micawber, on many other evenings while Mr Peggotty remained with us. He lived with us during the whole term of his stay, and his sister and my aunt came to London to see him. Agnes and I parted from him aboard-ship, when he sailed; and we shall never part from him more, on earth.

But before he left, he went with me to Yarmouth, to see a little tablet I had put up in the churchyard to the memory of Ham. While I was copying the plain inscription for him at his request, I saw him stoop and gather a tuft of grass from the grave, and a little earth.

'For Em'ly,' he said, as he put it in his breast, 'I promised, Mas'r Davy.'

CHAPTER 64

A last Retrospect

And now my story ends. I look back for the last time before I close these leaves.

I see myself, with Agnes at my side, journeying along the road of life, I see our children and our friends around us; and I hear the roar of many voices, not indifferent to me as I travel on.

What faces are the most distinct to me in the fleeting crowd?

Here is my aunt, in stronger spectacles, an old woman of fourscore years and more, but upright yet, and a steady walker of six miles at a stretch in winter weather.

Always with her, here comes Peggotty, my good old nurse. The cheeks and arms of Peggotty, so hard and red in my childish days, are shrivelled now; but her rough forefinger, which I once associated with a pocket nutmeg grater, is just the same, and when I see my least child catching at it as it totters from my aunt to her, I think of our little parlour at home, when I could scarcely walk. My aunt's old disappointment is set right, now. She is godmother to a real living Betsey Trotwood; and Dora (the next in order) says she spoils her.

There is something bulky in Peggotty's pocket. It is nothing smaller than the Crocodile Book, which is in rather a dilapidated condition by this time, with divers of the leaves torn and stitched across, but which Peggotty exhibits to the children as a precious relic. I find it very curious to see my own infant face, looking up at me from the Crocodile stories; and to be reminded by it of my old acquaintance Brooks of Sheffield.

Among my boys, this summer holiday time, I see an old man making giant kites, and gazing at them in the air, with a delight for which there are no words. He greets me rapturously, and whispers, with many nods and winks, 'Trotwood, you will be glad to hear that I shall finish the Memorial when I have nothing else to do!'

Who is this bent lady showing me a countenance in which there are some traces of pride and beauty? Near her stands a sharp, dark, withered woman, with a white scar on her lip. Let me hear what they say.

'Rosa, I have forgotten this gentleman's name.'

Rosa bends over her, and calls, 'Mr Copperfield.'

'You have seen my son, sir,' says the elder lady. 'Are you reconciled?'

Looking fixedly at me, she puts her hand to her forehead, and moans. 'Rosa, come to me. He is dead!' Rosa by turns caresses her, and quarrels with her; now fiercely telling her, 'I loved him better than you ever did!' – now soothing her to sleep. Thus they wear their time away, from year to year.

What ship comes sailing home from India, and what English lady is this married to a growling old Scotch Croesus? Can this be Julia Mills?

Indeed it is Julia Mills, peevish and fine, with a black man to carry cards to her on a golden salver, and a copper-coloured woman in linen to serve her Tiffin in her dressing-room. Julia is steeped in money to the throat, and talks and thinks of nothing else. I liked her better in the Desert of Sahara.

And lo, the Doctor, always our good friend, labouring at his Dictionary (somewhere about the letter D), and happy in his home and wife. Also the Old Soldier, on a considerably reduced footing, and by no means so influential as in days of yore!

Working at his chambers in the Temple, I come upon my dear old Traddles. His table is covered with thick piles of papers; and I say: 'If Sophy were your clerk, now, Traddles, she would have enough to do!'

'Those were capital days, in Holborn Court! Were they not?'

'When she told you you would be a Judge?'

'At all events,' says Traddles, 'if I ever am one –'

'Why, you know you will be.'

'Well, my dear Copperfield, *when* I am one, I shall tell the story, as I said I would.'

We walk away, arm in arm. I am going to have a family dinner with Traddles. It is Sophy's birthday; and, on our road, Traddles discourses to me of the good fortune he has enjoyed.

'I really have been able, my dear Copperfield, to do all that I had most at heart. There are our two boys receiving the very best education; there are three of the girls married very comfortably; there are three more living with us; there are three more keeping house and all of them happy.'

'Except –' I suggested.

'Except the Beauty,' says Traddles. 'Yes. It was very unfortunate that she should marry such a vagabond. However, now we have got her safe at our house, and got rid of him, we must cheer her up again.'

Traddles's house is one of the very houses – or it easily may have been – which he and Sophy used to parcel out, in their evening walks. It is large but Traddles keeps his papers in his dressing-room, and he and Sophy squeeze themselves into upper rooms, reserving the best bedrooms for the Beauty and the girls. There is no room to spare in the house; for more of 'the girls' are here than I know how to count. Here, established in perpetuity, is the poor Beauty, a widow with a little girl; here, at dinner on Sophy's birthday, are the three married girls with their husbands, and one of the husband's brothers, and another husband's cousin, and another husband's sister, who appears to me to be engaged to the cousin. Traddles, exactly the same simple, unaffected fellow as he ever was, sits at the foot of the large table like a Patriarch; and Sophy beams upon him, from the head.

And now, as I close my task, subduing my desire to linger yet, these faces fade away. But, one face, shining on me like a Heavenly light by which I see all other objects, is above them and beyond them all. And that remains.

I turn my head, and see it, in its beautiful serenity, beside me. My lamp burns low, and I have written far into the night; but the dear presence, without which I were nothing, bears me company.

Oh Agnes, Oh my soul, so may thy face be by me when I close my life indeed; so may I, when realities are melting from me like the shadows which I now dismiss, still find thee near me, pointing upward!

THE END

About this Compact Edition

David Copperfield was first published as a monthly serial from May 1849 to November 1850. This abridged version faithfully retains Dickens' language without additions, but cuts from the original edition have been made in overlong passages of description and dialogue. Scenes or incidents involving minor characters have also been reduced, but memorable eccentrics and vivid sequences are kept, together with the humour and pathos characteristic of Dickens. The narrative throughout is in the first person: David's life from childhood suffering to middle-life maturity and success – his autobiography having clear connections with that of his author – is poignant, funny, moving, graphic and, on occasions, tragic.